A BIT DIFFERENT

A BIT DIFFERENT

DISABILITY IN IRELAND

PAULINE CONROY

ORPEN PRESS

A Bit Different
First published in 2018 by
Orpen Press
Top Floor,
Unit K9,
Grants Road,
Greenogue Business Park,
Rathcoole,
Dublin,
Ireland.

e-mail: info@orpenpress.com
www.orpenpress.com

ISBN: 978-1-78605-060-1
Epub ISBN: 978-1-78605-061-8

Printed in Dublin, Ireland by SPRINTprint

Table of Contents

Acknowledgements

My first thank you goes to Pat McDonnell of UCD, who has been an inspiration in his dissemination of Disability Studies in Ireland. Tomás McEoin, author, encouraged me to keep going and stay focussed. Mary Fennessy kindly shared her insights into the dilemmas of social reform as did Katrina Goldstone, writer and journalist, who helped me update my thinking. Máire Meagher provided great moral support. Therese Caherty loyally supported me when she had no idea what I was discussing. Paddy Connolly of Inclusion Ireland has provided plenty of food for thought over the years, whether I wanted it or not.

I was greatly assisted by many individuals in relation to particular topics. Ruth O'Rourke, community researcher, baffled me with her ideas on the scandal of the Tuam Mother and Baby Home. Local historian Catherine Corless provided me and the rest of Irish society with an example of what a single person can achieve. Breeda Murphy and Sadie Cramer from the Tuam Home Survivors Network inspired me with new ideas on Mother and Baby Homes.

Lt. Col. Joe Ahern (Retd.) from the Association of Retired Commissioned Officers of the Permanent Defence Force kindly pointed out some necessary amendments. I acknowledge the contribution of Gerry Rooney ex-General Secretary and Ray McKenna, Health and Safety Officer of the Permanent Defence Force Other Ranks Representative Association (PDFORRA).

Harriet Coleman, Stewart Reddin, and Patricia Kelleher each kindly examined some chapters of the book and applied the scalpel knife. Elena Leteanu provided information on the geographical locations of asylums in Romania. I was lucky to have Mary Doyle available for advice on statistics. Stephen Cashell and Alex Fearon provided very speedy data entry. My brother Colin Conroy made some good suggestions on wars and disability, and Emma Loughran helpfully advised me on photo images. Sara Ferguson, image archivist of Oakland, California was especially helpful in locating an image for the book.

Finally, a special note of thanks is due to Shauna Daly, to publisher Gerard O'Connor of Blackhall Publishing and to James Kelly of Orpen Press for their supportive encouragement throughout the production process of this book. Thank you also to Cormac Jackson for his faith in me.

A Note for the Reader

Many of the terms used in this book would be regarded as offensive today. Words such as 'madhouse', 'lunatic' or 'defective' are demeaning. However, where these words were used in the relevant historical period being discussed, they are retained for historical clarity.

Ireland: Timeline of Important Dates

1684	Completion of the Royal Hospital Kilmainham for retired and invalid soldiers
1743	Hospital for Incurables founded in Donnybrook, Co. Dublin
1773	The House of Industry for destitute paupers of Dublin and the relief of some diseases is established
1788	King George III's mental illness becomes a topic of public discussion
1795	Philippe Pinel orders chains to be removed from insane women at the Salpêtrière Hospital in Paris
1810	Richmond National Institution for the Industrious Blind is founded in Dublin's Sackville Street (now O'Connell Street)
1814	Opening of Richmond Asylum for Lunatics and Idiots at Grangegorman, Dublin
1817	Claremont Institution for Deaf and Dumb is founded in Brunswick Street (now Pearse Street), Dublin
1822	First Catholic School for the Deaf is established in Cork by Dr Patrick Kehoe
1826	Section 61 of *Prisons (Ireland) Act* empowers inspectors of prisons to visit madhouses and places where idiots and lunatics are detained
1838	*Poor Law Ireland Act* extends workhouse system to the treatment of poor, elderly, epileptic, blind and deaf
1846	St. Mary's School for Deaf Girls opens in Cabra, Dublin
1847	*Poor Relief Act* implements Outdoor Relief, later known as Home Assistance
1850	Central Criminal Lunatic Asylum established at Dundrum, Co. Dublin
1857	St. Joseph's School for Deaf Boys opens in Cabra, Dublin
1858	Sisters of Mercy School for Deaf Girls opens in Cork
1866	Foundation stone laid for Irish Sisters of Charity Asylum for Female Blind at Merrion, Co. Dublin

Ireland: Timeline of Important Dates

1868   Irish *Industrial Schools Act* is passed

1869   Stewart's Institution at Palmerstown, Co. Dublin is opened for the mentally handicapped

1871   *Lunacy Regulation (Ireland) Act* transfers many powers of the mentally ill to the state

1892   St. Joseph's Institution for the Deaf opens in Co. Westmeath

1897   *Workman's Compensation Act* provides compensation for accidents at work

1903   Richmond Asylum Annex opens at Portrane, North County Dublin

1908   *Old Age Pension Act* is implemented for those over seventy years of age, subject to conditions

1908   *The Children Act* permits annual visits by an Inspector of Reformatory and Industrial Schools to such schools

1911   *National Insurance Act* provides sickness and unemployment schemes for those disabled workers aged sixteen and over

1920   Blind Pension is established

1923   *Electoral Act* Article 1(9) disqualifies persons in lunatic asylums and workhouses from the right to vote

1924   Lunatic asylums renamed as mental hospitals and given the names of saints

1924   Ireland signs ILO Convention CO12 of Workmen's Compensation (Agriculture) Convention 1921

1925   Lunatic asylums become mental hospitals under a local government act.

1926   First census is carried out in Ireland but includes little detail on people with disabilities living outside of institutions

1927   *Report of the Commission on the Relief of the Sick and Destitute Poor Including the Insane Poor* proposes that institutions for 'mentally defective' be inspected and have standards enforced

1931   National Council for the Blind of Ireland is founded in Drumcondra, Dublin

1942   First polio epidemic in Ireland

1945   *Mental Treatment Act* is passed

1947   *Social Insurance Act* is passed

1949   Rehabilitation Institute is founded for those recovering from TB

1951   Valerie Goulding and Kathleen O'Rourke found the Central Remedial Clinic in Clontarf, Dublin

1955   St. Michael's House Services is founded following the initiative of Mrs Patricia Farrell, who could not find a school for her child with Down's syndrome

1960   Irish Wheelchair Association is formed

1961   National Association for Mentally Handicapped is founded, today called 'Inclusion Ireland'

1961   Disability Federation of Ireland is established

1966   Occupational Injuries Benefit is established

1967   National Rehabilitation Board is established

1968   Prescribed Relatives' Allowance is established

1970   Invalidity Pension is established

1972   First Camphill Community is established at Duffcarrig, Co. Wexford

1973   Adoption of the *Rehabilitation Act* in the US

1975   Mothers who had been prescribed the drug Thalidomide are given a once-off compensation payment in Ireland

1980   Soldiers begin a series of cases against the Department of Defense for experiencing loss of hearing in the course of their work

1983   Commission on Social Welfare recommends against a Costs of Disability Payment

1984   In *Draper v. The Attorney General*, Mrs Draper – a person with a disability – loses her case and is not given the right to vote

1990   *Americans with Disabilities Act* is passed in the US

1990   Forum of People with Disabilities is established to lobby for the rights of people with disabilities

1992   Centres for Independent Living begin to be established in Ireland

1992   Trinity College Dublin and University of Bristol run first Irish Sign Language Interpreter and Deaf Tutor training programme

1994   Establishment of Commission on the Status of People with Disabilities

1995   Disabled Persons Maintenance Allowance is transferred to Department of Social Welfare and becomes the Disability Allowance

1996   Commission on Disability publishes its report: *A Strategy for Equality*

1997   Treaty of Amsterdam mentions 'disability' for first time

1998   *Employment Equality Act* includes disability as a ground of discrimination

1999   *National Disability Authority Act* provides for the establishment of a specialist agency under the Department of Justice, Equality and Law Reform

1999   Annie Ryan publishes *Walls of Silence*, her disturbing account of the treatment of patients and staff in mental hospitals in Ireland

2000   *Equal Status Act* includes disability as a ground for claiming discrimination in services

2000   National Rehabilitation Board is dissolved under Statutory Instrument 171

2000   Adoption of EU Directive 2000/78/EC on non-discrimination on the grounds of disability in employment

2001   *Mental Health Act* provides for reviews of involuntary detention in psychiatric facilities

2001   Kathy Synnott loses her Supreme Court Case on behalf of her teenage son to obtain a right to continue his education

2002   Central Statistics Office includes section on disability in the Quarterly National Household Survey

2002   Mental Health Commission is established

2004   *Education for Persons with Special Educational Needs Act* is passed

2005   *Disability Act* is adopted

2006   *Mental Health Act, 2001* commences after a five-year delay

2006   First National Disability Survey carried out but excludes most of those living in residential care

2006   A strategy for mental health services is published, entitled *Vision for Change*

2007   *Health Act* provides for establishment of the Health Information and Quality Authority (HIQA), which can set standards and inspect social care services for adults and children

2008   Section 68 of the *Civil Law (Miscellaneous Provisions) Act, 2008* is amended but retains the exclusion of those who are deaf

2009	The report of the Commission to Inquire into Child Abuse is published in five volumes and identifies cruelty toward children with disabilities
2010	Deaf and hearing impaired are permitted to sit on juries in Ireland following a challenge by Free Legal Advice centres
2007	Ireland signs the UN Convention (2006) on the Rights of Persons with Disabilities
2007	*Citizen Information Act* provides advocacy for people with disabilities
2009	Final report into the scandal of Leas Cross Nursing Home in Swords is published
2010	European Union ratifies UN Convention on the Rights of Persons with Disabilities as a collective entity
2012	Demonstration and sleep-in outside government buildings to resist cuts to services for people with disabilities
2013	European Court of Justice makes a landmark decision giving a wide interpretation of the concept of disability in a case involving two female employees who claimed they were disabled
2014	Oireachtas Committee on Public Accounts meets with management and board of Central Remedial Clinic over its financing
2014	Taoiseach Enda Kenny comments on REHAB charity controversy
2014	RTÉ's *Prime Time* shows undercover footage of ill-treatment of residents at HSE-run Áras Attracta care facility in Swinford, Co. Mayo
2015	The *Assisted Decision-making (Capacity) Act* is adopted but not implemented
2015	*Comprehensive Employment Strategy for People with Disabilities 2015–2024* is published
2015	Leigh Gath is appointed as confidential recipient of complaints in relation to disability services
2016	Finian McGrath TD is appointed Minister of State for Disability Issues
2016	Carers' Support Grant (Respite) is restored to its full amount in June of 2016
2016	Disability activist Martin Naughton dies

Ireland: Timeline of Important Dates

2016   Task Force on Personalised Budgets is appointed by Minister Finian McGrath TD

2017   New system of educational supports in schools is announced for September

2017   Budget 2017 provides a medical card to all children in receipt of the Domiciliary Care Allowance

2017   Disability (Miscellaneous Provisions) Bill creeps through the Oireachtas

2017   *Criminal Law (Sexual Offences) Act* is enacted

2017   Donal Toolan, actor and disability rights activist, dies

2017   Activists demonstrate outside the Dáil for Ireland's failure to ratify the 2006 Convention on the Rights of Persons with a Disability

2017   Minister Finian McGrath TD announces consultation on Personalised Budgets

2017   Disabled People of Ireland announced in October by Suzy Byrne

2017   Central Statistics Office publishes Census 2016 *Profile 9 – Health, Disability and Carers*

2017   Irish Sign Language is recognised in law

2017   First deaf person is called to jury service

2018   Ombudsman finds that Tusla and the HSE are not meeting needs of disabled children in care

2018   Government decides to ratify UN Convention on the Rights of Persons with Disabilities but does not ratify the Optional Protocol that permits complaints to be made to the UN

2018   Department of Employment and Social Protection consultations open on changes to disability payments

2018   Cabinet agrees that a bill should be drafted to allow carers obtain free GP care

2018   Mr Justice Gerard Hogan finds that Section 15.3 of the *Mental Health Act*, which provides for twelve months detention without review, is unconstitutional

2018   Government promises free GP care for carers at end of 2018

2018   A potential accessibility act is discussed in European Parliament in May

CHAPTER 1

Introduction

The historical legacy of nineteenth-century charity and containment underpinning the lives of people with disabilities persists in the twenty-first century. This legacy coexists, not always peacefully, with a myriad of new ideas and perspectives on individual rights, many of which are basic. In the chapters of this publication, important elements of this legacy are explored within Ireland and Europe. The book will explore which legacy, if any, is fogging up the glass of our understanding concerning the contemporary issues facing people with disabilities.

The historical barriers to full citizenship have yet to be lifted for and by people with disabilities. Despite extensive discourse concerning equal rights and equal status, some basic provisions are still lacking, some of which have been enacted in legislation that has never been fully implemented. Going to the theatre, enrolling your child in secondary school, entering the polling station – such are the major battlegrounds of rights and resources. The right to live independently with people of your own choosing, in a place of your own choosing, with the essential adjustments for everyday living – these are modest enough proposals in a modern democracy. The rights of disabled people are human rights. In a document contributing to the adoption of a new United Nations Convention on the Rights of People with Disabilities, Arthur O'Reilly writes: 'Human rights and fundamental freedoms are the birthright of all. This is the essence of the Universal Declaration of Human Rights and finds specific application in the International Covenant on Civil and Political Rights, the International Covenant on Economic, Social and Cultural Rights and other international instruments' (2003, 1).

Our present time, our era, is not a blank sheet – it is full of blotches from the past, ready to be smeared onto our current outlook. Inclusions, equalities, entitlements and rights are patched together from the threads of other epochs and times, adapting, deforming and delaying the articulations of our desire to eradicate prejudice and discrimination against those who are not like ourselves. Or so we believe. Difference can be real or imagined; difference can be a fact or a perception. The difference between the treatment of those with a disability or long-standing health conditions and those without is an unsustainable distinction. That distinction relegates, subordinates and oppresses those who have to experience it; these people receive no compensatory adjustment to realign their lives. Sadly, this is not just the case in Ireland:

- In Lithuania, 60 percent of polling stations are not accessible.
- In Hungary, the accessible polling stations can be far from where a voter with a disability lives, making it difficult for people with disabilities to reach them and exercise their right.
- In Germany, 85,000 people are not allowed to vote. These are people with dementia and people with intellectual or psychosocial disabilities.
- In Hungary, 56,000 people with disabilities are under guardianship; among them, 48,000 are not allowed to vote.
- In Portugal, people with intellectual disabilities cannot vote because voting information is not provided to them in an accessible, understandable way.
- In Ireland, people with disabilities have to search for an accessible polling station in order to exercise their right to vote.

In many EU countries, people with disabilities are locked within institutions and are not permitted to vote; they are not even aware that elections are taking place. Even if people with disabilities have the legal right to vote in certain countries, the lack of accessibility makes it impossible for them in practice. They often struggle with inaccessible polling stations; a lack of documents and information in accessible formats such as Braille, sign language or Easy-To-Read; complicated processes; and the lack of awareness about disability and accessibility (European Disability Forum, 2017).

Discrimination can be embedded in culture, a point made by the late Donal Toolan:

> The media continue to communicate a view that reinforces or, at a minimum, encourages prejudice about disabled people and their marginal place in society by using well-honed fears. Road safety

campaigns that use images of a victim using a wheelchair to deter people from driving too fast do not provide the best affirmation for the identity of those who chose to use a wheelchair as an efficient way of getting from A to B (2003, 173).

The Commission on the Status of People with Disabilities published its final report – *A Strategy for Equality* – on the eve of Ireland's economic boom in 1996. What followed was a mushrooming of new laws; public institutions; campaign movements; litigation; and the rise of organisations representing people with disabilities, their work colleagues and their families and friends. Yet so much second-class citizenship remains. Same-sex marriage has been enacted in law, women have become presidents of Ireland, child abuse has been exposed, there has been a peace process, the baptism barrier in national schools has become a public policy issue, and yet, people with disabilities have not been allowed to emerge from the margins of society.

Disability rights are the last of the civil rights yet to be accorded to citizens and residents in Ireland. Indeed, in some quarters, disability rights are not yet conceded as civil rights. That is why so much attention and expectation centred on Ireland's non-ratification of the United Nations Convention on the Rights of Persons with a Disability, 2006–2018. The carefully worded convention is a rights-oriented manifesto that defines people with disabilities as rights holders rather than charity recipients or users of services across all domains of life. The convention also prescribes the obligations of the state. It is ironic that while Irish governments provided excuses as to why the UN Convention could not be ratified, the same governments were supporting the implementation of the UN Convention through the Department of Foreign Affair's Irish Aid programme partnership with the International Labour Organisation (ILO).

Attitudes toward disability have vacillated between old charity ideas and the right to independent living, and policies toward children and adults with disabilities are frequently a heady mixture of both. Some oft-proclaimed strategies for reform have become enmeshed in excruciating medicalised assessments, while others have drifted from committee to taskforce, from steering group to working party, and finally faded into study groups and indifferent public forgetfulness.

There are 643,131 people in Ireland who declared that they had a disability in 2016 – 13.5 percent of the population. The number of children and young people with disabilities increased by almost 15,000 between 2011 and 2016. This has implications for schools and health and social services. Depending on how the statistical data is gathered, the proportion of people with disabilities could rise to 15 or 20 percent as the majority of us will eventually become older and frailer, with increasing propensity for the development of enduring health conditions that will interrupt the course of our lives. More and more of us will be directly affected by disability. Many people with disabilities still live in a disabling environment with restricted opportunities to live a self-determined life of their choice.

Some population groups have a higher-than-average experience of disability; this is the case for Irish travellers. Almost one in five Irish travellers had a disability in 2016; a rise of 1.7 percent from 2011. A total of 5,963 travellers had a disability of some sort in 2016, with many having more than one kind of disability in the form of chronic illness; difficulty in learning, remembering or concentrating; and difficulty with basic physical activities (CSO, 2017).

Social, cultural and economic forces have functioned to block the achievement of full citizenship status for people with disabilities. Among the obstacles are the scattered privatisation of service provisions, a related lack of transparency in how public expenditure is actually incurred and a reluctance to cede the autonomy and independent living arrangements that people with disabilities want and expect. To understand where we stand today, we need to look back to this heritage of exclusion, segregation and discrimination. It is impossible, even absurd, to advance proposals for change without examining the ideas and values, structures and administrations of previous regimes on which the new policies are expected to be an improvement. The chapters of this book examine the historical legacies facing policy makers.

End of the Heroic-Tragic Era

In relation to disability, the heroic-tragic era of policy, from the 1950s to the 1970s, has almost come to an end. This was a time when people with disabilities were regarded as without equal humanity or ability, save for a few exceptions; the exceptional persons were, and still are, held up as heroic, remarkable, extraordinary and unusual. Those with disabilities were not regarded as a reserve army of labour, since their work was not considered to have any human capital value. In this absence of value, it is unsurprising that deep segregation and disability apartheid were practiced. This now has to be undone, sector by sector, service by service, person by person.

During this time, there were champions: Lady Valerie Goulding, who started a rehabilitation movement; Christy Brown, who inspirationally touched a public nerve; Paddy Doyle, who told his story; and Annie Ryan, who wrote a book about mental health entitled *Walls of Silence*. The emergence of organisations – such as the National Association for Cerebral Palsy in 1948, the Polio Fellowship and Rehab in 1949, Liam Maguire and the Irish Wheelchair Association in 1960 and the National Association for the Mentally Handicapped of Ireland in 1961 (now Inclusion Ireland) – were radical departures at the time, but they did not subscribe to a rights-based approach to disability, or if they did, were not perceived to do so. Some of the negative attitudes toward disability in the 1950s are illustrated by the survivors of Ireland's polio epidemic and by the survivors of special residential institutions for children.

People with disabilities were regarded as tragically deficient or inherently without great capacity. In the case of the Catholic Schools for the Deaf, the fear that the souls of Catholic children would be stolen by the Protestant clergy was the main motivation in the establishment of religiously separate education for deaf children in the early 1800s (Crean, 1997, 36). Even though famine was sweeping the country and millions of Irish were dying or leaving on emigrant ships, an appeal was made across the country for funds to establish boarding schools: St. Mary's School for Deaf Girls and St. Joseph's School for Deaf Boys in Cabra, Dublin.

Following the nineteenth-century tradition of segregating those who were different by placing them in large, private, closed institutions, such as prisons, hospitals and asylums, people with disabilities were often separated from their parents at an early age and sent to residential schools. At these schools, they were prepared for manual and menial occupations or jobs reserved for people with disabilities. Many families believed or were persuaded that this was the right thing to do. Many did not have a choice in the matter as mainstream schools refused to enrol children with disabilities. There was never a question of opening up local services to children with disabilities as is the case today. Hence, their 'difference', combined with a perceived lack of productive capacity, formed the view that people with disabilities had little to offer and were essentially beneficiaries or recipients of charity bestowed upon them by others. Thus, they were effectively 'interned' in institutions. The 'personal tragedy' perspective was based on the perception of people with disabilities as having personal deficits and resulted in children and adults with disabilities being separated from their families in a form of institutional confinement. People with disabilities were to experience and suffer a particular form of social control: the era of segregation, which began in the nineteenth century, was restructured in 1922, and disabled people were displaced from the workplace and from public life (Barnes and Mercer, 2003). They became invisible and in terms of public policy – forgotten.

The Medical Model of Disability

While nowadays much is made of the humanitarian and charitable claims of the segregated system, this is an attribute that still needs to be demonstrated in evidence. With the twentieth century, the medicalisation of disability advanced, with an ever-greater emphasis on diagnostic treatment and curative approaches to efface, erase or make people with disabilities, as well as their impairments and health conditions, disappear. Rather than being locked away, children and adults with disabilities were to be normalised out of their differences. This normalisation persists today in the refusal of adjustments that would enable people with disabilities to interact with their environment.

A common assumption is that people with disabilities are unable to ensure a reasonable quality of life for themselves. This view is the basis for the medical model of disability. Pat McDonnell, in his sharp critique of said model, describes it as portraying a 'personal problem of and for the individual concerned, and solutions are offered primarily in terms of individual (re) adjustment' (2007, 182). Many professionals who accept the medical view of disability believe that people with a disability are incapable of managing their own lives (Oliver, 1990).

In contrast, a second explanation for this model is based on the social model of disability, developed by sociologist Mike Oliver (1990). This model proposes that the economic, cultural and social barriers faced by people with a disability are the main barriers to the attainment of their citizenship rights.

The new era of change saw the emergence of organisations *with* people with disabilities, rather than *for* people with disabilities, and segregated institutions and impairment-based charities were also challenged. By the late eighties/early nineties, international thinking was shifting with the UN adoption of the *Standard Rules for the Equalization of Opportunity for People with Disabilities* in 1993.

These rules did not confer any rights; they were not enforceable; they did not have the status of a convention or treaty. However, they had significant effects in many countries, including Ireland. Ireland established the Commission on the Status of People with Disabilities, which reported in 1996. The *Standard Rules* articulated the influence of many organisations of people with disabilities in developing a new concept of disability. This new concept established a relationship between the limitations experienced by people with disabilities and the design and structure of the environment, as well as the attitudes of the general population. This was the social model of disability, which was a critique of the medical model and saw the eventual expansion of the perspective on civil rights.

The Rights Model Takes Hold

The Commission on the Status of People with Disabilities was a landmark event in both process and outcome. The commission's report, *A Strategy for Equality*, marked the arrival of the disability social movement and the modernisation of concepts and practice. By 1995, there was a distinct turnaround in thinking concerning disability on the part of people with disabilities and their families, and on the part of many academics, intellectuals and public servants, including those in national and international organisations. Outside of this narrow radius, the views on disability remained locked in helpless stereotypes, charity collection boxes at supermarkets and intrusive and medicalised assessments.

The period from 1995 to 2001 was a period of rapid growth for Ireland in terms of employment, population, direct foreign investment, inward migration, and purchasing power and peace, with the Peace Process in Northern Ireland (O'Connell, 1999). An atmosphere of high optimism prevailed, and people dared to hope that improvements on the status of people with disabilities would finally take place, untrammelled by budgetary constraints, cultural backwardness, charitable concepts and endless certifications of one's disability.

This led to a flurry of innovative legislative drafting: *The Education Act, 1998*, which appeared to guarantee equal access to education for all – but did not; the *Employment Equality Act, 1998*, which included nine grounds for discrimination, one of which was disability; and the establishment in 1998 of the Equality Authority as a state agency promoting equality on a range of grounds of discrimination. *The Employment Equality Act* made statutory provisions for unequal pay between people with disabilities and people without disabilities in Section 35 (1), where their productivity is allegedly lower than a person without a disability. This laid a basis for wage subsidy-schemes and for the institutionalisation of unequal pay. *The National Disability Authority Act* was adopted in 1999. In the field of public and private services, an Equal Status Bill was published in 1999. This was not enacted due to legislative difficulties related to disability considerations the first-time round; the bill was later amended and enacted in 2000. The National Social Service Board was changed to Comhairle and conferred with new responsibilities for disability-related information provision. A Disability Bill was published in 2003 and was later withdrawn. *The Mental Health Act, 2001* was enacted, but much of it was not started for six years. The flurry of legislation did not meet public expectations, despite the efforts of forward-thinking TDs, senators, reform-minded civil and public servants and some lobby groups.

Establishing a new legislative framework was an essential prerequisite in turning ability/disability issues and their discourse away from the sacrificial frugalism of the past toward a more promising and statutory future. The Good Friday Agreement of the mid-nineties guaranteed the establishment of equivalent human rights commissions in the North and South of the island of Ireland and saw the publication of a Human Rights Commission Bill in 1999. The 1994 social partnership agreement, *Programme for Competitiveness and Work*, departed from practice and devoted an entire section to the reform of measures to remove certain policies that were barriers to people with disabilities, with much of the reform, such as the use of disability employment quotas in public employment, originating from the input of the Irish Congress of Trade Unions.

The outcome of those years produced several new state institutions and new legislation to provide for equal treatment for people with disabilities in a wide range of fields. A huge effort in consulting, drafting, considering and reflecting on the legislation and institutions was made by organisations of people with disabilities, their families and staff in the public and not-for-profit sectors. However, there was considerable resistance to change: certain not-for-profit services, public representatives with a charity-oriented perspective and housing and transport providers still saw disability rights as a financial burden. Despite their exhaustion from lobbying, various organisations, groups of people with disabilities, their families and supporters insisted on highlighting the flaws in the new battery of legislation, through seminars, conferences and parliamentary lobbying.

The Policy Landmarks of 2000

Many of the laws of the 1990s were amended and new laws were drafted to implement a more specific account of disability rights. This was a time of impatience: despite the initiatives of the 1990s, change was occurring at a slow pace, and some disabled people were not benefiting from the new services and approaches. *The Equal Status Act* of 2000 had to be amended in 2004 to comply with new anti-discrimination directives emanating from the EU that were specifically related to disability (Council, 2000).

The same occurred for the *Employment Equality Act* in 2004. Section 35 of the act was retained without any significant public commentary on unequal pay. *The Health Strategy Quality and Fairness: A Health System for You* was a policy document that caused an amount of excitement when it was released in 2001. However, the document was a lost opportunity in terms of providing people with disabilities immediate ease of access to services and an equitable distribution of resources and entitlements. *The Disability Act, 2005* was an achievement relative to the conditions of the 1990s and a disappointment in that it contained reforms but was not especially radical. Some saw it as overly restrictive in relation to definitions of disability and limited in scope. They regarded the assessment of need system as convoluted and complex. Article 2(1) of the act defined disability as follows: "'disability", in relation to a person, means a substantial restriction in the capacity of the person to carry on a profession, business or occupation in the State or to participate in social or cultural life in the State by reason of an enduring physical, sensory, mental health or intellectual impairment'. The article described disability as a *substantial* restriction, which appeared to limit the scope of the act. The absence of clear remedies, legal redress, complaints or appeals was a serious concern and a deficit noted by the Irish Human Rights Commission. The act obliged some, but not all government departments to produce disability plans. The definition of disability was not so medicalised as in the earlier *Employment Equality Act, 1998*, which described disability in medically deficit terms:

"disability" means—

(a) the total or partial absence of a person's bodily or mental functions, including the absence of a part of a person' body,

(b) the presence in the body of organisms causing, or likely to cause, chronic disease or illness,

(c) the malfunction, malformation or disfigurement of a part of a person's body,

(d) a condition or malfunction which results in a person learning differently from a person without the condition or malfunction, or

(e) a condition, illness or disease which affects a person's thought processes, perception of reality, emotions or judgement or which results in disturbed behaviour.

With this definition, it is hard to see where neurological and degenerative nerve disorders fit in, such as motor neurone disease, multiple sclerosis or Parkinson's disease. It would be inaccurate to describe these diseases as 'chronic' when they are in fact degenerative.

A new education act had to be introduced: *The Education for Persons with Special Education Needs Act, 2004*. *The Education Act, 1998* was not working for children with disabilities, and the *Comhairle Act* had to be amended in 2004 to provide for an advocacy service, since rights and information were not reaching people with disabilities. The establishment of a mental health commission by statute and the *Mental Health Act, 2001* broke the connections to that nineteenth-century approach to mental health difficulties. The act allowed for several new civil liberties checks and balances for persons in centres offering treatment for mental illness. The report published in 2006, *Vision for Change: Report of the Expert Group on Mental Health Policy*, succeeded in synthesising the many demands for forward-looking strategies for those at the margins of society. The adoption of the *Human Rights Commission Act* in 2000 led, eventually, and not without controversy, to the establishment of a human rights commission and commissioners under the chairmanship of Mr Justice Donal Barrington (RIP).

For many, the early years of 2000 will be remembered for the intense discussions concerning the need for a new disability act. This saw many rallies, assemblies and meetings organised by people with disabilities, their families, supporters and friends. A collaboration between large organisations, federations, service providers and lobby groups agreed on the core elements of a new bill in 2003. Independent needs assessment and advocacy figured high on their agenda. This progressive movement was sustained by the fact that 2003 was the European Year of Disability and that the Programme for Government committed to publishing a disability bill in 2002. *The Programme for Prosperity and Fairness 2000–2002* and the *Sustaining Progress: Social Partnership Agreement 2003–2005* contained progressive clauses on disability issues that added legitimacy to radical legislative reform.

In 2017, there were still legislative enactments awaiting commencement in:

- *The Education of Persons with Special Education Needs Act, 2004*
- *The Citizens Information Act, 2007*
- *The Disability Act, 2005*

On the surface, the Oireachtas had done its duty and enacted legislation. But the process was sabotaged as coalition after coalition declined to enact the same legislation up to thirteen years after its adoption as law. In the words of Annie Ryan: 'When people have no voice, silence is not always golden. Neither is it sufficient simply to break the silence. Revelations do not guarantee reform although they are an important step in ensuring improvement' (1999, ii).

Disability Services – a Private Affair on the 'Quasi' Market

Private bodies supply the majority of residential and day services as well as training and sheltered work-oriented services for people with disabilities.

This is especially the case for people with intellectual disabilities, where 90 percent of services are carried out by private providers. In the market of day services in Ireland, the Department of Health and Children and the Health Service Executive (HSE) are purchasers of services from a vast array of private suppliers. The fact that there may not be a profit in the transaction between purchaser and supplier is of no relevance to the market-based relationship. To add to the confusion, some of the suppliers are 'preferred' and obtain funding, using different articles of the *Health Act*, on a more advantageous basis than others, depending on whether they are providing services as a *substitute* for the state (valuable supplier) or as a *support* to the state (less valuable supplier).

The person using services has a relationship with the provider of services, such that they cannot purchase services directly; this is a characteristic of 'quasi' markets. The user is essentially secondary to the market, the terms of which are fixed by purchasers and suppliers. In contrast to financial services, for example, this is an as-yet relatively unregulated market with few fixed statutory standards to ensure equality of product or service between various suppliers for the same amount of money.

As in any market arrangement, niche markets and sub-sectors appear over time, specialising in workshops, vocational training and supported employment. As this occurs, so do monopolies manifest themselves in these sub-sectors and niches. This can be accompanied by mergers and acquisitions, whereby one service entity in say, Limerick, takes over the work of another in the same sector but in a different region of Munster or in a region adjacent to their own. The appearance of monopolies is not a moral issue; rather it is an inevitable consequence of market operations over time. However, it is of concern when there is an abuse of market position with implications for other suppliers, user regulation, standards and an actual distortion of the functioning of the market. There is evidence of some underlying resentment, where private not-for-profit providers reduce choice for adults, parents and children with disabilities.[1]

A study by the Comptroller and Auditor General (2006) suggested that Ireland had reached an advanced level in the economic relationship between purchasers and suppliers of disability services. In Ireland in 2005, within a market of competing bodies, 69 percent of all funding

---

[1] In this author's opinion.

to not-for-profit bodies in the field of disability went to just twenty-five organisations (Comptroller and Auditor General). The report was met with indifference. Eight years after this, a new study was initiated under the chairmanship of Lawrence Crowley. This proved to be highly complex because the HSE remained unable to provide the range or type of financial calculations that would normally be associated with the large-scale expenditure of public funds. According to an audit of disability services, the top 35 percent of disability service organisations funded by the HSE get 75–80 percent of funds; the remaining 65 percent of disability services had to make do with the remaining 20 percent of funds (Department of Health, 2012). The rationale for this was not at all clear.

Across the disability services market, 'battles' are fought with some suppliers, purchasers, groups of users and in combinations of all or none. Important among these issues has been the recognition and identity of people with disabilities. As with differences in sexual orientation or gender, the drive to assert difference and to develop claims on the basis of affirming, legitimising and articulating difference has been quite vocal in the last twelve years. Claims have been based on the disability rights attached to (often medicalised) categories and degrees of difference.

This institutional movement has prompted new, respectful interaction; it has also encouraged separatism, intolerance and even chauvinism. According to US theorist Nancy Fraser, the identity model suggests that failure to recognise difference is a misrecognition or harm. Battles over identity recognition and recognition of difference displace battles over redistribution. This problem can be codified in law or in a multitude of institutional sites. In relation to disability, the battle over recognition does not address the issue of redistribution of resources, such as day services, training resources, work and income-generating opportunities and support for independent living, rights and entitlements. Indeed, going a step further, an over-emphasis on personal identity could reduce surveillance on the maladministration of resources. This appears to have happened in the case of some not-for-profit service providers in the field of disability services.

Recognition of difference involves acknowledging the specificity of some groups (e.g., people with autism spectrum disorder or wheelchair users) and their difference. Redistribution, which is contradictory to recognition of difference, emphasises sameness and the rights of individuals and groups to be treated the same as others. The tension between the two principles can be frequently heightened to the point of hostility or blaming. This can take the form of 'blaming' the policies of the HSE for being overly oriented to difference and the recognition of identities while blaming the policies of others, such as government departments, for being overly oriented to sameness in offering entitlements to and opportunities for training and work.

Austerity

At the end of the first decade of the twenty-first century, individuals and families with disabilities, who had only just started having a say in policy development, found themselves bearing harsh cuts in paltry services and paying for their own services. Between 2008 and 2010, the basic social welfare payment for disabled individuals – the Disability Allowance – was cut, along with other social welfare payments. This affected 95,000 claimants. Adults living in residential centres on a full-time or part-time basis still have to hand over up to 80 percent of their social welfare payments to service providers. The hours of personal assistants to support independent living were reduced. An estimated 10 percent of special needs assistant posts for children with disabilities in mainstream schools and special schools were cut, a restoration of which only occurred in 2017.

The Legacy Issues

In this publication, the four opening chapters explore different legacies that impinge on our thinking today. From examining and reassessing the past, we can discern how 'rejected' ideas can infiltrate contemporary thinking and policy. Take a look at nursing homes, for example, where older and frailer people live out their last years, often without the choice of staying at home. As fast as nursing homes are being filled, other residential institutions offering services for people with disabilities are being emptied, under the name of 'congregated settings'. Some closed institutions, such as residential centres for people with disabilities, are now against public policy while others, like nursing homes, are favoured in public policy. This perversity of policy is not regarded as contradictory or peculiar because we are used to having closed public institutions as solutions to our private issues. Indeed, more than 1,000 individuals currently residing in nursing homes are under the age of 65 and perhaps should not even be there (RTÉ, 2017).

The treatment of people with disabilities under National Socialism in Germany and the occupied countries and in the US as part of the eugenics movement is a distinct legacy. Chapter Two analyses this specific inhumanity. This decision to sterilise without consent and kill people with disabilities was greatly ignored as a crime against humanity at the end of the Second World War. According to the Allied powers, it was not a war crime because it had occurred prior to the declaration of war; furthermore, compulsory sterilisation was widespread in many European countries and US states and consequently attracted approval rather than odium. The lack of challenges to eugenic thinking has diminished the dignity of humanity.

The national rise and spread of large asylums in the nineteenth century and their continued use in the twentieth century as places of simultaneous welfare and detention is still with us today. The story of Ireland's largest asylum, the Richmond Asylum at Grangegorman in northwest Dublin, and its annexe at Portrane in north County Dublin, the second-last asylum built, is recounted in Chapter Three. Using the census of 1901 and 1911, we now have a clearer profile of those who were confined in these city asylums, which were part of the massive asylum-building programme of the nineteenth century.

Were the lives of infants and children with sickness and disabilities, who died at the Tuam Mother and Baby Home, unworthy of saving? This is the question asked in Chapter Four, using new analysis on the data of the almost 500 deceased infants and children whose deaths were identified by Tuam historian Catherine Corless. A decision not to afford the dead a decent burial breaches a deep taboo in our culture: the dead are entitled to a dignified repose and a named place of memorial. Such a burial and memorial are among the requests of the Tuam Home Survivors Network.

Moving to more contemporary issues, a further legacy is our prejudice-laden attitude toward people with particular forms of disability, such as deafness, as illustrated in the army deafness cases of the twentieth century. This is explored in Chapter Five. The separation of deaf children and adults into religious-operated institutions can be viewed as a form of colonisation and proselytization that continued into the second half of the twentieth century. The practice of enclosing deaf people into closed institutions did little to improve public awareness of what it was to be deaf or have a hearing impairment. This lack of awareness became clear when mass claims by soldiers, sailors and airmen for occupational injuries to their hearing were presented before the courts in the 1980s. A combination of disdain for working-class claimants along with a prejudice against deaf people produced a toxic cocktail of confrontational engagement between the state and the soldiers. The claims were met with intense hostility and scorn by the mass media and many members of the Oireachtas. In researching this subject, it appeared that many people had forgotten about the issue and had forgotten that deafness is a cultural issue as well as a disability issue.

So where does the family figure in all this? The family is like yeast: it is expected to raise up its members and community and keep them risen through selfless care. However, not everyone with a disability has close family members, and this is addressed in Chapter Six. Many people with a disability live alone, have children or family members who have emigrated, live away from their family members, have never had a nuclear family, or have always lived away from their biological family. Almost 30 percent of people with a disability who live in private households are not immediate family members. The discussion on family care contrasts with the right to independent living and the right to autonomy of people with disabilities.

Chapter Seven navigates the difficult world of employment policies in relation to disability. Trade union policies under social partnership agreements made significant progress in developing public policy in favour of people with disabilities The role of trade unions in the politics of disability goes back to the *Workmen's Compensation Act, 1934*, which provided statutory compensation to workers wronged by accidents and diseases at work. Indeed, employment is simultaneously a source of disability and a solution to marginalisation. The right to economic independence through earned income has been stubbornly difficult to enforce in the labour market, despite the variety of systems deployed to do precisely this.

The detention of people with disabilities in their own best interests remains an outstanding and contentious issue. In Chapter Eight, the right to liberty and freedom as a fundamental right is put under the microscope. For some, the right to asylum and safe sanctuary should remain an entitlement. For others, the absence of consistent community-based mental health services propels them into frequent emergency detention under the *Mental Health Act, 2001*. They are not alone. Others with disabilities come into contact with the criminal justice system and end up in prison. Residents of facilities for individuals with intellectual disabilities and residents of nursing homes are often unable to leave and are presumed to have consented to their own containment. This presumption of consent is now being challenged. The dismantling of segregated services and arbitrary detention are just two of the demands of the civil rights movement of the twenty-first century.

Chapter Nine examines whether those who have survived childhood institutional abuse because of disability were victims of hate crime. Hate crime is motivated by contempt for particular target groups based on their perceived difference, such as their sexual orientation, age, nationality or disability. The findings of the 2009 Commission to Inquire into Child Abuse provides an opportunity to explore this hate crime. On the evidence of the witness testimony provided by the survivors as adults, it would appear that children with disabilities were not exempt from cruel and inhumane treatment; on the contrary, they were targeted for violent treatment because of their disabilities.

Getting the balance right between the regulation of services for people with disabilities and the control of the lives of citizens is treated in Chapter Ten. The demand for regulation to stamp out abuse may become disproportionate if everyday life is prescribed and determined by standards and inspections that are impossible to achieve. Perhaps in an eagerness to avoid abuse or the risk of abuse, the pendulum has swung too far in the direction of over-regulation.

The establishment of the independent living movement in Ireland in the early 1990s marked a tentative step away from the charity-oriented analysis of disability, as analysed in Chapter Eleven. The treatment of people with disabilities as a collective category and a move toward the identification of individualised rights accruing to individual persons has been difficult, despite the many person-centred policies and narratives. Many of the movement's objectives are embodied in the United Nations Convention on the Rights of Persons with Disabilities, which Ireland ratified in 2018. It is to the independent living movement that the credit must go for identifying 'the costs of disability' as a necessary prerequisite for full citizenship.

The rise of competitive markets in the provision of disability care services over the last decade has been one of the many manifestations of neo-liberal politics. Private, voluntary, not-for-profit bodies and for-profit companies, who provide a wide range of residential and day services, are funded by direct grants from the state; they deliver services on behalf of or in support of the state. Services such as home care are now and will increasingly be going out to market tender and will be provided by for-profit companies from Ireland or overseas. Services such as residential care for the elderly have been driven by tax incentives and public policies into a private for-profit sector at the same time as support for public nursing homes is withdrawn. The contributions that people with disabilities, both old and young, will have to pay for their own care are rising through the Fair Deal policy. The changing disability politics are moving services from charity to market. The privatisation of services makes regulation an imperative and has transformed the Health Information and Quality Authority (HIQA) into the Central Bank of disability services. HIQA was created in the *Health Act, 2007* and represented a new body for inspection and regulation. HIQA is charged with registering services; establishing standards; regulating, monitoring and inspecting a wide range of health and social services, including hospitals, medical technology, services to children, child detention centres, foster care, nursing homes and residential and respite services to people with disabilities. HIQA has more than 200 staff and is a statutory body reporting to the Minister for Health, with its own governing board and financial structures.

Social Movements

The future will be one of both gains and losses. The professionalization of services and the individualisation of entitlements will be markers of newly configured rights. Regulation and standards of service will play an ever-increasing role as expectations rise in terms of equality of treatment. The regulation of social services is on the rise. However, just because a service is regulated does not mean that abuse can be eradicated. But it is a start.

In October 2017, people with disabilities launched a new organisation called Disabled Peoples Organisation Ireland with the intention, amongst others, of registering for recognition with the United Nations as a non-governmental organisation of and by disabled people.

There have been earlier examples of organisations of people with disabilities: one of these is People with Disabilities Ireland, which was in operation from 2004 to 2011 (Lynch, 2011). It collapsed after funding was withdrawn by the Department of Justice on the grounds that insufficient amounts of funding were being transferred to the regional networks it intended to support. The Forum of People with Disabilities was an organisation of people with disabilities that engaged extensively with legislative reform around the issues of identity and rights. It functioned from 1994 to 2006 and received funding from the Atlantic Philanthropies. The first Centre for Independent Living was established in 1992 as a centre that advocated for independent living and has lobbied intensively for personal assistance to permit people with disabilities to participate in everyday life. A number of self-advocacy groups have also formed in recent years, especially among those with intellectual disabilities, with a strong emphasis on self-management and self-expression. They are strongly supported by organisations such as Inclusion Ireland. It is clear that there is a relatively wide range of organisations that attempted or continue to attempt to provide representation and expression to the views of people with disabilities.

The organisations of people with disabilities have frequently found themselves in competition with some service providers who, probably in a well-meaning fashion, want to be representatives of people with disabilities. If people with disability were listened to, the 'disability agenda' would probably change considerably, with some issues such as accessibility rising in priority. The situation is exacerbated by not-for-profit and voluntary organisations and associations holding meetings in inaccessible locations and failing to signal on their promotional leaflets whether the venue is accessible or not and whether there is signing or not.

Disability studies are a loose assembly of theoretical, analytical and statistical studies that explore, test and examine the relationship of disability and society at a national and international level. Disability studies have emerged as a result of the social movement of people with disabilities. This 'movement' has generated an entire range of questions that had not been previously asked. This new 'interrogation' of social policy, sociology, philosophy, politics and so on has created a new form of study entitled 'disability studies'. Disability studies are critical of existing ideas and practices and call into question much of what was previously regarded as 'obvious' and 'normal'. The field of disability studies challenges the existing expertise and knowledge and implies that our knowledge is deficient in relation to disability; it insists that the deficit cannot be remedied by adding on an extra seminar, providing an extra lecture or putting an additional appendix on a report. Rather, it claims that a whole new perspective on society and its components is essential to gain an understanding of the necessity to take account of and incorporate a disability dimension. Through disability studies, the relationship of disability to gender, racism and ageism can be explored.

Like women studies, African-American studies or ethnic studies, disability studies is a new arrival in the field of knowledge building. This field appeared in Ireland in 2000. Because of this, there are few books on disability studies in Ireland, both North and South. There are just a few university programmes that address disability studies and a limited number of dissertations and theses that could guide us on our way. Disability studies is at an exploratory stage, and the road map is not yet clear. Students with disabilities who study for degrees can make an important contribution to disability studies, as can many others. Disability studies require cultural studies, statistics, history, policy, eyewitness accounts, film and photographs. With disability studies comes new journals on disability issues, new magazines to discuss these issues and special university departments to pioneer disability research.

In the absence of the means to communicate, many people with disabilities have been unable to tell their stories; their views have not been incorporated into research; if they have sensory impairments of sight or hearing, their views have often not been communicated. This communication issue was institutionalised by the segregated living arrangements for people with disabilities, such that they were not seen in the street, heard on the radio or visible on television.

The field of disability studies has been expanding in universities, colleges and research institutes; in law, sociology, nursing; in mental health and in care work; in the field of social mapping and in social and civil rights. This publication will hopefully contribute to the expansion of knowledge research, lead to a more positive view of the rights of persons with disabilities and lend a more sensitive ear to their voices.

Chapter 1 References

Barnes, C. and Mercer, G. (2003) *Disability*, Polity Press, UK.

Council (2000) Council Directive 2000/43/EC, Council Directive 2000/78/EC, Directive 2002/73/EC. See preamble to *Employment Equality Act, 2004*.

CSO (2017) *Census 2016*. Profile 9 Health Disability and Carers, CSO, Dublin.

Comptroller and Auditor General (2006) Value for Money Report No. 52, Provision of Disability Services by Non-Profit Organisations, Government of Ireland, Dublin.

Department of Health (2012) *Value for Money Review of Disability Services*, Dublin.

European Disability Forum (2017) 10 October 2017. www.edf-feph.org.

Lynch, K. (2011) Statement in relation to People with Disabilities in Ireland (PWDI) by Kathleen Lynch TD, Minister for Disability, Equality, Mental Health and Older People, Department of Justice, 25 November 2011.

McDonnell, P. (2007) *Disability in Ireland: Ideological and Historical Dimensions*, Blackhall Press, Dublin.

Oliver, M. (1990) *The Politics of Disablement*, Macmillan, Basingstoke.

O'Reilly, A. (2003) *The Right to Decent Work of Persons with Disabilities*, IFP/Skills Working Paper No.14, International Labour Organization, Geneva.

O'Connell, P.J. (ed.) (1999) *Astonishing Success: Economic Growth and the Labour Market in Ireland*, Employment and Training Paper No. 44, International Labour Office, Geneva.

Ryan, A. (1999) *Walls of Silence – Ireland's Policy Towards People with a Mental Disability*, Red Lion Press, Kilkenny.

RTÉ (2017) 'More than 1,200 people under 65 living in nursing homes for the elderly,' https://ww.rte.ie/news/2017/0808/.

Toolan, D. (2003) 'An Emerging Rights Perspective' in S. Quinn, B. Redmond (eds.) *Disability and Social Policy in Ireland,* UCD Press, Dublin.

CHAPTER 2

Building Number 4 – Berlin

'T4' was the shorthand name for No. 4 Tiergartenstrasse, Charlottenburg in West Berlin, from where Adolf Hitler's National Socialist German Worker's Party (Nazi Party) directed a campaign of mass murder against adults and children with mental, intellectual, neurological and physical disabilities. This campaign started in 1933 with the forced sterilisation of people to prevent them reproducing individuals like themselves who would cause the so-called degeneration of the Aryan race. This was based on a new law entitled the Law for the Prevention of Offspring with Hereditary Diseases. The law came into operation in 1934 and extended to those with schizophrenia, inherited mental retardation, epilepsy, blindness, deafness or serious bodily deformities (Lewy, 2000, 39). Described sometimes as 'race hygiene', sterilisation was promoted to prevent the transmission of so-called hereditary 'inferiority' and promote the retention of offspring regarded as of superior physical status.

Abortion facilities and services were banned in 1933 (Bock, 1983, 400). In the first year of the campaign, 43,775 persons were sterilized. Overall, it is estimated that 320,000 were sterilised. The conceptual framework behind this forced sterilisation propagated that some life was unworthy of life. The births of those deemed unworthy of life were to be restricted by law, and in this way the German people, as an ethnic group or *Volk*, would become strong again because only the fittest would survive. There are other words meaning 'people' in German, such as *Menschen* and *Leute*, but *Volk* has the meaning of the 'popular masses' or 'nation'. Those selected for the sterilisation programme were those who were believed to be a financial or genetic burden on the state and who did not belong to the *Volk*: the mentally ill or intellectually impaired, who usually resided in institutions.

This was eugenics in practice; it was among the ill and those with cognitive and intellectual disabilities that the method for National Socialism's

Final Solution was tested, namely death by gassing. However, it started out as a sterilisation programme that soon moved to annihilation.

The National Socialists did not invent eugenic thinking. The idea of racial betterment was not uncommon at the time; this was due to the dissemination of eugenic ideas which fostered the notion that the human population could be improved by selective reproduction of those with positive physical traits and reduced reproduction of those with negative physical traits (Evans, 2010). Francis Galton (1822–1911), a cousin of Charles Darwin and an English scholar, is widely credited with being the founder of eugenic thinking in the late nineteenth century. His ideas were taken up with enthusiasm across the western world.

Involuntary sterilisation was common in Nordic countries, including Denmark, Norway, Finland and Sweden. Sweden is a case of special interest since it was introduced under a Social Democrat government and influenced by the eugenic thinking of the then internationally famous welfare thinkers Gunnar and Alva Myrdal. About 60,000 Swedish men and women were sterilised between 1935 and 1976 (Wielard, 1996). Interpretations vary as to why there were so many coerced sterilisations in the Nordic countries. Some argue that it was propelled by the desire to create a more perfect society and remove the reproductive capacities of the working class and institutionalised persons (Lennerhead, 1997, 156). So great was the interest in ensuring that the reproductive capacities of certain groups were restricted that the papacy intervened. Pope Pius XI condemned eugenic thinking in his encyclical in 1930 (Casti Connubii, 1930). His encyclical is better known for its condemnation of contraception and abortion: the treatment of eugenics takes up just one page. However, condemnation of negative eugenics by the Vatican posed a limited barrier to its widespread application in regions of devout Catholicism, such as parts of the US, France and southern Germany. The Pope's intervention shows that even in the early pre-war years, consensus was not widespread.

Despite some opposition, some thirty US states had passed compulsory sterilization laws by 1931 (Scally, 2002, 15); legal developments had laid a trail for the compulsory sterilization of people with disabilities. In 1927, the US Supreme Court ruled favourably in a landmark case that allowed the state of Virginia to sterilise a young, poor white girl named Carrie Buck who was in an institution for the 'feebleminded' (Cohen, 2016). The teenage Miss Buck had given birth to a child outside of marriage and was placed in the institution. It was wrongly alleged that both she and her baby were 'feebleminded'. She was not 'feebleminded'; she had been raped by a relative of the foster family with whom she had been living as a foster child, and that family wanted rid of her before they were disgraced. Her case went to the US Supreme Court. Her story is well told in a contemporary book by US journalist Adam Cohen. The Supreme Court stated: 'It is better for all the world, if instead of waiting to execute degenerate offspring of crime, or to let them starve for their imbecility, society can prevent those who are manifestly unfit from continuing their kind. The principle that sustains compulsory vaccination is broad enough to cover cutting the Fallopian tubes' (*Buck v. Bell*, 1927).

Carrie Buck later left the Virginia State Colony for Epileptics and Feebleminded, where she had been interned, and went on to marry twice, hold down jobs and stay in touch with her biological family. She regularly wrote letters to her mother and others, letters that showed little sign of the 'feeblemindedness' of which she had been accused. After Miss Buck was sterilised, it opened the doors for other states to eagerly and legally pursue their own population-control plans, which inspired the Nazis.

German health policy was not backward in the years before the Second World War. On the contrary, it was widely regarded as advanced. Public health policies decried the use of asbestos in workplaces and the smoking of tobacco, and restricted the use of pesticides and colorants. The consumption of wholemeal bread and vegetarian food was encouraged. Medicine and medical research played a crucial role in these public health perspectives (Cocconi, 2011, 9). The eugenic policies of sterilising and killing parts of the population were not based on ignorance: these decisions were made in the context of a relatively advanced and knowledgeable health system.

Important targets for sterilisation were the European peoples known in the majority language as 'gypsies'. Present in Europe from the fourteenth century and known under a variety of names, their persecution under National Socialism was, and is, just one of the many trials the Roma, Sinti and Yenish people had to face.[1] In 1935, Hitler announced

---

[1] The Yenish are the third largest nomadic group in Europe, living primarily in Germany, Switzerland, Austria, Luxembourg, Belgium and France. Their origins, unlike the Roma and Sinti peoples, are European.

his anti-Jewish laws, which were interpreted to apply to gypsies as well. A law limiting citizenship to those of German or related blood deprived gypsies of the right to vote. Local authorities proceeded to remove gypsies and part-gypsies (*Zigeunermischlinge*) from the electoral rolls. The Law for the Prevention of Offspring with Hereditary Diseases meant that prospective partners had to possess certificates that declared they were fit to marry; such certificates were not issued to those described as gypsy peoples. In addition, the origins of the entire gypsy population of Germany were researched by a special department in Munich, the Central Office for Gypsy Affairs, to determine their racial purity.

Such was the continued prejudice toward nomadic peoples over the centuries that when the European Convention on Human Rights was being drafted in 1950, after the Second World War, the right to liberty and security in Article 5 provided an exemption for 'vagrants'. States could not be accused of failing to protect nomadic peoples as they are not protected by the European Convention on Human Rights. When Ireland transposed the European Convention on Human Rights into Irish law in 2003 as the *European Convention on Human Rights Act 2003*, the 'vagrant' exemption under Article 5 (1)(e) was carried over into Irish law and now appears in the 2014 act.[2]

These developments are not merely of historic interest. In 2011, a young Roma woman accused the state of Slovakia of having sterilised her without her informed consent after giving birth by Caesarean section. She claimed this violated her right to safeguard her reproductive health. The European Court of Human Rights agreed that her rights had been violated. In the judgement: 'the Court could not but note a certain mindset on the part of the medical staff as to the manner in which the medical situation of a Roma woman should be managed [and] resulted in a medical intervention of a particularly serious nature being carried out without her informed consent' (*V.C. v. Slovakia*, 2011).

The situation of Roma women in the Czech Republic is no better, where a group of thirty Roma women came together to support each other after coercive sterilisations in 2005 (Holt, 2005, 927). Helena Ferencikova, one

---

[2] The author spoke about this exemption at Oireachtas hearings on the Human Rights Law on 16 January 2003 and was ridiculed by the representative of the Bar Council of Ireland.

of the thirty, sued the Czech health authorities and received an apology but no compensation. The group later expanded to eighty cases, with twenty more awaiting registration (Clifford, 2016; Open Society Foundations, 2011).

As recently as 2014, North Carolina was receiving applications for compensation from men and women who had been coercively sterilised between 1929 and 1974 on the orders of a state-wide eugenics board. Some had been as young as ten or twelve years old. Among the estimated 7,528 victims, some 73 percent were persons with intellectual disabilities, 22 percent had some form of mental illness and 5 percent had epilepsy. In other words, 100 percent of those sterilised had a perceived disability. A sum of $10 million had been set aside as compensation, but the number of survivors was unknown, so it was unclear whether all the budget could be distributed.

Among those who were ardent advocates of 'selective breeding' was Marie Stopes (1880–1958), who is best known today for her public campaigning on contraception at the turn of the last century and the name behind the Marie Stopes women's clinics. Despite her present-day association with progressive and feminist movements of her time, she was a member of various eugenic societies and a believer that only those 'fit to reproduce' should be allowed to do so. She favoured forced sterilisation if necessary, believing that many conditions were inherited and should not be allowed to manifest in children. In 1922, she decried that 'society allows the racially negligent, the thriftless, the careless, the feebleminded, the very lowest and worse members of the community to produce innumerable tens of thousands of warped and inferior infants' (Stopes, 1920, 236). Stopes's views in her book, as epitomised above, went to nine editions and were translated into eight languages.

Stopes's views were opposed by Dr Halliday Sutherland, who believed that she was mistaken about the inherited transmission of diseases such as tuberculosis (TB). Halliday wrote about his evidence on the infectious nature of TB in the *British Medical Journal*, basing it on his own work in Marylebone in London. Stopes and Halliday ended up in court three times over the issue. Halliday considered Stopes to be anti-working class and her determination to 'breed out' TB as both morally and clinically wrong. Halliday eventually won in court (Stopes, 1920, 1434).

Eugenic views were not confined to conservatives or scientists. Many other social democratic and socialist thinkers popularised eugenic views, including the so-called dangers of feeblemindedness in populations. Among the latter were George Bernard Shaw, writer and thinker; John Harvey Kellogg (the man behind Kellogg's Cornflakes), who established a race betterment society; Havelock Ellis, doctor and writer; H.G. Wells, author; and the founders of the London School of Economics, Sydney and Beatrice Webb (Shakespeare, 2008, 25).

Mr Arnold Marsh, a well-known Quaker and headmaster, wrote a reservation to the *Report of the Commission on Emigration* in 1956, disputing the views of the commission that to marry and found a family is a basic human right:

> I question the theory that the right to marry is absolute and inherent in the individual. In some circumstances, it may need to be withheld. A person should not found a family that is likely to be abnormally defective, and if it is accepted that to do so is morally wrong, I know of no reason why society should not put legal restraints on it as much as on other types of wrong-doing. Conversely, I should like to advocate a method of promoting the birth of more children who might be expected to be above the average, intellectually and physically, and morally too if that could be contrived [...] married people whose offspring might be expected to give special enrichment to the race might well be urged to consider it a special duty to enlarge their families (Marsh, 1956, 237).

In an analysis of the right to consent, the Law Reform Commission considered that 'while the worst features of the eugenic movement may be in the past, some echoes of it continue to linger' (2013, 17). The Department of Justice had earlier observed that prior to 1993, the legal protection in terms of sexual assault offered to mentally impaired women only extended to being 'carnally known'. There was no legal protection from other forms of sexual molestation or assault. This seemed to suggest that the rationale of the law was to prevent mentally impaired women from becoming pregnant but did nothing to preserve their dignity or protect them from abuse (Department of Justice, Equality and Law Reform, 1998).

Eugenics in Germany

Eugenic thinking, taken up by the National Socialist Party in Germany and copying the American legislative examples, was to have catastrophic consequences. 'Nazi medical experiments lay at the heart of the long process of eugenic purification through medicine [...](F)rom the summer of 1933, when a sterilisation law had identified a number of hereditary illnesses [...] threatening the purity of the German race, euthanasia programmes had been set up, foreshadowing the death camps, to select and exterminate those with mental or physical deformities' (Moorehead, 2011, 233).

The next stage in this life-unworthy-of-life-programme was to actually eliminate those whose very existence threatened the German and Austrian states (united in *Anschluss* since 1938). Unlike the sterilisation programme, this new phase was conducted in a deceitful and clandestine manner to avoid provoking public backlash. Parents of children with disabilities were encouraged to place their children in special institutions on the promise of treatment, where they were subsequently killed by drug overdoses or starved to death. State doctors were required to notify all births of infants with defects. Roughly 5,000 children and infants were killed (United States Holocaust Memorial Museum). Their parents were sent carefully worded letters, drafted using the children's files, stating that their children had passed away from a variety of childhood illnesses.

In the German monument for those who died under the T4 killing programme, the following stories illustrate the very different backgrounds and histories of the adult victims:

Fjodor W. Korso, 1905–41
In the Soviet-Finnish Winter War of 1939–1940, the Belarussian worker Fjodor Wassiljewitsch Korso suffered a serious head injury. Subsequent complaints led to his admission to the psychiatric hospital in Mogilev. After the German invasion of the Soviet Union, a German Special Commando Unit killed him in a purpose-built gas chamber, probably with the use of benzene gas. His family searched for him in vain.

Martin Bader, 1901–1940

The master shoemaker Martin Bader was admitted to hospital in 1938 because of Parkinson's syndrome and murdered by killing staff in Grafenek hospital, south of Stuttgart in 1940. From then on, his wife had to look after herself and their children alone. After the war the authorities did not recognise Martin as someone who had been persecuted by the Nazi regime and refused his family any compensation.

Ilsze Lekschas, 1895–1940

Ilsze Lekschas lived with her husband and two children in Memel, East Prussia, which was occupied by Lithuania in 1923. From 1925 she was treated by medical specialists for religious delusions while living with a foster family. After Memel was incorporated into Germany in 1939, she was moved to Soldau transit camp in Poland and was murdered there by an SS Special Commando Unit in a mobile gas chamber.[3]

Robert Lifton argues that the euthanasia programme involved a particular emphasis on the state, with the national collectivity or *Volk* having ownership over the death of its people. The life of the state had to be weighed against the death of some. Two German intellectuals contributed significantly to the discussion, namely Dr Karl Binding, legal theorist; and Dr Alfred Hoche, professor of psychiatry at Freiburg University. In a German language book entitled *Permission to Destroy Life Unworthy of Life*, they described direct medical killing as a healing treatment or healing work in relation to the *Volk*.[4] Their book is thought to have been extremely influential in converting intellectuals, both legal and medical, to a specific form of euthanasia. Their targeted subjects were the incurably ill, the mentally ill, the feebleminded and the so-called retarded and deformed children (Lifton, 1986, 46). According to historian Gisela Bock, after the demobilisation of the First World War, asylum patients were neglected and ill-treated so that they would not consume health resources, which ought to have been

---

[3] Edited extracts from the German and English text at the memorial to the victims of the Nazi T4 programme can be read at: gedenkort-aktion-t4-euthanasie-im-3-reich-berlin.

[4] German title: *Die Freigabe der Vernichtung lebensunwerten Leben*. 1920, Leipzig.

devoted to the returning soldiers. In addition, the returning soldiers had been exposed to or participated in war killings and death on a mass scale, which may have numbed them from empathising with the weaker members of society. These and similar arguments continue to be articulated up to the present day, providing new interpretations of historical analysis.

Shortly after this, adults were included in the euthanasia programme. Doctors all over Germany were asked to complete questionnaires on their patients as to their mental condition, whether they were German or not and whether they had been five years or more in an institution. The doctors were primarily, but not exclusively, psychiatrists and neurologists. The questionnaire could have appeared to be seeking statistical information.[5] Panels of three doctors would subsequently examine the questionnaires and mark those to be killed. Beginning in 1942, these patients were then removed from their institutions and transported in vans with dark-tinted windows to six specially constructed euthanasia centres, where they were murdered by gassing in shower rooms. These murders of people with disabilities represented the first use of gas as a means of killing people in an enclosed space.

Over 12,000 staff were employed in the programme, including those who had to take the bodies from the gassing facilities to the crematoriums. Families were given fictitious accounts of the deaths of their loved ones from a disease or during an operation, along with a false death certificate and an urn of ashes. Doctors and medical students spent weeks and months fabricating the letters and matching them to the patient's original files. The entire killing programme was conducted in a planned, systematic and deceptively bureaucratic manner but also in a medicalised and professional way (Lifton, 1986, 315). Hartheim Castle near Linz in Austria was the site of one of the first euthanasia gassing centres for people with disabilities as well as Catholic priests and bishops.

The collaboration of the German medical profession with the regime of the Third Reich was smooth, relatively turbulence-free and intertwined at all levels of the profession, including teaching, research, management and clinical practice levels. Describing how the Nazis took over TB clinics in Switzerland, Adam Lebor remarked: 'This was possible only through the cooperation of a great many German physicians, the majority of

---

[5] United States Holocaust Memorial Museum: www.ushmm.org.

whom willingly "coordinated" themselves with the regime and joined the Nazi party [...] with the exception of the teaching profession, none of the liberal professions showed such a large participation in the Nazi party as the German physicians' (Lebor, 1997, 158–9).

The collaboration involved institutions, universities and research centres who expelled their Jewish colleagues and those who were married to Jewish or part-Jewish partners. At least one hundred Jewish doctors ended up in Auschwitz concentration camp, where they were recognised as prisoner 'doctors' and allowed to do minor work in the camp 'health' centre.

Besides doctors, university professors and various university anthropology departments were involved in the thinking and analysis behind the sterilisation and euthanasia programmes, as well as in the practical work carrying out body measurements and cataloguing people as to their Aryan characteristics and general fitness. Eventually there was so much public disquiet that the euthanasia programme was officially 'ended', but notwithstanding this, it continued for some time after.

People with disabilities of a physical, cognitive and mental kind were the first to suffer mass murder under Hitler's National Socialism. The first gas chambers were designed, constructed, tested out and used to annihilate them. Thousands participated in this killing programme, including doctors, student doctors and nurses (Friedlander, 1995).

The significance of the sterilisation programmes and the treatment and mass murder of people with disabilities was somewhat underestimated by historians in the immediate aftermath of the war. There have been shifts over time in the interpretation of these events. Newer interpretations are constantly emerging, challenging previous perspectives and theoretical analyses. The ideologies that underpinned the mass murder of people with disabilities – ideas of inferiority, of being less human than others, less entitled to equal treatment – were not openly, publicly or widely challenged, and so, it may be argued, they persisted.

There were exceptions to this, such as the work of journalist and author Ernst Klee, who unearthed vast amounts of statistics and documents and reanalysed and published them (Klee, Dressen and Riess, 1996). He challenged previous conceptions about eugenics and demonstrated in his writings that the euthanasia of people with disabilities and the annihilations in the concentration camps were not the work of a small, demented minority but the undertaking of hundreds of professionals who assimilated the killing goals. He identified a large number of these professionals and published their jobs and locations in post-war Germany. Klee was the Julian Assange of his era. The Italian scientist Primo Levi wrote an account of his own arrest and time in Auschwitz as early as 1947 (Levi, 1979). He had some difficulties getting a publisher: publishing houses such as the Italian publisher Einaudi believed it was too early for such a book. The first publication had a very small print run, and it was not until later that translations reached a wider global readership (Sands, 2017). There were also the responses of Karl König and his friends, who founded the first Camphill school-community in Aberdeen, Scotland in 1940. König was a refugee who had fled Austria after it was taken over by Hitler. He was influenced by the ideas of Austrian educational philosopher Rudolph Steiner and Robert Owen's ideas of shared living and working. He believed that no human life was unworthy of living and that humans share an equal spiritual essence. Today, there are twenty Camphill Communities on the island of Ireland and three Rudolph Steiner schools.

However, even before the war trials by the Allied forces and the judgements of Nuremberg, some progressive-minded doctors mobilised at an international level to found the World Medical Association (WMA) in 1947 in order to establish a new standard of ethics in medicine. The importance of ethics during wars and the issues raised by experimentation were tackled by the WMA. This was manifest in the ethical code known as the Declaration of Helsinki. The Irish Medical Association was present at the founding annual general meeting. Between 1947 and 2015, no German doctor was voted chairperson. Nevertheless, a crisis did arise when German Vice President of the German Medical Association, Dr H. J. Sewering, presented himself as a candidate for the presidency of the WMA. It emerged that he had been a member of the *Schutzstaffel*, commonly known as the SS, the elite Nazi paramilitary force.[6] Sewering was forced to withdraw as a candidate and questions arose as to why his past had not been highlighted earlier, both in Germany and internationally (Sullivan, 1993).

---

[6] The *Schutzstaffel* or SS was a major and greatly feared paramilitary organization under Adolf Hitler and the Nazi Party. The SS was the organization most responsible for the genocidal killing of millions of Jewish people, among others. The SS were distinct from the secret police, known as the Gestapo (*Geheime Staatspolizei*), and the stormtroopers, known as the SA (*Sturmabteilungen*).

Some theories as to why eugenic ideas were still strong after the end of the Nazi regime may lie in the persistence of these ideas that had flowed through the Third Reich and had been insufficiently addressed and misinterpreted at the end of the war. This is the view of Hanuaske-Abel, who, in an extensive historical research document, argued that the German medical profession threw itself deliberately, consciously and enthusiastically into a downward spiral of criminal and unprofessional behaviour as early as 1933 by targeting mentally ill and disabled people (Hanauske-Abel, 1996). Abel specifically consulted original German-language sources to counter the oft-prevailing views that the medical profession had drifted into inhumane positions or were suddenly caught off-side. The professionals aligned with and pledged themselves to the state, rather than upholding independent, professional medical standards. They expelled Jewish doctors from the medical profession and conveyed the idea in their practice of medicine that some people were 'sub-human'. They collaborated in and organised large-scale murder.

Apart from the Doctors' trials at Nuremberg, further Doctors' trials took place in Germany after the war. Of those who registered for denazification after the end of the Second World War, 97.8 percent were acquitted, amnestied or received nominal sentences. This is unsurprising when one notes that 90 percent of lawyers had been Nazi Party members and that no judges from the Nazi era were prosecuted: they simply retook their places on the bench and resumed business as usual (Bower, 1995, 198–9). Winston Churchill and Konrad Adenauer are also reputed to have argued for the early release of the convicted Marshal Manstein, who had led the invasion of Poland and who was arrested and sentenced to eighteen years in prison but was released on health grounds after five years (Bower, 1995, 292). In another case of acquittal, Senator Joe McCarthy, from Wisconsin in the US, took it upon himself to defend Hans Schmidt, who officiated, every day for four years, at the shootings of prisoners at Buchenwald concentration camp.

Some doctors escaped judgement, such as Auschwitz's Josef Mengele, who fled to Latin America where he survived prosecution and eventually died in 1979. Some, like Dr Max de Crinis, concealed his role in the euthanasia programme. The influential and ruthless Dr Werner Heyde escaped from custody but was later found working as a doctor and was identified by Prof. H. G. Creutzfeldt (known for first recognising the Creutzfeldt-Jacob disease or 'Mad Cow' disease) who himself had been a supporter of the Third Reich. Heyde committed suicide before his trial began. Some, like the sadistic Dr Hermann Pfannmüller, were tried in German courts and received relatively short sentences of six years (Lifton, 1986, 103–32).

At the end of the Second World War, those who had been coercively sterilised prior to and during the rule of the Third Reich were generally denied any compensation on the grounds that it was undertaken under a law prior to the war and was not a war crime unless related to concentration-camp experiments. It was also proposed that the main victims were German and thus did not fall into a war category as there were similar eugenic laws in allied countries. Sweden's compulsory sterilisation law only lapsed in 1976. Compulsory sterilisation became a highly charged topic of discussion among female German historians in the 1980s, an exchange known as the 'Historians' Debate' or *Historikerstreit*, which was launched by the feminist historian Gisela Bock (Guba, 2009; Bock, 1984).[7] Bock argued that the compulsory sterilisation of women was part of the National Socialist gendered worldview. The German sterilisation law of 1933 remained on the German statute books until 2007. German victims of sterilisation had to prove that they were victims of Nazi persecution to obtain compensation. In the event, less than 1 percent of applicants received compensation payment. Nor was there any attempt to reverse male vasectomies (Weindling, 2014).

Eugenics in Norway

In a perverse turn of fate, the ending of the Second World War and the German occupation of Norway led to a disastrous situation for mothers who had become pregnant by German soldiers and their 10,000 children. Norway was a particular target of the Nazi regime, who considered the blonde and blue-eyed Norwegian women as ideal subjects to increase the Aryan 'race'. German soldiers and officers of the occupying army were encouraged to propagate the Aryan race by engaging in sexual relations with young Norwegian women. This was all part of Heinrich Himmler's

---

[7] This author attended a series of seminars on the topic presented by Gisela Bock at the European University Institute in Florence, 1987–1988.

Lebensborn (Font of Life) programme to generate a master race. *Lebensborn* clinics were constructed where future, usually young, Norwegian mothers could give birth in improved and private circumstances and receive material supports in the form of cash and kind for their contribution to the programme, which they may have been unaware of.

With the returning post-war government, the women and children were subjected to public violence, abuse, ill treatment and marginalisation for being 'collaborators' with an occupying power. There was no actual legal basis for their treatment (Elster, 2006, 324–28). The children were treated as pariahs in the years after 1945 (Dahl, 2006). The government determined, with the support of psychiatrist Ørnulv Ødegård, that about 4,000 of the children were feebleminded and/or carriers of defective genes (Simonsen, 2006, 30). These were the same arguments that had been used under the Nazis to sterilize and kill those regarded and classified as sub-human. Hundreds of the publicly despised children were rounded up and placed in adult asylums or centres for children and adults with intellectual disabilities; others were fostered, often to their own detriment. Hundreds of women were detained without arrest in a series of internment camps, and some fled with their children to Sweden. Among the latter was the child Anni-Frid Lyngstad (Frida), who went on to become a member of the Swedish pop group ABBA (Connolly, 2002). During the 1990s, some of the children, now adults in their fifties, began to protest at their treatment as children. Some 154 of them took a case to the European Court of Human Rights in 2003, seeking compensation from the Norwegian government for their treatment (ECHR, 2007; Paterson and Hall, 2001). Their case was lost, with the argument that too much time had elapsed since the post-war events in question, the claimants had not exhausted all the domestic remedies, and imprecise details had been presented to the court as to the wrongs done to them.

After the War

Were those who designed and implemented the programmes to sterilise and then murder the sick, the mentally ill and people with disabilities punished after the war when the Allies occupied Germany? Not really. The Nuremberg military trials concentrated mainly but not exclusively on those who had been responsible for the Holocaust during the war and those doctors who had carried out so-called experiments on internees in the concentration camps. At the first 'Doctors' trial', the prosecutors were faced with twenty or so doctors and health administrators who were accused of crimes against humanity. This was the first of twelve Doctors' trials. In all, sixteen of the doctors were found guilty, of whom seven were sentenced to death by hanging and executed on June 2, 1948. The evidence of the surviving 'prisoner doctors' in Auschwitz was important in these trials. Other doctors were tried later in German post-war courts.

Alice Ricciardi von Platen (1910–2008) was a doctor sent by the German Medical Union to attend the Nuremberg Doctors' trials and was mandated to write an account of the trials, where it was assumed she would side with the accused. She did not, and this meant that she never really had a medical career in Germany again (Ricciardi von Platen, 2000).

The denazification of Germany was intensely and widely opposed by sections of the British and American military and political forces during their occupation of Germany at the end of the war (Bower, 1995).[8] No German judge was prosecuted; all were permitted to return to the judiciary; some 90 percent of lawyers had been Nazi Party members. Of the doctors and nurses who presided over the Hartheim and Sonnenstein killing centres and who were responsible for up to 899 deaths, none were charged with murder. None of the convicted received more than a year's sentence. In farming, just six hectares of Nazi-confiscated land was taken back and redistributed. One of the limited successes of denazification was the German coal industry, where thanks to the miners' refusal to work under former Nazi overseers and foremen, a denazification process took place. In the American zone of occupation in 1948, of the twelve million persons registered as having worked with the Nazis, 97.8 percent were acquitted, amnestied or received nominal prison sentences.

This normalisation of those responsible for atrocities during the Nazi period included the business elite. For the company directors who had actively worked with the Nazi government, including Siemens, Thyssen, Bosch, Krupp, Deutsche Bank, Dresdner Bank, Flick Steel and IG Farben, it was business as usual.

---

[8] This paragraph is based on Tom Bower's (1995) *Blind Eye to Murder, Britain, America and the Purging of Nazi Germany – A Pledge Betrayed*, London: Little Brown and Company.

The Implications

So, what can we say about these events and their relevance for people with disabilities today? *The Lancet* presents the facts:

> Between 1933 and 1945 [...]doctors initiated and implemented an estimated 350,000 coerced sterilisations, the killing of 260,000 people with mental illness or disabilities and an estimated 25,000 human experiments, which led to the deaths of more than 2,000 research subjects[...](T)ens of thousands of bodies of the executed were delivered to German medical institutes for teaching and research, and in some departments bodies of Nazi victims were still used for these purposes until at least 1990 (Kolb, Weindling, Roelke, Seithe, 2012, 722–3).

It would appear that the German Medical Association waited for all the doctors active under the Nazi regime to die before apologising in 2012, sixty-seven years later, for the medical atrocities committed under Nazism; perhaps this late apology was timed to avoid dishonouring the profession and denigrating leading medical figures. From the 1950s to the 1990s, evidence emerged, bit by bit, of what medicine had become under Nazism: a killing machine. But denial was the order of the day. As recently as the 1990s, the German Medical Association had refused to publish the documents of the Nuremberg Doctors' trial. They were eventually published through private donations.

When considering the position of those who promoted eugenic thinking and particularly those who advocated the mutilation or killing of those with mental illness, cognitive disorders or intellectual disabilities, it is worth recalling that the medical professions in northern Europe and America were later the strongest supporters of the medical model of disability. This model defined people by their physical and mental deficits rather than their human attributes. If it has been hard to circumvent or replace the medical model of disability with a social or human rights model, it is partly because its roots go back decades, into the late nineteenth and early twentieth centuries. The medical model of disability has been normalised as common-sense thinking. It constitutes a serious obstacle to the rights of people with disabilities in relation to independent living and assisted decision-making in the twenty-first century.

In 2000, eugenics was specifically prohibited in the *Charter of Fundamental Rights of the European Union* with the words of Article 3 stating: 'In the fields of medicine and biology, the following must be respected in particular: the prohibition of eugenic practices, in particular those aiming at the selection of persons' (OJEC, 2000).

The public forgetfulness of people with disabilities, who were the victims of crimes against humanity, was somewhat remedied in 2014 when a memorial was unveiled at the site of Tiergartenstrasse 4 in Berlin.[9] Belatedly, recognition was given to those who had lost their lives because they were not deemed suited to survival of the fittest.

Conclusion

There should never be a hierarchical distinction among human beings that some humans are of greater worth than others, that the human essence of some people is worth less than others and that some humans are unworthy of living. The theme of humanity in all its imperfections and frailties should be oriented to understand the inherent dignity of all human beings. Eugenics is not the answer and neither is survival of the fittest. On the contrary, societies should be judged, if at all, by their treatment of the weak, the wounded and the unwell, their minorities and their undocumented.

Eugenic practices continued after the defeat of the Third Reich by Allied forces, after the ending of the Second World War and after the Nuremberg trials. These practices often were in the form of coerced or semi-coerced sterilisation. With involuntary sterilisation advocated by socialists and social democrats, it is not surprising that the issue has drifted into an underworld with little light at the end.

Eugenic thinking lingered on in society and can be found today both in Ireland and Europe in the reluctance to facilitate people with disabilities from leading an ordinary life outside of institutional constraints.

---

[9] Visited by the author in 2018.

Chapter 2 References

Bock, G. (1983) 'Racism and Sexism in Nazi Germany: Motherhood, Compulsory Sterilization and the State', *Signs: Journal of Women in Culture and Society*, Vol. 8, No. 3, University of Chicago Press.

Bock, G. (1984) 'Racism and Sexism in Nazi Germany, When Biology Became Destiny: Women in Weimar and Nazi Germany', *Monthly Review Press*, New York: pp. 271–96. First published in *Signs: Journal of Women in Culture and Society*, Vol. 8, No. 3 (1983).

Bower, T. (1995) *Blind Eye to Murder, Britain, America and the Purging of Nazi Germany – A Pledge Betrayed*, London: Little Brown and Company, pp. 198–99.

Buck v. Bell, 274 US 200 (1927) Opinion of the Court: scholarworks@gsu.edu. Accessed January 1, 2017.

Cocconi, G. (2011) *Il genocidio dei matti, Europa,* Casa Editrice Le Lettere, p. 9. www.ecostamp.it. Accessed September 1, 2017.

Casti Connubi, (1930) paragraphs 68–71, Libreria Editrice, The Vatican.

Clifford T. (2016) 'Government Admits Forced Sterilization', *Prague Post Magazine*, Budapest: www.praguepost.com/news/2902-government-admits-forced-sterilization. Accessed March 23, 2017.

Cohen, A. (2016) *Imbeciles: The Supreme Court, American Eugenics and the Sterilization of Carrie Buck*, New York: Penguin Press.

Connolly, K. (2002) 'Torment of the ABBA Star with the Nazi Father', *The Guardian*. Accessed July 20, 2018.

Crean, E.Y. (1997) *Breaking the Silence, The Education of the Deaf in Ireland 1816–1996*, Irish Deaf Society Publications.

Dahl, H. F. (2006) 'Dealing with the Past in Scandinavia' in John Elster (ed.) *Retribution and Reparation in the Transition to Democracy,* Cambridge University Press.

Department of Justice, Equality and Law Reform (1998) *The Law on Sexual Offences – A Discussion Paper,* Stationery Office, Dublin.

Elster, J. (2006) 'Redemption for Wrongdoing: the Fate of Collaborators after 1945', *Journal of Conflict Resolution,* Vol. 50, No. 3.

EUROCAT (2013) Press Release. 'Response to Inquiry into Abortion on the Grounds of Disability': http://www.abortionanddisability.org. Version Date: April 2013. Responding on behalf of EUROCAT: European Surveillance of Congenital Anomalies.

European Court of Human Rights, Application 187/12/03. *Thiermann and others v. Norway,* Press Release 153/2007 of 8 March 2007.

Evans S. E. (2010) *Hitler's Forgotten Victims: The Holocaust and the Disabled,* Ivan R. Dee Publishers.

Friedlander, H. (1995) *The Origins of Nazi Genocide: From Euthanasia to the Final Solution,* University of North Carolina Press.

Guba, D. A. (2009) 'Women in Nazi Germany: Victims, Perpetrators, and the Abandonment of a Paradigm'. Concept, V. 33: https://concept.journals. villanova.edu/article/view/327/290. Accessed September 14, 2016.

Hanauske-Abel, H. M. (1996) 'Not a Slippery Slope or Sudden Subversion: German Medicine and National Socialism in 1933', *British Medical Journal,* Vol. 313.

Holt, E. (2005) 'Roma Women Reveal that Forced Sterilisation Remains, *The Lancet,* Vol. 365, No. 9463.

Kolb, S. Weindling, P. Roelke, V. Seithe, H., (2012) 'The Art of Medicine – Apologising for Nazi Medicine: a Constructive Starting Point,' *The Lancet,* Vol. 380. 722–3.

Law Reform Commission (2013) Report: *Sexual Offences and the Capacity to Consent*, Dublin.

Marsh, A. (1956) *The Commission on Emigration and Other Population Problems, 1948–1954 Reports*, Stationery Office, Dublin.

Lebor, A. (1997) *Hitler's Secret Bankers: How Switzerland Profited from Nazi Genocide*, Pocket Books, London.

Klee, E. Dressen, W. and Riess, V. (1996) *Those Were the Days: Holocaust Through the Eyes of the Perpetrators and Bystanders*, Hamish Hamilton.

Levi, P. (1979) *If This is a Man* (1947) and *The Truce* (1963), translated into English by Stuart Woolf, Penguin.

Lifton, J. (1986) *The Nazi Doctors: Medical Killing and the Psychology of Genocide*, Papermac, London.

Lennerhead, L. (1997) 'Sterilisation on Eugenic Grounds in Europe in the 1930s: News in 1997 but Why?' *Reproductive Health Matters*, Vol. 5, No. 10, Elsevier, London, pp. 156–161.

Moorehead, C. (2011) *A Train in Winter: A Story of Resistance, Friendship and Survival*, Chatto and Windus, London.

Office of Justice for Sterilization Victims: www.ncadmin.nc.gov/about-doa/special-programs. Accessed December 2, 2016.

Official Journal of the European Communities (OJEC) (2000) C 364/14 18.12.2000.

Open Society Foundations (2011) 'Against Her Will – Forced and Coerced Sterilization of Women Worldwide', Budapest.

Paterson, T. and A. Hall (2001) 'Norwegian Government Sued over Children Nazis Left Behind', *The Telegraph*: www.telegraph.co.uk/worldnews/europe/Norway/1324127. Accessed September 25, 2017.

Ricciardi von Platen, A. (2000) *Il nazismo e l'eutanasia dei malati di mente*, Le Lettere. Italy.

Sands, P. (2017) 'Primo Levi: If This is a Man at 70', www.theguardian.com/books/2017/apr/22. Accessed September 20, 2017.

Scally, J. (2002) 'A Little Genetic Knowledge is a Dangerous Thing, *Studies*, Vol. 91, No. 361, Irish Province of the Society of Jesus.

Shakespeare, T. (2008) 'Disability, Genetics and Eugenics,' in John Swain and Sally French, (eds.) *Disability on Equal Terms*, Sage Publications Ltd.

Simonsen, E. (2006) 'Into the Open – or Hidden Away? The Construction of War Children as a Social Category in Post-War Norway and Germany', *NORDEUROPAforum*, No. 2. Berlin.

Stopes, M. (1920) *Radiant Motherhood – a Book for those who are Creating the Future*, G. P. Putnam and Sons Ltd, New York and London.

Sutherland, H. (1912) 'The Soil and the Seed in Tuberculosis', in *British Medical Journal*, (2), p. 1434.

Sullivan, P. (1993) 'Allegations about Nazi Past Force Resignation of WMA President-Elect', *Canadian Medical Association Journal*, Vol. 148 (6), pp. 995–96.

United States Holocaust Memorial Museum: https://www.ushmm.org/wlc/en/article.php/moduleId=10005200. Accessed September 9, 2016.

V.C. v. Slovakia, Case 18968/07 2011. Strasbourg, and Information Note on the Court's Case Law, No.146.

Weindling, P. (2014) Sterilization Compensation. Retrieved from http://eugenicsarchive.ca/discover/connections/535eeaff7095aa0000000217.

Wielard, R. (1996) 'Forced Sterilisation Exposed in Sweden, Belgium', Hartford Web Publishing: www.hartford-hwp.com. Accessed November 3, 2016.

CHAPTER 3

The Richmond Asylums at Grangegorman and Portrane

The two Richmond asylums located at Grangegorman in Dublin and Portrane in North County Dublin are separated by one hundred years and two different purposes. This chapter offers an analysis of the differing socio-political thinking behind their establishment, which helps us to reflect on their influence today. The two asylums were significant economic entities in their time. The social background of the residents of the two asylums in the years preceding Irish independence is presented in this chapter, drawing from a new database that holds the characteristics of the 3,000 people for whom the asylums were both a home and a site of confinement.[1]

The Richmond Asylum at Grangegorman

1801 was a bad year in Ireland. A rebellion had failed in 1798. There had been revolutions in France and America, and the passage of the Act of Union, forming a United Kingdom of Britain and Ireland, came into effect. The Irish parliament was abolished and the College Green building was to be sold to Bank of Ireland. Many businesses along with the entire Irish parliament moved to London and were soon followed by the occupants of the fine houses on Dublin's Gardiner Street and Summerhill. A great deal of manufacturing collapsed, creating a huge void in both capital investment and labour, which only increased with the advance of the century. This trend was so meticulously analysed by Alice Murray in 1903 (Murray, 1970).

---

[1] The database was constructed by extracting, patient by patient, the social characteristics of over 3,000 persons from the 1911 census and entering these onto an Excel sheet under several headings, from which a number of calculations could be made and profiles constructed.

Following the collapse of the French Revolution, the Napoleonic wars subsequently engaged England in large-scale protracted hostility against France until Napoleon's eventual defeat at Waterloo in 1815. War and domestic rebellion added to the sense of insecurity among the ruling class of Ireland. 'But the slump which follows a war brought about a fall in the price of wheat, a return to pasture and unemployment for the peasant population which, already large, was increasing fast' (Curtis, 1936, 357).

The population of Ireland was between four and five million, of whom hundreds of thousands lived a hand-to-mouth existence in rural and urban areas. The House of Industry at Grangegorman had been established by the *Act of Parliament, 1772* and opened in 1773. Its aims were to support those who were helpless due to age and infirmities; men who were (involuntarily) 'committed as vagabonds and sturdy beggars'; women who were 'idle, strolling and disorderly'; and deserted and fatherless children under the age of eight (House of Commons, 1828). The thinking was to contain and incarcerate the deserving poor, away from public view and off the streets.

The House of Industry in 1811 was noteworthy, according to a contemporary guide: 'This is a very spacious building established for the reception of the poor, who are received without any recommendation [...] There are also forty-six cells for lunatics [...] the beggars of Dublin, in general, have a strong aversion to this house; many of them, however, are compelled by force to enter' (Carrick, 1811).

It was also noteworthy for the poor of the city, who detested it: 'as the Black Cart of the institution went on its rounds collecting strolling beggars from the streets in order to compel them to seek work and shelter, riots sometimes broke out' (Maxwell, 1937, 131).

The five governors of the House of Industry in 1800 already possessed considerable prestige and not only in their respective emerging professions of law and medicine. As the governors of a rapidly expanding set of social and penal institutions, they enjoyed the patronage of the Lord Lieutenant of Ireland, who had approved their appointments. Governor James Henthorn was a surgeon, a member of the Royal College of Surgeons of Ireland (RCSI) and president of the RCSI in 1822, and of the Dublin Society, now known as the Royal Dublin Society (RDS). Governor Rev. William O'Connor was also associated with the RCSI. Edward Houghton was a barrister and member of the Dublin Society, and a member of the so-called 'Patriot' wing of Dublin Corporation, which opposed the tithe laws.[2] Rev. James Horner was a Presbyterian of the Scots Church and chaplain to the Four Courts Marshalsea debtors' prison. Governor Francis L'Estrange was a prominent surgeon with Mercer's Hospital, a member of the RCSI and its president in 1796. He was also a member of the Dublin Society and assistant surgeon at the House of Industry Hospitals.

The speciality of medicine was emerging as a distinct profession at this time. Henthorn, Houghton and L'Estrange were progressive-minded men in their membership of the Dublin Society, founded in 1731 to promote agriculture, arts, industry and science in Ireland. They appear to have astutely judged that the time was ripe for a major publicly funded collective initiative for the poor – a gigantic lunatic asylum for paupers and so-called 'idiots'. They believed that Ireland should have some welfare institutions. For a site, they merely had to look around the House of Industry.

Social Interventionism Begins

At the turn of the eighteenth century, this area, in the northwest of Dublin city, was a microcosm of the proliferation of institutions of confinement that were to expand on a national scale for the next century and a half. It became a zone for public intervention in social welfare institutions and a place of ever-increasing differentiation between categories of (using the terms of the day) paupers, beggars, idiots, lunatics, prisoners, orphans, debtors and about-to-be transported women prisoners (Nolan, 2013). The House of Industry governors had considerable experience of institutional governance at the House of Industry, as well as at various hospitals and prisons. Their idea for a new, specialised institution – a public lunatic asylum – was part of the dominant trend to collectivises, centralise, institutionalise and segregate. This was far from laissez-faire economics – it represented major state intervention in the functioning of civil society.

The district of Grangegorman was not part of Dublin city at this time. It was a very old area with a village (Stoneybatter) along with apple and pear orchards. Charles Stanley Monck of County Wicklow had voted for the Act of Union and in 1800 became a viscount (The Royal Kalender, 1822) and sold his land at Grangegorman to the state (Enniskerry Local History). 'Pensions, places and peerages were handed out to those whose

---

[2] A tithe was a tax to support the Church and its clergy.

votes were up for auction' according to historian Ó Tuathaigh (1972, 32). By 1760, the North Circular Road had been built and provided a site for the new asylum, the existing House of Industry and a new penitentiary (Dublin City Council, 2012, 2). The chosen site for the new asylum was beside the House of Industry, which became the North Dublin Union in 1838 (Moylan, 1945, 3; 1945a, 55; 1945b, 103). In proximity were Newgate Prison of 1773, the North Circular Road Orphan House of 1791 and the Richmond Bridewell.

The House of Industry was a secular powerhouse surrounded by quasi satellite institutions – all with a function of specialised confinement. They had national as opposed to purely city-wide or local missions. Local Bridewells – prisons – were attached to police stations and Poor Law Unions around the country tried to divest themselves of their pauper lunatics and have them placed in the Richmond Asylum via petitions to the Chief Secretary's office. The governors of the House of Industry were successful in highlighting the value of a public asylum to the Lord Lieutenant; accounts for the House of Industry in 1810 included a sum to launch the asylum. Public funding rose from £32,241 in 1809 to £48,628 in 1810 and up to £52,375 in 1813, the year before the Richmond Asylum officially opened (House of Commons, 1828, 3). The arguments in favour of a pauper's asylum were more likely to prevail in Ireland, since the prevailing system of private 'madhouses' hardly existed: 'The madhouse system had its roots in the practice of boarding unmanageable pauper lunatics at the parish's expense in private dwellings and of confining wealthier patients under the care of individuals, often medical men or clergymen [...] private madhouses [became] the principal institutions catering for pauper lunatics in anything approaching a specialized way' (1973, 659–60).

The system was open to appalling abuses. These private madhouses had never taken off in Ireland due to its poverty and the absence of a class of people of sufficient worth who had a house suited to such a purpose.

The architect for the new Richmond Asylum, chosen by tender, was Francis Johnston. He was extremely well known for his public buildings, such as the conversion of the Parliament Building on College Green for the use of Bank of Ireland, Hardwicke Place Church, Nelson's Pillar and the General Post Office (GPO). Johnston was influenced by what he knew of the Bethlehem Asylum in London. Bethlem was a notorious institution, which gave us the English word 'bedlam'. Up to the year 1770, paying visitors were allowed to amuse themselves by prodding the imprisoned lunatics through the bars of their cells.

Johnston designed a solid, square stone building with room for 250 patients. It had nothing of the classical columns he designed for the GPO or the aesthetic values of other commissions. While the site of the Richmond Asylum was being negotiated with the Monck family, the governors of the House of Industry received instructions to add more land to their purchase for the purposes of a penitentiary. The notion of confinement was deeply entrenched.

The proposers of the Richmond Asylum had a modern and European approach to their social venture and determined that they needed to know more about best practice overseas. In some regards they were 200 years ahead of their time. Dr Alexander Jackson, a physician at the House of Industry and later State Physician, visited no less than eighteen different lunatic establishments outside of Ireland. This was an enlightened approach to constructing an asylum and reveals perhaps something of the innovative influence of the Dublin Society in garnering new perspectives on problematic issues. There were new ideas in England and France about the treatment of lunatics that did not relate to the need for closed institutions but more to the conditions of incarceration inside them. One idea was the work of Philippe Pinel at the Bicêtre Asylum and the Salpetrière in southwest Paris, who cautiously began to dismantle the chains, shackles and imprisoning devices of some of the insane. The Society of Friends in York had established a Quaker retreat for the insane, employing more humane methods of incarceration. Dr Jackson came to a number of conclusions in his report for the governance of the new asylum, which were at considerable variance with dominant thinking:

- The asylum should be a hospital like any other; he rejected mere confinement.
- There should be a resident full-time medical superintendent and not a mere administrative governor.
- Patients – not inmates – should be examined prior to admission and not afterwards, as was the practice.
- The hospital should have no business other than as a hospital – no side lines in selling patient labour or manufactured goods, no exhibiting of patients for the amusement and spectacle of others.

From the outset, there was a lack of clarity as to the function of the new asylum among the other powerholders. For the Lord Lieutenant, the Duke of Richmond, it would deal with disorderly residents among the paupers in the House of Industry and was thus a poverty and social order issue. For the physicians and surgeons, it was an opportunity to expand into a new area of professional expertise by separating the insane from the destitute and confining them in a specialised institution (Finnane, 1981, 24). Contrary to Dr Jackson's suggestion, the first head of the asylum was 'Moral' Governor Richard Grace, who presided there from 1815 to 1830 and who was not a doctor. Doctors were appointed on a part-time basis and none were resident. Richard Grace lost no time in advancing himself personally and petitioned the Under-Secretary's office to ask for the appointment of Assistant Governor of the House of Industry. Therein, he claimed that the Richmond, under his management, had experienced 'an improvement … in the moral treatment of the insane, heretofore unknown in this country' (Chief Secretary, 1820).

The hopes of the founding governors of the House of Industry were further dashed when a separate fifteen-person board of governors was established by the Lord Lieutenant in 1815. Banking capital was emerging as a new force in Ireland with the Patriotic Assurance Company (1824), the Hibernian Bank (1825) and the Provincial Bank of Ireland (1825). This was reflected in changes to the board. The new board included a judge (Arthur Moore) and some bankers from the Huguenot La Touche family (John, David and Peter), who were associated with the Female Orphanage on South Circular Road. The hope of the founding governors that the asylum would receive mainly 'curable' inmates from the House of Industry, in the same line of specialisation as the adjacent Richmond Fever Hospital and Surgical Hospital, was dashed.

Despite its many learned and concerned promoters, there appears to have been quite a lot of administrative chaos in the early management of Richmond. Addressing by letter the House of Commons Select Committee on the lunatic poor in Ireland, the new Richmond governors admitted that they had no register of admissions or discharges from the asylum since residents first occupied it in 1814 (House of Commons, 1817, 32). Problems were already emerging at this stage as the asylum was filled to capacity and many 'lunatics' were awaiting admission from outside Dublin: 'not only was the asylum full to overflowing, but the house of industry was soon as full as before, and that as to finding accommodation for those at a distance, it was altogether out of the question' (Tuke, 1882, 4).

In 1827, a full 40 percent of residents of Richmond were categorised not as lunatic but as 'idiots' (Tuke, 1882, 7). The nearby lunatic wards in the House of Industry contained over 400 occupants. The push was for a greater number of asylums, and this was provided. The Richmond Asylum itself was in a continuous state of building and extension in 1814, 1815, 1816, 1849–51, 1854–55, 1887–89, 1895–96, 1898–99 and 1912 (Irish Architectural Archive).

The influence of the utilitarian ideas of philosopher and reformer Jeremy Bentham were important in the *Lunacy Act, 1845*, which saw insanity as a medical rather than a moral problem and the insane as persons of unsound mind rather than as rejects of humanity. It signalled the end to the 'Moral' governor's regime and the beginning of medical control of the asylums, epitomised in the significant appointment of Dr Joseph Lalor to Richmond in 1857 (Lalor, 1879, 361).

Table 1: The number of lunatics and idiots, as returned in census forms, 1851–1911*

Years of Census	At large	In Asylums	In Prisons	In Workhouses	Total
1841	*	*	*	*	3,258
1851	4,635	3,436	286	1,623	9,980
1861	7,277	5,016	294	1,511	14,098
1871	6,490	7,551	7	2,457	16,505
1881	5,491	9,443	*	3,479	18,413
1891	4,970	12,261	*	3,957	21,188
1901	3,868	17,350	*	3,832	25,050
1911	4,044	21,795	*	2,598	28,437

(Census, General Report, Ireland 1911, p. xli)
* Information not available or not applicable.

The census in 1851 began a comprehensive study of lunatics and idiots and created a series of research information and analysis, which continued until 1911.The new Free State series, starting in the 1926 census, discontinued the study of lunatics and idiots. In Table 1, we see that as the numbers of lunatics and idiots in the workhouses declined, the numbers in the asylums and at large rose at the turn of the nineteenth century. Of the 21,795 people in asylums in 1911, the vast majority were in public asylums (Census 1911, 188), and one in seven was in the Dublin City or County districts. Of the 21,000 people in asylums, it may be estimated that 1,000 had intellectual disabilities (Census, 1911, xli–xlii).

As early as 1817, a select committee was appointed to evaluate the situation of the mentally disordered and proposed the establishment of a national network of lunatic asylums for the poor. The Commission of General Control and Correspondence was established, which divided Ireland into districts containing between one and three counties each. Using an architectural model already developed by William Stark (1770–1814), whose most important work was the 1809 Glasgow Lunatic Asylum, which was influential in the development of hospital design, Francis Johnston (1760–1829) and William Murray (1789–1849) proposed two standard building types in a classical style, mixing the radial and the panoptic with corridors and landings projecting out from a central hub.

The building of the district asylums across Ireland was a large-scale enterprise mobilising architects, stone masons, quarry workers and general labourers. It was a massive economic intervention into the construction industry at a time when agriculture and manufacturing were in abeyance. The twenty-two asylums, built between 1814 and 1869, laid the infrastructure for a form of national public welfare, the management of which significantly devolved to regional authorities. This, unintentionally perhaps, promoted the emergence of an indigenous governing class; every asylum required a governing board.

A bill for converting the Richmond Lunatic Asylum in Dublin to the purposes of a District Lunatic Asylum was published on 28 April 1830 and provided for the expansion of asylums all over Ireland. They were to be regionalised by county or counties with other counties/parts of counties, with a size of between one hundred and 150 beds. This change represented a break with the concept of the parish and a move to strict county level with a centralisation of power over the regions. The purpose of these district asylums was to accommodate the lunatic poor and 'idiots' and hold custody of insane persons.

Table 2: Principal diseases of lunatics and idiots in Ireland, 1901 and
1911, at the Richmond Asylum at Grangegorman and Portrane, 1911.

Principal Diseases	Ireland 1901 Numbers	Ireland 1911 Numbers	Ireland 1911 %	Portrane 1911 Numbers	Portrane 1911 %	Grange-gorman 1911 Numbers	Grange-gorman 1911 %
Mania	11,190	11,053	39	533	34	581	35
Mania acute	547	2,131	8	-	-	-	-
Mania suicidal	12	47	(0)	-	-	-	-
Mania puerperal (1)	12	12	(0)	-	-	-	-
Melancholia	3861	5,389	19	352	23	451	28
Monomania	163	604	2	-	-	-	-
Paranoia	-	-	-	162	11	232	14
Idiocy (intellectual disability)	5,065	4,343	15	236	15	133	8
Idiocy with epilepsy	151	99	(0)	-	-	-	-
Dementia	3,552	3,570	13	217	14	187	11
Dementia with epilepsy	145	399	1	-	-	-	-
Epilepsy uncomplicated	302	496	2	16	1	9	1
Other (2) and Not known	49	294	1	34	2	47	3
Total	25,050	28,437	100	1,550	100	1,640	100

Source: Census, General Report, Ireland 1911, p. xliii; census 1911, Richmond Asylum at
Portrane.
(0) Numbers especially small.
(1) Puerperal psychosis after childbirth can be accompanied by psychotic episodes.
(2) Includes persons described as 'decrepit' and those who had diseases associated with syphilis.

The conditions that the patients suffered from cannot be assumed to be
exact. Psychiatry was still in its infancy, and exact categories of illness are
contentious to this day. Some definitions may have been more associated with one doctor compared to another. Melancholia, which may have
broadly indicated depression in patients, was associated with high proportions of patients at both the Richmond in Grangegorman and at Portrane.

Conditions such as epilepsy are today amenable to pharmaceutical treatment and would not warrant admission to a mental health facility. 'Paranoia' was a condition affecting 14 percent of patients at Portrane. Today it would be very likely regarded as a symptom of an underlying illness. The diagnosis of 'mania' was an important category at both Grangegorman and Portrane, as well as at a national level. It is not clear what precisely it described, but probably referenced patients with agitated behaviour or delusions.

A significant proportion of those held in asylums such as Portrane were not mentally ill. The asylums of the day included those with intellectual disabilities, persons with epilepsy and others whose conditions led to loss of lucidity on a temporary basis. A closer examination of those who were in Grangegorman and Portrane in 1911 (Table 2) reveals that apart from those who were described as melancholic or manic, there were persons described as 'idiots' who were intellectually impaired, persons with dementia and others who were deaf or blind. The allocation of a diagnosis appears to be arbitrary. The largest number of persons are described as 'manic', some of whom, one might speculate, had schizophrenia or bipolar disorder. There was also a perplexing underlying cause of mental illness known as 'seduction'. This category of underlying condition affected both men and women and may refer to a semi-coerced intimate relationship followed by abandonment.

Unfortunately, however, some of the categories used to describe the nature of the illness are so inexact as to be meaningless. Commonly used terms included 'mania', 'melancholia', 'monomania', 'insanity', 'moral insanity', 'derangement', 'dementia' and 'lunacy' (Malcolm, 1999, 328). There was a possible gender bias in that the underlying cause attributed to certain conditions were women-specific, such as childbirth, uterine disorders and climacteric (menopause).

Besides the Asylums

The revival of religiosity in nineteenth-century Europe prompted the expansion of European religious orders, societies and congregations in Ireland. Orders such as the Daughters of Charity, the Oblates of Mary Immaculate, the Holy Ghost Fathers, the Society of Jesus, the Marists and the Sisters of Charity of Jesus and Mary arrived between 1855 and

1861. There were many attractive endeavours for the female religious orders to save female souls from the damnation of unfettered sexuality. In parallel to asylum building, confining institutions for non-married mothers and abandoned women and girls were established by the private sector (Department of Justice and Equality, 2013). Some seventeen Magdalene-type institutions for so-called fallen women were founded between 1814 and 1843. The Good Shepherd Order, which specialised in providing 'asylum' to ex-prostitutes and unmarried mothers was one of thirteen French female congregations that established itself in Ireland between 1840 and 1900 (Clear, 1987, 137). The French Bon Secours – discussed in Chapter Four, were in fact late arrivals. However, the religious orders showed no interest in managing or operating asylums and left the so-called 'insane' to the state; this was to remain the case after 1922. The state was rather more ecumenical in its approach. At Portrane, there were two chapels, one Catholic (75 percent of patients) and one Church of Ireland (22 percent of patients). Into this religious mix can be added other different religions, religious associations, societies and fellowships such as Presbyterian, Jewish, Baptist, Methodist and Quaker.

The establishment of Poor Law Unions operated by guardians based on the 1838 *Poor Law (Ireland) Act* provided an additional governance outlet for the frustrated farmers and urban traders as well as a national boost to the quarrying and building industry. It also caused alarm to property owners liable to pay a rate to support the services. By 1843 there were 112 workhouses constructed or under construction out of an eventual 130 buildings. So great was the enthusiasm for this dismal solution to poverty that initially, there was gross under-occupation of the workhouses, with only 50,000 of the 100,000 places occupied before the Great Famine (Crossman and Grey, 2011, 70–71). Workhouses were solutions without a problem. Two years later, the Famine soon filled the vacant places and a further thirty workhouses were built between 1849 and 1853 during the second phase of building of the new lunatic asylums.

The Controversial Building of Portrane Asylum

The building of Portrane Asylum was controversial from the moment of its conception in the 1890s. It was conceived and built as an extension of the

Richmond Asylum at Grangegorman. While known as 'Grangegorman' and 'Portrane', they were actually two branches of the same asylum during the period under discussion in this chapter. The plan, design and costs of construction, indeed the very need for a new asylum, was heatedly debated among the intelligentsia. These discussions were articulated in extensive and often hostile exchanges in the House of Commons and the House of Lords from 1895 to the turn of the century. Portrane Asylum arose as a response to the chronic overcrowding in the Richmond Asylum at Grangegorman; it had been enlarged to house roughly 1,000 patients, but by the end of the century it was accommodating between 400 and 700 in excess of this provision (Hansard, 1895). The governors of the Richmond Asylum had explored the option of expanding Grangegorman, but the land around it was contaminated by cesspools and could not be built upon. This discovery led to calls to close Richmond and move the patients out to the north-Dublin coastal peninsula to the Portraine Estate (Hansard, 1895). These ideas were exacerbated by an outbreak of beriberi disease in Richmond in 1897 (Hansard, 1897). This was mistakenly interpreted as an infectious disease rather than a dietary deficiency of thiamine/vitamin B1.

As early as 1879, there had been appeals to stop the building of lunatic asylums in Ireland and switch instead to 'boarding out' patients in their communities and pay the families 'outdoor relief' to look after them (Hancock, 1876, 29; Hancock, 1879, 454). In the event, Portraine, later called Portrane, was to become a legal extension of Richmond Asylum at Grangegorman with over 3,000 patients eventually living on the two sites.

The competition for architects to design Portrane was yet another occasion for a controversy that is reminiscent of today. The design by George Coppinger Ashlin was the most expensive of the three finalists but was awarded the commission nonetheless. Ashlin was allowed to reduce his proposed costs without the other applicants being afforded such an opportunity (Clerkin, 2012). The site for the asylum was the vast Portraine Estate of 460 acres, situated on a narrow peninsula of land in the countryside of northeast County Dublin. Ashlin's gothic design style incorporated a number of interesting concepts which now reveal advances in the concept of mental illness. It envisaged different buildings not only for women and men but for the different classes of the insane according to the category or gravity of their illness, which was then quite an innovative perspective. Buildings for the patients were designed in a separated cascade on either side of a large clock tower, with the intention that patients be exposed to light. Lord Ashbourne, undoubtedly dreaming of English rural idylls, discussing the plan for the asylum in 1895, imagined that 'inmates could have the opportunity of gardening and moderate occupation in horticulture to relieve the mind' (Hansard, 1895).

The asylum opened bit by bit and by 1897 some 200 patients were already being moved to temporary buildings on the site (Hansard, 1897). By 1901 there were 398 patients and just thirty attendants (Census 1911 Enumerators Form). No medical superintendent had been appointed by 1898, giving rise to further exchanges in the House of Commons (Hansard, 1898). By 1911, Portrane was overcrowded, with 1,550 occupants, not long after building had been completed to accommodate 1,200 patients. Meanwhile, the Richmond Asylum at Grangegorman was as overcrowded as ever, with 1,640 inmates (Census, 1911).

The residents of the Richmond Asylums at Grangegorman and Portrane now numbered 3,190. It was a massive industrial scale of operation to manage and supply them with food, drink, bedding and asylum attendants. A multitude of events and perceived conditions could trigger a confinement in the asylums. An idea of this is conveyed in the *Report of the Inspector of Lunatics* (1912) on admissions to Richmond and Portrane. In 1912, some 537 new patients were admitted. Of these, none were admitted via the courts, by the inspector of lunatics, from Dundrum, (for the dangerous insane) from prison transfers or by the Navy. The vast majority – 91 percent of the 537 – were admitted by local medical officers (for a fee) or by someone reporting them as 'dangerous' and in seven cases, by someone 'paying' for them to be admitted.

Table 3 shows the occupational background of the residents of the Richmond Asylum at Grangegorman and Portrane in comparison with Ireland as a whole in 1911. The proportion of residents who were in the professional classes in the asylums (5 percent) coincides with that of Ireland as a whole. That they were in a pauper asylum might indicate that their circumstances or illness had brought them into hard times. A hundred years ago, we have evidence that mental and physical disability impoverished those who experienced it.

The proportion of those (mainly women) in domestic-service occupations is three times higher than Ireland as a whole (15 percent), reflecting the availability of live-in service jobs in the city. The proportion of residents holding agricultural jobs (5 percent), was five times less than Ireland as a whole; this is unsurprising.

What is most interesting is that a quarter of all residents of the two asylum sites had industrial occupations. These occupations were precise in description and ranged from printers to tailors to blacksmiths. From Table 3 there is evidence that the asylum population, allowing for an urban and rural context, was not especially different from Ireland as a whole. It reveals that about 60 percent of the asylum inmates had experience of specific occupations and were unlikely to have been part of a drifting and directionless mass swept into confinement. More than 60 percent of occupants were literate. The principal diagnoses were of 'melancholia' (25 percent) and of 'mania' (31 percent). In addition, some 8 percent of occupants were described as 'idiot'.

Table 3: The occupations of patients at the Richmond Asylum at Grangegorman and Portrane, 1911.

Class	Class of occupation	Total No. Ireland	Total % Ireland	Total No. P.	Total % P.	Total No. G.	Total % G.	Total No. G.+ P.	% Two R. Asylums
	Professional	128,389	5.2	79	5	86	5	165	5
	Domestic	133,220	5.4	199	13	268	16	467	15
	Commercial	92,910	3.7	91	6	88	5	179	6
	Agricultural	645,382	26.0	71	5	82	5	153	5
	Industrial	378,286	15.3	430	27	376	23	806	25
	Indefinite, non-productive	1,101,085	44.4	246	16	328	20	574	18
	Not known/ not clear	-	-	434	28	412	25	846	26
Total		2,479,272	100	1,550	100	1,640	(99)	3,190	100

Census of the Population of Ireland, 1911. General Report, Tables, extracted from Table 70, p.105; Richmond Asylum at Grangegorman and Portrane database: author's own, constructed from Census 2011 National Archives.

(P) Portrane Asylum
(G) Grangegorman Asylum
(R) Richmond Asylum

The Richmond Asylum at the Turn of the Century

The practice in Ireland at the turn of the century was to pack as many so-called 'lunatics', 'imbeciles', 'idiots' and blind and deaf people as possible into the asylums. Whether Ireland became more insane or whether more people were just admitted to asylums has been a subject of vigorous debate for more than a century. Speaking of the nineteenth century, medical historian Brendan Kelly argues: 'The minimal provision for the destitute mentally ill in Ireland gave way to a system of large district asylums dotted around the country, mostly filled to capacity and some twenty private asylums registered in 1893, located chiefly in Dublin and its surrounding towns' (2008, 22).

At the turn of the century, there was widespread concern at the rise in numbers of those being admitted to public asylums. So great was the worry that a special report from the Inspector of Lunatics was prepared on the increased prevalence of insanity in Ireland; it was published in 1894. The concerns are typified by the sardonic remarks of Edward Saunderson MP in the House of Commons in 1898: 'there is a large decrease in the population and a large increase in the number of lunatics. If this continues to go on the result will soon be arrived at when all the Irish people will be lunatics' (Hansard, 1898).

In a review of the subject, Walsh and Daly (2004) found it difficult to distinguish between new admissions to asylums and transfers from other institutions, asylums, workhouses and prisons. This was an impediment to determining whether more of the institutional population were being moved into asylums or whether more of the population were being diagnosed as mentally ill.

The number of persons classified as being a 'lunatic' or 'idiot' rose over the seventy-year period, from 1841 to 1911. This had been studied by Hancock (1876, 29–38). The increase between 1901 and 1911 was of 13.5 percent. Having examined and analysed admission papers to public asylums from this period, Malcolm noted that admission to an asylum was often triggered by an incident of violence in or around the family and concluded that: 'The diagnosis of hereditary disorder seems frequently to have been based on little more than gossip and hearsay … the Irish inmate, like the English one, was not marginal, either socially or economically' (1999, 181–2).

While this enormous capital project was being undertaken, the plight of workers and their families in the city was pitiful (Crowe, 2012). The chronic social conditions endured by Dublin's working class were documented in a British government inquiry: the Housing Conditions of Dublin's Working Classes, conducted between 1913 and 1914. According to this inquiry:

- 26,000 families lived in 5,000 tenements.
- 500 of these tenements were condemned as being incapable of ever being fit for human habitation.
- Over 20,000 families lived in a single room, of which 12,000 were occupied by three or more persons.
- 5,000 families had only two rooms in which to live.

Harold's Cross Road in south Dublin was described as: 'Fringed with rows of hovels as unsightly as they are, from a sanitary point of view, dangerous' (Mulhall, 1999, 58). The death rate in the city in the first decade of the twentieth century was 24.8 per 1,000, and the infant mortality rate in 1910 was 142 per thousand births. This compared with a figure of 103 per thousand births in London. Almost one-third of the population of the city lived in the slums, in conditions described thus: 'the Gothic pinnacles of St. Patrick's Cathedral … look directly down upon the quarter of the Coombe where the degradation of human kind is carried to the point of abjectness beyond that reached in any city of the Western world, save perhaps Naples' (Wright, 1914).

The appalling conditions in which people lived undoubtedly contributed to the spread of disease and to stress because of the overcrowded conditions.

'Landlords left their properties in a squalid condition, meanwhile tenants sublet corners of rooms to sub-tenants. Washing facilities were negligible, clothing and bed clothes were flea- and lice-ridden' (Jones and Malcolm, 1999, 131).

The causes of diseases were attributed in the census reports to a variety of factors. By far the most significant was the hereditary factor. Apart from this, an amazing mixture of causes appear, including anxiety, terror, grief, religious excitement, seduction and reversal of fortune. Among the physical causes were intemperance, malformation of the brain, epilepsy, head injury, sunstroke, childbearing and nervous diseases. Other physical causes were claimed to arise from bronchitis, pneumonia, kidney and liver disease, alcohol and opium.

The Asylum Children, 1911

The Richmond Asylums at Grangegorman and Portrane also accommodated a number of children and young people in 1911. There were fifty-four children and young people under the age of twenty-three. The majority were boys and were in Grangegorman. There is no explanation in reports as to how these young people came to be admitted to an adult asylum.

J. M. from Dublin was seventeen years old in 1911 and was in Grangegorman. He was able to read and write and had been suffering from 'mania' since he was thirteen years old. T., aged seventeen and from Dublin, was a tailor who had been suffering from depression from the age of twelve, while thirteen-year-old P. M. from Dublin was in Portrane and was described as an 'imbecile' from birth. On the same page of the census return, with the same description, was ten-year-old J. McM., also from Dublin.

In Grangegorman, P.C. was only five years old – a pauper child from Dublin. He was described as an 'imbecile' and as blind – conditions he apparently had had since birth. P.B. was just seven years old, from Garristown in north Dublin. He too was intellectually impaired and unable to speak. Nine-year-old R. from Dundalk was incarcerated, and besides being intellectually impaired, was also described as deaf and dumb. Fourteen-year-old G. was from a Church of Ireland family in Dublin. He was described as having had 'mania' since birth.

Between 1901 and 1911, the population of Ireland decreased by 1.7 percent from emigration, the Great Famine of 1845, and the rising age and low rate of marriage and family formation. The proportion of persons classified in each census as mentally ill or intellectually disabled rose from one in every 657 in 1851 to one in every 154 by 1911. In contrast, in Dublin, the population rose between the 1901 and 1911 census by 6 percent. In the province of Leinster, which includes Dublin city and county, the ratio of lunatics to non-lunatics was as high as one in every 136 of the population (Census, 1911, xlii).

Entering an asylum would not necessarily improve one's chances of survival since the diseases of the time also entered and took hold. In the Grangegorman and Portrane asylums in 1910 there were cases of erysipelas, enteric fever, scarlet fever, measles and dysentery, which gave rise to nine deaths among patients and staff (The Sixtieth Annual Report, 1911). The kind of diseases to be found in Ireland in 1912 that people died from were: tuberculosis: 10,294; whooping cough: 1,045; influenza: 1,025; measles, diphtheria, scarlet fever, tetanus, dysentery and typhus fever: 34 (Registrar General, 1913, 136; Prunty, 1999, 160).

The reliability of data on infectious diseases has to be cautioned, as one in five deaths were not certified and not all burials were registered. In Dublin's Glasnevin Cemetery, 800,000 people are buried in either 'poor ground' or in 'unpurchased graves' (MacThomáis, 2012, 109). Between 1908 and 1989, about 5,000 former patients were buried on the grounds of the Portrane Asylum in unmarked graves (Kelly 2002).

Moving from the general to Dublin more specifically, Table 3 illustrates the wide range of locations where those who were insane or had related conditions were reported to be found. These locations altered between 1901 and 1911, with less recorded as being in workhouses in 1911 and more recorded as being 'at large' in the community or in asylums, as mentioned above. The social administrators of the time took a broad view of this and made no assumptions that the insane were to be found only in hospitals.

The occupational picture of Portrane is that of a city. Although a public asylum, the proportion of professional persons is the same as that which prevailed nationally: 5 percent. In the overcrowded conditions of Dublin living at the time, it is easy to imagine that an incident or incidents of real or threatened violence or eccentricity could prompt a family to place a relative in the Richmond Asylum or in Portrane.

About 25 percent of residents were migrant workers from within Ireland or abroad. The origins of the asylum residents were collected quite carefully, as the cost of paying for their presence in the asylum would be laid on the local authorities of their county of origin. The catchment area of Richmond was supposed to be Dublin, Louth and Wicklow. Of the 1,041 for which information was recorded, 75 percent did in fact come from those three counties. The remaining 25 percent came from every one of the thirty-two counties of Ireland, from Donegal to Kerry and from Down to Wexford. This made the Richmond Asylum a somewhat 'national' system. In addition, a small number came from England, Scotland, Europe and America.

Table 4: Place/Country of origin of residents of the Richmond Asylum at Grangegorman and Portrane, 1911.

Origin	Persons at Grangegorman	% of all known at Grangegorman	Persons at Portrane	% of all known at Portrane
Dublin, Kingstown (Dun Laoghaire), Wicklow, Louth	890	73	786	76
Elsewhere in Ireland	274	23	218	21
UK	40	3	28	3
America and Overseas	16	1	9	(0)
All known origins	1,220	-	1,041	
Origin Not known	420	-	509	-
Totals	1,640	100	1,550	100

(Database of Richmond Asylum at Grangegorman and Portrane, extracted from Census 1911, National Archives).

Of the 20,021 persons who were defined as lunatics or idiots in Dublin City and County in 1911, just 3,630 persons were in public asylums, of which 3,161 persons or 87 percent were to be found in the Richmond Asylums at Grangegorman and Portrane.

The method of assessing literacy in the census was a simple three-point indicator of 'can read and write', 'read only' and cannot 'read or write'. Literacy levels in Portrane were on par with the literacy levels of other asylums (64 percent literate) when one combined those who could read and write together with those who could read. Levels were lower than in the general population of Dublin City and County (Census 1911, p. xliii; Census 1911 General Report; Table 131, p. 238).

Unlike Grangegorman, there was plenty of work for patients at Portrane, and the institution ran itself profitably in the years 1911–12. A part of its income came from the farm on its 469 acres of land, a part of which was given over to buildings, grassland and woods and a quarter of which was cultivated to provide food to Portrane, Grangegorman and to the open market. The asylum had its own tailor's workshop, henhouses, piggeries, calves, cow barns, stables, harness rooms and turf stores (Inspector, 2013). Although only nine residents from the 1,550 were described as agricultural workers, that is the work with which many residents were provided.

The asylum was managed on a military model with a 'general' – the chief superintendent, Dr. H. M. Cullinan; a small number of 'officers'; a resident doctor; the matron: Miss J. E. Hughes (1902–12); the chief attendant, chief gardener, storekeeper: Mr. W. Smelzer; and gatekeeper, Mr. J. Clancy. There were also a small number of nurses and a large number of untrained attendants who relied on not-very-insane residents to assist them. The matron, Miss Hughes, is worth a specific mention as one of the founders of the Irish Nurses Association, the Irish Matrons Association and a strong supporter of professional nurse training, especially in mental health (Luddy, 1995, 226; BJN, 1910, 69; BJN, 1913, 430). The census indicates that sixty-four staff members and their families were living in houses on the grounds, and an estimated fifty-six staff appeared to live in the asylum buildings or were on duty there on census night (National Archives, 2013).

By 1911, trade unions were emerging and expanding in Ireland. As early as 1896 an association of asylum attendants was formed in England which became the National Association of Asylum Workers. Between 1896 and 1905, the Asylum Attendants of Ireland Trade Union was formed and was registered as the Asylum Workers Union between 1905 and 1910 (COHSE, 2013; Warwick, 2013). This development worried the asylum governors, and staff candidates who were offered a job at Portrane were obliged to sign a form declaring they would not join the union.

1922: No Freedom, No Franchise

By 1923/1924, the issue of what to do with the entire institutional frame-work for detaining and retaining people came up in Dáil committees, questions and debates. The Office of Justice of the Peace was abolished and replaced by commissioners who could certify people into asylums under Section 10 of the *Lunacy Ireland Act, 1867*. In 1923 it was determined that persons in prisons, lunatic asylums and workhouses were not to be regarded as resident there for the purposes of voting in elections; their disenfranchisement was confirmed in law. Under the *Local Government (Temporary Provisions) Act, 1923*, the workhouses were to be emptied (to some extent) of their occupants. But not to freedom. The designated occupants were dispersed to other institutions. The *Local Government Act* of 1923 abolished workhouses, centralised social administration at a county level, provided for the establishment of new institutions and permitted the poor to receive relief in or out of the newly renamed workhouses – now county homes. Section 69 of the Local Government Bill, 1924 provided that:

> All district lunatic asylums maintained by county councils under Section 9 of the *Local Government (Ireland) Act, 1898*, shall henceforth be styled and known as district mental hospitals, and the title of every such district lunatic asylum shall be and is hereby amended by the substitution therein of the words 'mental hospital' for the words 'lunatic asylum'.

The position of patients with mental illness, persons with intellectual disabilities, epilepsy and other conditions is well outlined from the dominant political and social perspective in 1927. In that year, the *Report of the Commission on the Relief of the Sick and Destitute Poor including the Lunatic Poor* was published (Commission, 1927). The report anticipated a continuing rise in admissions to asylums, now renamed as mental hospitals. This was due to the transfer of ever greater numbers from the workhouses to the hospitals. As for the so called 'idiot' children, the report advised that they should be transferred to other institutions, but as to where exactly, they were unclear. They had sought advice from the Stewart Institution at Palmerstown but were discouraged there as the hospital did not think it was achieving much success (Commission, 1927, p. 111, 443).

At the committee stage of the Local Government Bill in 1923, the government was accused of having no 'mind' or 'ideal' as to what do about the Poor Law by the famous Labour TD Thomas Johnson. Johnson was right in that the new state had no perspective of a life without institutionalising and confining the unwanted and the troublesome. The core of the proposal was to rearrange the names of the institutions in a saintly fashion and reshuffle the cards by redistributing the occupants in a different way. Ninety years later, the implementation of the mental health policy: *A Vision for Change*, is still awaited.

Conclusion

In the absence of a national parliament, the great lock-in of poor, peasant and working-class men, women and children was a form of nation building by collective public institutions such as asylums, industrial schools, Magdalene laundries and workhouses. In the words of Maurice Craig (1971, 59), 'The most conspicuous buildings of nineteenth-century Ireland are the innumerable gaols, workhouses, orphanages and county homes with which the landscape is so richly embellished.' The absent state manifested itself across the country through these ideologically impregnated buildings in which thousands were confined and many more deposited there as unwanted. These early institutions provided an opportunity to practice governance among Catholic, Protestant and Presbyterian middle-class men and, in some instances, women too. Ireland's welfare state was composed almost in its entirety of closed institutions.

The question is not whether the Irish were more insane than other nationalities or more likely to be scooped up into involuntary detention than elsewhere, but rather why did we get into the habit of normalising the incarceration of so many of our fellow men, women and children? The asylums, such as the Richmond, were a huge economic project on a mass scale. In the absence of manufacturing and the flight from the land, asylum building and maintenance was a state subsidy to the economy. The asylums were never a religious endeavour but always secular and multidenominational.

The practice of providing welfare to sick adults and children within enclosed institutions was at its height at the turn of the last century. This is epitomised in the management and growth of the aforementioned asylums. The design of Portrane articulated some, but not all, of the then new thinking about 'inmates' as patients who could benefit from productive daily activity as well as air and sunlight. The finding of children in the adult asylums in 1911 is not a scene from the past; children are still admitted to adult mental health facilities over one hundred years later in 2018.

The majority of those in the asylums had been placed there by family members. This undermines the myth that people were swept up by the state into institutions. Indeed, so hated were the workhouses that it may well have made an asylum appear as an inviting alternative.

The New Portrane

Life has come full circle. There is to be a new 130-bed Forensic Mental Health Service built at Portrane, on the grounds of the old asylum. There is a plan to have a child and adolescent mental health service there. Building was to begin in 2017 with completion in 2020. This is an improvement on an earlier plan to build the hospital on a site at Thornton Hall on the Dublin/Meath border and move Mountjoy prison beside it. That would have replicated the prison/hospital neighbourliness of two hundred years ago at Grangegorman, when custodial institutions were located together. The Portrane site is still on a peninsula, twenty-three kilometres outside Dublin, once again creating distance between patients and wider society.

Chapter 3 References

British Journal of Nursing (1910) January 22, 1910. Archive of the Royal College of Nursing, London.

British Journal of Nursing (1913) May 31, 1913. Archive of the Royal College of Nursing, London.

Carrick A. J. (1811) *A Picture of Dublin for 1811 Being a Description of the City and a Correct Guide*, Bachelors Walk, Dublin.

Census, General Report, Ireland, 1911.

Chief Secretary (1820) Chief Secretary's Office, NAI, CSO/RP/1820/4602 of 24.8.1820, Record 421.

Clear, C. (1987) 'Walls within Walls – Nuns in 19th Century Ireland,' in Curtin, C. Jackson, P, O'Connor, B. (eds.) *Gender in Irish Society*, Galway University Press.

Clerkin P. (2012) '1900 – Lunatic Asylum, Portrane, Co. Dublin,' *Archiseek*: www.archiseek.com. Accessed July 22, 2018.

COHSE (Confederation of Health Service Employees) (2013): www//:cohse-union.blogspot. Accessed January 17, 2013.

Commission (1927) *Report of the Commission on the Relief of the Sick and Destitute Poor including the Lunatic Poor*, Dublin Stationery Office, Saorstát Eireann.

Craig, M. (1971) *The Personality of Leinster*, Mercier Press, Cork.

Crowe, C. (ed.) (2012) *Dublin 1911*, Royal Irish Academy, Dublin.

Curtis, E. (1936) *A History of Ireland*, Methuen and Co. Ltd, London.

Department of Justice and Equality (2013) *Report of the Interdepartmental Committee to Establish the Facts of State Involvement with the Magdalene Laundries*, Dublin.

Dublin City Council (2012) Planning Scheme 2012 Grangegorman, Chapter 6, p. 2.

Enniskerry Local History (no date) 'The Moncks and Charleville Estate': www.enniskerryhistory.org/home/index.php/archives/1238. Accessed July 23, 2018.

Finnane, M. (1981) *Insanity and the Insane in Post-Famine Ireland*, Croom Helm, London.

Hancock, W. N. (1851) 'Should Boards of Guardians Endeavour to Make Pauper Labour Self-Supporting or should they Investigate the Causes of Pauperism?' *Transactions of the Dublin Statistical Society*, Vol. II, Session 4, 1850/51, pp. 1–3.

Hancock, W. N. (1859) 'On the Importance of Substituting the Family System of Rearing Orphan Children for the System now Pursued in our Workhouses,' *Journal of the Dublin Statistical Society*, March, pp. 317–333.

Hancock, W. N. (1876) 'On the Legal Provisions in Ireland for the Care and Instruction of Imbeciles, Idiots, Deaf and Dumb, and Blind, with Suggestions for Amended Legislation,' *Journal of the Statistical and Social Inquiry Society of Ireland*, Vol. VII, Part XL, 1875/76, pp. 29–38.

Hancock, W. N. (1879) 'On the Report of the Irish Lunacy Commissioners, and the Policy of Extending the English Law for the Protection of Neglected Lunatics to Ireland,' *Journal of the Statistical and Social Inquiry Society of Ireland*, Vol. VII, 1878/79, Part LV, pp. 454–61.

House of Commons (1828) *Accounts of House of Industry and Foundling Hospital*, Sessional Papers, Vol. 22, Sub vol. 1: www.dippam.ac.uk. Accessed January 1, 2015.

House of Commons (1817) *Report from the Select Committee on the Lunatic Poor in Ireland and an Appendix*, 25 June and 2 July.

Inspector (1912) *Report of the Inspector of Lunatics, 1912*, Appendix B, Table XI.

Inspector (1913) *Report of the Inspector of Lunatics, 1913*, Appendix B, Table XVII.

Jones, G. Malcolm, E. (eds.) (1999) *Medicine, Disease and the State in Ireland 1650–1940*, Cork: Cork University Press.

Journal of the Statistical and Social Inquiry Society of Ireland, Archives, 1847 Complete Collection.

Journal of the Statistical and Social Inquiry Society of Ireland, Archives, 1870–76, Vol. VI, Parts XL–XLIX.

Kelly, B (2008) 'Mental Health Law in Ireland, 1821 to 1902: Building the Asylums', *Medico-Legal Journal,* 76, Round Hall, Dublin.

Kelly, R. (2002) 'Portrane Groups Welcome Work on Graveyard,' *Fingal Independent*, Dublin. www.fingal-independent.ie. Accessed November 26, 2012.

Lalor, J. (1879) 'On the Use of Education and Training in the Treatment of the Insane in Public Lunatic Asylums', *Journal of the Statistical and Social Inquiry Society of Ireland*, Vol. VII, Part LIV, 1878/79.

Luddy, M. (1995) *Women in Ireland 1800–1918: A Documentary History*, Cork, Cork University Press.

MacThomáis, S. (2012) *Dead Interesting: Stories from the Graveyards of Dublin*, Mercier Press, Cork.

Malcolm E. (1991) 'Women and Madness in Ireland, 1600–1850' in MacCurtain, M. and O'Dowd, M. (1991) *Women in Early Modern Ireland*, Wolfhound Press, Dublin.

Malcolm, E. (1999) '"The House of Strident Shadows": Family and Emigration in Post-Famine Rural Ireland', in Jones, G. Malcolm, E. (eds.) *Medicine, Disease and the State in Ireland, 1650–1940,* Cork, Cork University Press.

Maxwell, C. (1937) *Dublin under the Georges, 1714–1850,* George Harrap and Co. Limited, London.

Moylan, T. K. (1944–5) *Dublin Historical Record,* Vol. VII, 2. The District of Grangegorman, Part 1.

Moylan, T. K. (1945a) *Dublin Historical Record,* Vol. VII, 3. The District of Grangegorman, Part 1.

Moylan, T. K. (1945b) *Dublin Historical Record,* Vol. VII, 4. The District of Grangegorman, Part 1.

Mulhall, D. (1999) *A New Day Dawning – A Portrait of Ireland in 1900,* Cork: The Collins Press.

Murray Collection, Irish Architectural Archive, Merrion Square, Dublin.

National Archives (2013) Census 1911, Enumerators Reports for Portrane Asylum, Dublin.

Nolan, B. (2013) 'The Grangegorman Depot and the Transportation of Irish Convict Women – Power, Punishment and Penance, 1844–1853', Communication to the Stoneybatter and Smithfield People's History Project, Cobblestone Bar, Dublin, October 5.

O'Sullivan, E., O'Donnell, I. (2012) *Coercive Confinement in Post-Independence Ireland – Patients, Prisoners and Penitents,* Manchester University Press.

Ó Tuathaigh, G. (1972) *Ireland before the Famine, 1798–1848,* Gill and Macmillan, Dublin.

Parry-Jones W. L. (1973) 'English Madhouses in the Eighteenth and Nine-teenth Centuries,' *Proceedings of the Royal Society of Medicine,* Vol. 66, July, London, pp. 659–664.

Prunty, J. (1999) *Dublin Slums, 1800–1925 – A Study in Urban Geography,* Dublin: Irish Academic Press.

Raftery, M., O'Sullivan E. (2001) *Suffer the Little Children – the Inside Story of Ireland's Industrial Schools,* Dublin: New Island Books.

Registrar General (1913) *Forty-Ninth Annual Report of the Registrar General for Ireland, Containing a General Abstract of the Numbers of Marriages, Births and Deaths Registered in Ireland during the Year 1912,* London, HMSO.

Reuber, M. (1996) 'The Architecture of Psychological Management: the Irish Asylums 1801–1922, *Psychological Medicine,* Vol. 26. (6) Cambridge University Press, pp. 1179–1189.

Saorstát Éireann (1927) *Commission Report into the Poor and including the Lunatic Poor,* Stationery Office, Dublin.

The Sixtieth Annual Report of the Inspectors of Lunatics (Ireland), H. M. Stationery Office, London, 1911.

Tuke, D. H. (1882) *Chapters in the History of the Insane in the British Isles,* Kegan Paul, Trench & Co., London.

Walsh, D., Daly, A. (2004) *Mental Illness in Ireland, 1750–2002,* Dublin, Health Research Board.

Warwick (2013) Warwick University archives on trade unions: dscalm.warwick.ac.uk. Accessed January 1, 2013.

Wright A. (1914) *Disturbed Dublin: the Story of the Great Strike of 1913–14 with a Description of the Industries of the Irish Capital,* Dublin, Forgotten Books Series Classic Reprint.

CHAPTER 4

Tuam – The Disappeared Children

It was not Bosnia looking for mass graves after the war. It was not Argentina searching for the disappeared during the fight against dictatorship, or Chile, where the mothers of the disappeared searched for their grandchildren born in captivity. It was a quiet town – Tuam – in the West of Ireland, in the County of Galway, in 2014. There, a local historian, Catherine Corless, unearthed 796 death certificates for children who died in the local Mother and Baby Home run by the Sisters of Bon Secours. Catherine had painstakingly obtained individual death certificates from the Registrar of Births, Marriages and Deaths in Galway for the children who died at the institution between 1925 and 1961, after which it closed. But where were their graves? She found only two individual graves for the 796 dead children (Keely, 2017, 2).

The publication of her research attracted global media attention. For *Le Monde* in France, 'convent ghosts were haunting the Irish town of Tuam' (Bernard, 2014). Germany's *Allgemeine Deutsche Zeitung* considered that the nuns 'treated the babies as rubbish,' (Buchsteiner, 2014) while for Italy's *Corriera della Sera* it was 'Catherine and the Lost Babies of Ireland' (*Corriera della Sera*, 2017).

Not everyone believed the story of the 796 children with no graves. The public relations expert Terry Prone, who did PR for the Bon Secours sisters, allegedly denied that there were any unburied bodies at the former Mother and Baby Home in Tuam (Weber, 2014). She later retracted her view during a television interview in 2017 (Griffin, 2017, 14).

In 2015, the Minister for Children and Youth Affairs, Dr James Reilly, presented a motion to the Dáil to establish a commission of inquiry into Mother and Baby Homes. He admitted that he initially thought that the issues were straightforward but then discovered they were not. There were issues of adoption, consent to adoption and children adopted and sent overseas (Reilly, 2015, 11).

The sisters of Bon Secours were founded as the *Soeurs de Bon Secours de Notre Dame Auxiliatrice de Paris* in 1824, and like many French and European Catholic religious orders, they post-dated the French Revolution of 1787–99. The Poor Clares were established in 1825, the Society of the Sacred Heart in 1779, the Marists in 1817, the Faithful Companions of Jesus in 1820, the Sisters of Charity of Jesus and Mary in 1803, and the Vincentians in 1832. In all, thirteen French congregations came to Ireland between 1840 and 1900 (Clear, 1987,135). The Bon Secours did not reach Ireland until 1861, after the Famine, at which time the Good Shepherd Sisters were already involved in running the Magdalene Asylums and, therefore, might have been called upon to open a Mother and Baby Home for 'fallen women' in Tuam. They were not.

The Bon Secours' mission is, amongst other goals, dedicated to the redemptive significance of suffering and death. Their specialisation was, and still is, health care but not specifically maternity care. Today, the Bon Secours health system is the largest independent healthcare provider in Ireland, employing 2,500 staff across the country.

Who Were the 796 Who Died?

The 796 children were born to mothers who were unmarried, pregnant and whose families did not want them. They sought admission themselves to Tuam Mother and Baby Home out of forced destitution or were placed there by relatives unable to bear the shame of illegitimacy in the family. Some were undoubtedly victims of rape or incest, had been taken advantage of by older men, were cognitively impaired or were children and could not have given consent to sexual relations. A proliferation of Magdalene Asylums appeared across Ireland from 1809 to 1890 in Dublin, Carlow, Waterford, Galway, Cork, Limerick, Derry, Antrim, Down, Belfast, Dundrum and Dun Laoghaire (Department of Justice and Equality, 2013). It would appear that Ireland needed a profusion of carceral institutions to maintain sexual control over women. There were no institutions for wayward men. All forms of contraception were illegal for most of the period during which the Tuam Home was functioning. Contraception was legal between 1922 and 1938. However, Section 17 of the *Criminal Law Amendment Act, 1937* was adopted by the Dáil and came into force in 1938:

73

(1) It shall not be lawful for any person to sell, or expose, offer, advertise, or keep for sale or to import or attempt to import into Saorstát Éireann for sale, any contraceptive.

(2) Any person who acts in contravention of the foregoing sub-section of this section shall be guilty of an offence under this section and shall be liable on summary conviction thereof to a fine not exceeding fifty pounds or, at the discretion of the court, to imprisonment for any term not exceeding six months or to both such fine and such imprisonment and, in any case to forfeiture of any contraceptive in respect of which such offence was committed.

A fine of £50 was an enormous sum of money in 1937. It was considerably more than a labourer's typical annual wage, when labourers earned about fifteen shillings or less than £1 a week. The threat of prison for six months was a heavy sentence for bringing a packet of condoms back from England on the boat. In the absence of contraception and any form of legal pregnancy termination, the position facing unmarried pregnant women was stark (Smith, 2007; Lloyd Roberts, 2016, 55–79).

Infanticide was one 'solution' to which some women – urban and rural – resorted (Rattigan, 2012, 204). Besides deaths in the institutions, there was also individual cases of infanticide, which were prosecuted as murder of infants or concealment of births. Historian Clíona Rattigan identified 913 such cases between 1900 and 1919 and a further 999 cases between 1927 and 1950. Only 5 percent were found guilty of murder; judges and juries alike preferred to avoid such harsh punishments and evade the obligation to hang young girls if they were found guilty of murder.

Having an abortion in England under the limited legal grounds of the *Infant Life (Preservation) Act* of 1927 was available until 1967 and the passing of the *Abortion Act* of 1967. This was a possibility for a few who knew about it and could afford it. Going to England and having the baby there was also an option. The baby could be given up for adoption or both mother and baby could stay there together if the mother could find work and childcare. The third option was to go into a Mother and Baby Home in Ireland and give birth there. Mothers were then required to work for up to a year or more to pay off the costs of their keep. Some mothers left after they had paid off their debt. Thus, at any time, there would be more children than mothers living in the Tuam institution. The children attended the local national school and left the Tuam home at six or seven years or after they had made their First Communion. Some were adopted, but there was no adoption act until 1952, so adoption was a relatively easy and informal arrangement, be it in Ireland or overseas (Milotte, 2012).

At the Confidential Committee of the Commission to Inquire into Child Abuse (CICA), 29 percent of witnesses described themselves as 'non-marital children who as a consequence of the circumstances of their birth were generally in some form of institutional care for most of their childhood, and in industrial schools in particular' (CICA, 2009, 111–119, 263–265 and 313). Some women succeeded in having themselves admitted to County Homes or former workhouses. While pregnant, many women became destitute and homeless. The stigma of being pregnant or with child while unmarried was deep and pervasive, stretching across all classes and levels of society. There were some exceptions in working-class areas where a mother would add her daughter's child to her own children and the child would be reared as a sister of his/her mother.

Unmarried pregnancy spoiled a family's honour and brought shame to them in the eyes of their immediate and wider community. The spoiling of family honour would impact on the chances of brothers and sisters being able to marry well, if at all. The only response to this dilemma was to cut off the rotten branch from the good tree by expelling the potential mother from family and community to England, to a Mother and Baby Home, to a County Home somewhere, anywhere, as long as they were far away and out of sight. According to a survivor of Tuam, the second-class status of illegitimate children continued as they got older: they were never picked to go on a sports team, ever. They could not be altar boys at Mass or enter the priesthood (Anonymous, 2017).

The ostracising of the unmarried mother was embodied in law: she had no right to public housing or social welfare. Private landlords had the right to refuse to let flats to unmarried mothers and did so. It was not until 1973 that a small means-tested Unmarried Mothers Allowance was provided for in law. Children's Allowances had been introduced in 1944 but were only available to households with three or more children. Unmarried mothers were thus disqualified from social welfare entitlements such as Home Assistance, which later became the Supplementary Welfare Allowance, or

Children's Allowance for the period during which the Tuam Mother and Baby Home was functioning. Barry Desmond, Labour TD, had this to say in 1972:

> Recently I had the case of an unmarried mother who applied for children's allowances and, even though I sent in a covering letter to the Department stating that this was an application by an unmarried mother, in thick red pencil back came the form saying it must be signed by the head of the household. Eventually the Department was prepared to accept her father as head of the household. She was the mother of the child. This reveals a lack of sensitivity, of which I rarely accuse the Department. I think it gets a great deal of abuse which it does not deserve. However, there is need for change in the certification of application forms (1972).

While there had been a Cherish campaign to obtain such an Unmarried Mothers Allowance for those who needed it, it was significant that its arrival came in 1973, just a few years after the UK *Abortion Act, 1967*, which Irish women made use of from its first year of operation in 1968. The number of women with Irish addresses going to the UK for pregnancy terminations was doubling each year, from sixty-four women and girls in 1968 to 577 in 1971. This increase was starting to cause unease among Dáil deputies (Dáil Eireann, 1972). One Family, the old name for the Cherish organisation, describes the situation at the time:

> In 1972 … single pregnant women were often thrown out of their homes, lost their jobs and were rejected by their communities. It was extremely difficult for them to keep and raise their children themselves. Cherish was set up to provide such women and children with a voice, empowering women to help themselves and their families (One Family, 2017).

A description of mothers in Tuam in the late 1940s was written by a child born there: 'There was a continuous cycle of expectant mothers coming in and then leaving for God knows where, and rumours were rife. It was widely accepted that children were being sold to wealthy childless couples in Ireland, England and America' (Rodgers, 2005, 89).

From the 1920s onwards, there was awareness that children were dying at an inexplicably high rate in institutions. The well-known and later controversial Secretary to the Department of Local Government, E. P. McCarron, who was Registrar General of Births, Deaths and Marriages in the 1920s and 1930s, made this abundantly clear. In his report for 1931, he devoted a special section in his opening summary entitled: 'Deaths of Illegitimate Infants'. The report states:

> Based on the number of illegitimate births, the resulting mortality rate is 267 per 1,000 births for both sexes […] in other words, one out of every four illegitimate infants born alive in 1931 died before the completion of its first year of life […]
>
> The illegitimate infant mortality, as derived from the records of 1931, is more than four times the mortality among legitimate infants, which was 62 per 1,000 births for both sexes, 69 per 1,000 for males and 55 per 1,000 births for females […] It would appear that […] at every period of life the mortality among illegitimate infants is much in excess of that for all infants (Department of Local Government and Public Health, 1932).

The report goes on to analyse where the infants died at different ages (Department of Local Government and Public Health, 1932, 23). McCarron demonstrated that 92 percent of all illegitimate infants under the age of one died in institutions across Ireland in 1931. Of the thirteen born in Galway, just three died outside an institution; in Offaly, all ten illegitimate infants died in an institution. Matters did not improve much over time. In the Registrar General's report for 1940, there were 1,824 illegitimate children born, and the illegitimate death rates of infants were again highlighted. One in four were dying before their first birthday. Of the 449 illegitimate infants who died before their first year, 87 percent died in institutions. In Galway, just one of the fifteen illegitimate infants born in 1940 died outside an institution. Dr Noel Browne became Minister for Health in 1948 and quickly moved to action on infectious diseases and the BCG vaccination for children (*The Irish Times*, 1948.) He later went on to say that he intended 'to make a serious attempt to reduce the incidence of child mortality' (*The Nationalist and Leinster Times*, 1930, 1).

For fear his readers might not get the message, E. P. McCarron had a special table prepared for his *1931 Annual Report*, which contrasted the infant mortality rates of legitimate and illegitimate children aged one year or less for a nine-year period from the date of the foundation of the state. This is illustrated in Table 5 below.

Table 5: Deaths of legitimate and illegitimate infants under the age of one and the rates per 1,000 of corresponding births, 1923–31.

		Infant mortality of infants under one year old, 1923–1931								
		1923	1924	1925	1926	1927	1928	1929	1930	1931
Deaths of Legitimate Infants	Numbers	3,539	4,014	3,739	3,999	3,748	3,467	3,556	3,498	3,421
	Death Rates/1,000	59	65	62	67	64	60	63	62	62
Deaths of Illegitimate Infants	Numbers	559	529	477	553	506	549	546	467	514
	Death Rates/1,000	344	315	287	322	288	307	295	251	267

Source: Department of Local Government and Public Health 1932; *Annual Report of the Registrar General, 1931,* Stationery Office, Dublin, Table 14, p. 22.

In Table 5 we observe that in 1923, for example, there were 3,539 legitimate births and the infant mortality rate was fifty-nine per 1,000 births. There were 559 illegitimate children born that year, and their infant mortality rate was six times higher at 344 infant deaths per 1,000 births. The infant mortality rates for illegitimate infants fluctuated considerably over the nine-year period – improving and deteriorating from one year to the next. In contrast, the infant mortality rate for legitimate children showed a more constant pattern, with the rate showing an even and gradual decline from 1926 to 1931.

There are some problematic issues with using data collected at one source for a specific purpose, such as certifying deaths, and comparing it with data from a different source for a different purpose. There is a certain process that must be adhered to following a death. The first stage of the historical process was to determine whether all deaths of infants and children were certified by a medical doctor and whether a certificate was issued for that death. The second stage was whether the death was notified to the local registrar as a death within his district and so become a registered death. This was particularly important in the case of deaths from infectious diseases, for which special regulations applied. This was also imperative in order to prevent crimes or accidents leading to death from being hidden. The third stage involved all the registered deaths for an area being transmitted to the Registrar General at the Department of Local Government and Public Health in Dublin. The fourth stage involved the burial records.

The data from the Registrar General's annual reports does not align with the data from the Tuam Mother and Baby Home. According to the certified deaths at Tuam, there were twenty-five infant deaths of children under one year in 1938. According to the Registrar General, there were just eighteen deaths of illegitimate children in the County of Galway in 1938, of which just sixteen took place in unnamed institutions. Even allowing for the fact that death certificates are for a specific day and the Registrar General is assembling data returned to him by the county from a medical officer, the discrepancy is puzzling. It may be that the local medical officer was not being notified of all of the deaths at the Mother and Baby Home in Tuam and therefore could not return all of them to the Registrar General. Unmarried mothers were to be found not only in Tuam but also in the Galway County Home. This is clear from the Galway County Council Archives Registry of Interments in Galway County, under the *Burial Grounds (Ireland) Act*. As a result of this discrepancy, the infant mortality rate for infants under one year old at Tuam may have been even higher than the Registrar General's data suggests.

The discrepancy appears again in 1941. In that year, the Mother and Baby Home at Tuam had thirty-two certified deaths of infants under one year, while the Registrar General records only twenty-seven infant deaths in County Galway, twenty-two of which were in an institution (Department of Local Government and Public Health, 1942, 19). Again, the Mother and Baby Home had an excess of ten deaths which do not seem to have appeared in the Registrar General's data. None of the Tuam deaths were in December, and so they were not at risk of being carried over in the data to the subsequent quarter returns from Galway.

Many deaths occurred in Ireland during the period from the 1920s to the 1960s that were not registered. While nationally about 6 percent of deaths were unregistered in 1960, in the West of Ireland, it was 15 percent (Registrar General, 1960). In 1938, some 38 percent of deaths were unregistered in the province of Connaught. There was a casual indifference to death in general in terms of involving the state in the affairs of the deceased. As the Tuam Mother and Baby Home had an assigned and well-known doctor, Dr Thomas Bodkin Costello, it is surprising that there is a discrepancy in the data. In the context of the time, the majority of poor families had no direct access to a doctor such as Dr Bodkin Costello and were not in the care of nursing sisters. Thus, one might reasonably expect infant deaths in an institution to be less common than infants born at home.

As for E. P. McCarron, he was summarily dismissed from his job in 1936, in a controversial move by the Government Executive, for his apparent refusal to sanction appointments in mental hospitals that had not been processed by a public appointments procedure (Dáil Éireann, 1937). Like author John McGahern, he was put out.

Intellectuals Ponder the Issue

Some argue that the Tuam Mother and Baby Home should be seen in the cultural context of its time (Scolairebocht, 2014). The Registrar General's reports reveal that there was no consensus that the high infant mortality rates of illegitimate children should be ignored at that time. The 1954 Commission on Emigration and Other Population Problems came across the issue and was surprised at the absence of explanations. They made enquiries in England, in London, Birmingham, Liverpool and Lancashire and found that there were about 250 illegitimate births taking place in England of infants who were conceived in Ireland (the thirty-two counties). They raised the issue of infanticide but decided not to proceed further with it. They noted that while the infant mortality rate for legitimate children was forty-five deaths per 1,000, for illegitimate children it was seventy-eight deaths per 1,000.

At the time, the Department of Health was asked by the commission to report on its welfare arrangements for unmarried mothers and their children. The department appeared to be very satisfied with their own system of subcontracting mothers and children to religious orders. The Department and Public Assistance Authorities were offering between £15 and £60 per year for children fostered out or £52 for a child placed in an industrial school, but there was no way in which the actual mother could obtain such significant sums of money. The department made it clear that if a mother and her child attempted to leave the Mother and Baby Home in circumstances that the religious orders did not approve of, her child would be taken into care (Commission on Emigration and other Population Problems 1948–1954: Reports).

The carceral regime laid out for unmarried mothers is well described by Charles Eason in a 1928 article, and it was precisely that regime which caused unease in the 1954 Commission on Emigration. Eason reported that the argument had advanced:

> The local authority should have power to detain the inmates for a period of one year in case of a first admission, for two years in the case of a second admission and in the case of third or subsequent admissions for such period as they think fit. The Report goes on to say that such detention is not intended to be in any sense penal but for the benefit of the woman and her child (1928, 23).

Of interest is Mr Eason's passing comment that the Bon Secours' special institution in Tuam was reported to have failed to carry out necessary building repairs, as arranged with the Board of Health.

Other religious institutions in Northern Ireland had issues of public concern in 1945. Major David Anderson, Chairperson of the Church of Ireland Hopedene Hostel for unmarried mothers, raised concerns about: 'The heavy mortality figures among illegitimate children […] for want of proper supervision many unwanted babies die because of indifference of those who look after them […] (this) is worthy of government consideration and enquiry' (Torney, 2017, 9).

What is under discussion is not a Catholic issue or a Protestant issue, but a wider global issue of the societal discarding of parts of humanity.

The Failure to Bury the Children

Unburied bodies are nowadays a source of horror and shame for those who see and hear about them: 'reverence for the mortal body in its final dissolution has been continuously rising; the reason lies in its compact with individuality, a compact reaffirmed by DNA, iris scanning and other forensic recognition techniques that presuppose absolute uniqueness' (Warner, 2017, 20).

Feelings about funeral and burial rites run deep and vary from culture to culture and epoch to epoch (Warner, 2017, 19). The desire for memorials can be deep-seated, and the absence of a body or corpse can trigger intense emotions. The practice of selling indulgences, forms of remittances that could buy the dead out of purgatory while awaiting their admittance to heaven, was a major cause for the split in the Church during the Reformation.

In relation to the Tuam Mother and Baby Home, the failure to bury the infants and children and to place the bodies in a disused sewer tank was illegal. The disposal of bodies by burial in a coffin was the only lawful means of dealing with the deceased at the time of the operation of the Tuam home. The *Local Government (Ireland) Act, 1898* gave the then local authorities the power to regulate burials. The act stated:

> [...]it shall be lawful for the Local Government Board to order that no new burial ground shall be opened in any city or town or within such limits, without such previous approval, or that after a time mentioned in the order burials in any such city or town, or within such limits, or in such burial grounds, or places of burial, shall be discontinued wholly or subject to any exceptions or qualifications.

There were restrictions in law on places in which bodies may be buried:

> 44. (1) Subject to the provisions of subsection (4) of this section a person shall not, without the consent of the Minister, bury the body of a deceased person in a place which is not a burial ground for the purposes of this section.
> (2) The following (and no other) places shall be burial grounds for the purposes of this section—
> (a) a place which is in lawful use as a burial ground and which was, immediately before the commencement of this section, in lawful use as a burial ground,
> (b) a place as respects which the Minister has, after the commencement of this section, given his approval to its being used as a burial ground,
> (c) a burial ground provided by a burial board under the Acts (*Local Government Sanitary Services Act, 1948*).

The act made it clear that only regulated burial sites could be used. Even greater detail had been provided earlier in the *Public Health (Ireland) Act* of 1878, which provided for burial ground regulations and local Burial Boards for each district. Burials had to be registered and a register maintained with details of all those buried. These laws carried the presumption of constitutionality when Ireland became Saorstát Éireann in 1922. The powers of the former Burial Boards were transferred to Irish local authorities in 1925. Those who breached burial laws committed an offence. While the Tuam home was still open, further regulation came with the local *Government (Sanitary Services) Act* of 1948. Section 44(5) of that act provided for fines not exceeding £50 or prison of not more than six months, or both, for those found guilty of offending against the burial laws. The Bon Secours sisters had to have known that: 'a person shall not … bury the body of a deceased person in a place which is not a burial ground' (*Local Government Sanitary Services Act, 1948*).

Given the presumption that all the infants and children were baptised, there was no barrier to their being buried in consecrated ground in a graveyard, the designation of which had been approved by Galway County Council. That graveyard could be the cemetery used by the order for their own sisters or a new graveyard for which there would be County Council approval, since they owned all the workhouse land on which the home operated. In the Galway County Council Archives, there are records for the Tuam Cemetery for periods up to 1922. These records show, amongst other information, which plots those who died in institutions were buried in. This included the Tuam Workhouse and Tuam Infirmary (Galway County Council Archives). There was a consecrated burial ground where the Bon Secours sisters were buried on the grounds of the Grove Hospital in the town of Tuam.[1] When that land was sold, the bodies of the nuns were exhumed, memorial plaques removed and all were reinterred in another cemetery. But the hidden bodies were left behind.

It is of note that the *McAleese Report of the Inter-Departmental Committee to Establish the Facts of State Involvement with the Magdalene Laundries* (2013) upheld that there was no law restricting or regulating Bon Secours' burials in the 1920s and 1930s. This is repeated by the Interdepartmental

---

[1] Visit to the grounds of the former Grove Hospital and cemetery, Tuam, on September 9, 2017.

Commission in an inaccurate citation drawn from the McAleese Committee. Why the sisters did not exhume and bury the bodies of the infants is a mystery to this day.

Infant and Children's Deaths

The number of deaths may have considerably exceeded the 796 that have been brought to public attention. When the 796 deaths are analysed by the age at which the children died, a gap appears. No deaths were reported for infants aged from birth to one month before 1938. Suddenly, in 1938, deaths of small infants appear at all ages, including from a few hours old to four weeks old. It is not at all clear why this gap in deaths from 1925 to 1938 exists.

Would the children have survived if they had been vaccinated against infectious diseases? The answer is no. Legitimate children were also exposed to infectious diseases, however, it is unknown whether their death rate was the same or less than illegitimate children suffering from the same diseases. The important vaccination programmes for infectious diseases did not exist between the 1920s and the 1960s. Vaccination programmes for measles were only implemented in 1988, whooping cough in 1996 and influenza in 1998. The only vaccination available, for TB, was introduced in 1949, largely thanks to the campaigning of Dr Dorothy Stopford Price (1890–1954) (Stopford Price, 2017). However, the TB vaccination may not have provided complete security against catching the various types of TB. Price had imported the BCG vaccine into Ireland and had discovered that much of rural Ireland had never been exposed to TB: the people of rural Ireland were in urgent need of a vaccination programme, a view she shared with Dr Noel Browne.

From 1941 onwards, the sisters of Bon Secours would nevertheless have been alerted to the risks of infectious diseases by the obligation in law of their doctor to provide a notification to the local health authority of any infectious diseases (Statutory Instrument No. 13 of 1941). They could not have failed to notice the headlines of *The Irish Times* on the subject of TB in 1948. If they did not care to read a 'Protestant paper', they could have consulted *The Connacht Tribune* (1948, 1). Specific guidance on infectious TB was given in a series of mass-produced leaflets by the

Anti-Tuberculosis Section of the Irish Red Cross Society, warning of the importance of good food and the risks of infection from proximity and overcrowding (National Library of Ireland, 2017).

The Causes of Deaths

The largest single cause of death, almost one in five, was attributed to various causes associated with weakness. Today, such a child would be described as 'not thriving'. In an already weakened state, the children would have quickly acquired infectious diseases and, lacking resistance, died of TB, measles, whooping cough and other infections or of malnourishment. Up to 1950, TB was a killer and accounted for forty-eight deaths at the Tuam Home and was mentioned in an additional eight cases. Pneumonia, together with bronchitis and respiratory illness, accounted for sixty-one deaths at the Tuam Home and was cited in many others. Influenza was a recurring cause of death year after year until 1952. This is in contrast to the nature of diseases such as measles or whooping cough, of which there appeared to be four specific outbreaks between 1933 and 1948. One can only speculate that there was overcrowding at the Tuam home and that children with infections were in close proximity to others.[2] It may be that those children experienced a lack of basic hygiene and nursing care when ill.

Vaccines as well as formula milk being developed by British companies were tested out in several Mother and Baby Homes, such as at Bessborough in Co. Cork, St Patrick's in Co. Dublin, Castlepollard in Co. Westmeath and Dunboyne and Stamullen in Co. Meath. The companies involved were Glaxo Smith Klyne and Wellcome Laboratories in the UK. As many as 2,000 children were involved in tests between 1930 and 1935 (Fátharta, 2017, 4). This practice of experimenting on humans who cannot give consent seems unethical.

The majority of children who died – 82 percent – did not survive their first birthday and died within their first year of life. Of these, 5 percent died within a week of birth, which must have been extremely sad for their mothers. Conditions did not spare the toddlers, some 15 percent of whom

---

[2] A former resident expressed the view that Tuam Home was constantly overcrowded. September 13, 2017.

died before their third birthday alongside older children aged four and five years old.

Table 6: Age groups of deceased children at Tuam Mother and Baby Home, 1925–1960*

Age of children at death	Numbers of deaths	% of all deceased
Aged 0 to 7 days	43	5
Aged 8 days to 12 months	608	77
Aged 13 to 36 months	115	15
Aged 37 months and older	26	3
Unaccounted	4	0.8
Total	792	100

*No information for four children.
Database constructed from Catherine Corless's 2014 study.

To find out about the deaths of children at the Tuam Mother and Baby home, Catherine Corless examined all the deaths with an address at the Tuam home in the deaths register for the County of Galway. She identified 796 deaths, one by one, in the archives.

There were children up to four years old and older who attended the local school and who stayed either in the home or with foster families until their First Communion. Some children remained while their mothers left and went to work to pay for their keep in the hope of being reunited later. According to Catherine Corless, mothers may have thought their child was in the home when in fact the child had been fostered out, and the mother's money continued to be accepted along with the weekly state capitation payment.

The large-scale abandonment of illegitimate children in Ireland, to their death, is not a new phenomenon. Historian Diarmuid Ó Gráda observed that in the Foundling Hospital of Dublin:

> The children concerned got no medicines save for a tranquilliser called diacodium that allowed them to die quietly.[3] In the period

---

[3] Diacodium is a syrup opiate that was formerly made from poppies.

1810–16 well over five thousand children were killed in this way…
Thousands of children suffering from smallpox were likewise
dispatched to the infirmary and left there to die (Ó Gráda, 2015,
184; Kelly, 1992, 5–26).

Table 7: The principal underlying cause and single causes of deaths of
796 children at Tuam Mother and Baby Home, 1925–61.

Principal Causes of Death	Numbers	% of total
Diseases of the heart	27	3.4
Pneumonia	21	2.6
Bronchitis, rhinitis, respiratory illness	40	5.0
Gastritis, colitis and digestive system conditions	38	4.8
Congenital malformations	25	3.1
Diseases peculiar to early infancy and immaturity	50	6.3
TB all forms	48	6.0
Syphilis	13	1.6
Scarlet fever/sore throat	8	1.0
Whooping cough	46	5.8
Measles	80	10
Infective/parasitic diseases	3	0.3
Cancers all forms	-	-
Anemia	7	0.7
Meningitis	23	2.8
Birth injuries	6	0.8
Influenza	77	10.0
Febrile convulsions/fits/epilepsy	43	5.4
Weakness/debility/marasmus	152	19.0
Other/abscesses, oedema, otorrhea, eczema, ecthyma	88	11.1
None cited	1	-
Total	796	(99.8)

Calculated from author's database of thirty-seven causes of deaths and their classification using
part of the Registrar General's method in his 1960 Annual Report.

Religion, at both state and community level, was a factor in the dispar-
aging and disrespectful treatment of sick infants and children in Tuam.
The particular religious belief system of the time deprived illegitimate
children of the same right to life as legitimate children. This was the view

of the Tridentine Catholic Church, which became obsessed with securing the absolute allegiance of its nominal adherents [...] a knowledge of the Catechism that took precedence over fidelity to the ethical code (Murphy, 2008, 366.). The case of Romania and its treatment of disabled children dispels the anti-clerical notion that ill-treatment is confined to locations where Church and State are joined as one. While controversy over the State Inquiry into Mother and Baby Homes in Ireland continued to attract media attention during 2016 and 2017, another baby deaths' scandal was emerging on the other side of Europe, in Romania.

Romania – the 771 Damaged Children

The disabled children at the hospital homes of Cighid in Ghiorac, on the Hungarian border; Păstrăveni in Nemat County, Moldavia; and the Home for Deficient Irrecoverable Minors from Sighetu Marmatiei in Mara-mures were classified as 'irrecuperable' by the dictatorial regime (1965–89) of Nicolae Ceauşescu in Romania. They were neither recoverable nor partly recoverable (i.e., fit to become the workers of a 'worker's state'). These children were among the 10,000 children abandoned to remote regions, deprived of care, warmth, clothing, food and medical attention. The so-called hospitals of Cighid, Pastrevani and Sighetu are cited in the significant legal proceedings of 1 June 2017, lodged in a Bucharest court, alleging that crimes of brutality and neglect were committed in the 771 deaths of children at these centres, a number uncannily close to the 796 death certificates of Tuam in Ireland. The two public enquiries were running at the same time in Ireland and Romania. The concepts of 'recu-perable' and 'irrecuperable' are not far from the concepts of 'educable' and 'uneducable mental defectives' referred to in a report of the Irish Poor Law Commission in 1928 (Eason, 1928, 23).

The three centres where the children were abandoned are located in remote, underdeveloped regions of Romania. Sighetu, for example, is a place where Hungarian as well as Romanian is spoken, since it had been part of Hungary. It was used as a form of 'Siberia' for political pris-oners, former ministers, writers, scientists and dissident intellectuals in the post-war period of the 1950s. Seven to eight hours from Bucharest by road, it is a place of traditional villages and national park areas. Sighetu had a thriving 'shtetl' or Jewish community until the Second World War. In the shtetl communities, Jewish people could live close to each other, follow their own traditional dietary and religious beliefs, worship in their own way, speak Yiddish and celebrate their own feast days.

Nicolae Ceaușescu was head of the state in Romania from 1965 to 1989 and held some bizarre beliefs. He believed that economic growth and industrialisation could be forced in the then predominantly agricultural country. He determined that the country needed more people to attain economic growth. From this emanated a pro-natalist policy of banning contraception and pregnancy terminations and insisting on women producing as many children as possible, with a minimum of five. This was not unlike Ireland, where in 1961 the average size of a family was just under five children. Those who did not comply with the state's reproductive exhortations were subjected to threatening gynaecological interviews. Many women died in childbirth or from botched backstreet abortions. Families on subsistence wages could not afford indefinite numbers of children and took to leaving them at the doors of orphanages. Amongst those abandoned were many children with disabilities.

The children with disabilities were classified and categorised, and those with apparently more serious disabilities were banished to the north of Romania. They were left in the hands of untrained local staff with no professionals to speak of. The children were deprived of nutritious food, were not taught how to walk or speak, were not touched or handled and in some cases, never saw the sun. Children spent days and weeks in their cots without being lifted out. The infants, toddlers and children who survived up to the age of eighteen were regarded as worthless. When the Romanian government fell in 1989, there was a strong sense of bitterness over what the country had become. Nicolae Ceaușescu and his wife Elena were executed after a very short summary trial in 1990. It was then that western journalists photographed the outrageous conditions of the orphanages and permitted the western world to see the depths to which humanity can fall.

Before embarking on their court case, the Institute for the Investigation of Communist Crimes and the Memory of the Romanian Exile visited more than twenty institutions and gathered evidence, including eye-witness testimonies. From ten particularly bad institutions they selected just three for the court case (www.iicr.ro).

The press conference announcing the court case was attended by Izidor Ruckel, one of the children admitted to Sighet Hospital and adopted in 1991 by a family in the United States, at the age of ten. He recounted his experiences during the time he spent at the orphanage. He described extreme violence, beatings and injections with sedatives. Izidor had had polio and had been abandoned by his parents in a hospital. He met his biological family much later in his life but was extremely angry with them for having abandoned him (www.iicr.ro, 2017).

As in other instances of abandoned children, these little human beings become commodified when it comes to inter-country adoption. They unknowingly have monetary value as potential adoptees. In 1990, Romania was besieged with parents from western countries seeking to adopt Romanian orphanage babies and children. While some couples were sincere in wanting to save a child from orphanage life, others paid intermediaries or individuals in order to adopt children who, in many instances, had living parents whose consent was not sought. So great was the risk to children's welfare from trafficking that Emma Nicholson, a Conservative MEP for the UK, then European Parliament Rapporteur on Romania, campaigned to have all adoptions halted in Romania. She and her campaign were successful.

Closer to home, the Scottish Child Abuse Inquiry and the child survivors of the Smyllum Park children's home, run by the Daughters of Charity of St Vincent de Paul was the occasion for the discovery of a mass unmarked grave of an estimated 400 children. Research undertaken by BBC Radio 4 found that the mass grave was in St. Mary's Cemetery. As in Tuam, death certificates had to be identified one by one from the archives. No burial sites were found with the exception of two children. The BBC programme *File on 4* raised questions about child deaths at the orphanage before it was closed in 1981 (BBC Radio 4, 2017). The discrepancy between the death certificates and burial records arose in the context of the Scottish Child Abuse Inquiry which began in 2017 (childabuseinquiry.scot/news, 2017).

Derek Leinster's campaign to find out the fate of children who attended a Protestant children's home, called the Bethany Home, in Dublin prompted the erection of a monument to the estimated 222 children buried in an unmarked mass grave there. Niall Meehan has described the struggle of the children of the Bethany Home to uncover the truth of their past and the discovery of bodies in an unmarked mass grave in Mount St Jerome's Cemetery. Some 219 children died at the home between 1922 and 1949. The home was not included in the terms of reference of the Commission of Inquiry into Child Abuse (Niall Meehan, 2010, 10; Hilliard, 2017, 2).

Conclusion

In Ireland, Scotland and Romania, unwanted children were 'banished babies', in the words of Mike Milotte. They were unprotected by the state and their rights, including their right to life, were ignored and hidden. In both countries, public authorities and citizens are being obliged to consider and reconsider their treatment of outlawed children with illness and disabilities.

The Tuam story illustrates the importance of research and action undertaken by individuals and small local groups connected to survivors of the containment institutions. They have unravelled the myths and reality of a past that shamed women and girls into subordination. The critical approach of intellectuals such as Charles Eason, public servants such as E. P. McCarron and the members of the Commission on Emigration challenges the idea that what happened in Tuam was part of the consensus culture of the first half of the twentieth century. It was not. It was critiqued and independently explored. The treatment of pregnant, unmarried girls and women was definitely not accepted by a number of opinion formers of the time. Cultural relativism, which suggests that acts should be appraised by the populist morality of the time, has no place in the story of the Tuam Mother and Baby Home. It was and is wrong to neglect infants and children. It was and is an offence to fail to provide a decent burial.

Chapter 4 References

BBC (2017) *The Secrets of Smyllum Park* (see also BBC Radio 4). Reporter: Michael Buchanan: http://www.bbc.com/news/uk-41200949.

Bernard, P. (2014) 'Par Tuam, Irlande, Les fantômes du couvent hantent la ville irlandaise de Tuam', *Le Monde* http://www.lemonde.fr/europe/article/2014/06/14/les-fantomes-du-couvent-hantent-la-ville-irlandaise-detuam_4438048_3214.html#qGoTv4sRXxZLgAZU.99.

Buchsteiner, J. (2014) 'Massengrab im irischen Tuam, Babys waren für die Nonnen Abfall,Irland steht nach dem Fund von 800 Babyleichen in Tuam unter Schock. Der Skandal fördert nicht nur die Abgründe der meist katholischen, Fürsorge-Einrichtungen zutage, sondern eine Kultur des Vergessens und Verdrängens'. *Frankfurte Allgemeine Zeitung*: http://www.faz.net/aktuell/politik/massengrab-im-irischen-tuam-babys-waren-fuer-die-nonnen-abfall-12978532.

Scottish Child Abuse Inquiry (2017) https://childabuseinquiry.scot/news 2017.

Corriere della Sera (2017) 'Catherine e i bimbi perduti d'Irlanda. La tenacia di una madre ha permesso di fare luce sul «segreto di Tuam»: ritrovata una fossa comune con 800 piccoli corpi' *Corriere della Sera, 6 March*: https://www.pressreader.com/italy/corriere-della-sera/20170306/281792808818215.

CICA Commission to Inquire into Child Abuse (2009) *Report*. Vol III, Confidential Committee.

Clear, C. (1987) 'Walls within Walls – Nuns in 19th-Century Ireland', in C. Curtin, P. Jackson, B. O'Connor (eds.), *Gender in Irish Society*, Galway University Press.

Commission on Emigration and other Population Problems 1948–1954: Report, (1954) Dublin, Stationery Office, pp. 111–113 and p. 313, Table 25 and pp. 263–265.

Department of Justice and Equality (2013) *Report of the Interdepartmental Committee to Establish the facts of State Involvement with the Magdalene Laundries,* Dublin, Appendix 3. The report drew on earlier research by Maria Luddy.

Desmond, B. (1972) Dáil Éireann Debate, Vol. 263, No. 4, Paragraph 713, 3 November 1972.

Dáil Éireann Debates (1972) Vol. 263, No. 3, Paragraph 514, 3 November.

Department of Local Government and Public Health (1932) *Annual Report of the Registrar General, 1932*, Dublin, Stationery Office, p. xxxix, p. 23, Table 15.

Department of Local Government and Public Health (1941), *Annual Report of the Registrar-General 1940*, Dublin, Stationery Office, p. 19, Table 13.

Department of Local Government and Public Health (1942) *Annual Report of the Registrar General 1941*, Table 13.

Dáil Éireann (1937) Motion to Appoint Tribunal, Vol. 65, No.1. paragraphs 55–144.

Eason, C. (1928) *Report of the Irish Poor Law Commission Paper to the Statistical and Social Inquiry Society of Ireland*, 26 January 1928, *JSSISI*, Vol. XIV, No. 5.

European Court of Human Rights (2004) *Case of Pini and others v. Romania*, (Application Nos. 78028/01 and 78030/01) Judgement Strasbourg, 22 June 2004.

European Court of Human Rights (2004) Chamber Judgement in the Case of *Pini and Bertani and Manera and Atripaldi v. Romania.*

Griffin, N. (2017) 'Tuam families ask Prone to Apologise in Person', *Irish Mail on Sunday*, October 15.

Hilliard, M. (2017) 'Memorial Held for Children in Collective Grave', *Irish Times*.

Institute for Information on the Crimes of Communism (IICR) (2017): www.iicr.ro/en/. Accessed September 18, 2017.

Keely, O. (2017) 'Galway Historian Receives Human Rights Award,' *Irish Times*.

Kelly, J. (1992) 'Infanticide in Eighteenth Century Ireland', *Irish Economic and Social History Journal*, Vol. 19, pp. 5–26: http://www.jstor.org.stable/24341845. Accessed January 1, 2017.

Lloyd-Roberts, S. (2016) 'Irelands Fallen Women,' *The War on Women And the Brave Ones Who Fight Back*, Simon & Schuster, London.

Local Government Sanitary Services Act, 1948.

Local Government Sanitary Services Act, 1948a. Section 44.

Meehan, N. (2010) 'Church and State Bear Responsibility for the Bethany Home', *History Ireland*, Vol. 18, No. 5.

Milotte, M. (2012) *The Banished Babies: The Secret History of Ireland's Baby Export Business*, Dublin: New Island Books.

Murphy, J. H. (2008) 'The Role of Vincentian Parish Missions in the Irish Counter-Reformation of the Mid-Nineteenth Century,' in N. C. Fleming and Alan O'Day (eds.) *Ireland and Anglo-Irish Relations since 1800: Critical Essays*, Volume I, Ashgate, Hampshire, UK.

National Library of Ireland (2017) See: Sample in *The Revolution Papers, 1948, The Campaign against Tuberculosis*.

Ó Fátharta, C. (2017) 'New Bessborough Revelations Show Wider Range of Products Tested on Children,' *Irish Examiner*. The article quotes from the work of Dr Michael Dwyer, Department of History, University College, Cork.

Ó Gráda, D. (2015) *Georgian Dublin: The Forces that Shaped the City*, Cork University Press, Cork.

One Family (2017) https://onefamily.ie/about-us/our-history.

Rattigan, C. (2012) *"What else could I do?" Single Mothers and Infanticide Ireland 1900– 1950'*, Irish Academic Press, Dublin.

Reilly, J. (2015) Dáil Éireann Debates, Vol. 864, No. 2 p.11.

Registrar General (1960) *Annual Report of the Registrar General 1960*, Dublin, Stationery Office, Table XXXIX.

Rodgers, J. P. (2005) *For the Love of my Mother*, Headline Publishing Group, London.

Scolairebocht (2014) 'The Statistical, Biological and Other Reasons why the Tuam Home Mortality Rate is Misleadingly High: http://www.politics.ie/forum/current affairs/227620-statistical. Accessed September 24, 2017.

Smith, J. M. (2007) *Ireland's Magdalen Laundries and the Nation's Architecture of Containment*, Manchester University Press.

Statutory Instrument No. 13 of 1941, The Public Health (Infectious Diseases) Regulations under which Measles, Pneumonia, Whooping Cough, Diphtheria, Dysentery, Scarlet Fever, and Malaria were notifiable.

Stopford Price, D. (2017) dh.tcd.ie/pricediary/about-dorothy-price-her family/dorothy-stopford-price-and-the-irish-tubercuulosis-epidemic Accessed July 1, 2017.

The Connacht Tribune (1948) 'Minister Outlines Emergency Drive against T.B.' March 20.

The Irish Times (1948) 'Sanatorium in Castlerea will be in use by Summer,' February 26.

The Irish Times, (1948) 'Health Inspection will Not be Compulsory for Children,' March 20.

The Nationalist and Leinster Times (1930) 'No Alien Health Schemes for Ireland,' October 30.

Torney, K. (2017) 'Unwanted Children are Allowed to Die,' *Irish Times*, June 15, 2017.

Warner, M. (2017) 'Back from the Underworld – The Work of the Dead: A Cultural History of Mortal Remains by Thomas Laquer,' *London Review of Books*, Vol. 39, No.16, p. 20.

Weber, S. (2014) Letter to journalist Saskia Weber, reprinted in 2014 at: www.kettleontherange.com/2014/11/01.

CHAPTER 5

Hostile Engagements – An Analysis of the Army Deafness Claims

The discovery of hearing impairment in thousands of Irish soldiers through occupational injury in the 1990s attracted ridicule and hostility in the media and in the Dáil. Decisions in the courts to award compensation to soldier-claimants for acquired hearing impairment – deafness – opened a period of hostile engagement between rank and file uniformed members of the Defence Forces and their employers. Accusations of malingering, fraudulent compensation claims, trickery in medical assessments and the deliberate demoralisation of the army were poured onto a group of men whose job was to defend the nation state but who were losing their hearing in doing so.

Blood contamination, hepatitis C, planning corruption, the beef industry, child abuse – these are the topics that have attracted tribunals of inquiry when hundreds or thousands of people are affected by the action of the public authorities and which, to varying extents, attracted approval in the media and in commentaries from the general public. But not soldiers. The scale of their injury in the form of hearing impairment was viewed as incredible, impossible to prove and not susceptible to scientific diagnosis or verification. Soldiers who had been gradually injured over the years were cast as unfit to be treated with the same legitimacy as other citizens. Theirs is a story of a disability that was disbelieved.

The Military-Civil Context

The Defence Forces are made up of three entities: the Army, the Air Corps and the Naval Service; this is the Permanent Defence Force (PDF), of which the army is by far the largest force. In addition, there is the Army Reserve, which is the land component of the Reserve Defence Forces and a Naval Reserve. It is the second line reserve of the army and acts as an auxiliary (An Fórsa Cosanta Áitiúil or FCA) to the PDF. These were later restructured: the Reserve Defence Force consists of the Army Reserve and the Naval Service Reserve. The army element is designated the Army Reserve (Cúltaca an Airm). The naval element is designated the Naval Service Reserve (Cúltaca an Seirbhís Chabhlaigh).

While the Defence Forces have their own military command, the civil power resides with the government through the Minister for Defence and the Department of Defence. Historically, studies in civil-military relations rarely address the views of the enlisted man or woman. The majority of civil-military studies are based on the relationship between the state and military leadership (Martin, 2016). This is in sharp contrast to cultural representations of war in films such as *Dunkirk*, *Apocalypse Now*, the TV series *Band of Brothers* or the very popular video game series *Call of Duty*, which views war through the eyes of the lowly soldier or sergeant – a view from the bottom-up rather than the top elite.

Military organisations are closed and opaque organisations with many 'secretive' or unpublished features that are not easily visible to the outsider. This is equally the case of prisons, churches or boarding schools, where the organisation develops its own culture and own way of conducting its business. In the Defence Forces, obedience is of paramount importance in its culture through a clearly delineated hierarchy, which is visible through titles, language, uniforms and insignia. Orders may not be queried or discussed: they are to be obeyed. The Defence Forces did have an internal complaints system but it emerged over time that it was functioning poorly and attracted little confidence among the rank and file of soldiers, sailors and aircrew members. This was addressed in 2004 with the introduction of a civilian Ombudsman for the Defence Forces, both serving and former members, whose first full year of operations was in 2006.

The Irish Defence Forces are unique compared to other countries in that soldiers do not generally live in barracks but in the community among other citizens; their children attend local schools and they buy their groceries, like everyone else, at local shops and supermarkets. In response to a severe economic crisis in the late 1980s, the then government agreed with the Irish Congress of Trade Unions to underwrite a very radical partnership agreement involving the state, private and public employers and farmers. The agreement, called the *Programme for National Recovery, 1987* was to set wages and working conditions through a centralised collective bargaining system. Individual trade union members of the Irish Congress of Trade Unions would no longer negotiate wages locally – all would be centralised into the partnership forum. Soldiers were not at the negotiating table and remained excluded up to 2017. Partnership did not extend to the Defence Forces, and in the face of the emphasis on the partnership method, some soldiers wondered why they were excluded.

Pay and conditions were regarded as a central issue by rank and file soldiers and other members of the PDF. On duty at the Northern Irish border, they saw the better pay and treatment of Gardaí in supporting the civil power.

The Gardaí had hot lunches brought to them in aluminium trays and got overtime payments. Soldiers got cold sandwiches and no overtime pay. Providing armed escort duty to cash-in-transit, soldiers could observe the advantages of other employments such as security work. Members of the Defence Forces may not engage in political activity and are prohibited by law from joining political parties or secret societies (Clonan, 2007).

Since they could not act themselves, their wives took to the picket lines and air waves. In 1988, the National Army Spouses Association (NASA) formed in a relatively loose and informal way and began to picket barracks and political meetings in support of improved pay and conditions for their husbands who were prohibited in law from taking such action or speaking to the media. NASA demanded the right for soldiers to form a representative organisation similar to a trade union. This was unsurprising since trade unions had been elevated to one of the main drivers of economic recovery. Three army wives stood as candidates in national elections to the Dáil; they did not obtain seats but they severely frightened some TDs with the volume of votes they attracted. Meanwhile, soldiers and other members of the PDF began to quietly visit their TDs and even the Dáil itself.

Initially, there was deep opposition to the formation of a representative body for the Defence Forces, as illustrated in this reply from Michael Noonan TD to Dáil questions from Michael Bell, TD for the Labour Party and Tomas McGiolla, TD of the Workers Party:

> I am advised that the formation by members of the defence forces of associations or unions having a system of organisation and control separate from that of the defence forces, would be incompatible

with the system of command essential in any defence or military force contemplated by Article 13 and 15 of the Constitution and provided for in the Defence Acts and the regulations made under those Acts. Apart from objections based on the legal considerations involved there would be fundamental policy objections to any development towards the creation of unions of associations in the Defence Forces (Oireachtas, 1988).

The position was not sustainable. Despite deep and sincerely held opposition in the hierarchy of the Defence Forces and in the Department of Defence, the government – the civil power – decided to engage with the protests. The government took the usual route by establishing a committee to look into the matter; this was called the Brady Commission, named after Vincent Brady, TD. The Brady Commission's full title was the *Report of the Inter-Departmental Committee on Defence Forces Pay, Allowances and Conditions*: it reported in December 1988. In the event, the Brady Commission did not recommend an increase in basic pay for soldiers other than what all employees would get under the national partnership agreements, where they were not represented. It did propose an increase in pensionable allowances. This caused huge disappointment and annoyance among the rank and file of Defence Force members.

The content of the Brady Commission caused such anger and outrage that the Gleeson Commission was eventually set up in 1989, headed by the well-known Senior Counsel and former Attorney General, Dermot Gleeson, to look into pay and conditions. The Commission on Remuneration and Conditions of Service in the Defence Forces was established on 29 July 1989 to: 'carry out a major review of the remuneration and conditions of service of the Defence Forces having regard to their separate and distinct role and organisation and to make recommendations' (Signal, 2012).

This was the first independent commission in the history of the state to examine pay and conditions in the Defence Forces. It was also the first opportunity that members of the Defence Forces had to make a case on their own behalf directly to an independent body. This provided soldiers, members of the Naval Service and Air Corps, as well as officers, with a novel opportunity to systematically formulate their views and perspectives. There were three groups representing privates and non-commissioned officers and six members representing the East, South and Western Commands, as well as Air Corps and Naval Service representatives. There was very active engagement with the commission and a feeling of optimism among rank and file. This seemingly fragmented structure for consultation may have had the unintended consequence of developing coherence in the presentation of the ideas of Defence Force members.

Ireland was changing: more and more soldiers had a better education and more officers were now obtaining university-level education. A few decided to quietly canvass views with the idea of forming a representative body for the non-commissioned ranks. They based themselves on Article 40.6.1 (iii) of the Constitution, which affirms 'the right of the citizens to form associations and unions'.[1] This article had not been tested in the courts in relation to military law and is not an unfettered or absolute right in any case. Nevertheless, the government decided to concede the right to soldiers to form an association with a new law containing the outline of a new association, but it was not necessarily the association the soldiers had in mind and wanted, which was The Permanent Defence Forces Other Ranks Representative Association, or PDFORRA.

Labour Deputy Seán Ryan TD spoke during the extensive debate on the new law:

> The Bill raises a whole series of fundamental questions because it is so badly thought out and prepared. Perhaps its worst feature is the position in which it places people who have been campaigning, perfectly democratically and legitimately, to establish an association which is now in place with over 8,000 signed up members. The association has a constitution which explicitly recognises 95 per cent of the aspects contained in the Minister's speech here this afternoon. Its officials are clearly people who have the interests of a professional army at heart. Having met some of them I can vouch for that. However, the effect of this Bill will be to outlaw the association and to make it illegal. People will not be able to seek membership of the association when this Bill is passed. Indeed, it will be a criminal offence for anyone to seek to recruit members to it. In other words, this Bill places democratically organised soldiers

---

[1] In Irish: *ceart na saoránach chun comhlachais agus cumainn a bhunú.*

in exactly the same position as the provisional IRA, an illegal organisation. This is not just absurd, it is scandalous (Dáil Eireann, 1990).

The government dropped the plan for a governmental non-governmental organisation. A governmental non-governmental organisation is a body or association established and funded by governments to pursue governmental aims and represents itself as a civil society organisation when it is patently not. The soldiers won the right to form representative associations very similar to trade unions.

On 6 May 1991, PDFORRA was officially established. PDFORRA is a representative organisation, affiliated to other similar bodies in Europe through EUROMIL (European Military Representative Associations), in which it takes an active role and has a member on the EUROMIL's board. Through EUROMIL, PDFORRA has been appointed to the Organisation for Security and Co-operation in Europe as expert observers in situations of conflict in Europe. It is reasonable to say that PDFORRA takes a social democratic perspective, but it is probably modelled on typical public service trade unions and staff associations. In addition, officers are represented by the Representative Association of Commissioned Officers (RACO) and the Reserve Defence Forces Representative Association. There is also an Association of Retired Commissioned Officers (ARC), an Irish United Nations Volunteers Association, and an Organisation of National Ex-servicemen and women Association.

Despite several petitions over the years by PDFORRA, there remains a ban on them joining or affiliating with the Irish Congress of Trade Unions. Instead, a form of internal arbitration has been established to allow them to process grievances; an army Ombudsman has also been established. Replying to a priority question from Deputy Sean Ryan of Labour, the then Minister of State, Paul Keogh of Fine Gael, responded:

PDFORRA has requested on a number of occasions, in 2002, 2009, 2012 and 2014, to become either affiliated to, or to take up associate membership of, the Irish Congress of Trade Unions. These requests raise significant challenges from a governmental and societal perspective, including the risk of subverting the military chain of command requiring consideration. Appropriate systems have been put in place to ensure that the concerns of Defence Forces personnel can be dealt with in an appropriate manner through the conciliation and arbitration scheme. This includes access to independent adjudication (Oireachtas, 2016).

Despite considerable reform, the Defence Force personnel remain locked out of the ICTU.

Prevention of Disability

While soldiers' representation was being thrashed out in the Dáil, another momentous policy change was taking place in factories and offices across the country. This was the new obligation on employers to exercise a duty of care in relation to the health and safety of their employees, the development of regulations for dangerous activities outside of factories and for the provision of safety representatives among employees. The prevention of disabilities and disease acquired in the workplace has not always been at the top of public or private agendas. It has been a casual affair. Up until recent decades, the emphasis has been on systems of compensation for accidents and work-originating diseases, after the damage has already been done. The identification of risks, workplace safety campaigns and enforcement of safe practices are all relatively new arrivals on the labour market, almost one hundred years after the first *Workmen's Compensation Act* of the nineteenth century. The *Health and Safety Act* of 1989 had to be substantially updated by a new act in 2005, prompted by European Union directives driving forward a new trans-European framework to protect workers' health and prevent injury on a large scale. The 1989 act provided for the establishment of a Health and Safety Authority.

Only since 1998 have there been enforceable disability rights in employment in Ireland. The exclusion of the Defence Forces from the scope of large areas of the *Employment Equality Act, 1998* continued a pattern whereby the Defence Force opted out of legislation affecting their members, specifically the equality of treatment with other workers in terms of disability. The opt-outs for employees of the Defence Forces are to be found in Section 7 (discrimination), Section 37 (allowing discrimination on age and disability grounds), Section 77 (job interviews) and Section 104 (no access to the Labour Court). There has been no visible lobbying among non-governmental organisations in the field of disability or social affairs to lift the opt-outs for soldiers.

From the point of view of most people in society, hearing loss is a disability. From the point of view of many people who are deaf, hearing loss is not a disability, as they can communicate through signing with their hands and have a language called sign language. They argue that sign language is a different language from English and for 5,000 of them, it is their first language. This means they make a strong distinction between speech on one hand and language on the other. Irish sign language is a full language in that it has its own grammar and rich vocabulary. This is especially significant for those who have been deaf since birth and have lived with sign language for all of their lives. From this perspective, Irish sign language is, therefore, part of Irish culture and heritage, and it is not a disability. The Irish Sign Language Bill was enacted in 2017.

While the media at the time referred to army deafness claims, the extensive and protracted discussion of army deafness in the houses of the Oireachtas barely touched on the phenomena of deafness at all and concentrated on the cost of the claims to the exchequer. There were many references in the debates to what was called 'deaf handicap'. This was quite surprising, because the same Oireachtas was, in the early 1990s, preparing an Employment Equality Act, enacted in 1998, which prohibited discrimination on nine grounds, one of which was the ground of disability. The term 'handicap' was already falling out of use as a discredited and backward term.

In one of the few analyses of a specific disability such as that of deafness, Edward Crean argues that huge mistakes were made in segregating deaf children into special schools during their education and forbidding the use of sign language as the first language of communication (1997). Despite the prohibition on using sign language, the children resisted, and sign language went underground. In the words of an adult describing his experience as a child, 'We used to sign in the toilets. In the dormitory, we could open the curtains to let in a little light. We used to sign away for hours' (McDonnell, 2007, 111).

Despite spending years in schools for the deaf, many exited the education system with poor or no qualifications and little capacity to advance themselves or obtain decent employment. The long-standing discriminatory and often demeaning treatment of people with hearing impairments in Ireland interacted negatively with the army deafness cases. Educated separately in 'schools for the deaf', people with hearing impairments or those who were deaf were outside the experience of children educated in mainstream schools. Subjected to so-called 'normalisation' programmes, which forbade the use of sign language, there was an insistence, without pedagogical evidence, that the children should learn to speak with sound rather than sign. This ideological perspective is called oralism.

Public attitudes toward sight and hearing disabilities are not improving over time. In a survey of attitudes toward disability, Irish respondents were asked if they would object if a child with a disability was in the same class as their child. In 2006, 5 percent of respondents answered that yes, they would object if a child with a hearing or vision disability was in the same class. This percentage doubled to 11 percent in 2011 (NDA, 2011, 29). The proportion of negative responses to the same question for children with mental health difficulties, intellectual disabilities and physical disabilities also rose over the 2006 to 2011 period. We cannot assume that prejudice automatically fades over time. This has to be demonstrated on a case by case basis.

Occupational hearing loss occurs frequently in some manufacturing, ship-building, steel, aircraft manufacture and construction sectors. This was recognised in the *1955 Factories Act* and subsequently in the *1975 Factories (Noise) Regulations, Statutory Instrument No. 235* on workplace noise, followed by further regulations in *Statutory Instrument No. 157* in 1990, which aimed to protect workers from exposure to noise. There was no dearth of regulations on noise-level damage, but they simply were not applied by the Department of Defence. How could this be? Maybe it was because soldiers were not factory workers. Perhaps it was a continuation of the typical opt-out attitudes from general labour legislation. There may have been an element of machismo; a thinking that soldiers are above and beyond injury. We simply do not know. At a wider level, the Defence Force was considered unique and exceptional in its status, requiring very specific responses.

The Beginning of the Hearing Loss Claims against the State

Claims for compensation for hearing loss began to trickle into the civil courts as personal injury claims in 1992. While they were called army deafness claims, they included some claims by members of the Naval Services, the Air Corps, the FCA and retired army personnel. The soldiers claimed that their hearing had been damaged by excessive noise while they were employees of the Department of Defence during firing exercises or in the field overseas. They argued that audiometry tests showed their hearing was damaged and that this was as a direct result of negligence or neglect of a duty of care toward them on the part of their employers, the Defence Forces. In legal terms, they were alleging that a wrong had been done to them, a wrong that could have been foreseen and avoided.

The hearing loss, they argued, was permanent damage that could not be repaired and, therefore, they were entitled to compensation for the wrong/injury done to them.

If the Department of Defence and military authorities had lost round one in the recognition of PDFORRA, they were determined not to lose round two as the Defence Force members moved into the judicial arena, albeit one by one. The Department of Defence vigorously defended themselves against accusations of failure to protect the hearing of soldiers and others. They argued that plastic hearing plugs had been issued and that cotton wool had been available, but while they had records of their purchase, they had no records as to their use. In some instances, soldiers bought their own ear protectors and put them on but were subsequently ordered to take them off as they were not Defence-Force issued.[2] The cases made by the claimants were generally successful, and they were awarded damages and the costs of engaging lawyers.

If information as to the consequences of exposure to work-based noise was missing on the part of the state, they did not have far to go to get it. Ireland was party to the European Council of Ministers Resolution on Health and Safety in 1978, which included a specific reference to workplace noise and to a a European health and safety action programme in 1984 (OJEC, 1978 and 1984). European surveys on working conditions were edited at Loughlinstown, Co. Dublin (Paoli, 1993; Paoli and Merllié, 2001). Ireland adopted a council directive on the protection of workers from the risks of workplace noise by way of a statutory instrument in 1990 (OJEC, 1986; S.I. 1990). As early as 1992, researchers in Loughlinstown were identifying noise-induced hearing loss as a large-scale problem

---

[2] Discussion with member of PDF.

across Europe and by 2000, it was one of the most reported occupational diseases in nearly all of the disease-reporting schemes across Europe.

It was much earlier, in the 1960s, that some armies became aware of hearing loss and various hearing conservation issues. The UK Ministry of Defence introduced plastic ear plugs and ear muffs in 1966, but Ireland only followed suit with limited preventative measures seven years later in 1973. There were big problems at the time, including difficulties putting the plugs in and taking them out. Some plugs became stuck in the ear and medical officers had to be called to remove them. This discouraged soldiers from adopting safety measures. During the 1970s and 1980s, soldiers and officers continued to be exposed to noise levels that were thirty-three times higher than the legal limit (RACO). In the three years prior to 1985, 40 percent of disablement claims were for hearing disabilities (PDFORRA Archive). By 1985, some 40 percent of army disablement claims were due to noise-induced hearing loss (RACO, 1998, 4). In the words of Michael Bell (1936–2011), Labour TD:

> I was the first Defence Force officer in 1981–82 to equip his team with proper ear protection in the all-Army shoots. Up to that there was no provision for the issuing of proper equipment as per Defence Force Regulations [...] the Department and the Government of the day deserve what they got because they were guilty of negligence of the highest order (PAC, 1998, 41–42).

Concerns over safety and hearing loss were found not only among soldiers but also among members of An Garda Síochána.[3] In 1996, members of the Garda Traffic Corps, who use motorbikes, were worried that their hearing might be permanently affected by wind noise. They were also aware that the *1989 Health and Safety Act* placed new duties on employers to examine risks to employees. Wind noise was an issue familiar to Guards who used motorbikes and from which they could effectively defend themselves by using ear protectors. Wind noise could reach very high decibel levels within minutes of starting to ride. The traffic unit members were about one hundred in all and initially, their superiors thought they might be preparing a claim for hearing loss. This was not actually the case. What

---

[3] Discussion with former member of the Garda Traffic Corps, 2017.

they wanted were tests to see what kind of ear protection they should wear. The Garda riders picked out a noise breaker that could be customised to fit each member and was washable. In the event, a cheaper version was selected, which consisted of a small, disposable foam plug that was less expensive.

The Department of the Defence denied that they had been negligent toward soldiers, insisting that there were various measures to protect hearing over the years, but that the soldiers had ignored the protective devices such as cotton wool or generic ear plugs. Alternatively, the department argued that if there was some hearing loss experienced by soldiers, it was not so great as to cause 'a handicap'. Even if it was a 'handicap', it was not so great that it should attract significant compensation. RACO argued that the expenditure on hearing protection for soldiers between 1972 and 1983 was three and a half pence per soldier – the price of a pint of Guinness was three shillings and eight pence. RACO went on to argue that 'We expected artillery officers to become deaf and most of them did. It was the norm' (CPA, 1998).

In the absence of a trade union, it fell to PDFORRA to mount a defence for the right of their members to protect their health and safety, affected by these mass industrial injuries, by having individual access to the courts. However, PDFORRA was then a very new organisation, and the deafness cases were effectively happening outside of their control.

State Responses to Deafness Claims

Hearings on the army deafness claims were held in the Oireachtas by the Public Accounts Committee in 1998. At these extraordinary and little-publicised hearings, the 'strategy' to undermine the soldiers' claims became clear in the evidence of witnesses. An interpretation from a reading of the testimony is that medical experts, journalists and lawyers – the middle-class professionals who could align with the soldiers – had each been the subject of a campaign organised by the state to create difficulties between the soldiers with hearing disabilities and the professionals.

As the numbers of cases brought by soldiers increased in the mid-1990s, alarm began to spread within the higher echelons of the Department of Defence and within the political parties at the volume of cases and their success in the courts. The policy of the state was to oppose every case to the steps of the court and then settle there and then or allow them to go to a hearing. RACO was critical of this strategy. Referring to the strategy, the Secretary General of the Department of Defence conceded: 'We have not been very successful in Court. There is no question about that. Those cases we brought to Court were pretty worthless. They really were the bottom of the barrel' (Committee of Public Accounts, 2000).

In the face of mounting claims, which suggested that a type of class action suit was occurring, state bodies attempted to develop a 'strategy'. One arm of the discrediting strategy was to belittle the soldiers by suggesting that some claims were for minor impairments of hearing, were part of a compensation culture or that paying out on the claims would lead to cuts in the defence budget. Relations between the government and PDFORRA deteriorated to the point that at their AGM in 1998, an emergency motion was passed asking the then Taoiseach, Bertie Ahern, to fire Minister Michael Smith TD for his handling of the army deafness controversy (Brady, 1998). The Department of Defence told the all-party Committee of Public Accounts that fraudulent claims may be occurring, that people with little or no handicap were getting substantial sums of money, that it was possible to doctor audiogram results by attending a loud disco prior to the test and that there was a huge assault on the exchequer. The chairman of the committee said 'anybody who thinks this is not a scam must be blind'. Pat Rabbitte TD, a committee member, was reported to have said that the increase in claimants was 'virus-like' (O'Sullivan, K, 1998).

A second arm of the strategy was to try and influence the judiciary in relation to the size of the compensation awards. This was a highly controversial approach since under the Irish Constitution, the powers of legislature, executive and judiciary are separate from each other and are not supposed to encroach upon each other. The doctrine of the separation of powers between the three spheres is the basis of contemporary democracy. The notion of telling judges how to make compensation awards would have been a momentous innovation and unconstitutional if it had been permitted. It was not. Despite this, the Department of Health and Children established an expert group to devise a way of measuring different levels of hearing loss or disability against various sizes of awards and to take account of measurement systems in other countries, such as the UK and the US. The intention was that the eventual expert group report could be voluntarily considered by judges, if they so wished, prior to making an award in a successful case involving a soldier. The report of the expert group emerged and came to be known as the *Green Book* in contrast to the UK's *Blue/Black Book* of 1983.

To get the judiciary to actually read the *Green Book* and use it required a change in legislation so that the *Green Book* could be placed on the judge's bench during a trial of the case. This triggered the *Civil Liability (Assessment of Hearing Injury) Act, 1998* (Dáil, 1998, 18). The act could not order a judge to make a particular level of award, but he could voluntarily consult the *Green Book* for guidance if he so wished. The act stated that: 'Judicial notice shall be taken of the Report in all proceedings before a court claiming damages for personal injury arising from a hearing injury'.

Minister Smith was aware of the thin line he was walking:

It is important to point out that there is no directive element in this legislation. Accordingly, the question of interfering with the independence of the Judiciary does not arise. If the legislation has the desired effect it would be because the courts are persuaded by the rationale of the Green Book. The courts, under this legislative approach, will remain free to adopt whatever attitude they wish in dealing with this issue.

The act was just four pages long and contained a formula for measuring deafness at different degrees of severity and the type of compensation that might be attached to each degree, extracted from the *Green Book*. The minister argued that the Dáil should adopt new legislation because:

Deputies on all sides of the house will appreciate that resources are scarce and should be spent in the most beneficial way for society at large. I do not wish to labour the point, but in the context of there being many worthy demands upon the exchequer, we must stop and consider whether the expenditure of hundreds of millions of pounds on individuals who are suffering minimal or no handicap in their daily lives is justified (Smith, 1998).

The hearing loss court case of Private Kevin Hanley from Limerick was an important landmark for the Department of Defence. The state had appealed an award of £50,000 to Private Hanley, who had been in the army for eighteen years and had been a mortar operator for many years without ear protection. The state appealed his award until it reached the Supreme Court. There, the judges decided that Private Hanley could keep his £50,000, but in the future, things would be different. A formula of an amount of compensation per degree of hearing loss should be applied in most cases with some degree of flexibility for the courts. This would halve the amount of compensation paid out to soldiers and reduce legal costs.

Could the administrative and legal mess have been avoided? Yes. Some of the complexities could have been addressed by changing the law to allow for what is called a class action: when numerous persons pursue the same employer through the courts on similar grounds. The Law Reform Commission later studied this question and proposed a reform, Multi-Party Action, to deal collectively with similar cases (Law Reform Commission, 2005). Individuals affected would opt-in to the multi-party law case if they so decided. Otherwise, hundreds of cases have to be taken separately and individually with the associated duplication of time and resources. A class action procedure enables individuals to get broader access to justice and favours those who are disadvantaged and out of reach of the courts and legal professionals. Soldiers would fall into this category. Of note is that the strategy of the Department of Defence had all the hallmarks of a class action in that they wanted all claims to be dealt with in a similar manner by judges, without judicial discretion. A Multi-Party Actions Bill was published by the Oireachtas in 2017.

The difficulty with the Minister of Defence's search for an objective standard of the so-called hearing handicap is that the Department of Defence was using a medical model of disability policy. This model is based on individuals having measurable deficits in their mental, physical or sensory capacities. This approach was already falling out of favour internationally in the early 1990s. Alternative models of disability were emerging, of which the most significant was the social model. In this policy model, disability was the interaction between an individual with an impairment and the environment surrounding him. A blind student who was offered a regular book to read would not be able to read it. If offered the book in Braille, the student could read it and would no longer be disabled in that regard.

A soldier with hearing damage was not going to be able to continue to function in environments where they would be exposed to very loud noise, be it of prolonged duration or short-lived spurts. Once such damage was done, it generally could not be reversed. Hearing damage, once detected, could limit the career path of a soldier, restricting their ability to be posted overseas, go on courses, fire certain weapons or go for promotion. These are serious obstacles for a workforce whose career options were already limited by incomplete secondary education, which was typical for a soldier in earlier decades.

The minister made it clear that the majority of claims made by the soldiers were not credible or were exaggerated. However, socialist TD Joe Higgins argued that: 'In the past, protecting their hearing seemed to be the only matter left to the discretion of soldiers. Everything else, from the time they got up in the morning to the type of uniform they wore, was decided for them' (Higgins, 1998*)*.

A third strategy to reduce the costs to the state of the soldiers' claims was focussed on the legal profession, who represented the soldiers in the courts. Many barristers and solicitors were also engaged by the Department of Defence to prepare, design and implement the state's defence against the claims. In 1999, the Minister of Defence, Michael Smith TD began preparations to establish a tribunal for army deafness cases, either inside or outside the Defence Force. However, a tribunal was never established. Instead, in the year 2000, closed meetings between the Department of Defence, the Office of the Chief State Solicitor and some soldiers' solicitors took place, with the Law Society acting as facilitators. The result of this and related initiatives led to an agreement that the services of barristers would be kept to a minimum, that negotiated settlements could increase and that some court cases could be adjourned to see if they needed to go ahead (*Law Society Gazette*, 2000, 7). In the same period, a further legislative change was introduced, expanding the functions of the National Treasury Management Agency to encompass that of a state claims agency managing most of the litigation against the state and public bodies. By that point, 16,807 claims by soldiers had been made against the state for noise-induced deafness and tinnitus, which is an untreatable ringing or buzzing noise in the ear.

Table 8: The number of cases where the state briefed lawyers in relation to the Army Deafness Claims, 2003–11*

Up to 2003	2003	2004	2005	2006	2007	2008	2009	2010	2011
13,913	750	357	1304	1,616	124	59	6	0	0

*A number of cases were withdrawn or the claimant died.
Source: *The Irish Times* 2014 based on FOI request and Press Release, Dept. Defence, No. PRD054. August 12, 2003.

Frances Fitzgerald TD, from an army family, disagreed with Minister Smith's strategy:

> I question some aspects of the State's strategy and some of the underlying assumptions that may be directing thinking on the matter. There has been a tendency to rubbish the cases and to stereotype claimants. There has been great concern about ambulance chasing solicitors who are dealing with the matter in an opportunistic way. While I accept there is a problem, we cannot stereotype all solicitors or lawyers dealing with the matter [...] The matter has been left to the courts and when this has not produced the desired results, judicial decisions have been queried. Whatever we may wish to assume, we cannot dismiss the claimants involved. Leaving aside the Irish situation, there is adequate global evidence of hearing disability being caused in the manner described by many claimants (Dáil, 1998b).

The Law Society was also extremely enraged with its treatment by ministers and speaking to the Public Accounts Committee, stated firmly: 'We wish to suggest that neither we nor you should allow the solicitors' profession to be made a scapegoat' (Dáil Éireann, 1998, 162).

PDFORRA felt the same in relation to their members, telling the Public Accounts Committee that 'attempts have been made to pillory, bully and embarrass soldiers and ex-soldiers' (Dáil Éireann, 1998, 107).

Conclusion

The decision of 16,000 Defence Force members to sue their employer for industrial injuries remains the largest case of mass industrial injury claims since the foundation of the state. The army deafness cases of the 1990s have to be read in the context of an emerging and confident movement of soldiers, sea farers and aircrew members of the 1980s. The articulation of the voices and views of the rank and file soldiers and subsequently commissioned officers broke a silence that had hung over the Defence Forces since their establishment in 1924. While representation was achieved in the recognition of the PDFORRA as a legitimate representative organisation, it is questionable as to whether the hoped-for improvements in pay and conditions have been delivered. This remains the case, particularly for post-1994 recruited ranks. Their net pay in 2017 was not much more than their social welfare entitlement.

In many regards, the army deafness cases were an issue of social class – of mainly working-class people claiming a right and using the judiciary to vindicate it.

The strategizing in relation to undermining the soldiers' deafness cases and its vigorous implementation leaves one with an uneasy feeling. With the distance of time, the aggressive handling of the army deafness cases may have incorporated an element of pay-back following the establishment of PDFORRA as a representative body. PDFORRA and RACO had little if anything to do with the soldiers, sailors and aircrew personnel taking their individual cases to the courts other than to defend their right to do so.

As part of the resolution of the army deafness cases, there is now a State Claims Agency, which is indeed a positive development. The change of law to allow *Green Books* be placed on judges' tables is more worrying since it gave the appearance of indirectly 'influencing' how judges carry out their role independently. This borderline status was admitted by the minister of the time. In this regard the army deafness cases raised issues of the separation of powers between legislative, executive and judicial in a democracy.

There have been some positive safety changes. There are now signs stating that particular zones are noise-induced hearing-loss areas. 'Check hearing' is now a command prior to the use of firearms. The ear defenders now in use, in contrast to earlier ones, can be worn with a helmet. Soldiers, sailors and aircrew personnel with specific grades of hearing loss can be restricted in the duties they are permitted to undertake, but this is not positive for those concerned. In 2017, PDFORRA was allowed to engage with the Workplace Relations Commission for the first time.

Wars have had a significant effect on how disability is viewed for those defined as patriotic. The First World War prompted a rush of hospitals in Ireland to receive the wounded and injured soldiers in 1918 and after. War had an effect on how invalided soldiers and others were treated in Germany after 1918, as discussed in Chapter Two. The end of the war in Vietnam coincided with the beginning of the independent living movement in the US, discussed in Chapter Eleven.

The deafness and tinnitus cases revealed the great reluctance on the part of many journalists and members of the Oireachtas to appreciate the significance of acquired workplace injuries (effectively permanent and disabling), to understand the need for hearing preservation and to show some respect for the army rank and file who defend the nation. The situation of the army claimants was and is that of many people who lose some or all of their hearing and find themselves excluded occupationally, subject to discrimination and isolated from social relationships by their inability to hear. The deafness experienced by soldiers and others in the Defence Forces brought to the surface a latent antagonism bordering on the hostile among opinion formers in Irish society. It was as if the soldiers of Ireland did not have the right to be disabled.

Chapter 5 References

Brady, T. (1998) 'Soldiers in Call for Sacking of Minister', *Irish Independent*: http://www.independent.ie/irish-news/sdoldiers-in-call-for-sacking-of-minister-26171137.html. Accessed January 11, 2017.

Clonan, T. (2007) 'Civil Control of the Military and the Police in Ireland: the Armed Forces', Dublin Institute of Technology: arrow.dit.ie/cgi/viewcontent.cgi?article=1019=aaschmedbk. Accessed January 11, 2017.

CPA Committee of Public Accounts (1998) *First Interim Report on the Appropriation Accounts 1996*, Oireachtas.

CPA Committee of Public Accounts (2000) *Annual Report of the Comptroller and Auditor General and Appropriation Accounts*, Vote 37. 29 June.

Crean, E. J. (1997) *Breaking the Silence – The Education of the Deaf in Ireland, 1816–1996*, Irish Deaf Society Publications, Dublin.

Dáil Éireann, Defence Amendment Bill (1990) Second Stage, Vol. 396. No. 9, Paragraph 2370.

Dáil Reports (1988) Questions, Vol. 385, No. 3. Paragraph 653, 7 December 1988.

Dáil Reports (1998) Debate, Vol. 490, No. 5, Paragraph 490, 6 May 1998.

Dáil Reports (1998a) Debate, Vol. 490, No. 5, Paragraph 870, 6 May 1998.

Dáil Éireann (1998) Committee of Public Accounts, *First Interim Report on the Appropriation Accounts*, 1996.

Dáil (2016) Debate, Vol. 922, No. 1. Paragraph 27314/16, 27 September.

Department of Defence (2015) *Wellbeing in the Defence Forces – Report on the Defence Forces 'Your Say' Climate Survey 2015*: www.defence.ie/system/files/media/file-uploads/2017-12/df-climate-survey-report-2-16.pdf.

EU Directives published in the *Official Journal of the European Communities*, No. L183 on June 29, 1989 and in No. L206 on July 29, 1991.

European Communities (Protection of Workers) (Exposure to Noise) Regulations, 1990.

Higgins, J. (1998) 'Army Responsible for Deafness Claims', *The Irish Times*, 8 May 1998.

Law Reform Commission (2005) *Report – Multi-Party Litigation* (LRC 76–2005), Dublin.

Law Society Gazette (2000) Army Deafness Litigation Update, July.

McDonnell, P. (2007) *Disability and Society – Ideological and Historical Dimensions*, Blackhall Publishing, Dublin.

Martin, M. (2016) *Breaking Ranks – The Shaping of Civil-Military Relations in Ireland*, The History Press.

NDA (2011) A National Survey of Public Attitudes to Disability in Ireland, NDA, Dublin.

OJEC (1978) *Official Journal of the European Communities*, No. C 165 of July 11, 1978 and No. C 67 of March 8, 1984.

OJEC (1986) *Official Journal of the European Communities*, No. L 137 of May 24, 1986 and Statutory Instrument No. 157/1990.

O'Sullivan, K. (1998) 'False Army Hearing Loss Claims may Push the Final Bill to £2bn', *The Irish Times*, November 28.

Pascal Paoli (1993) *First European Survey on the Work Environment 1991–1992*. European Foundation for the Improvement of Living and Working Conditions, Dublin.

Pascal Paoli and Damien Merllié (2001) *Third European Survey on Working Conditions 2000*, European Foundation for the Improvement of Living and Working Conditions, Dublin.

RACO (1998) The 'Army Hearing Claims' Issue, Presentation to the Committee of Public Accounts, Oireachtas, February 3, 1998.

RACO (2012) *Signal*, Vol. 11, Issue 1, 2012, *Journal of Representative Association of Commissioned Officers* (RACO).

Smith, M. (1998) Dáil Éireann, Vol. 490, No.5, May 6, 1998.

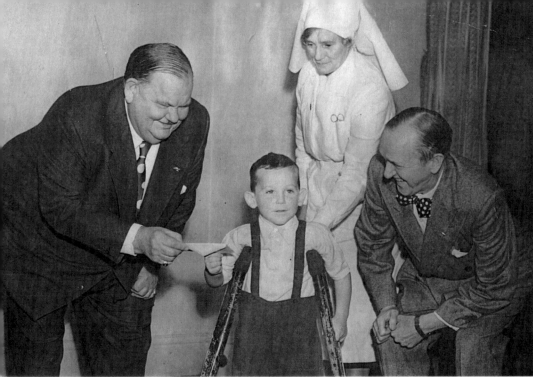

Comedians Stan Laurel and Oliver Hardy present a cheque to Willie Nolan on their visit to St Marys, Baldoyle, in 1953. Courtesy of The Irish Times.

Donal Toolan (1967-2017) artist and activist at RTÉ Radio Station in 1988. Image is courtesy of RTE Archives

Rosemary Kennedy (1918-2005)
sister of John F. Kennedy on a visit
to Kilcroney, Co Wicklow around
1938-40.
Copyright © John F. Kennedy
Library Foundation.

Nurse at prams outside a
Lebensborn (Fountain of
Life) home under an SS
flag, 1940s.
Bundesarchiv Bild
148-1973-010-11

The author at statue of Philippe Pinel (1745-1826) an early and radical psychiatrist, outside the Salpetrière Hospital and former asylum in Paris, 2018.
Photo: Izzy Kamikaze

AU DOCTEUR
PHILIPPE PINEL
BIENFAITEUR DES ALIÉNÉS
1745 - 1826

LA SOCIÉTÉ MÉDICO-PSYCHOLOGIQUE
DE PARIS

People with disabilities protest outside the Dáil in 2016 to demand
ratification of UN Convention on Rights of Persons with Disabilities.
Courtesy of office of Senator John Dolan, Photographer Doreen McGee.

Tom Johnson Leader of the Labour
Party (left), Thomas Foran and Seamas
Hughes of the ITGWU being arrested
by the Black and Tans, Dublin, after a
raid on Liberty Hall, January 1 1920.
Image is courtesy of RTE Archives,
Cashman Collection.

Activists Don Galloway and Ed Roberts founders of the Independent Living Movement on Berkeley Campus of University of California in 1974. Photo Ken Okuno.

Suzy Byrne, Disability rights activist and advocate.

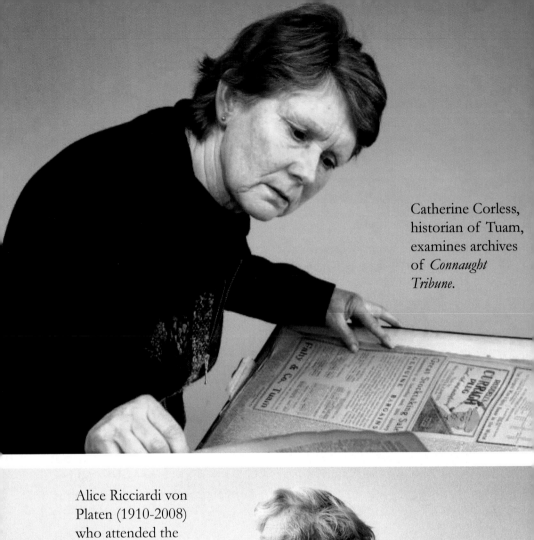

Catherine Corless, historian of Tuam, examines archives of *Connaught Tribune*.

Alice Ricciardi von Platen (1910-2008) who attended the Nürnberg trials of Nazi doctors. Photo Miguel Ferraz.

CHAPTER 6

It's a Family Affair

For many persons with disabilities, their family has been and remains a source of empowerment and advocacy. For others, however, their family has been overprotective, restricting their growth as individuals. Tragically, for others still, their family has viewed them with stigma or shame, and has become a source of abuse and neglect (Secretary General, 2007).

The relationship of the state to people with disabilities and their families has always been fraught since the rise of capitalism, which ended home-based work, to which all family members, including those with disabilities, could contribute. When home-based activities such as weaving, leather work and food preparation moved into factories, family members with disabilities got left behind at home or in institutions.

In the Constitution, the family is defined as a basic and natural unit of society, yet in the past families were encouraged to remove their children from the family and place those with disabilities in various institutions. Even today it is difficult for children and adults to obtain comprehensive treatment for mental illness outside of hospitals. It was as if, for the family to survive as a unit, its troublesome members had to be expelled. Sometimes this created family secrets – the secret of family members who were not present in the family.

This was the basis of *Rain Man*, the film starring Dustin Hoffman and Tom Cruise, with Hoffman starring as Raymond, the brother with autism who has been secretly institutionalised for years and is only 'discovered' by his brother (Tom Cruise) when their father dies. The character of Raymond was based on several real people, including Kim Peak from Utah (1951–2009). Kim could memorise vast quantities of data but had issues in managing his shirt buttons. The writers of *Rain Man* met with Peak, and from these meetings, as well as meetings with others, they developed Dustin Hoffman's character, later inviting Peak to join in the publicity for the film and in its success.

A less happy outcome awaited Rosemary Kennedy, sister of US President John F. Kennedy. Rosemary had a learning disability, which she struggled to deal with in a large family of very competitive and ambitious parents, brothers and sisters. She could read, write and mix socially to a limited extent, and she had done well under the teaching methods of Maria Montessori. However, Joe Kennedy and his wife Rose were preoccupied with how to conceal the nature of her disabilities as she became a teenager and young woman. Joe Kennedy decided to approve of an invasive surgical procedure for his daughter: a frontal lobotomy was performed on her when she was twenty-three years old. His hope was that the surgery would improve her learning difficulties. This was a high-risk and controversial brain surgery at the time and was in the early period of its use. For Rosemary, the operation was a disaster. She lost most of her powers of speech and coordination, as well as many other skills she had striven to achieve, and she suffered amnesia with regard to her own early life. Joe arranged for her to be sent to a Catholic convent in Wisconsin where he had a house built for her near the grounds of Saint Coletta Institution (Larson, 2015, 190). The public were misled as to the nature of her disabilities, and she was rarely discussed in family stories and interactions. For the next twenty years, her parents barely visited her. Her younger sister, Eunice Shriver Kennedy (1921–2009), maintained a close relationship with Rosemary and took her on outings and visits to Eunice's family home with her husband Sargent (1915–2011) and children. The Saint Coletta Institution, managed by the Sisters of St. Francis of Assisi, was 900 miles away from Boston, Massachusetts. It was there that Rosemary Kennedy passed away in 2005 (Larson, 2015).

The secrecy involved in 'hiding', not speaking about and supressing the existence of a family member in an institution affected some of their siblings painfully in later life, according to Canadian research (Burghardt, 2015, 1071). A very simple question like 'How many children are there in your family?' could throw brothers and sisters off course in admitting that there were more children in the family than resided in their home. Secrecy may be associated with shame at having a child with disability or the family's failure to care for the child. With many people today lies the memory of the frequent practice of 'giving children away' to other relatives, families or institutions. The practice was not believed to be wrong, damaging or untoward. In the 1960s, family sizes were still very large, with one third of all births being the fifth child or more in the family, and the temptation to give away the seventh or eighth child must have been great for families of modest means. Either way, the secrecy altered family dynamics and impacted on the child.

The problem of secrecy was well known. A social worker in 1952 described the problem:

> Unfortunately, the idea is prevalent that it would attach a stigma to the family. In many cases, the defective hidden away in the home is a constant source of worry and irritation to the family as a whole. The mother continues to treat the child as a complete infant, this being the easiest method to adopt (Kelly, 1951, 58).

The giving up of a child was a sacrifice expected of parents so that the core family unit could survive both socially and psychologically. It was quite a common practice in rural Ireland to send children to live with childless relatives up until the 1960s. Children with disabilities were viewed as so great a 'burden' that it was assumed a typical family could not sustain itself in supporting such a child. Children with disabilities were not the only children subjected to this sacrifice. Illegitimate and impoverished children were also separated from their parents and placed in industrial schools or given up for adoption. Despite a strong family-oriented discourse in the public domain, the family unit was denied to many people with disabilities. While concealment and secrecy has diminished, it continues to affect those who have been living in large institutions and who still live there.

The author recalls visiting a residential care service for people with intellectual disabilities and meeting there a young man called 'John'. He described with eloquence the efforts of care staff to reconnect him with his family of origin. They eventually tracked them down, but, John reported, his family of origin did not want to be involved with him after so many years of separation. Undeterred, the staff located a cousin, aunt and uncle who agreed to be a family for John and invite him to their home for Sunday dinners. 'They are now my family,' he stated with some satisfaction (Meagher, 2017). There are other moments of success.

Suzanne had lived in residential care for a long time and always in proximity to other people. She frequently expressed anger. Relations with her family were tense. When the service decided to offer her a 100 percent person-centred option of living in a house on her own with a care worker,

Suzanne's life was transformed. Being on her own seemed to suit her, and her periods of frustration were reduced. Her family, especially her mother, re-engaged with her and accompanied her to swimming lessons as well as on her first train trip and overnight stay to visit relatives in the west of Ireland. Suzanne found family members who cared about her, could connect with her and were happy for her to live in a house nearby.

The Dilemmas of Mothering

It is often erroneously assumed and unspoken that women and men with disabilities do not want or should not want to fall in love, have relationships, form a family/household/partnership and have children. Why this is so is never spelt out, but the belief may have eugenic undertones. It may reflect a belief that equality does not apply to people with disabilities.

Mothering in a disabling society is how Goretti Horgan has framed her analysis of motherhood in Ireland when said mothers have a child with a disability (Horgan, 2004). Horgan singles out the disempowering effect of professional attitudes on mothers, who have to struggle for years to get a diagnosis for their child, without which they are eligible neither for services nor for additional supports at pre-school or school. While the majority of women expect to become mothers and see this as normal, women with disabilities reported that this was definitely not the case for them. Society did not expect them to become mothers (Horgan, 2004). It may be that women with a disability were presumed to be devoid of sexual feelings and desires and were somehow 'asexual' or too inherently 'incompetent' to be mothers.

Advocate and blogger Suzy Byrne has argued that issues such as abortion rights deeply affect people with disabilities. Speaking to a conference in Dublin, she described some of the assumptions about women with disabilities:

Disabled women are hugely affected by the Eighth Amendment (to the Constitution). Disabled women are not seen as sexual, not allowed control over their bodies when giving birth. It hugely impacts on disabled women and yet we haven't been talking about it loudly enough. We are so busy fighting for our mere existence. We need to debate these things in the open (Dunne, 2017, 4).

It is as if the designation of a 'disability' automatically supresses all other identities such as that of mother or father, sexual orientation, religious beliefs or profession. We are all intersectional and carry multiple and changing identities into our everyday lives. People with disabilities are also parents, gay, Catholic and a multitude of other identities, apart from having a disability.

Hunting for a Diagnosis

For most children, obtaining an official diagnosis is the passport to services: no diagnosis means no services. There are extensive delays in getting children assessed under the *Disability Act, 2005*, which varies from county to county. Some families have had to go to the High Court, demanding that their child receive an assessment to which they are entitled under the aforementioned act (*Irish Examiner*, 2017). According to the solicitors for those families affected, in 2017 there were 3,960 children overdue for an assessment of need by the health authorities. Once assessed and armed with a statement of need, there starts the unending search for the quality and quantity of services that correspond to the diagnosis, such as speech and language therapy or support needs at pre-school. This can involve a further level of delay as families wait for appointments for services or lodge appeals against schools who refuse enrolment or lodge appeals when services are refused.

Despite the several references to children with disabilities in the *Education Act, 1998*, the boards of management of schools can agree on and publish enrolment systems which, in practice, exclude children with disabilities from enrolment. These decisions can be appealed, but the outcomes are not especially promising. As long as the school has abided by its own enrolment system, the appeal will not be successful. Here is how one South Dublin national school words its special needs policy:

> The school principal, acting on behalf of the Board of Management, will meet with the parents/guardians of the child to discuss the school's suitability or capability in meeting those needs. If necessary a full case conference involving all parties will be held, which may include parents/guardians, school principal, class teacher, learning support teacher, teacher for special needs or psychologist and other professionals as appropriate.

In addition, schools are not obliged to enrol children with disabilities where the school considers that they do not have the resources to meet the special educational needs of a child. This is slowly changing for the school year 2017–2018 in relation to the employment of special needs assistants. However, this does not alter the fact that schools can refuse to admit children with disabilities. So, while every child has the right to an education, they are not entitled to admission to a particular school (Banks, Maître, McCoy and Watson, 2016).

This has become more complicated in recent times as publicly funded therapeutic services in large charitable institutions have been reduced, often with theoretical replacements in local health care services. The major charitable bodies in this arena find themselves in crisis, as one parent described:

> My child waited 9 months to be seen by a Speech and Language Therapist; he has never spoken a word and he's 2.5 years old. The therapist noted he had a disorder not a delay but made no diagnosis and instead simply placed him back on the list for another 12 months and placed him on a list for therapy that is 7 to 9 months long. We since paid to go private, received an appointment within 2 weeks and a diagnosis. Therapy began that day with regular weekly appointments […] we are now having to pay €55 for each appointment. He has a severe speech condition which requires early intervention as he will spend many years in therapy and it is important to begin that work as early as possible as it will affect his daily communication, his ability to make friendships and more importantly it will affect his ability to learn in a mainstream school (Barnardos, 2017).

Parents become understandably distressed and fraught when they cannot get the right services for their children that they know will benefit them. Equally frustrating is having to pay privately for services that should be available publicly because of taxation.

The Labour Market

Having a child with a disability involves a lot of additional tasks both inside and outside the home. There are doctors and specialist appointments to be made, forms to be obtained with certificates completed by doctors or professionals and forms to be delivered to schools and clinics to obtain services. There is transport to and from venues or different schools, often with other children in tow. Typically, the partner with the better paying job stays at work and the other partner withdraws from the labour market. As remarked in recent Irish research: 'Typically, child disability is associated with much lower rates of employment for mothers than for children without a disability' (McGinnity, Murray, McNally, 2013, 13).

This reorganisation of family life can have significant implications. A mortgage may have been obtained on the assumption of two or at least one and a half salaries to pay for it. This assumption goes out the window. The strain of this family adjustment can hit couples hard and may even lead to estrangement. It is unknown whether the rate of marriage breakdown among couples with a child with a significant disability is higher or the same as equivalent couples whose children have no disabilities. What we do know is that in 2011, the proportion of carers who were separated or divorced was higher than in the general population.

In Europe, women are more likely than men to have developed a disability by the time they reach the age of sixty-five. This can be calculated by comparing men and women, aged fifty to sixty-four, under five different kinds of restrictions they could experience. Only in levels of work activity are older men and women almost equally restricted. Differences are quite marked in restrictions due to health conditions and mobility. This is illustrated below.

Table 9: The proportion of men and women aged 50 to 64 experiencing life restrictions in Europe.

Types of Restrictions	% of Men 50-64 years	% of Women 50-64 years
Activities of daily living	5.5	6.1
Instrumental activities (e.g., climbing stairs)	3.7	6.4
Mobility	13.8	21.0
Work participation	19.3	20.0
Limits due to health conditions	31.0	35.6

Source: OECD, 2017 'Gender, Health and Labour Force Participation', in *The Pursuit of Gender Equality – An Uphill Battle*, Table 22.2. Data from 2013.

The Social Protection of Families

Ireland ratified the UN Convention on the Rights of Persons with a Disability in early 2018.

The preamble to the convention includes a reference to families:

> [...] convinced that the family is the natural and fundamental group unit of society and is entitled to protection by society and the State, and that persons with disabilities and their family members should receive the necessary protection and assistance to enable families to contribute towards the full and equal enjoyment of the rights of persons with disabilities.

Later in the convention, a clause on respect for home and the family is to be found in Article 23. Its section (3) states:

> States Parties shall ensure that children with disabilities have equal rights with respect to family life. With a view to realizing these rights and to prevent concealment, abandonment, neglect and segregation of children with disabilities, States Parties shall undertake to provide early and comprehensive information, services and support to children with disabilities and their families.

Many families with a child or adult with a disability are in need of social transfers to maintain any decent standard of living. There is no doubt that disability impoverishes and erodes savings that have accumulated over years. It takes only one special bed and an electric wheelchair (€1,000) to knock out years of savings. The costs of disability are recognised as a policy issue by the World Health Organisation, who reports that the additional costs for Ireland could consume from 20–37 percent of weekly income (WHO and World Bank, 2011, 43). Changes to eligibility for the housing adaptation grant and increased prescription charges in recent years are just two of the extra costs of disability that deplete family savings and expose families to the risk of poverty. Table 10 shows that half of family carers (101,400) get an annual carer support payment, which is intended to pay for respite care or other costs related to disability. Just one third (33 percent) of family carers (64,772) receive a weekly payment.

Table 10: The number of carers in receipt of state payments, 2015.

Persons with Carer's Allowance and Carer's Benefit 2015 (1)	Persons in census describing themselves as carers 2016 (2)	Persons in receipt of Carer Support Grant, 2016 (Estimate) (3)	Proportion of carers (Col. 2) who are recipients of Carer's Allowance and Carer's Benefit (Col. 1) (4) %
64,772	195,263	101,400	33%

Source: Department of Social Protection, (2016) *Annual Statistical Report, 2015*, Table E2. CSO (2017) Census 2016, Preliminary Results, *Profile 9 – Health Disability and Carers*.

The Carer's Allowance is relatively new, dating back to 1990. It gradually replaced two unwieldy and odd payments called the Prescribed Relatives' Allowance and the Constant Attendance Allowance, which had originally been designed to help low-income families look after elderly relatives. A small number of individuals are still receiving Prescribed Relatives' Allowance.

The majority of home-based carers (195,263 men and women; column 2) do not receive any financial support because they cannot pass the means test, have insufficient social welfare contributions, are working more than fifteen hours a week outside the home, the person for whom they are caring for is judged not substantially sick/disabled enough as to require full-time or part-time care or they are living too far away from the care recipient. Refusals can be appealed, and in some instances, are reversed on appeal. As the population ages, carers are becoming older and less able to offer care without additional support. About half of carers are aged forty to fifty-nine, with those aged fifty to fifty-four accounting for almost 15 percent of all carers. In 2016, 60.5 percent of carers were women and 39.5 percent were men.

In terms of numbers, some carers also receive a Domiciliary Care Allowance (DCA) once a month until their child or children reach the age of sixteen years, at which point the child can apply for weekly Disability Allowance. This is one of the rare occasions when a child of sixteen years can receive a welfare payment in their own right. In 2015, some 29,305 parents received a monthly DCA for their child. Roughly a quarter of all applicants are refused, but many subsequently obtain the payment on appeal. This was one of the grounds for the formation of a virtual campaign on Twitter and Facebook in 2016 called 'The DCA Warriors' to campaign for greater flexibility in awarding the Domiciliary Care Allowance to families (Baker,

2016). Since parents can receive the Domiciliary Care Allowance and Carer's Allowance at the same time, the Domiciliary Care Allowance recipients have not been included in Table 10 so as to avoid double counting.

> The DCA was first introduced by the Minister for Health in 1973 by way of circular 24/73. The payment was specifically designed to help parents/guardians of severely handicapped children between 2 and 16 years of age who were being cared for at home. To qualify the child had to have a severe disability requiring constant care and attention substantially in excess of that needed by a child of the same age, which was likely to last for at least 12 months. The means of the child, not the parents/guardians, was taken into consideration. In 2000 the scheme was extended to include children under 2 years of age (Department of Social Protection, 2012, 10).

The Domiciliary Care Allowance was the first cost-of-disability payment in that it was not based on working status or income but was a family-based payment to mitigate the additional costs of caring for a child with a 'severe' disability. This is a specification that one finds repeatedly in legislation and involves considerable medical validation in terms of what exactly is a social payment. A payment of this type had been floated in 1965 in the *Report of the Commission of Inquiry on Mental Handicap*, and there it languished on the pages of the report. It was not until Brendan Corish TD, of the Labour Party, became Minister for Health that it was actually introduced, eight years later. It was one of several radical and socialist proposals advanced by the Labour Party under what was then described as their New Republic policy. It is of note that in his adherence to the principal of universality of service provision, he did not recommend a means test to obtain the allowance. The Domiciliary Care Allowance was reviewed in 2012 (Domiciliary Care Allowance Working Group, 2012).

The definition of 'severe' was medically defined and validated. Why the parents had to wait until the child was two years old is unclear. Jonathan Irwin, then CEO of the Jack and Jill Foundation, suggested at one point that it was because the state were hoping that a number of the children would be dead by then (Conroy, 2010). Irwin went on to lobby the government to remove the two-year wait for the allowance: the limitation was eventually removed.

There are a range of other illness and disability support schemes. These include the Disability Allowance, Illness Benefit, Injury Benefit, Invalidity Benefit, Disablement Benefit and the Blind Pension. Each has its own separate origin and rules of entitlement and administration.

Some of those providing care for others are children themselves, under the age of fifteen years; 3,800 such boys and girls were identified in the 2016 census. Of those, 831 were nine years old or less (CSO, 2017). To expect or accept children to act as carers of others for a prolonged period is quite unacceptable. While most children provided just two hours of care per week, a minority were caring for up to twelve hours a week. The number of child carers fell between 2011 and 2016, mainly due to reductions in the younger age groups. The involvement of older teenagers remained almost the same. When children become known to the organisation Family Carers Ireland, the family can be visited and arrangements can be made so that external carers can begin providing help in the home (McGrath, 2017, 20).

At the other end of the spectrum, some carers are themselves quite old: more than 5,000 are aged seventy-five to seventy-nine years; over 3,000 are aged eighty to eighty-four years and an amazing 1,700 are aged over eighty-five years.

The withdrawal of a parent from the labour market is recognised by the existence of a Carer's Allowance, which is granted on, among other conditions, the agreement of the carer to care for a person and not to take up more than fifteen hours of waged employment or education per week, equivalent to three hours a day. In some instances, a half-rate Carer's Allowance can be granted. The rationale for the restricted hours is that the Carer's Allowance is a form of wage substitution, and caring is a form of labour and is not recognised as a voluntary activity or labour of love. Interestingly, the Carer's Allowance is the only social welfare benefit or allowance that requires recipients to work for their welfare payment.

The chances of participating in the labour market decline sharply for carers who provide even greater numbers of care hours at home. Carers providing up to fourteen hours of care a week were twice as likely to be on the labour market compared with those providing care for forty-three or more hours per week. The higher proportion of women caring in the home is a gendered issue for labour market access. Without ongoing vocational training or professional development, their chances of competing for jobs will be weak. If they are self-employed, they will find themselves without a client base. The Carer's Allowance continues for twelve weeks after a death, at which point the carer must claim Job-Seeker's Allowance, which requires them to search for paid employment; this is a position they may not have held for many years and for which they are often ill-prepared.

Table 11: The number of child carers, 2011–16, providing regular, unpaid help, by age group and hours worked.

Age of children	1–14 hours, 2011	1–14 hours, 2016
0–4 years	409 children	352 children
5–9 years	519 children	420 children
Age of children	15–28 hours, 2011	15–28 hours, 2016
0–4 years	12	7
5–9 years	56	52
Total	996	831

Source: CSO (2017) *Census 2016*. Statbank. Part 2, CSO (2017) Census 2016. *Profile 9 – Health, Disability and Carers*.

The impact of emigration on care work is underestimated. As the numbers of immediate family members shrink in size, the remaining members take on a caring role with fewer family members with whom to share it. This can quickly lead to inter-familial resentment between brothers and sisters at home and abroad. Many brothers and sisters reported being ignored in their care support, according to research from Cork:

As children, the participants reported being largely ignored by professionals. Yet it is clear from their accounts that many of them undertook direct care tasks for their brother or sister and almost all provided some form of support, which helped their parents with care tasks. It is also evident that as children, the participants were very familiar with the likes, dislikes, routines, needs and challenges of their brothers and sisters with ID/ASD.[1] This would suggest a

---

[1] Intellectual Disability/Autism Spectrum Disorder

need for professionals and service providers to recognise the roles that siblings undertake and acknowledge them as active agents in the support structure within families. Recognition of sibling roles and engagement with siblings from an early age, would facilitate future planning in a gradual way and would set the foundations for subsequent beneficial, collaborative and cooperative sibling relations with professionals and service providers (Leane, Kingston and Edwards, 2016).

Support to Home Carers

Some home carers have to be supported by professional carers due to the complexity of the support provided to a family member. The professional carer might be a personal assistant, a home helper, a health care assistant, or in some instances, a nurse. While the assessment of need may be carried out by the HSE, the actual carer is likely to be employed by one of many private care supply companies who have contracts with the HSE. This privatisation of social care is quite problematic.

The private care providers are usually for-profit companies who must make enough money to cover training, insurance, administration, travel, social contributions, recruitment and human resource management. However, the competitive commissioning process may force down their costs such that the conditions of employment become precarious for their care workers, triggering a high turnover of staff. From the point of view of the care recipient, the time- and task-based system of assessment can lead to low quality care.

There is no statutory right or entitlement to home care. The public policy decision to privatise home care via for-profit agencies was not discussed in the public arena. It simply happened. Agencies/companies were invited to express interest in providing services in a number of locations and were then funded to do so. Neither the family nor the person with a disability had any say in which agency operated in their area. Their choice is limited to those agencies, which have been approved and selected by the HSE for that geographical HSE community care area. There are more than twenty companies nationally that are members of the trade association of Home and Community Care Ireland (HCCI), which represents some of these private home-care providers. Those who pay privately can use any agency or hire a carer directly if they wish. Some families start the day with a HSE carer for thirty minutes to one hour and then have a private or family carer to help them for the rest of the day.

So, despite the HSE spending €370 million on home care services each year, there is no individual statutory entitlement to it. The HCCI are in favour of statutory regulation of home care. If a request for home care services at public expense is refused, there is little anyone can do about it except reapply or complain to the Ombudsman. Types of services as well as their frequency and standards vary from county to county. In 2017, a new home care system of delivery of services was allegedly being explored. However, what was actually being investigated was the HSE's delivery of services such as home help and home care packages. The entitlement to a personal assistant, a visit from a public health nurse or a housing adaptation were not explored, despite these being integral aspects of home care and support (Department of Health, 2017).

The Irish system of privatised home care is modelled on the UK's system. The private care system in the UK is under huge pressure and heading for a crisis. Some UK home care service providers are no longer bidding for contracts or have actually handed back the contracts they have as they are not sustainable (Koehler, 2017, 6). There are several reasons for this, among which figure the increasing numbers of older and frailer persons, additional costs of recruitment of staff and cuts in local authority budgets. In the words of a UK report: 'Too often people are expected to receive care in slots of time that are too short – either because commissioned visits are short in duration or because visits are cut short through a practice known as call cramming' (Koehler, 2017, 5).[2]

In the absence of employment, family carers can feel quite stranded when the person for whom they are caring passes away or moves to a nursing home. The centre of their life and existence is suddenly gone, often without recognition, leaving them in a situation for which they are often unprepared, both emotionally and financially.

Some campaigners in the disability movement view the 'carer debate' as undermining their aim, which is to seek independent living for all

---

[2] Call cramming refers to scheduling so many visits per hour/per day that there is no flexibility for the client.

individuals with disabilities. The family carer, they would argue, cares 'for' a person with a disability rather than allowing the person with a disability to have the autonomy to choose how and where they want to live. Caring for, or being cared for, is not the same as living with independence. This is how the European Disability Forum (EDF) views the question:

> For the European Disability Forum, the right for disabled people to choose and to make choices in life must be inviolable. Disabled people want to freely enjoy […] their most fundamental rights and to live independently in the community as affirmed in Article 19 of the UN Convention on the Rights of Persons with Disabilities. Persons with disabilities should be able to enjoy good quality services that will make [it] possible for them, in the long run, to fully exercise their citizenship, their right to dignity and enable them to participate in society.

Suzy Byrne, a vocal campaigner for independent living, criticised Finian McGrath, Minister of State for Disability in 2017, stating he did not 'address disabled people' directly and 'nor was he accountable to us'. Instead he was 'being led by parents and carers' and '[…] now we are seeing the rebirth of the charity model for service delivery. We have people incarcerated in nursing homes' (Dunne, 2017, 4).

The absence of choice is a major issue for disability rights campaigners, who rely on the UN Convention on Rights of People with Disabilities for their rationale:

> Article 19: Living independently and being included in the community:
> States Parties to the present Convention recognize the equal right of all persons with disabilities to live in the community, with choices equal to others, and shall take effective and appropriate measures to facilitate full enjoyment by persons with disabilities of this right and their full inclusion and participation in the community, including by ensuring that:
> a) Persons with disabilities have the opportunity to choose their place of residence and where and with whom they live on an equal

basis with others and are not obliged to live in a particular living arrangement;

b) Persons with disabilities have access to a range of in-home, residential and other community support services, including personal assistance necessary to support living and inclusion in the community, and to prevent isolation or segregation from the community;

c) Community services and facilities for the general population are available on an equal basis to persons with disabilities and are responsive to their needs.

Article 19 (b) of the convention states that people with disabilities should not be obliged to live in a 'particular living arrangement'. Despite this standard, the most common arrangement is a community group home shared with others. The move to individualised living arrangements has occurred, albeit very slowly. In some instances, this has altered for the better the relationship between individuals and their families of origin, who are now more involved and connected to their family member (Harnett and Greaney, 2015). For some individuals with autism or mental health difficulties, living in such close proximity to others generates high levels of stress and anxiety. The battle of ideas and practice between care 'for' and 'care with and by' is only getting started.

The Family as a Private Zone

Accepting professional carers into the family home alters the household dynamic from one of intimacy and privacy. The home becomes a place of employment and a care-site for another person. The presence of the non-family member in the home can lead to altered behaviour on the part of family members toward each other, and there may be a sense of unease as to what is acceptable for a professional carer to do or be asked to do. Family members who are not the principal carers can be ambivalent as to whether a professional carer is actually needed. This can coincide with persons with a disability or long-standing health condition refusing to accept non-family carers in the home. This is all the more difficult when the family is a zone of privacy, a refuge from the outside world or a place where you feel that you can 'be yourself'.

The provision of 'respite care' to families is a controversial issue. The concept of 'respite' is based on the premise that caring for a person with a disability is a difficult burden that can be alleviated by periods of time when this burden is lifted and the person with a disability enters a residential institution for what is called 'respite care'. In international discussions, the use of the term 'short break' has replaced the term 'respite'. In addition, a Department of Social Protection annual grant, traditionally known as the Respite Care Grant and now called the Carer Support Grant, is paid to family carers once a year so that they can afford a holiday. It is not a pro-rata payment (Crowley, 2015). The grant comes in the form of a direct payment (€1,700 in 2017) and can be paid to some of those who are/are not in receipt of the Carer's Allowance or Benefit. Along with the Domiciliary Care Allowance, this is a further example of a direct payment in relation to disability.

While the Carer Support Grant and services are welcome to many families and individuals, the concept of connecting disability to a 'burden' is distasteful to some organisations and individuals with a disability. Their preferred alternative is a cost-of-disability-payment. The entire discussion of 'respite' is repugnant to those who are seeking independent living opportunities, a theme discussed in Chapter Eleven. The focus on care *for* individuals undermines, in their opinion, the lack of opportunities and empowerment for people with disabilities to care for themselves.

Year by year, the opportunities for carers to avail of short break care have shrunk. This is partly due to the rising demand for short breaks and the static level of provisions. It is also due to the HIQA demanding higher standards in the actual provision of services. The practice of offering short breaks to parents with caring responsibilities has gradually been discontinued over the last five years. In the absence of residential care spaces, some respite care space has been filled with emergency admissions to residential care. This is not supposed to happen, and those care spaces are no longer available for short breaks.

It is not known to what extent the closing down of residential institutions has contributed to the crisis of short breaks. Change in policy has played a part, with the HSE encouraging families to offer short break care in their homes to other families under a home sharing or home contract agreements. Some large service providers such as Cheshire Ireland, St. Michael's House and Walkinstown Association for People with an Intellectual Disability have launched new carer support services and are within a voluntary network of short break providers. However, the relevance of such home-based solutions for those with considerable needs is questionable and unresearched. The combination of these factors sparked many complaints to TDs and questions in the Dáil during the 2016 and 2017 periods, the replies to which did not explain what was happening in the field of carer support. In a reply to Louise O'Reilly TD, Minister of Health Simon Harris TD stated:

> The Deputy is correct, and there is no point in beating around the bush. There is no centrally maintained list of people awaiting these services. It is not that I have an answer that I am simply not providing the Deputy. This is done on a community health organisation, CHO, level. As with our waiting list conversations, we must find a way of seeing the full range of needs (2017).

In some instances, the presence of a family member with complex and pervasive disabilities and health conditions can medicalise the home and significantly change its atmosphere. This arises when special beds, hoists and multiple carers are present in the house often in an average sized dwelling, alongside family members. It can be easier if the house or apartment is extended or modified to better accommodate a family member with a disability. That has now become quite problematic and complex to manage. Those who have household incomes of up to €30,000 can get a local authority grant for 95 percent of the cost of adaptation, capped at €30,000. Households with income above €60,000 get nothing. Incomes in between are means tested, including the income of other family members, such as students living at home. Family members who build or part-build extensions, put in their own plumbing or build their own ramps themselves do not get reimbursement. This is regrettable and exhibits the promotion of a dependency culture that impedes families from expressing their self-reliance.

Households

Many people with intellectual disabilities have a home with one or two parents. Of those who live outside residential settings, roughly 63 percent of those with an intellectual disability are in a conventional home situation.

However, roughly 37 percent are not in a conventional home: i.e., a family-type home but not with parents. For example, many live with a brother or sister. The presumption that most people with disabilities live in their nuclear family homes is not borne out by census data. Some are with other relatives or non-relatives while others have been adopted or are in foster care/boarding-out. While the variety of arrangements is advantageous, some of this has come about by chance. In fact, sometimes the roles can reverse and people with intellectual disabilities are themselves trying to care for a lone older parent and need support as carers.

People with disabilities are themselves heads of households or are the spouses of heads of households. In 2011, more than 160,000 people with disabilities were the head of a household, while more than 110,000 people with disabilities were the spouse/partner of a head of household. Often in this situation are those who have acquired a disability or long-standing health condition in later life, such as a neurodegenerative disease, a heart condition or an age-related condition. In this context, support to the family implies support for a couple to remain together in their own home with their children; this is easier said than done. Parents with disabilities can find themselves deprived of their children, as lawyer Kate Butler described in relation to court hearings:

> Whenever an order was being sought – in other words, where the State was moving to take a child into care, or to heavily supervise their care in the family home – the report found that 15.4% of the time, the reason for seeking the order was parental disability (intellectual, mental, physical). Shockingly, this was the most frequently cited reason for seeking an order. Neglect, at 15.3%, was the second most frequently cited reason.
>
> The prevalence of disability as a reason for seeking an order is of huge concern. It raises questions about whether parents in this group are receiving adequate supports, whether social workers are educated about the kinds of specialist supports that are required, and whether these parents face a bias on the part of some social workers in relation to their parenting ability (Butler, 2016).

It was not just parents with disabilities who had issues presented to the Family Court, but children also. Coulter noted that: 'One of the most striking issues about the children who were the subject of applications was the high proportion who had special needs. Almost one in three cases (30 percent) involved a child or children with special needs' (Coulter, 2014, 6).

As we expect more and more services to be provided by families and households and within families and households, we need to rethink families. Most children in care (94 percent) are now fostered in relative's or other people's families, as illustrated in Table 12. Separated children seeking asylum are also fostered. At the end of 2016, there were 6,258 children in the care of the state, the majority of whom were in foster care. The question that arises is whether a disproportionate number of children with disabilities are being taken into state care – children who, with different supports, might have stayed at home or spent more time at home.

In a searing and sharp critique, the Office of the Ombudsman for Children reported an indifference to the specific needs of children with *disabilities* in care by Tusla, the child welfare agency, while the HSE were indifferent to the needs of the child *in care* when specific disability supports were requested (Office of the Ombudsman for Children, 2018).

The results of Carol Coulter's reports suggest that, once again, a nineteenth-century practice is reappearing: the removal of children with disabilities from the care of their family of origin without evidence of a comprehensive examination of whether, with some support, they could care for the children themselves.

Pregnancy and Choice

In the twenty-first century more is known about the origin of certain disabilities with which babies are born. For example, up to 70 percent of neural tube defects can be prevented by lawfully incorporating folic acid into food fortification. Ireland does not do this. However, 30 percent of neural defects still cannot be prevented or foreseen. Other preventative measures include public health campaigns to reduce the exposure of women with diabetes or epilepsy to the use of medication that is damaging to a foetus and ensuring that disadvantaged households have sufficient income to purchase nutritious food.

Table 12: The profile of children in care in Ireland at the end of Quarter 3, 2016[*]

Type of care for children	Numbers of children	% of total
Foster care general	4,133	66
Foster care with relatives	1,772	28
Residential care general	312	5
Residential care special	9	1
Totals	6,226	100

[*]103 children not in table data.
Based on: Cahal McHale and Dr Valerie O'Brien (2017) *Foster Care: Envisioning the Future – A Discussion Paper* – February, Social Workers in Foster Care. See also
Family Carers Ireland pre-budget Submission, Budget 2018 at familycarers.ie/wp-content/uploads/2017/07/2018.

Serious chromosomal anomalies, such as neural tube defects, increased in Ireland between 2009 and 2011 (McDonnell, Delany, O'Mahony, Mullaney, Lee, Turner, 2014). In a scientific study of 225,998 births (2009–2011), 236 neural tube cases were identified. Of these, 45 percent had anencephaly and 6 percent had encephalocele.[3] Of the 236 cases, an estimated 22 percent of women had a pregnancy termination abroad.

There is no certainty with the subject of fatal foetal abnormality. However, it is certain that responding to a growing prevalence of chromosomal anomalies through public health actions could reduce the incidence of these circumstances and reduce the need for some, but certainly not all, pregnancy terminations.

Founding a family complete with children throws up new choice questions about disability. These are pregnancies often welcomed with joy but incompatible with sustainable life.

Conclusion

The family has increasingly become the focal point for the delivery of social services: large-scale residential services and mental hospitals have

---

[3] Anencephaly is the failure of the neural tube to fuse. In encephalocele, a part of the brain protrudes outside of the skull.

declined in importance. The large nineteenth-century psychiatric hospitals are being closed down as they are incompatible with modern health care. The equally large-scale residences for people with disabilities are being closed down to permit a more mainstream life for the residents. This has heightened a very gendered demand for efficient home-based services and effective therapeutic services for those living in group homes. This is further explored in Chapter Eleven.

However, not everyone has a family or household. Census 2016 identified 1,871 homeless men and women with a disability. The most significant difficulty was emotional or psychological. We do not know if their mental disabilities arose as a result of being homeless or whether the negative environment they encountered in relation to their disability propelled them into homelessness. Others are in hospitals or nursing homes and are deprived of the right to attain the goal of independent living.

Carers, both women and men, boys and girls, continue to offer support to their relatives and are the only social welfare recipients obliged to work for welfare payments. The risk of a child with special needs ending up in state care is surprisingly high, reverting to the nineteenth-century practice of segregating children with a disability from mainstream family life.

Chapter 6 References

Baker, N. (2016) Thousands of 'DCA Warriors to press candidates on doorsteps', Irish Examiner, 3 February 2016, www.irishexaminer.com/election2016-news-and-analysis. Accessed July 25, 2018.

Baker, N. O'Loughlin, A. (2017) 'Families sue HSE for delays assessing needs of Disabled children', Irish Examiner, 9 May 2017, www.irishexaminer.com/breakingnews/ireland/families-sue-hse-for-delays-assessing. Accessed May 9, 2017.

Banks, J. Maître, B. McCoy, S. Watson, D. (2016) Parental Educational Expectations of Children with Disabilities, Research Series Number 50, ESRI, May, Dublin: www.esri.ie. Accessed September 7, 2017.

Barnardos (2017) Waiting List Briefing Paper, May 23 2017: www.barnardos.ie. Accessed September 7, 2017.

Burghardt, M. (2015) '"He Was a Secret": Family Narratives and the Institutionalization of People with Intellectual Disabilities', *Disability and Society*, Vol. 30. No.7–8. UK: Taylor and Francis.

Butler, K. (2016) 'Lessons from the Courtroom', *Frontline*, Issue 104: frontline- Ireland.com/lesson-courtroom. Accessed February 23, 2016.

Conroy, P. (2010) Communication to the Author and Attendees at the ISBA (International Short Breaks Association) Conference, Galway, June 9, 2010.

Clifford Larson, K. (2015) *Rosemary – The Hidden Kennedy Daughter*, Houghton, Mifflin Harcourt, Boston, US.

Coulter, C. (2014) Child Care Law Reporting Project, *Second Interim Report*, Department of Justice and Equality: https://www.childlawproject/wp-content/uploads/2014/10/interim-report-2-web.pdf. Accessed July 24, 2018.

Crowley, C. (2015) Making the Respite Care Grant a Pro-Rata Payment, Carers Alliance, Cork.

CSO (2017) *Census 2016*, Profile 8, Health Disability and Carers, CSO, Dublin.

Department of Health (2017) Improving Home Care Services – Have Your Say: homecareconsultation@health.gov.ie.

Department of Social Protection (2012) *Report of the Review Group on the Domiciliary Care Allowance*, Final Report, December 21, 10: www.welfare.ie. Accessed July 24, 2018.

Dunne, S. (2017) 'Both Sides of Abortion Debate "Abuse Existence of People with Disabilities"' in *The Irish Times*. Dublin.

European Court of Justice (ECJ) (2008) *S. Coleman v. Attridge Law and Steve Law*, Judgement of 17 July 2008, Case C-303-06.

Harnett, A. and Kathleen Greaney (2015) Next Steps – the Journey so Far – Sharing Learning to Inform the Movement to Individualised Supports, National Federation of Voluntary Bodies, Galway, Ireland.

Harris, S. (2017) Dáil Éireann, Debates, 28 September.

Horgan, G. (2004) in P. Kennedy (ed.) *Motherhood in Ireland*, Mercier Press, Cork.

Kelly, B. (1951) 'A Social Problem', *Loreto Annual 1951*, The Argus Press, Dublin.

Koehler, I. (2017) The Human Cost of Cut-Price Care, London: LGiU and Mears: www.lgiu.org.uk. Accessed August 24, 2017.

Leane, M. A. Kingston and C. Edwards (2016) *Adult Siblings of Individuals with Intellectual Disability/Autistic Spectrum Disorder: Relationships, Roles and Support Needs*, National Disability Authority, Dublin and School of Applied Social Studies, University College Cork.

LoveBoth Project (2017) 'Eight Reasons to Protect the 8th Amendment', Brochure, Dublin.

McDonnell, R. Delany, V. O'Mahony, M.T. Mullaney, C. Lee, B. Turner, M.J. (2014) 'Neural Tube Defects in the Republic of Ireland in 2009–2011', *Journal of Public Health*, Vol. 37. No. 1. Oxford University Press, UK. pp. 57–63.

McGinnity, F. Murray, A. McNally, S. (2013) *Growing Up in Ireland – Mothers' Return to Work and Childcare Choices for Infants in Ireland.* Department of Children and Youth Affairs, Stationery Office, Dublin.

McGrath, P. (2017) 'Young Carers – Ireland's Hidden Army', *Healthy Ireland Magazine*, Autumn, Dublin.

Meagher, M. (2016) Unpublished research discussed with author in 2017.

Office of the Ombudsman for Children (2018) *Molly's Case: How Tusla and the HSE Provided and Coordinated Supports for a Child with a Disability in the Care of the State* – An Investigation by the Ombudsman for Children's Office, January: www.oco.ie. Accessed January 10, 2018.

Parliamentary Inquiry into Abortion on the Grounds of Disability (2013) UK, 17 July 2013.

Secretary General of the United Nations (2007) Message on the International Day of Families, New York, United Nations, 15 May.

Termination for Medical Reasons (TFMR) Submission to the Citizens Assembly, December 14, 2016: team@TFMR.com. Accessed December 16, 2016.

WHO and World Bank (2011) *World Disability Report*, Geneva, Switzerland.

CHAPTER 7

The Right to Work – Denied

When Swiss lorry driver Sven Glor was called up for military service in 2004, little did he know that it would be the start of a legal battle over employment with repercussions all over Europe. Sven, aged twenty-six, was judged unfit for military service due to his Type 1 diabetes, although that condition did not prevent him working as a lorry driver. However, the Swiss authorities decided that despite his illness, he should have to pay a tax payable for not undertaking military service. The tax would be levied on his salary until he was at least thirty-four years old. Exemptions from the tax and alternative civil/non-military service were only available to conscientious objectors; Sven wanted to complete his military service. Sven appealed against his treatment to various tax and legal authorities in Switzerland mainly without legal representation, but in vain. Finally, with his father's support, he engaged a prominent lawyer and had his case presented to the European Court of Human Rights in Strasbourg, France.

In a wide-ranging judgement, the court found that Sven Glor's human rights had been breached on three counts (Glor, 2009). The court found that the state of Switzerland had breached his rights by imposing a disability tax on him in a manner over which he had no control and from which he could not be exempted. The court found no justification in imposing a situation where some persons paid the tax and others did not. The court considered that the Swiss military authorities should have admitted him to military service and provided him with a post that did not require the physical effort they judged essential in recruits. The court was also of the view that Sven was entitled to reasonable accommodation and an adjustment or redeployment within the military that fitted his disability. Making explicit reference to the UN Convention on the Rights of Persons with Disabilities, the court confirmed that the UN Convention was now the global norm to prevent disability discrimination, even though Switzerland had not ratified the convention at that time (they did so after the case in

2014). Sven Glor received no compensation because he had not asked for any. His legal costs were eventually paid. His story raises many of the issues at the heart of the treatment of people with disabilities in relation to employment: discrimination, reasonable accommodation, the right to work and health.

Quotas in Employment Policy

In Ireland, the first attempt to establish a legal basis for the right of people with disability to work dates back to the second half of the last century. The then Minister for Labour, Michael O'Leary TD (1936–2006) was in favour of employment quotas, namely that a fixed percentage, such as 3 percent of all employee posts in the public service, should be reserved for people with disabilities. The quota system arose in Europe after the First World War when Germany and Austria wanted to force employers to hire former soldiers and war veterans, who were facing a very uncertain future (Thornton, 1998). The issue was discussed at the post-war Inter-Allied Conference of 1920. On the assumption that disabled veterans were unable to compete equally with other workers, quotas were seen as a way of equalising opportunities between workers and were widely supported by trade unions. The use of quotas as an employment practice spread across Europe, including Central and Eastern Europe and later Japan. They subsequently became embedded as a policy and became 'nationalised' in various ways across various countries, with diverging scope and depth and with different emphasis and exemptions. Quotas were frequently accompanied by levies on employers who had not implemented their quota obligations. The US and Canada did not take on quotas as in Europe. Together with the UK, they moved directly toward anti-discrimination legislation as a way of opening employment opportunities for people with disabilities. Confusingly, Ireland has both: a voluntary quota in the public sector and anti-discrimination legislation for both public and private sector employers.

Minister O'Leary wanted to implement quotas on a statutory basis in the public sector in Ireland but could not persuade his cabinet colleagues to agree with him. Due to cabinet confidentiality, which prohibits us from reading their discussions or his proposal, we will never know what arguments the minister put forward and what replies he received. He had to rely on a voluntary system of quotas, aiming for 3 percent of jobs in the public sector to be filled by people with disabilities. There was no legal basis for this and so no enforcement. This remained the case in 1984 when a government *Green Paper* stated that: 'The Government do not consider it desirable at this time to impose an obligation on private sector employers to recruit a fixed number of disabled workers' (Lunt and Thornton, 1993, 52). Quotas in the public sector were put on a statutory basis in *The Disability Act, 2005*, twenty-eight years after the initial proposal.

In addition to the voluntary quota, there were some 'reserved occupations', such as telephonists who were typically blind, or making and repairing cane chairs in sheltered workshops. Sheltered workshops are closed or protected places of work where employment is reserved for people with disabilities. Quotas were revived in Ireland with the employer-labour agreement of 1991, called the Programme for Economic and Social Progress (PESP), which devoted a whole page of reforms to 'People with Disabilities'. Among the proposed changes, mainly impelled by the Irish Congress of Trade Unions, was a commitment to 'increasing on a gradual and sustained basis the number of people with disabilities employed in the public service' (PESP, 1991, 41).

Discrimination

Not everyone was convinced that quotas, restricted to the public sector, were the way forward. Once again, this view was legitimised from overseas. The United Nations' *Standard Rules on the Equalization of Opportunities for Persons with Disabilities* were adopted by the General Assembly around the same time in December 1993. Although not a legally binding instrument, the *Standard Rules* represented a strong moral and political commitment on the part of governments to take action to attain equality of opportunities for persons with disabilities (UN, 1993). In the US, policy was headed in a very different direction compared with Europe. The *Americans with Disabilities Act of 1990* (ADA) was a far-reaching federal measure to combat discrimination in line with US civil rights perspectives in relation to race, sex, national origin and religion. The approach was significantly different from the idea of quotas. The ADA obliged almost all employers and training bodies to adjust their advertising, recruitment, employment, training and retention policies so that employees with disabilities could enter the workforce on an equal basis with others. The adjustment required in this process was termed providing 'reasonable accommodation.'

Not to be outdone by the Americans, the EU Treaty of Amsterdam in 1997 contained a mention of disability in its Article 13:

> Without prejudice to the other provisions of this Treaty and within the limits of the powers conferred by it upon the Community, the Council, acting unanimously on a proposal from the Commission and after consulting the European Parliament, may take appropriate action to combat discrimination based on sex, racial or ethnic origin, religion or belief, disability, age, or sexual orientation (European Union, 1997, 26).

The new European Treaty article was carefully worded so as not to give any new rights to people with disabilities directly in Europe; it merely allowed the European institutions and member states to take 'appropriate' action to combat disability discrimination. In contrast to the Treaty of Rome, which gave the right of a 'direct effect' to men and women alleging gender discrimination, regardless of whether their government had incorporated the directive into national law or not, disability discrimination had no 'direct effect' on individuals until member states based a non-discrimination law on it.

Following the treaty, organisations across Europe representing people with disabilities began lobbying strongly for a new European law to prohibit discrimination against people with disabilities, both in and out of the workplace and across European borders. This law would take the form of a European Directive on employment and occupation. The Directive 2000/78/EC embodied the following principles in relation to disability:

- Non-discrimination,
- Protection for rights,
- Equal labour and trade union rights,
- Access to technical, vocational and continuing education and training,
- Employment opportunities and career advancement,
- Opportunities for self-employment,

- Public and private-sector employment,
- Provision of reasonable accommodation in the workplace,
- Promotion of work experience, and
- Promotion of vocational and professional rehabilitation, job retention and return-to-work programmes.

The Court of Justice of the European Union has played a major and central role in addressing disability discrimination in Europe through the judgements of the court and the opinions of the Advocate General. A case of particular interest in defining the scope of European disability law was that of *S. Coleman vs. Attridge Law and Steve Law* (ECJ, 2008). Ms Coleman claimed that she had been harassed by her employer when she returned from maternity leave and then had to take some time off to care for her new baby who had a disability. The court found that unwanted conduct amounting to harassment 'by association' had taken place. It also arises when an employee's conduct suffers from disability that is not their own but is related to the disability of his/her child, whose care is provided primarily by that employee. Such conduct is contrary to the prohibition of harassment under Council Directive 2000/78, which provides a framework for equal treatment in employment and occupation, specifically in Article 2(2)(a).

The definition of what exactly constitutes a disability was further expanded in two joined European Union court cases from Denmark in 2013 (ECJ, 2013). In these, the court found that the concept of disability must also include a medically diagnosed illness with physical, psychological or mental impairments that, together with various barriers, impede and restrict a person's long-term participation in working life compared with other workers. The cases had been brought by the Danish trade union HK Denmark (Handels-og Kontorfunctionærernes Forbund), where the employees were looking for reasonable accommodations in the form of part-time work/changes in working hours. The Danish cases built on an earlier 2006 case from Spain, known as the Sonia Chacón Navas case, which dealt with the difference between disability and sickness in the Equal Treatment Directive of 2000/78 (ECJ, 2006).

One of the most common issues in the workplace is mental health and mental illness. A 2017 study found that 60 percent of employees in the UK had experienced a mental health issue due to work or where work was a contributing factor at some point in their career. Almost one in three had been 'diagnosed' with a mental health condition at some point in their lives. Symptoms such as depression, anxiety and panic attacks were common, as were changes in appetite, irritability and mood swings as well as raised blood pressure, dizziness and headaches (Business in the Community, 2017, 10). However, many employees believed they would be penalised if they reported their problem, and managers had not been trained to deal with the presentation of such issues in the workplace.

The Need for Assistance and Adaptation at Work

It is logical to believe that people with disabilities might take up employment if there were some supports they could rely on. Throughout Europe, there are specific needs, varying by country, that some people require on an everyday basis. These needs include personal assistance; special aids; and equipment that enables them to get in and out of bed, undertake shopping, cooking and other basic activities of everyday life. Specific groups have greater need for these services, including women, those living alone, those on lower incomes and those aged sixty-five years and over.

Having taken account of everyday needs, what about supports at work? The European Union's statistical office – Eurostat – has identified the principal supports that people need in order to obtain and remain within employment. There were huge variations between countries. In the Netherlands, for example, 67 percent of men with a disability and 65 percent of women with a disability had not used any workplace assistance. In Ireland, 94 percent of men and 93 percent of women had no workplace assistance. When it came to personal assistance, it had been used by 11 percent of men and 10 percent of women in the Netherlands. This compared – poorly – with just 1.7 percent of Irish men and women in total. In the absence of visible supports to obtain or remain within employment, many people with disabilities will not risk even attempting or exploring entry to the labour market. They are economically inactive and remain so.

Some countries seem to have an enabling environment for employment while others do not. This can be measured and compared by looking at the activity rates (employment and job-seeking persons as a proportion of those of working age) of those with and without restrictions arising from their disability/environment.

Table 13: The activity rates of people aged 15 to 64 with/without restrictions in Ireland and Finland, 2011.

2011	Proportion of persons economically active who had difficulty in basic activities		Proportion of persons economically active who had no difficulty in basic activities
European Union	53.8%		74.1%
Ireland	36.3%		71.4%
Finland	66.9%		79.2%

Source: Eurostat: http://appsso.eurostat.ec.europa.eu/nui/

In the European Union, of twenty-eight member states, 74 percent of those of working age who had no restrictions in their daily lives were at work or seeking work (Europa, 2014). However, only just above half of those with a restriction (53.8 percent) were at or seeking work. In Finland, 79 percent of people with no restrictions were in work or seeking employment and almost 70 percent of those who had restrictions in basic activities of living were in employment or on the labour market – much higher than the EU average (53.8 percent). The gaps between the economic activity rates vary widely from country to country. It would seem that lifting barriers to employment is more successful in some countries than in others.

In 2016, there were 176,445 persons of all ages with a disability in the Irish labour force, giving a labour force participation rate of 30 percent compared with a rate of 61 percent in terms of those without a disability; that 31 percent difference means a lot of inequality. This comparison includes people over sixty-five years, so, looking at the differences for those aged fifteen to sixty-four years only, the rates are different. Among the total population, the participation rate was 78 percent for men and 66 percent for women, whilst for those with disabilities the rates were 51 percent and 42 percent – a 27 percent gap for men and a 24 percent gap for women. As for unemployment, persons with a disability had twice the rate of unemployment – 26.3 percent, as people with no disability – 12.9 percent (2016). For those with specific difficulties, their unemployment rate was far higher: it stood at over 40 percent for individuals with an intellectual disability (CSO, 2017).

There is a large and measurable underutilisation of the energies and resources of people with disabilities. This is evident whether measured by unemployment rates or connections to the labour market. The status of people with disabilities varies from one labour market to another. So, some measures for labour market entry are working; the problem lies in identifying which ones.

Reasonable Accommodation

The American and European approach to non-discrimination in employment was quickly taken up in Ireland by non-governmental bodies who demanded Irish non-discrimination legislation. This was duly delivered in the form of the *Employment Equality Act, 1998*. The *Equal Status Act* was not so quick, and two years were to pass before it was adopted, with disability being the ground on which objections were made. The reasonable accommodation provision was and is one of the more contentious issues in employment for people with disabilities. Section 16 of the act describes it as follows:

'appropriate measures', in relation to a person with a disability
(a) means effective and practical measures, where needed in a particular case, to adapt the employer's place of business to the disability concerned,
(b) without prejudice to the generality of paragraph (a), includes the adaptation of premises and equipment, patterns of working time, distribution of tasks or the provision of training or integration resources, but
(c) does not include any treatment, facility or thing that the person might ordinarily or reasonably provide for himself or herself.

The types of appropriate adjustments that might be considered and applied are many and varied according to individual situations. The following are some of the adjustments:

- Adjustments to the premises
- Allocating some of the disabled person's duties to another person
- Transferring him or her to fill an existing vacancy
- Altering hours of work or training
- Assigning him or her to a different place of work or training

- Allowing him or her to be absent during working or training hours for rehabilitation, assessment or treatment
- Giving, or arranging for, training or mentoring, whether for the disabled person or any other person
- Acquiring or modifying equipment
- Modifying instructions or reference manuals
- Modifying procedures for testing or assessment
- Providing a reader or interpreter
- Providing supervision or other support
- Creating a new job for a disabled employee (Stacey, 2012).

In the case of lorry driver Sven Glor, applying Section 16 (b) meant that the Swiss authorities should have *redistributed tasks* to Sven Glor in line with his health condition. They would not, under sub-section (c) be obliged to provide him with insulin injections, which he should provide for himself.

Equality is treating everyone the same; this is the common reflex response to the question 'what is equality?' But in the case of disability discrimination, the law says that people with disabilities should not be treated the same. On the contrary, people with disabilities in the work-place, in training, promotion and in recruitment, should be provided with those adjustments that enable them to be on a level playing field with everyone else. People with disabilities are entitled to be treated differently in order to be equal to others.

Many people are still surprised at the idea of reasonable adjustment or accommodation, although it is now more than twenty years since the idea was first introduced in law and then implemented. What appears to be difficult to grasp is the concept of adjusting the working environment or conditions for an individual with a disability rather than for a category or group of people.

Take, for example, transport to work by train. Iarnród Éireann expects travellers with wheelchairs or walking frames to phone or email them twenty-four hours in advance of using the train station so that ramps or personal assistance are available. This seems quite unreasonable compared with other train passengers. What is even more unreasonable is that to use their website to find out if a station is wheelchair accessible takes ten to twelve navigations, for just one station. The practice of reducing station staff does not help matters when two wheelchair users need the single old-fashioned ramp to get on or off the train. The DART train system had a six-month pilot project during 2018, but users still had a requirement to telephone in advance. The plan was rejected by the Irish Wheelchair Association.

Examples of interesting accommodations were observed in France while the author was visiting there. Local municipal authorities at a beach resort had provided plastic wheelchairs so that people with disabilities could enter the Mediterranean and float with ease. A second useful adjustment was at an airport car park: before entering the airport building from the car park, there was a low stand with a button to press for assistance. This signalled to staff inside the airport that someone outside needed assistance.

Obtaining Reasonable Accommodations or Adjustments

During a consultation with public sector employees with disabilities, the author found some strange workplace situations. An employee with a hip complaint was given the task of going up and down ladders to replace file boxes. The employee could not perform this task and was sent home on full pay for several months. A deaf employee was allocated a job as a clerk in the courts, where he had to sit with his back to the judge, which meant he could not lipread the judge; the employee asked to be redeployed. In another example, two employees, one of very short stature, the other with a back injury from his previous employment, asked for different chairs, one a higher chair and the other a highbacked chair. They both had difficulty obtaining them. One of the employees waited a year for his chair.

On the positive side, several blind employees were able to work with talking software and were satisfied with their job of opening all general emails coming into the building and forwarding them to the right person. A young man in a low-grade job was able to easily fix computer problems. He was offered a promotion and was pleased with the offer but declined it on account of a mental health difficulty that he felt prevented him taking on responsibility for others. A hospital, very short of nurses, did a call-back invitation to retired nurses. A nurse who had retired due to depression was quickly rehired into a desk job, away from the clinical frontline. This suited everyone.

For Trade Unions engaged in collective bargaining, providing and advising on individualised workplace adjustments can be awkward and difficult. On the one hand, they have collective agreements covering all employees; on the other hand, they are obliged to facilitate solutions and adjustments for and with individual employees with disabilities. It is not always clear to whom an employee with a disability should address herself/himself: to a trade union shop steward if there is one, to their immediate supervisor, or to management? Management can often be perplexed about how to handle issues. The Irish Congress of Trade Unions has reached out to employers by providing them with information, examples and policies in the field of disability.

Of particular concern are manual workers: they are more likely to experience physical injuries. Manual workers also experience high levels of depression, the precise reasons for which are still unknown. A harbour authority employee was informed by a tugboat employee that due to a heart condition, he had been told not to jump from boat to boat. As a manual worker, he could not be redeployed to a desk job as there were none. The harbour authority was reluctant to pension him out as he had not worked long enough to have a decent pension. The situation could only have been resolved if there were agreements between a range of public sector bodies to accept redeployed workers from other agencies.

In another example, a local authority parks department worker developed depression and was taking medication. With the medication, he was not supposed to drive grass-cutting machinery, which was a requirement of his job. He asked his shop steward what to do. The shop steward advised him not to disclose his situation to the employer until the union could figure out a solution to propose. The employee could not be redeployed to desk work as he did not have the education to carry out desk work.

An employer might not have to provide these types of appropriate measures if it meant that the employer would suffer a 'disproportionate burden'. In order to establish what a 'disproportionate burden' is for the employer, several factors are taken into account. These include:

- the financial cost of the measures involved;
- the other costs involved, such as staff time or impact on productivity;
- the size and financial resources of the employer's business.

Before an employer can argue a 'disproportionate burden', the employer must have checked whether there are grants available to subsidise adjustments. The reasonable accommodation needed may cost nothing – it might be a slight adjustment in work tasks or a change in car-parking facilities. An alternative approach for an employer who finds that the only solution to reasonable accommodation too expensive would be a tax concession against the cost of the adjustment.

Disclosure

Disclosing a disability or health condition to an employer involves telling the truth. The truth may not be palatable to an employer or to other employees, and the results of this may be very unwelcome to the employee. If employees do not disclose a disability, especially hidden disabilities, their public-sector employer will have very few people with disabilities on their payroll and will not meet their disability quota target under the *Disability Act*. The reasons why people do not want to disclose a disability or health condition can be many and varied (NDA, 2009). Many simply do not want to bring their personal identity into the workplace.

There is another angle to this: if an employer has provided workplace adjustments such that employees with disabilities are able to do their job as well as their colleagues, then logically, they are no longer in a 'disabling' environment and will answer the questions on disability with a 'No, I do not have a disability'. In this scenario, the modern-minded employer will return lower levels of quota compliance than the employer who may have high disclosure levels but less practical measures to address disability.

Disclosure can become an issue in other ways. An employee may have to take sick leave for a health condition that they have not discussed with their workmates or colleagues. Their fellow workers will frequently have to do some of their work while they are out sick, and they will be curious at the prolonged absence. The employer will know their condition from the 'sick certificate' but may not disclose it to other staff members under any circumstance, even though staff are wondering when the employee will return to work.

The Sheltered Workshop versus Supported Employment

Up until the 1990s, the most common form of employment opportunity offered to people with disabilities, especially intellectual disabilities, was work in sheltered workshops. Workshops attached to large voluntary-service providers ranged from excellent pottery workshops to quite monotonous work stuffing envelopes. Sometimes the contracts of the workshops were intermittent, which led to participants having nothing to do. The sheltered workshops offered

- a closed segregation from mainstream employment on the open labour market;
- a classification by operators as therapeutic work rather than waged employment;
- the payment of weekly trainee allowances rather than weekly wages.

There was quite a lot of ambiguity regarding sheltered workshops. For those who attended, they appeared as work. For some service providers, they were a form of useful day services. For others, they provided vital and specialised skills that would enable participants to eventually get an outside job and were a special form of vocational rehabilitation. The International Labour Organization estimated that there were roughly 8,000 persons engaged in sheltered workshops in Ireland in the 1990s (Visier, 1998, 349).

The ambiguity and diversity of goals can be attributed to the different strands of history and the historical origins of sheltered workshops in the US and the UK. A particular strand was the growth of sheltered workshops for the blind in the early twentieth century so that the blind could become self-sufficient and avoid reliance on welfare. A further strand in history was the aim of churches to retain people with disabilities within their orbit of influence. The prevention of people with disabilities appearing in the public labour market was an additional strand of thinking that fed into segregationist approaches to employment (Matson, 1990). As described in Chapter Three, the Richmond Asylum in Portrane operated a very successful farm, which at one point contributed to the feeding of over 3,000 asylum residents.

As it became apparent to large voluntary organisations and to the Department of Health that some workshops were in fact enterprises and their trainees were wage earners, many workshops closed down. However, this was not the only reason for their closure. Some found that the private contracts for which they did work were no longer available. Others discovered that they might have to establish private companies to continue with the workshops; this could have been against the ethos of the service provider or not worth the extensive paperwork involved. Others turned to the alternative of Supported Employment or developed their own person-based approach to job placements. Person-based or person-centred approaches involved looking at the capacities of individual potential workers and finding a good match for their abilities in employment

Supported Employment

An example of person-based approaches included persons with intellectual disabilities visiting households of the elderly accompanied by a care worker and collecting their empty bottles for delivery to the local bottle bank. A second example included a young man who was on the autism spectrum who went to the library of a local monastery where he entered data on a computer, in a silent and isolated environment. These examples involved short working hours and were, therefore, not part of the State Supported Employment Programme and did not benefit from Supported Employment subsidies.

Supported Employment provides individual placements with a temporary job coach for people who would otherwise be unable to obtain a regular job on their own. Jobs of a certain duration in terms of hours per week can receive state subsidies and can be paid at the level of minimum wage or more. Supported employment schemes can also involve the use of public transport to get to work and the opening of a bank account.

If a person works at least twenty-one hours per week and holds the job for six months, wages can be subsidised under certain conditions. A person with a disability and in receipt of the Disability Allowance can also earn up to €120 a week in 'therapeutic' work without losing their welfare payments, medical card or free travel pass. As a consequence, many individuals arrange their working hours so as not to go over the €120 threshold or twelve hours work per week. While Supported Employment brings some people with disabilities closer to mainstream employment, many essentially remain welfare recipients with a temporary part-time job. Attempts to address some of these obstacles are being made (DSP, 2017, 26). The thinking behind wage subsidies is worth questioning. One rationale for the subsidies is that employees with disabilities work slower and have lower productivity, which should be compensated by a subsidy. A second rationale is that employers do not want, or are prejudiced against, individuals with a disability and need to be financially incentivised to overcome their prejudices. It is not clear which is the prime motivator of supported employment.

The Right to Work

What is interesting about Sven Glor's case is that he wanted to work and felt entitled to do so on being called up for military service. He did not want to opt out or pretend to be a conscientious objector. He just did not want to be punished for having diabetes.

Of the total 643,131 persons with a disability in Ireland, 130,067 were at work in 2016, amounting to just 20 percent of people with a disability of working age (CSO, 2017). This very low proportion implies that the value and worth of the labour of large numbers of men and women is not being realised, and the labour market is being deprived of that value. More importantly, large swathes of citizens are being deprived of the opportunity to work and contribute to society. The low employment rate includes those who were born with a disability and never had access to the open labour market as well as those who acquired a disability during their working life. This is mirrored among the forty million individuals with a disability in the other twenty-seven member states of the EU; the employment rate of people with disabilities in Ireland is low by European standards (Watson, 2017, 4). It further exemplifies the absence of the right to work as far as many people with disabilities are concerned. Employment is not always about wages: it is also about independence, companionship, discussion, socialising and sharing.

The potential employees and the self-employed among people with disabilities are often statistically invisible: they are hidden among those described as 'economically inactive'; in other words, those with no apparent connection to the labour market (Eurofound, 2017). Even those with supported employment jobs can be described as 'inactive' because social welfare is their primary income, and their jobs can be described as therapeutic activity.

Creating more employment opportunities for people with disabilities could be achieved by greater use of the special disability clauses in the public procurement regulations. The new regulations derive from the EU's decision to insert social clauses into mainstream rules and regulations for state bodies who seek expressions of interest in supplying goods and services. This could be viewed as a form of 'socialising' in the economic sphere. It may also be viewed as an attempt to mitigate the harshness of the competitive labour market and the worst effects of globalisation. One of the provisions of the new regulations involves making it easier for sheltered workshops to bid for work contracts when 30 percent of their employees have disabilities. Some public contracts, under specific conditions, can be reserved for social disability enterprises only. Public authorities can also insert social clauses into the award criteria for contracts so that enterprises employing up to 30 percent of employees with disabilities can be favoured compared with those who employ none or less.

Across Europe, a wide variety of approaches are being implemented to promote the employment of people with disabilities (Optimity Matrix, 2015). They range from various quota arrangements, promotion of social enterprises, anti-discrimination measures and other labour market incentives. What is common to countries is the lower employment rates for people with disabilities (49 percent) compared to those who do not have a disability (72 percent). The absence of paid employment may be one of the causes of the higher poverty rates among households containing a person with a disability.

Among individuals with an intellectual disability over the age of eighteen, the employment rate is negligible in Ireland. In 2004, just seven out of every one hundred persons with an intellectual disability had employment that was on or 'near' the open labour market. As the number of persons with an intellectual disability rose in the growing population, the employment rate gradually fell over the next twelve years, reaching just four out of every hundred persons with an intellectual disability in 2016 (HRB 2004–2016). A target to double this rate would still only yield 8 percent of those with an intellectual disability and of an age to work having a job. This is puzzling given the hundreds of millions of euros of expenditure in the area of disability every year. Since the majority of jobs are in supported employment programmes, one has to assume that lack of public investment in Supported Employment may be one of the causes of the decline in the employment rate. Supported Employment is located as a policy measure in the Department of Social Protection, as a welfare measure, and not in the Department of Jobs, Enterprise and Innovation, where it belongs.

Employment Strategy

In 2014, the government announced its *Comprehensive Employment Strategy for People with Disabilities* for the period 2015–2024. It has six priorities for action: building skills, capacity and independence; providing bridges and supports into work; making work pay better than living on welfare payments; promoting job retention; providing co-ordinated and seamless support; and engaging employers. Surprisingly, the strategy did not prioritise combatting discrimination on the grounds of disability on the labour market. This was despite evidence from the Economic and Social Research Institute that discrimination was a factor in employment prospects: 'Discrimination may be one factor that affects the employment prospects of people with disabilities […] Discrimination faced by people with disabilities in areas such as transport and healthcare may have an indirect impact on their capacity to take up work or remain in a job' (Watson, 2017, 4). The strategy does not identify what policies had existed in the past that worked or did not work, and whether there were lessons to be learnt from these.

Many of the actions that emanate from the strategy are broadly scattered across a range of policy terrains. The engagement of employers, for example, cites twenty-two different actions to be undertaken for or by employers or their representatives, or other bodies, or in conjunction with others. It might have been advisable to have only two well-developed actions, such as the employer helpline and the establishment of the employer-trade union partnership. In the event, the results of the strategy for the first period of the plan, 2015–2017, were mixed. Many actions in the plan were described as being in the 'partially undertaken' category, according to the chair of the implementation group.

A major obstacle to obtaining employment and advancing within it is the level of education of people with disabilities. This is recognised in the Employment Strategy. People with disabilities are more likely to have only reached primary education or lower-secondary education compared with those without a disability. People with disabilities were twice as likely to have ended their education in the first years of second level education (28 percent) compared with those without a disability (12 percent). A study for the National Council for Special Education found that many students with special education needs did not want 'inclusive' education in mainstream schools. They put great value on their Special School experience and the care offered by their teachers there. Some found that being called out of mainstream classrooms for resource teaching was intrusive and prevented them 'fitting in' with other school pupils (Squires et al., 2016).

To obtain assistive technology for individual pupils in a school, the school principal has to jump through many hoops. They have to write a report on why the pupil needs the technology and the alternatives that were tried and failed. The principal needs written permission from the parents, the school board of management, a professional and the local special education needs organiser. All of this must be done before the file even reaches the Department of Education. This is evident from reports of the National Council for Special Education (NCSE, 2018). These requirements suppose that each school has a large administrative infrastructure to process such an application system. They do not. The incorporation of so many screening levels for each application implies that claims for technical assistance are potentially fraudulent and unless subject to repeated confirmatory stages, will evolve into a scam.

Fiscal Policy

A surprising omission from the Comprehensive Employment Strategy is the area of fiscal policy. Tax policy is already in use in a limited way. There are useful tax credits aimed at households and persons with a disability. They include duty exemptions for some car users and the costs of adapting a car and some exemptions on the VAT component of home-owner's contributions to housing adaptation. Disability tax credits are not present. Such credits are within the UK tax system, at €3,350 for a disability and an additional €1,421 on top of that for a severe disability. It would compensate, for taxpayers with disabilities, the additional and recurring costs of using taxis to get to work, paying for childcare and the purchase and replacement of working clothes.

It is unclear why fiscal policy is avoided as a national redistributive device and job retention strategy for people with disabilities, particularly those with disabilities acquired during their working life. This might be due to the fact that employment for people with disabilities is still viewed through charity-tinted glasses and is regarded as a job for the Department of Health and the Department of Social Protection. There is no disability unit or desk at the Department of Jobs, Enterprise and Innovation. Unsurprisingly, there is a disconnect between general employment strategy and disability job policies. Making a comprehensive employment strategy mainstream for people with disabilities is utopian in this context. In a two-hundred-page departmental brief to the Minister for Employment in 2017, disability is mentioned just three times, and only in relation to copyright rules.

It would have been useful, even logical, if the strategy had recognised that employment is not universally beneficial; it is also a source of disability, illness and fatality (see Chapter Five). Thus, a main task of employers is to prevent workplace injury and ill health by providing a safe workplace to employees. This is all the more relevant when we learn that occupational injury and ill health in Ireland rises during a boom and declines during a recession (Russell, 2015). The numbers at risk are quite significant, with 10,485 workers claiming Occupational Injury Benefit (ESRI, 2015, 95; HSA, 2017). The spectrum of risk ranges from a few days' absence to fatal injury but with important differences between men and women. Men are more likely to experience injuries (construction/agriculture) while women are more likely to experience ill health (services/hospitality). The economic sector with the highest proportion of illnesses reported is, ironically, the health and social sector.

Globally, the most significant factor in workplace absences due to illness is in the field of mental health, and more specifically, depression. It is also an area that carries continued stigma and potential for discrimination. Employees do provide inaccurate sick certificates for their absences. They are fearful, and rightly so, that any mention of a mental illness will damage their job and their career prospects. If an able body was a prerequisite for employment in the nineteenth and twentieth centuries, it is an able mind that is required in the twenty-first century, as noted by writer Colin Barnes (Barnes, 2000, 441). Many facets of modern employment are outside the reach of those with mental health difficulties. The knowledge economy, with its emphasis on learning and psychological attainment, team systems of working, just-in-time production systems and the inter-personal skills expected of frontline staff working with the public are all minor landmines that waylay employees with mental health difficulties on their winding path to inclusion or exclusion in the workplace (Conroy, 2005, 44).

Conclusion

Across Europe there is evidence of labour market exclusion of people with disabilities, with considerable variation between countries. Paid employment on the open labour market is not a priority for everyone with a disability and is furthermore a source of injury and illness, namely disa-bilities. The position of people with intellectual disabilities on the labour market is negligible. Court cases at a European level have been an impor-tant source of vindication for the rights of people with disabilities at work and in terms of accessing employment.

Ireland has combined a policy of employment quotas in the public sector with anti-discrimination policies for all employers in the public and private sectors. This is quite confusing. The location of employment policy for people with disabilities in a 'welfare' department of government signals the mindset of public policy. Despite decades of information, many employers and providers of public services still cannot grasp the mandatory obligation of making simple adjustments for individual workers with disabilities.

Independent living with personal assistance is a priority for some (see Chapter Eleven), while the right to the education and housing of one's choice are top of the list for others. For the EDF, accessibility in all its forms is key to equality of treatment, be it websites or buildings. The voices of people with disabilities, advocating for themselves, remain often distant and unheard, and this is certainly true within the workplace.

Chapter 7 References

Barnes, C. (2000) 'A Working Social Model? Disability Work and Disability Politics in the 21st Century', *Critical Social Policy*, Vol. 20, No 4. Sage Publications, UK.

Business in the Community (2017) *Mental Health at Work Report*, National Employee Mental Wellbeing Survey Findings. YouGov and Mercer, UK: wellbeing.bitc.org.uk/all-resources/research-articles/mental_health_at_work_report-2017.pdf. Accessed October 4, 2017.

Cases C-335/11 and C-337/11, *Ms J. Ring vs. Dansk almennyttigt Boligseskabs and Ms L. Skouboe Werge vs. Dansk Arbejdsgiverforening*, Denmark. Press Release No. 42/13, Luxemberg, April 11, 2013: www.curia.europa.eu. Accessed August 8, 2017.

Case C-13/05, *Sonia Chacón Navas v. Eurest Colectividades SA*. Press Release No. 55/2006: www.curia.europa.eu. Accessed August 8, 2017.

Conroy, P. (2005) 'Mental Health and the Workplace' in S. Quinn and B. Redmond, (eds.) *Mental Health and Social Policy in Ireland*, UCD Press, Dublin.

CSO (2017) *Census 2016*, Preliminary Results, CSO, Dublin.

CSO (2017a) *Census 2016*, Profile 9: Health Disability and Carers, StatBank Tables E9009 and E9011.

CSO (2017b) *Census 2016*, Profile 9: Health Disability and Carers: http://www.cso.ie/en/releasesandpublications/ep/p-cp9hdc/p8hdc/p9chs. Accessed August 10, 2017.

Department of Social Protection (2017) *Ministerial Brief*, June, Part A: www.welfare.ie/en/downloads/Ministers-Brief-2017. Accessed May 10, 2017.

Eurofound (2017) Reactivate: Employment Opportunities for Economically Inactive People, Loughlinstown, Dublin, October. www.eurofound.europa.eu/publications.

Europa (2014) News Release 184/2014, Eurostat: http://ec.europa.eu/eurostat/statistics-explained/index.php/Disability_statistics_-_barriers_to_employment. Accessed December 2, 2014.

European Commission (2017) Commission Staff Working Document – *Progress Report on the Implementation of the European Disability Strategy (2010–2020)* SWD(2017) 29 final, Brussels.

European Union Treaty of Amsterdam, Amending the Treaty on European Union. The Treaties Establishing the European Communities and Certain Related Acts, (1997) Luxembourg.

Finlay, F. (2017) *First Report of the Chair of the Implementation Group on a Comprehensive Employment Strategy for People with Disabilities*, Dublin.

Glor (2009) *Glor v. Switzerland*, Application No. 13444/04, Judgement of April 30, 2009. European Court of Human Rights, Strasbourg.

Health and Safety Authority HSA (2017) *Summary of Workplace Injury, Illness and Fatality Statistics 2015–2016*, Dublin. Figure 2.9: www.hsa.ie. Accessed January 1, 2018.

HRB (2004–2016) *The Annual Reports of the Intellectual Disability Database Committee, 2004–2016*, Health Research Board, Dublin. See Table 3.7.

Judgement of the European Court of Justice (ECJ) *Coleman v. Attridge Law and Steve Law*. July 17, 2008, Case C-303/06. Luxembourg.

Lunt, N. and Thornton, P. (1993) *Employment Policies for Disabled People – A Review of Legislation and Services in Fifteen Countries*, Department of Employment, UK.

Matson, F. W. (1990c) 'Sheltered Workshops and Blind Alleys' in *A History of the Organized Blind Movement in the United States, 1940–1990*, National Federation of the Blind, Baltimore, Maryland.

National Disability Authority (2009) *Disclosing Disability in the Workplace – A Review of Literature and Practice in the Irish Public Sector*. NDA, Dublin.

National Council for Special Education (2018) Application Forms under Circular 10/2013: www.ncse.ie. Accessed September 14, 2017.

Optimity Matrix (2015) Reasonable Accommodation and Sheltered Workshops for People with Disabilities: Costs and Returns of Investments, Employment and Social Affairs Committee: www.europarl.europa.eu/studies. Accessed July 25, 2018.

PESP Programme for Economic and Social Progress (1991) Stationery Office, Dublin.

Russell, H. Maître, B. Watson, D. (2015) *Trends and Patterns in Occupational Health and Safety in Ireland*, Research Series No. 40, Table A1.3, ESRI, Dublin.

Stacey, M. (2012) The Anti-Discrimination Directives 2000/43 and 2000/78 in Practice. Communication to Disability – EU Jurisprudence and the UN Convention on the Rights of Persons with Disabilities Seminar for Members of the Judiciary, Trier, 4–5 June. ERA Conference Centre, Trier, Germany: http://www.era-comm.eu/oldoku/Adiskri/07_Disability/2012_June_stacey_EN.pdf.

Squires, G. Kalambouka, A. Bragg, J. (2016) *A Study of the Experiences of Post Primary Students with Special Education Needs*, NCSE, Trim, Co. Meath.

Thornton, P. (1998) Employment Quotas, Levies and National Rehabilitation Funds for Persons with Disabilities: Pointers for Policy and Practice, ILO, Geneva: DigitalCommons@ilr.cornell.edu/gladnetcollect.

UN *Standard Rules on the Equalization of Opportunities for Persons with Disabilities*. Adopted by the 48th Session of the General Assembly, December 20, 1993.

Visier, L. (1998) 'Sheltered Employment for Persons with Disabilities' in *International Labour Review*, Vol. 137, No. 3. ILO, Geneva.

Watson, D. Lawless, M. Maître, B. (2017) *Employment Transitions among People with Disabilities – an Analysis of the Quarterly National Household Survey*, Research Series No. 58, ESRI, Dublin.

Chapter 8

Detention in your Best Interest

If you have not committed a crime, you cannot be detained – right? Wrong. Thousands of people with disabilities as well as many others are locked into their residences or detained against their will in hospitals and nursing homes every year. Liberty or freedom is not absolute. Their detention is judged to be in their own best interests or the interests of society. In 2016, there were 2,414 involuntary admissions of people to mental health facilities; that amounts to six admissions a day, every day of the year (Mental Health Commission, 2017, 5).

The deprivation of liberty is one of the most serious human rights issues imaginable. The first Saorstát Éireann Constitution of 1922 contained a provision in Article 6: 'The liberty of the person is inviolable, and no person shall be deprived of his liberty except in accordance with law'. The 1937 Constitution of Ireland, which replaced the Irish Free State Constitution, kept a liberty provision. Article 40.4 of the 1937 Constitution provides:

4 1° No citizen shall be deprived of his personal liberty save in accordance with law.

4 2° Upon complaint being made by or on behalf of any person to the High Court or any judge thereof alleging that such person is being unlawfully detained, the High Court and any and every judge thereof to whom such complaint is made shall forthwith enquire into the said complaint and may order the person in whose custody such person is detained to produce the body of such person before the High Court on a named day and to certify in writing the grounds of his detention, and the High Court shall, upon the body of such person being produced before that Court and after giving the person in whose custody he is detained an opportunity of justifying

the detention, order the release of such person from such detention unless satisfied that he is being detained in accordance with the law.

Any kind of detention, regardless of its name or good intent, must be underpinned by law and not merely by practice.

A complaint that a person is being wrongfully detained can be brought before the High Court, and the person in question must be produced before the court, and if it is considered that the law used was wrong, then the person can be brought before the Supreme Court. The complaint or order is referred to in Latin as *Habeus Corpus*, meaning 'you may have the body'. The human rights instruments of the United Nations, the European Union and the Council of Europe all declare that the right to liberty and freedom must be treated as a fundamental right of an individual. However, the Irish Constitution goes on to argue in Article 40(4) that a situation of armed rebellion or refusal of bail to an accused person may be occasions for the restriction of liberty. In this regard, internment without trial was lawful for many decades under the *Offences Against the State Act, 1939–1998*.

Personal autonomy is one way to describe freedom in practice: making decisions about your life free of the interference or constraints of others; and being able to move about or travel, express one's views, choose a household to live in and choose your friends, partners or companions to share your life with. Consent (i.e., the absence of coercion, whether physical, social, psychological or financial) goes hand in hand with autonomy.

Consent

Consent has many different aspects, including understanding what you are doing, having the choice to do it or not, and appreciating the consequences of doing/not doing it. Consent functions in a real world of practical choices. When, for example, a person wants to leave a residential centre, and if they believe that they cannot leave the residential centre and nobody has told them that they may leave, and if the doors are locked, their apparent consent is arguably coerced. They do not know that they have a choice or maybe they believe that they have no choice. Freedom is not an abstract: it operates in tangible circumstances in the here and now. Detaining people can seem like common sense. It is not. Detention is an issue of fundamental rights.

Article 14 of the 2006 UN Convention on the Rights of Persons with a Disability addresses freedom:

1. States Parties shall ensure that persons with disabilities, on an equal basis with others:
    (a) Enjoy the right to liberty and security of person;
    (b) Are not deprived of their liberty unlawfully or arbitrarily, and that any deprivation of liberty is in conformity with the law, and that the existence of a disability shall in no case justify a deprivation of liberty.

2. States Parties shall ensure that if persons with disabilities are deprived of their liberty through any process, they are, on an equal basis with others, entitled to guarantees in accordance with international human rights law and shall be treated in compliance with the objectives and principles of the present Convention, including by provision of reasonable accommodation.

Both liberty and security are mentioned in Article 14(1). Security ensures that people with disabilities, or indeed any detained person, should not be needlessly exposed to violence or aggression from others, whoever they may be, whether family, co-residents, cellmates, carers, members of the public or professionals. Article 14(2) indicates that specific laws in relation to the enforcement of individuals are necessary if they are to be deprived of their freedom. Here we enter a highly populated and extremely grey zone. If we take people with a disability or with a health condition, or people with an intellectual impairment living in a nursing home, community residence or residential service, it is currently commonplace for hall doors to be locked with a key or keypad and for the residents not to have the freedom or the right to go in and out of said doors. But there is no law at present that embraces these situations, and the individuals concerned have not been asked or consented to this situation in which they find themselves.

If social carers kept the doors open and permitted the residents to walk out, they could be accused of neglecting their duty of care to the resident. Family members may expect doors to be locked and believe that they have the right to demand this. However, no one has the right to impede the freedom of another, except in accordance with the law. In the absence of a law, we have a lawless situation in relation to the care services. The HIQA has repeatedly drawn unfavourable attention to locked or key-padded doors during its inspection visits to centres for people with disabilities. Its criticisms ranged from the health and safety implications through to the apparent lack of justification for the practice. The practice may be in place for the protection of one person, but the rest of the residents in the same residence have to endure it.

Appearing before a hearing of the United Nations Committee against Torture in Geneva in July 2017, a number of non-governmental organisations highlighted detention in places other than prisons, both historically and currently. These included the Justice for Magdalene Research and the Irish Council for Civil Liberties (ICCL). Liam Herrick of the ICCL argued that the problem of ill treatment was acute in what he called 'closed spaces':

> The key issue for Ireland in meeting its obligations under the UN Convention is to put in place sufficient and effective safeguards to ensure that vulnerable individuals are not victimised. In particular, the Convention requires that the State protects those who find themselves subject to detention – recognising that it is in closed spaces, where the most serious violations of human rights can take place.
>
> Ireland has a troubling history of failing to protect those we have placed in such closed spaces. In that context, it is essential that we now move to put in place a strong National Preventative Mechanism which can ensure that no place of detention – prison, police cell, hospital or care home – is beyond the reach of comprehensive and rigorous inspection (Herrick, 2017).

In 2017, the Department of Health belatedly opened a consultation process in relation to the deprivation of liberty and safeguarding proposals concerning people living in nursing homes, residential centres for people with disabilities and voluntary patients in some mental health centres (Department of Health, 2017). This issue was prevalent in 2006 when Ireland signed the UN Convention on the Rights of Persons with Disabilities, specifically Article 14, which was related to liberty. The draft deprivation of liberty safeguards came in the form of a bill to be inserted into the *Assisted Decision-Making (Capacity) Act, 2015*, which had then only a minority of its articles in force. The 2015 act includes persons living in centres under the *Mental Health Act, 2001*. The deprivation of liberty proposals was to apply to people living in centres, where they:

- were under continuous supervision and control
- were not free to leave
- lacked the capacity to decide to live or continue living in that facility.

The bill proposed that the moment of detention occurred at admission. At that point, the person in charge or other medical experts would be required to obtain or search for at least six documents including those relating to the capacity of a person, their decision-making representative, and their property or assets, and potentially await a court order, for which there would be legal aid. In 2017, the waiting list for legal aid was six to twelve months. A person could be admitted in an emergency/temporary decision, that is without said documentation, for a period of twenty-five days only. There were separate proposals for persons already living/ detained in a residential centre. The proposal was immensely complex, even for experts, and even allowing for the fact that it locked in two other pieces of complex legislation.

Detention with a Capacity to Decide

John Rogers SC and former Attorney General has argued that a person can only be deprived of their liberty in highly specified circumstances. Such a specification would be a tightly worded law. Until recently, this was not the case for people detained against their will while being mentally ill. Prior to the *Mental Health Act, 2001*, individuals could be detained in what might appear as an arbitrary fashion; they did not have a regular, independent review of their situation of detention. This is still the case for some patients in the Central Mental Hospital, now called the National Forensic Mental Health Service. 'The right to travel is part and parcel of the right to liberty. The precise terms of the Offences Against the State, 1939, show, for example, how the restriction of that right can only be attained in the most strictly construed circumstances' (McDonagh, 1992, 28).

An interesting case of the pre-2001 era was that of Martin D. in 1970, a politically active left-wing student attending University College Dublin who was arrested at a student protest at Belfield, Dublin and was subsequently committed with his friends to Mountjoy Prison. From there he 'disappeared' from view until he was tracked down to the Central Mental Hospital in Dundrum. He spent three months there, and it was very difficult to get him freed, despite the reporting of journalist Dick Grogan (1938–2016) and a Dáil intervention by Noel Browne TD, who stated in the Dáil: 'Would the Minister not inquire into the circumstances surrounding the transfer of young D. to the Central Mental Hospital where it is by many people believed that he has been transferred because of his dissident political views' (Oireachtas Debates,1970, column 449). Noel Browne was then interrupted by the Ceann Comhairle (Dáil chairman) to stop him speaking any further on this topic, but he refused and continued: 'Is the Minister aware that there is very serious public disquiet that this individual who is acting in a very honourable tradition of refusing to recognise the institutions of this State, an attitude which is a long time in existence in Irish history?' (Oireachtas Debates,1970, 9 December, column 449).

It is of note that Martin D.'s father was a psychiatrist. At court hearings, from which he was absent, he was described as a 'psychopath'. When a Habeus Corpus application was finally made by Donal Barrington SC to the High Court, through the intervention of the ceaselessly active Margaret Gaj, he was granted immediate release from the Dundrum Central Mental Hospital. After some time, he left Ireland and went to live in the UK (ucdhiddenhistory, 2017).

Today, those who are transferred from prison to the Dundrum Central Mental Hospital have their cases reviewed every six months by the Criminal Law Review Committee, assisted by a panel of lawyers. Since some prisoner-patients are released after five months, they never have a review. Others have had a review of their case up to twenty-five times and remain unreleased (Criminal Law Review Committee, 2017, 13). Prisoner-patients whose sentence expires while they are in Dundrum can be re-detained under the *Mental Health Act, 2001* and are not in fact 'released' at all, except on paper. In addition, there are prisoner-patients in Dundrum who have been judged unfit to plead in court on the grounds of a serious mental illness. They too stay there until they have completed their treatment and become sufficiently fit to plead. They can then be tried for the original alleged crime in court.

There are, as a consequence of complex and ad hoc policy-making, two systems of inspection for one Dundrum Central Mental Hospital.

There are inspections under the *Mental Health Act, 2001* and inspections of different patients or the same patients with now changed status, under the Criminal Law Review Committee. How patients are expected to understand this complexity is unclear.

Detained in Prison

Prison is not just for criminals, however. Of the 12,579 men and women in prison in 2016, some had been sentenced for a crime. Of those ordered by the courts to be committed to prison, 2,976 were there on remand without bail, awaiting trial or on trial; thirty-seven were being held in prison awaiting extradition to another country for trial; 401 were detained on immigration issues such as having no visa or right to remain in Ireland and were awaiting deportation; twenty-two had not paid debts; and five were detained in contempt of court. In addition, there were thousands of committals to prison for non-payment of court-ordered fines. After the debtor's law was amended, convicted debtors who refused or could not pay the fine or undertake community service could still be committed to prison. Given that a staffed prison costs the state more than €60,000 a year, having people in prison for not paying a fine or having an expired visa on their passport is an expensive way to address administrative and social issues.

People with disabilities are not always to be found where we expect them to be. Prison is a case in point. There were just under 1,000 people with disabilities detained in prison in 2016. This is a large proportion of the 3,791 prisoners in all prisons in the state on census night (2017). The single largest group were those prisoners who had 'a difficulty learning, remembering or concentrating' (CSO, 2017). The causes of so many individuals with a disability being in prison and their circumstances were mixed and could range from a mental illness, an intellectual disability, a learning disability, a brain injury, attention deficit disorder or the effects of unprescribed drugs or alcohol. Roughly 120 prisoners were recorded as having an intellectual disability; roughly the same number had a serious sight impairment. A psychological or emotional condition was identified among 331 prisoners. These numbers are unlikely to be an exaggeration since census forms in prisons are completed by management. Undoubtedly, prison can exacerbate a pre-existing health difficulty or even trigger an illness where none was there before.

There are prisoners who are entitled to leave but cannot. This has been pointed out by the parole board:

> The Board reviewed the cases of three life-sentenced prisoners who have each been in prison for over 17 years. In all three cases, the Board was of the view that the individuals concerned should be recommended for temporary release. However, two of the prisoners had serious psychiatric problems and the other prisoner had an intellectual disability. It was not possible to recommend them for temporary release because the essential community supports were not available. As hundreds of prisoners have serious psychiatric or intellectual disability problems, this is going to become a more regular occurrence (The Parole Board, 2016).

Brendan Kelly, Professor of Psychiatry at Trinity College, in a letter in 2016 to the *Irish Times* stated that prisons are toxic for the mentally ill:

> People with enduring mental illness might no longer be in psychiatric institutions, but they are more likely to be unemployed, under-employed and homeless, compared to those without such illness. They are also more likely to be arrested in similar circumstances and remand is more probable even for lesser offences. Prisons are toxic for the mentally ill. This inequality sets in early in life: people from lower socio-economic groups develop mental illness at a younger age than those from higher socio-economic groups and have longer durations of untreated illness (associated with poor prognosis) (Kelly, 2016).

A small number of prisoners with mental illness can be transferred from prison to the Dundrum Central Mental Hospital voluntarily or involuntarily. There, beds are reserved for the Irish Prison Service prisoners/patients, and there is usually a waiting list for those beds. In 2017, prisons had referred twenty prisoners with mental illness to Dundrum, but there were no beds available and they had to go on a waiting list (Dunne, 2017). Dundrum has an in-reach service to some prisons but not all prisons have the nursing staff, the separate accommodation or the psychologists to follow this up. Ideally, all health services in prison should be part of mainstream community-based health services. Prisons cannot recreate inside their walls all the requisites of a health service.

Some prisoners with a serious mental illness never get a bed in Dundrum because they do not want to go there and be labelled as a 'psycho' or as 'mental' in their neighbourhoods: such is their fear of the stigma of mental illness. Prisoners can be and are transferred there against their will. Some do not get a bed because their illness is judged to be unamenable to treatment. Prisoners in these circumstances, who might be a danger to themselves and/or others, can end up spending long periods of time locked up in a cell for twenty-one to twenty-two hours per day.

You would expect to find a number of young people with disabilities in a children's detention centre. However, in Ireland, this is not the case. The Children Detention Campus at Oberstown in North Dublin makes no particular mention of children under the age of eighteen with mental disabilities or psychological and emotional difficulties in its publications. This was reconfirmed by an answer to a HIQA query during a 2017 inspection (HIQA, 2017). 'Data provided to inspectors showed that there were no children with a disability (as defined under the *Disability Act, 2005*) on the campus'. The same report noted that there had been 3,027 'incidents' of behaviour by the child residents during 2016, and 150 'incidents' during January 2017, over the course of just thirty-one days. Following these incidents, children were put in isolation in their rooms. One child had no access to fresh air until the eighth day of his detention, one until the fifth day of detention and one had no fresh air until the seventh day of detention. HIQA found this treatment unacceptable. The children may have been better off in prison where such treatment of prisoners is against the statutory *Prison Rules* of 2007.

Voluntary and Not So Voluntary

Since 2006, people with a mental illness, which conforms to the definition of a 'mental disorder', can be detained against their will in a mental health facility in an approved general hospital or psychiatric hospital. A mental disorder is specifically defined in law as:

- A mental illness, severe dementia or significant intellectual disability <u>and</u> there is a serious risk that you may cause immediate and serious harm to yourself or to others.
- A mental disorder is also a mental illness, severe dementia or significant intellectual disability and your judgement is <u>so impaired</u> that your condition could get worse and treatment can only be given in a hospital.

Thus, not all mental illnesses are mental disorders that lend themselves to an involuntary admission. Even where the mental illness is a mental disorder, you can be refused admission to the state forensic facility, the Central Mental Hospital, if it is believed that the admission would not improve your mental health.

These definitions lend a somewhat Kafkaesque appearance to what is already a complex situation. Merely having an addiction to drugs or alcohol, having a personality disorder or being deviant are not sufficient grounds in themselves to justify an involuntary admission to a mental health facility. Trying to explain the subtleties of what is and is not a mental illness to a mother who wants her son admitted to a secure hospital is difficult. Yet, the law is quite unambiguous: Mental Illness equals No to admission; Mental Disorder equals Yes to admission.

To make matters even more confusing, some are nevertheless admitted to the Central Mental Hospital even though they do not have a known mental illness or mental disorder. This happens when the legal representative or guardian of a patient appeals to the 'inherent jurisdiction' of the court, or the judge's own discretion. In such instances, the patient can be moved to the Central Mental Hospital. With inherent jurisdiction, a superior court can make a decision for which there is no existing statute, law or rule. However, inherent jurisdiction, in relation to vulnerable adults, risks interfering in their right to a private life and to privacy. It carries a totalitarian aroma, even when benevolently or beneficially intended.

On March 3, 2011 Mr Justice Birmingham delivered a judgement in the High Court that a man aged twenty-six, who was found not to be of unsound mind, not suffering from a mental disorder and not having a mental illness could be detained in the Central Mental Hospital as requested by the HSE and with which his representative, known as a guardian ad litem, agreed.[1] The man had a personality disorder and some characteristics of Asperger's syndrome since childhood. He manifested extreme aggression, first displayed on his expulsion from nursery school aged four. He was eventually placed and detained in a secure health facility in England, and the HSE and his sister wished to repatriate him to Ireland. The only suitable placement was in Dundrum. Exercising his power in terms of the inherent jurisdiction of the court, Mr Justice Birmingham agreed that he could be so detained. The hospital agreed to receive him. He was to be detained indefinitely. His detention was to be reviewed by order of the courts every two months (J.OB., 2011). In this case, the High Court had to consider if it had inherent jurisdiction to direct the involuntary detention of a patient in circumstances where the involuntary detention provisions in the *Mental Health Act, 2001* did not apply. The application was novel as JOB was not suffering from a mental illness or mental disorder as required by section 3 of the Mental Health Act 2001 and therefore, the provisions of that act did not apply. Thus, the main question to be determined was whether, in a situation where an adult lacks capacity and where there was a legislative lacuna so that the adult's best interests could not be served without the intervention by the Court, the High Court had jurisdiction to intervene. Mr Justice Birmingham answered in the affirmative.

With the increase in the number of persons judged 'not guilty by reason of insanity' under the *Criminal Law (Insanity) Act, 2006* and committed to the Central Mental Hospital, the number of beds available for the transfer of mentally ill prisoners to Dundrum shrank in 2016. This resulted in nineteen prisoners detained in prison and on the waiting list for psychiatric care. Some could have been released without ever accessing in-patient care. The inspector of mental health services is of the view that:

> Prisoners with mental illness should have the same level of mental health care as the rest of the population … There are a number of serious concerns about the provision of mental health services to mentally ill prisoners and there is an inadequate number of forensic beds for those prisoners who require in-patient psychiatric treatment (*Mental Health Commission* Annual Report, 2016).

---

[1] A guardian ad litem is a professional or adult appointed by a court to represent the interests of adults and children.

The fact that a prisoner does not obtain access to a bed in the Central Mental Hospital or does so only after a long delay does not signify that their human rights have been breached or that they have experienced cruel and unusual treatment. This and several judgements related to human rights and mental health are discussed in a 2015 human rights report on Ireland: *A Report on the Application of the European Convention on Human Rights Act 2003 and the European Charter of Fundamental Rights: Evaluation and Review* (Kingston and Thornton, 2015).

The Mental Health Tribunals

Each decision to involuntarily admit a person to a mental health facility, which is locked and which they cannot leave, is reviewed by a mental health tribunal. The tribunals are Ireland's main defence against accusations of unreasonable removal of freedom and detention of individuals. The tribunals operate under the auspices of the Mental Health Commission. The tribunals are composed of a chairperson who is a barrister or solicitor, a consultant psychiatrist and a lay person. They are convened into mental health facilities to hold a hearing on whether the decision to admit a person involuntarily was correct or not. These people are selected from panels that are established for a three- or four-year period. Their decisions can be appealed to the Circuit Court and High Court and overturned. The tribunals are, therefore, quasi-judicial.

The first hearing is within three weeks of a decision to commit a person, and further hearings to renew decisions are held at three, six-month or yearly intervals. Tribunals are held behind locked doors: all one can know is the outcome of the tribunal: to detain or not to detain, and on which grounds. When a tribunal decision is challenged in the courts, the members of the tribunal (apart from the chairman) who made the decision are not informed; neither are they informed of the final outcome nor are they individually represented in court. The whole process is quite opaque. To make matters worse, in the past, tribunal members had to sign a confidentiality document that strongly resembled a 'gagging order'. This document prohibited them from speaking not only about the tribunal (which was justified) but also about anything else they observed or heard in the hospital (not so justified).

Theoretically, the patient should be present at the hearing, though this may not always happen, especially if the patient is too frail or disoriented to understand what is happening, if there are insufficient staff to accompany the patient or if there is a lack of interpreters to translate what the patient is saying. A hospital psychiatrist speaks on behalf of the mental health facility at the tribunal, and a lawyer, provided for free, represents the patient. 'Represent' is a word to be used carefully here: patients may be incapable of issuing instructions to their lawyer, may not understand why the lawyer is asking them questions or may issue apparently inconsistent instructions such as 'yes, I want to attend the tribunal' but 'no, I do not want anyone reading my medical files'. The impaired capacity of the patient to issue instructions places the lawyer in an invidious position, obliging him/her to act in the best interests of the patient insofar as they can determine what these are.

Besides the hospital psychiatrist and the tribunal psychiatrist, a third psychiatrist also reads the patient's file and gives an opinion on it. Members of the patient's family can attend if they are informed that a tribunal will take place. Psychiatric nurses who care for the patient on a day-to-day basis have no right of attendance, nor do psychologists, social workers or psychotherapists. The system becomes a tyranny of experts, daunting for the patient, as well as making it very expensive. A single hearing costs more than €4,000.

The room in each facility where tribunals take place has to be approved by the Mental Health Commission. This apparently mundane requirement has a logic of its own. Prior to this, once a room had been approved, some hospitals had the habit of convening the tribunals in alternative rooms, often locked, sometimes with no door handles, often too small and sometimes too claustrophobic for the patients and participants alike.

The review of patients admitted against their will to hospitals is very different in England and Wales. Patients or their representatives apply to have a tribunal hearing: it is not automatic. More people can be invited to give evidence and are present at the hearing, such as the nurse, who knows the patient best. The hearing can recommend not only the end of detention but a range of other possibilities such as temporary leave or transfer to another hospital. Patients diagnosed with a personality disorder are included in the *Mental Health Act* in the UK, unlike Ireland.

A Little Bit Detained

With the ongoing discussion on the implementation of the legislation to confer rights on persons who lack some or most capacity to make decisions, the issue of those who are 'voluntarily' in a psychiatric facility has arisen. It had been assumed by many that if you were not detained under the *Mental Health Act*, you were in a facility of your own free will. A person can enter a hospital for treatment voluntarily and be compulsorily detained while there. This can be both surprising and unnerving for a patient. The default position that all patients in mental health facilities are there voluntarily is now being seriously questioned. It is not clear what exactly 'voluntary' means.

It has been the case since 2006 that a person who entered and stayed in a mental health service could be prevented from leaving by an application of the *Mental Health Act* to them when and if they expressed an intention to leave against the advice of their medical team. This could and can create anxiety among voluntary patients. The presumption that a voluntary patient has consented or is in agreement to being in a mental health facility is flawed, if not entirely mistaken. There have been few tests of whether patients in hospital have given authentic consent to being there. Patients in these circumstances are frequently unable to give their consent, to articulate their lack of consent or can only partially consent. Even if they do appear to give their consent by not physically attempting to leave, their circumstances may be coercive in that they have no means to leave the facility, obtain or use transport to go anywhere and may have nowhere to go. The consent is flawed and unreal.

The scenario for voluntary patients will become immensely complex when the articles of the *Assisted Decision-Making (Capacity) Act, 2015* are implemented. With this act, voluntary patients will have decision-making 'representatives'. Such a representative, appointed by the courts, could intervene in decisions made by consultant psychiatrists in relation to whether the patient should be discharged/not discharged. The representative will be a new form of patient advocate who will have legitimate standing within the health services and who is intended to boost the rights of patients using mental health services. At present, although the patient has a free legal representative before a tribunal, her/his lawyer is not allowed to represent the patient in any other context. The 'free' legal representation only covers the tribunal and narrowly defines and excludes the patient's objections and concerns with their social welfare, housing or issues related to their wider treatment in hospital.

The coalition of organisations known as the Mental Health Reform made a start on this issue by proposing, with the support of Fianna Fáil, a series of amendments to the *Mental Health Act, 2001*. This was called the Mental Health (Amendment) Bill, 2017. Their proposals made it obligatory for voluntary patients to consent to their admission and then to their treatment, including consent with support to their decision-making. The principle of the 'best interests' of the patient was replaced by clauses from the *Assisted Decision-Making (Capacity) Act, 2015*, such as 'respecting the will and preference of the person'. Patients also had the right to 'the least restrictive care' (Mental Health Reform, 2017).

Perhaps not every involuntary patient needs to have a series of tribunal hearings. The number of tribunal hearings could be reduced by restricting them to those patients or family members who wish to have one, or whose solicitor seeks one or in special identifiable cases. One of the more contentious issues is in relation to how a person, whose GP thinks they have a mental disorder, is physically admitted to hospital. In many instances, they are accompanied by a member of An Garda Síochána. However, while waiting to be seen and admitted, the person is free to walk away and legally, they cannot be stopped as they are not yet under the *Mental Health Act*. A variety of experiments were tried by the HSE and the Mental Health Commission with 'authorised persons' and private transport services, but the issue remains problematic.

The right of a person to seek refuge in a hospital and to be temporarily protected from the torments they experience has been much neglected by those who advocate the closure of the old asylum hospitals, as described in Chapter Three. The 'community' is not particularly caring toward those who are visibly mentally ill. Some are so alienated from family and former friends that they become homeless and adrift; some of them end up in hospital, some in prisons and others on the street. This issue has been exacerbated by the closing of the old asylums and the absence of a well-organised programme for patients to resettle outside. There occurs a coincidence, for some, of abject homelessness and mental illness.

Conversely, a surprising number of individuals drift into Ireland from mental health services overseas: from Spain, the UK, the US and Poland. By the time of their arrival, they have stopped the medication they were prescribed and are very unwell. In some instances, the patient is admitted involuntarily to an Irish mental health facility, some end up being apprehended by the Gardaí for public order offences and imprisoned without bail as they have no fixed residence in Ireland and others have to be repatriated once their identity is known.

The 2017 Mental Health (Amendment) (No. 2) Bill proposed a number of important changes to the rights of patients. One of these changes includes the right of the patient to be afforded the highest attainable standard of mental health, consistent with least restrictive care, autonomy, privacy, bodily integrity, dignity, equality, non-discrimination and with due respect for the person's own understanding of his or her mental health. The bill also proposed that anyone who becomes a voluntary patient must have the capacity to do so. This is in line with the *Assisted Decision-Making (Capacity) Act, 2015* (Kelly, 2017).

Care Homes

Older persons with the onset of age can develop mental disorders such as dementia and are no longer able to look after themselves without social support. Their capacity to remember, concentrate or carry out their daily routines can become impaired. Ireland's answer to this is the provision of mostly private nursing-home care, subsidised by the individual, their family and the state under the so-called 'Fair Deal'. In many instances, older people have not chosen to reside in a nursing home: their family members are no longer able to care for them unaided, and so it is the only choice. Others are in nursing homes because their relatives have died and their children have emigrated. Consent to leave a family home and enter a residential setting is becoming a more contentious issue as concern rises as to how choices are made and who is making them. This will come to the fore with the implementation of the *Assisted Decision-Making (Capacity) Act* which may occur in 2018 or later.

The act will eventually wind down the system of wardship, which affects the frail, elderly and those with complex and pervasive needs. Some 2,600 people with extensive and complex needs are 'wards of court'. Wardship is a legal process which transfers all the legal rights of a citizen to the state. Wardship replaces or extinguishes the rights and obligations of parents and places those rights and obligations in the hands of the state. Wardship, once granted, is managed by the Office of Wardship. An average of 119 persons a year with an intellectual disability are taken into wardship. The largest single group are those with dementia or other neurological and degenerative conditions. Wardship is an old law from the time of the British Empire. It was termed *The Lunacy Regulation (Ireland) Act* of 1871.

Table 14: Wards of Court – reasons for admittance to wardship – active cases, 2013–16.

Reason for admission	2016	2015	2014	2013
Acquired brain injury	64	55	54	47
Elderly/mental infirmity	142	155	159	148
Learning/intellectual disability	123	122	122	112
Minor child	3	5	6	6
Psychiatric illness	93	96	95	101
Residential abuse	2	2	2	2
Total	427	435	438	416

Source: *Annual Reports*, 2014–2017; Statistical Archive of the Courts Service

Wardship is a grave matter in that a person loses their legal personality in every regard. A visit to the dentist needs court permission; a daytrip needs court permission. The process is cumbersome, and the reporting system is overly detailed and fails to recognise that individuals who may lose their capacity to manage their financial affairs can still make other decisions. A form of wardship more akin to guardianship is prevalent in parts of Europe. It has been the subject of shelves of cases to the European Court of Human Rights in Strasbourg due to abuse of those in guardianship. The questioning of wardship was one aspect of the Swedish author Stieg Larsson's anti-heroine Lisbeth Salander in *The Girl with The Dragon Tattoo*.

Conclusion

People with disabilities are not always where we expect them to be or where we are solicited to find them. Circumstances, which in the past we viewed as voluntary, do not appear so voluntary in the light of modern-day thinking. Passivity cannot be assumed to be consent. Striking the right balance between freedom and detention is protective of human rights. We now know that detention is not confined to prisons – there are many closed spaces. Closed institutions are still part of the resolution of depositing people with perceived social problems and social issues away from society. As fast as some institutions close, such as residential centres for people with disabilities, others seem to spring up, such as nursing homes or small-scale institutions. Inside a closed institution, individuals are highly dependent on functioning complaints systems; external inspections; monitoring and active, independent advocacy. With these four principles put into practice, individuals can hope to defend their rights and be heard and treated with dignity.

Chapter 8 References

Criminal Law Review Committee (2017) *Annual Report, 2016*. See: Appendix C.

CSO (2017) *Census 2011*, StatBank: Population Enumerated in Communal Establishments (number) by Type of Communal Establishment, Sex, Disability Type, Age Group and Census Year. Accessed July 21, 2017.

Dáil Éireann – 09/Dec/1970 Questions, Oral Answers – Central Mental Hospital. oireachtasdebates.oireachtas.ie. Accessed July 21, 2017.

Department of Health (no date) *Deprivation of Liberty: Safeguard Proposals Consultation Paper*. http://health.gov.ie/consultations/. Accessed February 9, 2018.

Dunne, S. (2017) 'Bed Capacity at Central Mental Hospital at "Critical" Level, says HSE', *The Irish Times*. https://www.irishtimes.com/news/health/bed-capacity-in-the-central-mental-hospital-at-critical-level-1. Accessed September 18, 2017.

Hidden History of UCD (2009) https://ucdhiddenhistory.wordpress.com/2009/04/30/update-april-09/. Accessed July 21, 2017.

HIQA (2017) *Oberstown Children Detention Campus, Inspection Report*. HIQA, August.

Herrick, L. (2017) 'ICCL to meet with UN Committee Against Torture', Irish Council for Civil Liberties. www.iccl.ie/archive/iccl-to-meet-with-un-committee-against- torture/. Accessed July 25, 2017.

J. O'B (2011) and in the Matter of the Inherent Jurisdiction of the High Court, Between the HSE (Plaintiff) and J. O'B, Represented by his Guardian ad Litem, (H. O'B) Citation 2011 IEHC 73.

Kelly, B. (2017) 'Professor Brendan Kelly reflects on the advances and shortcomings of care in Ireland', *Irish Medical Times*, 14 July. See also,

Kelly, B. (2016) *Hearing Voices: The History of Psychiatry in Ireland,* Irish Academic Press.

Kelly, B. (2014) 'Focus on Mental Health Services', *Irish Times*, Letters, 16 July.

Kingston, S. Thornton, L. (2015) *A Report on the Application of the European Convention on Human Rights Act 2003 and the European Charter of Fundamental Rights: Evaluation and Review.* Report commissioned by The Law Society of Ireland's Human Rights Committee and Dublin Solicitor's Bar Association.

McDonagh, S. (ed.) (1992) *The Attorney General v. X and Others – Judgements of the High Court and Supreme Court and Legal Submissions made to the Supreme Court.* Incorporated Council for Law Reporting for Ireland, Law Library, Dublin.

Mental Health Commission (2017) *Annual Report 2016,* July.

Mental Health Reform (2017) *Briefing Note on the Mental Health (Amendment Bill 2017,* July 13, 2017: mentalhealthreform.ie.

The Parole Board (2016) *Annual Report 2015,* Dublin.

CHAPTER 9

Hate Crimes against Children with Disabilities

More than one hundred countries have ratified the United Nations Convention on the Rights of Peoples with Disabilities, which came into force in 2006. The European Union itself ratified the convention on January 5, 2011, the first time in history that the EU has become a party to a human rights treaty (Europa, 2011). The convention does not create new rights for people with disabilities. Its fifty articles spell out in detail the rights and freedoms of people with disabilities and the obligations of governments. These rights and obligations had previously been scattered across a range of international laws and instruments (UN, 2006).

Articles 15 and 16 are of particular interest to people with disabilities who have experienced violence and abuse. They are equally of interest to their families and supporters as well as public and private providers of services. Article 15 provides that people with disabilities will have 'freedom from torture or cruel, inhuman or degrading treatment or punishment'. Article 15 prohibits medical or scientific experimentation on any person without their free consent. Article 16 declares 'freedom from exploitation, violence and abuse'. The convention describes five areas of state obligation or duty toward people with disabilities. Firstly, governments must do all that is possible to protect people with disabilities from exploitation, violence or abuse at home or outside the home. Secondly, governments must take actions to prevent violence and ensure that people with disabilities are able to recognise and report violence and abuse. Thirdly, states must ensure that facilities designed for people with disabilities are independently monitored. Fourthly, public authorities have the duty to promote the physical and mental recovery, rehabilitation and integration of persons who have experienced abuse, exploitation or violence in an environment that promotes dignity and autonomy. Fifthly, states must have legislation and policies, including with gender and child-focused dimensions, in order to identify, investigate and prosecute instances of exploitation, violence and abuse. The Convention on the Rights of Persons with Disabilities has to be read in conjunction with the UN Convention on the Rights of the Child (1989), and in particular Article 19, which states that:

> States Parties shall take all appropriate legislative, administrative, social and educational measures to protect the child from all forms of physical or mental violence, injury or abuse, neglect or negligent treatment, maltreatment or exploitation, including sexual abuse, while in the care of parent(s), legal guardian(s) or any other person who has the care of the child (UN, 1989).

Children with disabilities have been identified as one of the more vulnerable groups of children among the eight million children in residential care across the world; these children also experience violence and abuse in care (UN, 2006). Children may be subject to abuse not only by staff, but also, as a consequence of neglect, by their peers. The *International Save the Children Alliance Report* (2003) noted that children with disabilities are often in residential care, not because they need nursing or medical care, but because they have been abandoned or rejected. Wendy Cousins demonstrates that despite policy narrative to the contrary, high proportions of disabled children spend time in residential schools, hospitals and respite centres (Cousins et al., 2003). Jenny Morris has repeatedly stressed that young people with high levels of support needs rarely get a chance to give their own opinions and feel more restricted by the absence of support than by their impairment (Morris 2001; 2001a).

The UN Convention has had an influence in Europe. It is shaping the European Union's disability strategy for the period 2010–2020 (European Commission, 2010). The strategy proposes to support 'national efforts to achieve the transition from institutional to community-based care'. The strategy, however, makes no reference to the violence and exploitation experienced by adults and children with disabilities, despite long-standing support for such actions through the EU DAPHNE programme to combat violence against women and children, administered by the Commission's Justice Directorate. The DAPHNE programme supported more than thirty large multi-country projects on violence against adults and children with disabilities between 1997 and 2007 (European Commission, 2008). With implications wider than the European Union, the European Court of Human Rights, in the Sven Glor case described in Chapter Seven, made reference to the UN Convention as a new standard, whether countries like Switzerland had ratified it or not. In the case of Switzerland, it had failed to ratify the convention.

The slow pace of policy change toward the rights of people with disabilities at the level of the European Union may be found in the unresolved past of eugenic influences on public policy in the 1930s and 1940s, particularly among the medical profession in Germany (Weindling, 1987; see Chapter Two). The belief that some lives are unworthy of living and that some human beings are subhuman spread widely and enthusiastically among scientific and intellectual circles within Europe. Some authors consider negative eugenic concerns to be reappearing in new guises in the field of genetic testing and the treatment of certain mental illnesses (Weiner et al., 2009; Hanauska-Abel, 1996).

Ignoring or neglecting the phenomena of violence against persons with disabilities renders it quite invisible despite its high prevalence (Morris, 1997, 241–258). The first findings of the largest known survey of crime against people with disabilities have been published in the US by the US Department of Justice (US Department of Justice, 2009). The findings confirm that people with disabilities are more likely to be victims of crime. Children and youths aged twelve to nineteen years had experienced violence at nearly twice the rate of children and youths without a disability. The US National Crime Victimisation Survey is based on a sample survey of 76,000 households containing 135,300 adults, children and youths aged twelve years or more.

Persons with a disability experienced a rate of rape or sexual assault that was more than twice the rate for persons without a disability. Women and girls with a disability had a higher victimisation rate than men and boys with disabilities. The rate of victimisation of women and girls was almost twice the rate compared with women and girls with no disability.

The survey explored victimisation rates between six different 'types' of disability: sensory, physical, cognitive, able to care for one's self, able to go outside the home alone, and limitations in employment or business. The survey found that people who had a cognitive disability had a higher rate of crime victimisation compared with those who reported other types of disability. Persons with a cognitive disability experienced higher rates of rape, sexual assault, robbery and aggravated assault than those with a sensory disability. This was the case for both men/young boys and women/young girls with cognitive disabilities. Even here, the victimisation rate for women/girls with a cognitive disability was higher again than those for men/boys with such a disability: this gender bias is reinforced by other studies (INWWD, 2010; Nixon, J. 2009).

The US survey is consistent with the Mencap study in the UK which found that 82 percent of children with a learning disability – 280,000 children – are bullied, with many of them too frightened to leave their own homes (Mencap, 2007). Others manage to cope with the support of friends (Burke et al., 2010). An example of bullying cited by the Mencap study was a physical assault requiring eighteen stitches in the forehead of a child with a learning disability. In this regard, the conceptualisation of violence against people with disabilities as a form of hate crime makes complete sense (Chakroborti, 2010).

There is no specific hate law related to crimes against people with disabilities in Ireland. How one would go about drafting such a law is complex, and this is one of the issues addressed by the Hate and Hostility Research Group at the University of Limerick, with support from other centres. A specific anti-hate law on several grounds could be drafted, which would create a new 'crime'. Alternatively, hate crime could be inserted into existing laws, making hate an aggravating factor. A further approach is to add the targeting of specific groups in a crime, such as gay people or people with disabilities, and make it an additional factor in the sentencing, which judges may take account of or which judges would be obliged to take into account. These options are explored in a new 2017 publication (Haynes, 2017). An expert group on crime statistics reported in 2017 that victim assessment was part of mandatory crime reporting and included a requirement to record motive for a crime, specifically where discrimination could be a motive, including on the grounds of disability (CSO, 2017).

In 2016, a bill in relation to hate crime was published by the Oireachtas. The Criminal Justice (Aggravation by Prejudice) Bill, 2016 was a Private Members Bill proposed by Deputies Fiona O'Loughlin and Margaret Murphy O'Mahony, both members of Fianna Fáil. The bill proposes that where an accused is charged with an offense, the offense would be 'aggravated by prejudice', where the offense was accompanied by prejudice relating to colour or ethnic origin, disability, sexual orientation or transgender identity. The bill did not specifically include prejudice on the grounds of religion or membership of the traveller community. In October, the bill was referred to a select committee on justice and equality, following some debate.

However, it is complicated to criminalise hate crime if the crime is based on the intention of the perpetrator, who may deny it, or the action may not be based on the targeting of a person with a disability because they are disabled but because they appear vulnerable. Evidence of prejudicial motivation is difficult to gather in a form of evidence suitable to be brought before a court.

The Case of Ireland

The public and private treatment of children in care, and in residential care in particular, has been a highly sensitive and controversial topic as well as an unresolved policy concern in Ireland for the last decade (Coldrey, 2000, 7–18; Rafferty and O'Sullivan, 1999). Within the context of the unfolding scandals of abuse of children in residential centres run by religious orders, the widespread abuse of young boys by priests, as well as a systemic neglect of children in need, there was a reluctant acceptance of the abuse that had occurred. Bob McCormack, writing of Ireland, observed that: 'The realisation that children with disabilities were at risk of sexual abuse was slow to be acknowledged. The thought that the most vulnerable children in society were the most abused was so abhorrent as to (be) inconceivable to many' (McCormack, 2005). McCormack's views are consistent with those of the National Society for the Prevention of Cruelty to Children (NSPCC), writing in the UK in the same period (NSPCC, 2003).

In a 2002 study of sexual abuse and violence in Ireland, which addressed the sexual abuse of people with learning disabilities, the authors found that staff and directors of two centres refused to participate in the study unless the questions about the reporting of cases were removed from the questionnaire on the grounds that the study might 're-traumatise the participants' and 'no resources were available to mitigate the trauma' (McGee et al., 2002). This minimisation and refusal to accept the threat of violence against children with disabilities is a persistent challenge to child protection policies. Add to this the particularity of clericalism in Ireland and a noxious mixture is created. Authoritarianism and defensiveness feed each other (Walsh, 2009; Flannery, 2009).

A build-up of allegations that children had been and continued to be abused in residential institutions run mainly by Catholic religious orders mounted at the end of the nineties and subsequently lead to the exposure of the abuse at the Protestant Bethany homes (Meehan, 2010). Cultural activism played an important role in generating doubt and unease among the general public concerning the bona fides of such charitable institutions. Cultural influences played a part in bringing the subject to the fore (Smith, 2007). The UK film *Lamb* (1985) starring Liam Neeson was loosely based on real events that occurred in Ireland and Scotland in 1978 when a care worker took a child in care to England with him. The late Louis Lentin's 1996 film *Dear Daughter* revealed allegations of the vicious treatment of girls in the care of the state in an institution run by the Sisters of Mercy in Goldenbridge. The Sisters of Mercy denied the allegations. Journalist Mary Raftery's (1958–2012) three-part TV documentary *States of Fear* in 1999 brought the systematic ill-treatment of children in care in religious-run industrial schools to a wider Irish public.

In 2000, the Irish government established the Commission to Inquire into Child Abuse, which published a five-volume report in 2009 (Commission to Inquire into Child Abuse, 2009). The commission was placed on a statutory basis and was chaired by judges; first Justice Mary Laffoy and on her resignation, Justice Seán Ryan. The commission explored the treatment of former residents in relation to physical, sexual and emotional abuse and neglect. The commission itself travelled to the UK and the US to hear testimony from Irish emigrants. Over the decade 1999 to 2009, 1,500 adults who had lived in a variety of care settings came forward or engaged with the commission. The commission held public hearings where state officials and religious orders were questioned about the allegations of abuse. Some survivor witnesses opted to claim compensation at a Redress Board. Over 1,000 former residents gave evidence of their experiences to a special confidential committee made up of commissioners (Commission, 2009). No questionnaires were used, and witnesses could tell their story in their own way. Witnesses could have an accompanying person with them when telling their stories. Sign language interpreters were employed by the commission.

Some fifty-eight witnesses to the confidential committee reported the abuse they had experienced as children in what were called 'special schools' prior to the 1970s and up the 1990s. Witnesses had often been in special residential schools for the deaf, for the blind or for pupils with learning difficulties. Of the fifty-eight witnesses, twelve reported having no knowledge of their family of origin: all they had was their name. Their identity had been lost from the moment of their admission to an institution – a cruel forgetfulness.

One woman described her experience as a child: 'I was looking for my mother, there was no answers... I heard girls talking about their mammies, and I had nobody to come up to see me. I knew nothing (about family) ... so I took these fits of temper. I was a handful' (Commission, III, 250).

The former residents described being severely physically punished by staff:

There was a whole load of them [...] who'd slap me across the face or with the strap on my legs [...] they just kept slapping me the whole time and they all said I was a troublemaker (Commission, III, 241).

There is the whole issue of (mannerisms) [...] people have sort of mannerisms maybe, shaking backwards and forwards, you'd be beaten for that (Commission, III, 241).

The mannerism of rocking in children can be a symptom of stress or of an underlying mental disorder. Among the behaviours which attracted severe physical abuse were making mistakes in the classrooms or workshops, using sign language, not using disability aids properly, losing or damaging disability aids, disclosing abuse, talking to co-residents and being forced by violence to carry out sexual acts (Commission, II, 241). 'We were punished for signing [...] it was very, very difficult to control [...] it was our language. It was the way we communicated. It was natural for us to use gestures. We were deaf' (Commission, II, 242).

Some of the former residents of the special schools were traumatised by witnessing or hearing violence against other children: 'and you could hear the screams, the screams, he was very violent. He was a big, strong, fit man. I was petrified of him, it came back to me in dreams, the dreams of it returned' (Commission, II, 241).

Peter Tyrell, a former child detainee at the age of eight, wrote in his memoir of the treatment of other boys at Letterfrack Industrial School, which was managed by the Christian Brothers:

Boys who are not good looking or are in any way deformed, are laughed at, and ill-treated. Tom x, a big lad for his age, has one leg, and is made to do serve duties and washing up and scrubbing floors, etc. I have seen him beaten by (Brother) Vale on the stump of his bad leg. He works in the tailor's shop and is a good tailor, he plays handball very well, and he can beat me easily (Tyrell, 2006, 82).

Peter Tyrell himself died by suicide on Hampstead Heath, London, in 1966. His life story was published after his death.

Many witnesses provided the confidential committee with graphic accounts of the sexual abuse they experienced while living at special schools from the age of seven years and upwards. Witnesses described being shown pornographic films or taken to pubs and given alcohol prior to being sexually assaulted or violated. Witnesses reported bribes and inducements such as money and cigarettes.

Residents described:

'Brother X used to do dirty things to me at night [...] He used to wake me at night and took off all my clothes' (Commission, III, 244).

afterwards (the rape) he gave me a bar of chocolate and told me to keep quiet about it, I was very shocked (Commission, III, 245).

From the time I was 7 until I was 14, maybe three nights a week, maybe 4, 2 or 3 (religious) Brothers sexually abused me [...] Sometimes they would follow me behind the toilets in the day time and do it again, they would pretend to dry [...] (me)[...] with a towel and they would do that, mess with you (Commission, III, 245).

There was another Brother, he brought me into his room, I didn't like it, he did things, and he hurt me. I was crying [...] it was at night time, he made me do things [...] he did things to me [...] he hurt me [...] Sometimes he took me into his room (Commission, III, 244).

A resident described her experience as a small girl sent out to a holiday family:

I was abused, I was sexually abused, it was a man (the father) [...]
I was sent out nearly every weekend and holidays and it went on for
years and years of my life [. . .] I can't get over it, it just gets to me.
I was 7 years of age (Commission, III, 247).

Deaf witnesses described being forced to use oral communication instead
of sign language:

I was very, very disappointed with myself, because I couldn't learn
through oralism, and then they would hit you, if you didn't understand and so we pretended to understand to avoid being hit all the
time (Commission, III, 248).

Pupils with special needs, far from being treated with any care or respect,
reported being humiliated and sneered at and their intelligence ridiculed.
The perpetrators were not only religious and lay staff, as well as holiday
home members, but also older or stronger co-residents who were allowed
to bully and molest them, a phenomenon also reported by children with
disabilities in Canada (Odell, 2011, 49).

A number of witnesses with intellectual disabilities attended the confidential committee and remained frightened at the prospect of speaking
about what had happened to them. Some sought reassurances from the
commissioners and their accompanying persons that they would not 'get in
trouble' for attending the commission (Commission, III, 246). Describing
the effects on their adult lives, forty-nine former residents with disabilities
described a wide range of impacts, injuries and mental health problems.
The highest number reported feeling suicidal, in need of counseling and
unable to forget the abuse (Commission, 2009).

Children with disabilities were physically, sexually and emotionally
abused in hospitals, as well as neglected. Thirty-one former hospital residents brought their accounts to the confidential committee. Among these,
twenty-three had spent periods from two to ten years in eighteen institutions that were described as hospitals:

I remember one morning [...] I was about five and I was sat up in the
bed [...] and I heard a voice behind and there's a very tall nun looking
down on me and she's not pleased, I can tell by her face. She said I'd

offended God, she called me a cripple. I remember it's the first time I was ever called a cripple [...] She said before I was fit to meet him (God) again, I'd have to be broken, and she just picked me up out of the bed and she threw me down onto the ground [...] she'd just kick the shit out of me, picked me up and punched and beat me [...] after that I kept very, very quiet [...] invisible [...] where you think if you don't speak you're not going to get beaten (Commission, III, 333).

The abuse of children in hospitals was reported as perpetrated by doctors, nurses, religious sisters and older patients. The former child patients described being used as 'exhibits' for visitors. They were teased and made fun of. They were frightened after observing the treatment and deaths of other patients on the wards. The sweets and gifts sent from home were removed from them and consumed by staff or distributed to other patients. One patient described her lack of personal identity: 'They used to have a discussion when they were bathing me, on my head, the size of my head and I remember them saying "this one has a very small head, I wonder will she be alright?" I remember thinking what am I going to do about my small head?' (Commission, III, 240).

One patient who reported being beaten to a relative was believed and the relative confronted the religious Sister. Subsequently, the mother received a letter asking her to stop the relative's visits. While ten of the thirty-one witnesses disclosed the abuse at the time, for others, the confidential committee hearing was the first time they had recounted their experiences.

In addition to the witnesses who had been abused as children in schools and hospitals, there were survivors who were deaf or blind. Twenty-one complaints were made to the commission's Investigation Committee concerning St. Mary's School for Deaf Girls in Cabra, North County Dublin. Twenty of the complaints concerned excessive physical punishments by nuns, teachers and lay staff using a variety of implements. Some of the complaints alleged the children's hands were tied behind their backs to stop them using sign language. Complaints included emotional abuse, fear, bullying and humiliation. The nuns denied to the commission that they had 'beaten' children or used punishments for signing (Commission, II, 555). Similarly, in the case of the Mary Immaculate School for Deaf Children in South Dublin, the nuns denied the twenty allegations against six nuns that children were beaten with a stick or ruler for using sign language; that the children were forced to use the toilet 'on demand' by systematically administering laxatives to them; and that they were denied an education through the use of oralism.

The commission investigated in detail accounts of the sexual abuse of children at St. Joseph's School for Deaf Boys in Cabra, managed by the Christian Brothers. The complaints dated back decades and up to the 1990s. While the order acknowledged that individual Brothers had sexually abused boys in their care, they insistently denied that it was systematic or a 'phenomenon'. The commission concluded that:

> the management in Cabra failed to protect children from sexual abuse by staff. When complaints were made, they were not believed or ignored or dealt with inadequately. The level and extent of abuse perpetrated by one lay worker, as late as the 1990s, was an indication of the lack of proper safeguards [...] the investigation revealed a pattern of physical and emotional bullying that made Cabra a very frightening place for children who were learning to overcome hearing difficulties (Commission, I, 578).

The school for deaf girls – St. Mary's in Cabra – was operated by the Dominican Sisters. There were complaints of abuse at the school:

> Allegations were made of sexual abuse by visiting priests and the congregation admitted such an allegation was made against a priest, who left shortly after that and never returned [...] All of the complainants alleged emotional abuse in respect of prevention of the use of sign language, segregation from other children based on hearing impairment, fear, bullying or humiliation (Commission, II, 555).

With the exception of admitting that an allegation against a priest had been made, all other complaints were denied by the Dominican Sisters.

The Commission to Inquire into Child Abuse conducted a limited investigation into a third school for deaf children: the Mary Immaculate School for Deaf Children, operated by the Belgian congregation of the Daughters of the Cross of Liège. There were twenty statements of complaint, but the commission could not find any evidence to corroborate them, and the congregation denied them (Commission, II, 560).

St. Conleth's Reformatory School at Daingean in County Offaly closed in 1973, but its name still causes a shiver for its notorious brutality toward the boys who were sent there because they had been taken into care or taken in by the courts. It was managed by a Catholic congregation, the Oblates of Mary Immaculate, who had come to Ireland in 1856. The commission heard that the Oblates were aware that severely psychiatrically disturbed children ended up in Daingean via the courts. They also accepted that they had failed to meet the special needs of pupils with psychological or emotional difficulties (Commission, I, 62). The commission found that children were sexually abused at Daingean and that cruel punishments were administered to the boys, including flogging. Far from being an educational or childcare facility, the commission determined that it had neither a remedial or reformatory practice. Because it was not officially a prison, the commission stated that there was an absence of legal and administrative protections for detainees. The commission noted that an earlier report on the Daingean boys found that after Daingean: 'a surprising number went to Britain, where they finished up sleeping rough and declining into alcoholism. A large proportion went to other places of detention in Ireland or Britain' (Commission, I, 689).

A Brother who had worked at Letterfrack Industrial school in County Galway remarked pithily to the commission:

> The boys in Letterfrack were disturbed. How will I say this? If they weren't disturbed before they got to Letterfrack, they were disturbed when they got there [. . .] the very fact of sending them there, they did become disturbed, they became sort of unhappy and quiet – not quiet – into themselves, introverted. Generally unhappy (Commission, I, 380).

In this regard, the system of residential institutions, hospitals and industrial schools injured and damaged children. They literally impaired the children, generating new disabilities. In that sense, the treatment of children with disabilities cannot be confined to the 'special' schools to which children are sent but to all institutions, be they hospitals or reformatories. The children were treated cruelly, despite the various schools being managed by a variety of separate religious orders and congregations. Addressing the report, former President of Ireland Mary McAleese described the treatment of the children as 'cruel, inhuman and degrading' (McGarry, 2009, 8). The inspection system of the state failed to identify the abuse and where it was reported to them, generally ignored the reports. This response is not unique to Ireland. Events in Italy confirmed a pattern of refusing to accept the truth of what children with disabilities disclosed as adults.

Italy – the Victims of Catholic Schools for the Deaf Speak Up

The north Italian city of Verona is best known as the setting for Shakespeare's *Romeo and Juliet*. In September 2010 it was the location of an extraordinary public meeting of deaf adults who described their abuse when children in the Catholic Istituto Provolo in Verona, a Catholic residential centre for deaf boys in the town at San Zeno di Montagna and at a summer camp at Lake Garda. The Istituto Provolo is run by the congregation of the Company of Mary. The meeting was the culmination of two years of the former residents' attempts to open dialogue with the Catholic Church on their experiences as abused children. Some sixty-seven former pupils met as an association, declaring that the numbers of abused children ran into the hundreds. Many, aged in their fifties and sixties, were not interested in court cases or compensation – the time limits for these had long expired. They wanted to denounce the systematic and repeated physical and sexual violence they had experienced as children in a Catholic and charitable institution. Calling themselves 'We the Victims of Paedophile Priests', they invited the *Espresso* newspaper to publish a number of their testimonies. As children, the majority came from poor families, often small landholders in the surrounding Verona countryside, which confirms the close association between poverty and the treatment of children perceived to be disabled (Barnes, Sheldon, 2011, 771).

A former priest and abuse victim, Salvatore Domolo, chaired a press conference at which he declared that clerical paedophilia was a 'crime against humanity' (Tessadri, 2010; Agnew, 2010). 'Bruno' became deaf at the age of eight and began attending the Provolo Institute, where he stayed until the age of fifteen years. A handsome child, from the third month after his admission to the age of fifteen, he was repeatedly sexually abused by priests and brothers. He had a list of sixteen abusers and reported an occasion where he was brought to an ecclesiastical palace at the age of eleven. The rapes there damaged him psychologically and permanently. The deaf adults described a life of terror as children, of beatings, of being taken from their beds at night, of being abused in the chapel, the confession box and at the church altar.

The victims had a sense of being treated as inhuman or less than human. The three associations of Sordi Antonio Provolo, Non-Udenti Provolo and Sordi Basso-Veronese-Legnago intended to work together and connect with other associations in the US and Europe to combat organised paedophilia in the Catholic Church and to have it recognised as a crime against humanity.

In response to the press conference and newspaper accounts, the diocese of Verona said that these events occurred long ago, that they know nothing of the specifics of the accusations, that the accusers may have monetary motivations, that none of the named priests were currently in contact with children and that the diocese would continue to adhere to canon law (Callaghan, 2010, 343). On October 31, 2010 the Verona victims met with European and American victims of Catholic abuse at a demonstration in Rome in front of Catholic buildings, demanding that the Pope stop protecting paedophile priests. This constituted an important step in the internationalisation of the struggle by disabled people against the sexual violence and abuse perpetrated on them.

Ireland and its Standards

The standards established by the UN Convention on the Rights of Persons with Disabilities do not remove all inequalities, such as inequalities of class, ethnicity and social origin. Nevertheless, they constitute an important benchmark for countries like Ireland, if Ireland were ever capable of reaching the standards. Children with disabilities in Ireland have experienced violence, cruelty, and inhumane and degrading treatment. In terms of the need for monitoring and vigilant inspection, residential institutions where more than 300 children with disabilities are living are now inspected by the HIQA.

Children diagnosed with acute mental illness and believed to be at risk to themselves or others continued to be placed and detained in adult psychiatric hospitals by the state. During 2010, ninety-one admissions of children under the age of eighteen took place (Bonnar, 2010). In 2016, while 96 percent of children and adolescents were admitted to child and adolescent facilities, 4 percent of children continued to be admitted to adult wards. The practice continued into 2017, when forty-four children were admitted to adult mental health facilities (Mental Health Commission, 2017).

Attempts to investigate reports of sexual and physical abuse in a residential service for persons with intellectual disabilities from the 1970s to the 1990s, when the residents were children, drifted into disarray in 2008 (McCoy, 2007, Hynes, 2008).

Conclusion

Children with disabilities in the care of the state, in hospitals, industrial schools and special schools, suffered physical, psychological and emotional abuse and damage in the form of hate crime. Crimes against children with disabilities are not unique to Ireland, as the Italian story reveals. These children were beaten on damaged parts of their body, punished when using their own language, sexually violated and called demeaning names such as 'cripple'. A conservative estimate of the numbers of adults with disabilities who reported to the Commission to Inquire into Child Abuse is 131. Some former residents, like Peter Tyrell, were already dead. Some still feared speaking out.

What has been unique to the developments of the last decade has been the slow emergence of voices and associations of those adults with disabilities who have lived in, endured and been survivors of residential institutions as children. It is significant that the UN Convention describes the reality of such experiences with words such as 'inhumane', 'cruel', 'torture', 'exploitation' and 'degrading'.

Chapter 9 References

Agnew, P. (2010) *Irish Times*, Dublin, September 25, and *Irish Times*, Dublin, November 1.

Barnes C, Sheldon, A. (2011) 'Disability, Politics and Poverty in a Majority World Context', *Disability and Society*, Vol. 25, No. 7, Routledge.

Bonnar, S. E. (2010) *Report for the Mental Health Commission on Admission of Young People to Adult Mental Health Wards in the Republic of Ireland*, Mental Health Commission, Dublin.

Burke, S. Burgman, I. (2010) 'Coping with Bullying in Australian Schools: how Children with Disabilities Experience Support from Friends, Parents and Teachers', *Disability and Society*, Vol. 25. No. 3, Routledge.

Chakroborti, (2010) '"Mate crime": Ridicule, Hostility and Targeted Attacks against Disabled People', *Disability and Society*, Vol. 26, No. 1, Routledge, London.

Callaghan, B. (2010) 'On Scandal and Scandals, the Psychology of Clerical Paedophilia', *Studies – An Irish Quarterly Review*, Vol. 99. No. 393–396, Dublin.

Coldrey, B. (2000) 'A Mixture of Caring and Corruption: Church Orphanages and Industrial Schools', *Studies – An Irish Quarterly Review*, Vol. 89, No. 353, Dublin.

Commission to Inquire into Child Abuse, CICA (2009) *Commission to Inquire into Child Abuse, Report*, Volumes I–V, Stationery Office, Dublin.

Cousins, W. Monteith, M. Kerry, N. (2003) 'Living Away from Home: The Long- Term Substitute Care of Disabled Children', *Irish Journal of Applied Social Studies*, Vol. 4 (1) Spring, Article 6.

CSO (2017) Report of the Expert Group on Crime Statistics: http://www.cso.ie/en/media/csoie/methods/recordedcrime/report_of_the_expert_group_on_crime_statistics_2017.pdf. Accessed July 26, 2017.

Europa (2011) Press Releases of the European Union, 'EU ratifies UN Convention on Disability Rights,' No. IP/11/4 of January 5, 2011, Brussels.

European Commission (2008) Violence and Disability – Daphne, European Communities, Luxembourg.

European Commission (2010) Communication from the Commission to the European Parliament, the Council, the European Economic and Social Committee and the Committee of the Regions, COM(2010)636 final, Brussels.

Hanauske-Abel, H. M. (1996) 'Not a Slippery Slope or Sudden Subversion: German Medicine and National Socialism in 1933', *British Medical Journal*, Vol. 313, No. 7070:1453, BMJ Publishing Group Ltd. London.

Haynes, J. J. Schweppe, S. Taylor (eds.) (2017) *Critical Perspectives on Hate Crime – Contributions from the Island of Ireland*, Palgrave Macmillan, UK.

Hynes, J. (2008) *Review of the Circumstances Surrounding the Elapse of Time in Bringing to Completion the Western Health Board Inquiry into Allegations of Abuse in the Brothers of Charity Services Galway*, HSE, Dublin.

INWWD (International Network of Women with Disabilities) (2010) *Document on Violence against Women with Disabilities*: http://groups.yahoo. com/group/inwwd. Accessed May 17, 2017.

International Save the Children Alliance, (2003) *A Last Resort: The Growing Concern about Children in Residential Care*, Save the Children, London.

Morris, J. (2001) *That Kind of Life? Social Exclusion and Young Disabled People with High Levels of Support Needs*, Report published by SCOPE, London.

Morris, J. (2001a) 'Social Exclusion and Young Disabled People with High Levels of Support Needs', *Critical Social Policy*, Vol. 21(2) Issue 67, Sage Publications.

Morris, J. (1997) 'Child Protection and Disabled Children at Residential Schools', *Disability and Society*, Vol. 12, No. 2, Routledge.

Mencap (2007) Bullying Wrecks Lives: The Experiences of Children and Young People with a Learning Disability, London, Mencap.

McCormack, B. (2005) *The Power Relationship in Sexual Abuse: An Analysis of Irish Data relating to Victims and Perpetrators with Learning Disabilities*, Paper to the Seminar of the National Disability Authority 'Violence Against Disabled People', November 29, 2004. Published on the website of the National Disability Authority, Ireland at www.nda.ie.

McCoy, K. (2007) *Report of Dr. Kevin McCoy on the Western Health Board Inquiry into the Brothers of Charity Services in Galway*, HSE, Dublin.

McGarry, P. (2009) 'Findings Demand Focus on Children – McAleese,' *The Irish Times*, June 26, Dublin.

McGee, H. Garavan, R. De Barra M, Byrne, J. Conroy R. (2002) *The SAVI Report – Sexual Violence and Abuse in Ireland,* Royal College of Surgeons in Ireland, Liffey Press, in association with the Dublin Rape Crisis Centre, Dublin.

Meehan, N. (2010) 'Church and State and the Bethany Home' in *History Ireland*, Vol. 18. No. 5, Dublin.

Mental Health Commission (2017) *Annual Report*, MHC, Dublin, July.

Nixon, J. (2009) 'Domestic Violence and Women with Disabilities: Locating the Issue on the Periphery of Social Movements', *Disability and Society*, Vol. 24, No. 1, Routledge, January.

NSPCC (2003) *It Doesn't Happen to Disabled Children: Report of the National Working Group on Child Protection and Disability*, NSPCC, London.

Odell, T. (2011) 'Not your Average Childhood: Lived Experience of Children with Physical Disabilities Raised in Bloorview Hospital, Home and School from 1960–1989', *Disability and Society*, Vol. 26, No. 1, Routledge, UK.

Quarmby, K. (2008) Getting Away with Murder – Disabled People's Experiences of Hate Crime in the UK, SCOPE, London.

Rafferty, M. O'Sullivan, E. (1999) *Suffer the Little Children: The Inside Story of Ireland's Industrial Schools*, New Island, Dublin.

Smith, J. M. (2007) *Ireland's Magdalen Laundries and the Nation's Architecture of Containment*, Manchester University Press, Manchester.

Tessadri, P. (2010) 'Noi vittime dei preti paedofili,' *L'espresso* 22 January, Gedi Gruppo Editoriale S.p.A: espresso.repubblica.it.

Tyrell, P. (2006) *Founded on Fear*, Irish Academic Press, Dublin.

United Nations (2006) *Report of the Independent Expert, Paulo Sérgio Pinheiro, for the United Nations Study on Violence against Children*, United Nations, General Assembly, Sixty-first session, Document A/61/299, New York.

United Nations, (2006) Convention on the Rights of Persons with Disabilities, New York.

United Nations, (1989) Convention on the Rights of the Child, New York.

US Department of Justice (2009) National Crime Victimization Survey – Crime Against People with Disabilities 2007, Bureau of Justice Statistics, Washington D.C.

Walsh, A. (2009) 'The Challenges Facing the Church in Ireland in the Aftermath of the Ryan Report', *Working Notes*, Issue 62, November, Jesuit Centre for Faith and Justice, Dublin,

Weindling, P. (1987) 'Compulsory Sterilisation in National Socialist Germany', *German History – The Journal of the German History Society*, Vol. 5, (1) Oxford Journals, OUP, UK.

Wiener, D. Ribeiro, R. Warner, K. (2009) 'Mentalism, Disability Rights and Modern Eugenics in a "Brave New World"' in *Disability and Society*, Vol. 24, No. 5, August, Routledge.

CHAPTER 10

The Role and Rise of Service Regulators

Historical Context

With Ireland's long history of mistrust of centralised power, the regulation of social services has been slow to take effect. The British tradition of establishing inspectorates for prisons or lunatic asylums in the nineteenth century was not endorsed with any enthusiasm by Saorstát Éireann in 1922. The very presence of the poor and ill as persons entitled to recognition was reduced to nought. In 1923, it was determined that persons in prisons, lunatic asylums and workhouses were not to be regarded as resident there for the purposes of voting in elections; their disenfranchisement was confirmed (Dáil, 1923, 639–640). Live-in servants and farm labourers were also denied the vote. The *Electoral Act, 1923* stipulated that:

> A person employed in a house, part of a house or other premises at a salary shall not be treated as thereby occupying the same for the purpose of his trade, profession or business within the meaning of this Section.
>
> A person who is an inmate or patient in any prison, lunatic asylum, workhouse, poorhouse, or any other similar institution shall not by reason thereof be treated as ordinarily resident therein or as occupying the same within the meaning of this section (*Electoral Act*, 1923).

When the act was being debated in the Dáil, Darrell Figgis, author, journalist and an independent but Sinn Fein-minded TD (1922–1923) and Tom Johnson TD (1872–1963), a former dockworker and leader of the Labour Party, queried the exclusionary sections. Ernest Blythe TD for the Cumann na nGaedheal Party defended them, and they were inserted into the act.

This less-than-inclusive view of democracy was part of a significant elitist undercurrent in the early years of the state; it was an undercurrent that viewed labourers, the poor, the sick and the disabled as an underclass who were probably unfit for democracy and should be excluded from democratic participation if at all possible.

Cumann na nGaedheal established a commission on the relief of the sick and destitute including the insane poor, which reported in 1926 (Saorstát Éireann, 1927). The commission members visited institutions around the country and took evidence from witnesses. They laid considerable emphasis on overcrowding in County Homes and other institutions and recommended that auxiliary institutions be established to provide further accommodation. They observed that 18,000 people were in asylums and that these numbers were rising annually. They recommended that the inspector of mental hospitals should also visit other approved institutions. They mentioned just one institution for 'defective' children – Stewart's Hospital in Dublin. A substantial part of their discussion was taken up with whether the right people were in the right institution, rather than querying the internment or placement of so many people in a variety of closed institutions.

In this historical context, the notion of regulating social services to ensure that recipients received the services to which they were entitled was difficult and problematic. There were precedents, however, that could have been built upon. Section 61 of the *Prisons (Ireland) Act* of 1826 gave prison inspectors the power and obligation to visit both public and private places of detention of 'lunatics and idiots'. This was a far-seeing development that recognised the obligation of the state to have a measure of accountability and duty of some care in the management of institutions. By 1846, an independent Inspectorate of Lunacy was established, with one inspector who submitted annual reports to the then Lord Lieutenants and Governor Generals of Ireland (Walsh and Daly, 2004, 18). Later, the *1908 Children Act*, Section 2, provided for each local authority to appoint 'infant protection visitors' to inspect where children in care were being housed. That legislation was to be the principal protective legislation for children until the 1990s. That reformist and philanthropic impulse found in Britain was absent in Ireland, or if present, was ignored and dispensed with after independence.

The Contemporary Drive to Regulate

The provision of services to children and adults with disabilities takes place in a quasi-market of services today. This almost-market of services has supply and demand factors like any market, levels of quality issues and not much transparency as to how it functions. The market in social and health services alone absorbs more than €1 billion of state funding annually. Instead of the state being the single supplier of disability services, it buys in services from a range of providers who are for-profit or not-for-profit. The buy-in is carried out through grant aid and service-level agreements, under which the service provider pledges or contracts to supply a fixed quantity of services to a public body. In this arrangement, the ultimate user, the person with a disability, has no say whatsoever. The market players make the decisions as to what is on offer: day services, therapeutic services, short break services, housing services, residential services or special transport services (Le Grand, J. and Bartlett, W. 1993).

The expansion of the public budget for disability services and the disquiet as to how the money was being spent were among the factors which prompted the Department of Health to invite the Comptroller and Auditor General to undertake an in-depth value-for-money study of services for people with disabilities in 2012 (Department of Health, 2012). The final report provided seventeen pages of recommendations. Among the recommendations were coordinated research between state bodies, an insistence on greater detail in how money is spent on individuals, a move toward an individualised funding system, ensuring standards are maintained in day services, the promoted sharing of resources between service providers, the collection of data on how budgets are spent and ensuring that for-profit service providers meet the same standards as required of other bodies providing services.

The report identified 105 for-profit providers in Ireland (five were in Northern Ireland and the UK) who obtained €22 million in purchasing funds from the HSE in 2011. It noted that: 'information is not available on the number, age or disability of clients who are receiving services from private for-profit providers, the service provided or the outcomes for the service users. It is therefore not possible to comment on the efficiency or effectiveness of the services provided' (Department of Health, 2012, 77).

Many of the large charities which deliver disability services are complex, national corporate-style bodies, although they do not aim to make a profit from their work, though they may generate a surplus. St. Vincent's Health Care Group of the Sisters of Charity has a net worth of approximately €233 million and 3,889 staff members. In 2015, the Brothers of Charity had an income of €192 million and employed 3,686 staff members. Together, the two bodies employed more people than Google Ireland, which had 6,000 employees.

The Irish not-for-profit sector is much larger than those bodies incorporated as charities. The scale of the funding involved is huge. The top ten charities in Ireland had an income of €3.06 billion in 2009 and €2.79 billion in 2011. Besides the Charity Commission and Philanthropy Ireland, funding data is collected by Boardmatch Ireland and the private body 2into3 (Power et al., 2016).

Table 15: The top twelve charities in Ireland by turnover, and other unincorporated bodies, 2011.

Rank	Name	Income (millions)	Activity
1	St. Vincent's Health Care	€363.3	Hospitals
2	Mater University Hospital	€257.6	Hospitals
3	St. Patrick's Hospital Cork	€224.1	Hospitals
4	Bon Secours Health System	€221,7	Hospitals
5	The Rehab Group	€176.6	Rehabilitation services
6	Concern Worldwide	€160.2	Overseas aid
7	St. Michael's House	€87.1	Disability services
8	Society of St. Vincent de Paul*	€79.9	Relief of poverty
9	Trócaire*	€63.0	Overseas aid
8	Cope Foundation	€62.0	Disability services
9	GOAL	€61.0	Overseas aid
10	Irish Wheelchair Association	€53.1	Disability services
11	Enable Ireland	€49.0	Disability services
12	Rehabcare	€44.7	Disability services

* Not incorporated as charities
Source: Boardmatch Ireland, 2013, Charity 100 Index 2011, December, p. 1 and 5.

The top charities in terms of income are concentrated in hospitals, disability services and overseas aid. Besides state funds, charities have to raise their own funding. A UK study revealed that charities in the UK in 2013 obtained just £3.16 for each £1 spent on fundraising (Fiennes, 2017, 7). From this, it is clear that being a top charity does not automatically mean efficiency.

The Regulatory Motorway

The motorway of regulation has several different lanes running in parallel. The emergence of private and public as well as public-private services in the market of disability service-provision has prompted a demand to regulate the variety of bodies in receipt of public funds. A second driver of change is the international social and labour standards for services, emerging through the European Union in Belgium, the United Nations in New York, the Council of Europe in France and the International Labour Organisation in Switzerland. These international bodies require an inspection of services to ensure that they conform with the human rights of people with disabilities. They operate in the same manner as motorway toll booths, proposing and setting standards for organisations driving along the motorway.

At the same time, global business regulation has seen severe challenges with the emergence of digital-based companies such as Uber and Airbnb (Stone, 2017). These new companies have challenged standards, systems, rules and benchmarks and have driven taxi drivers and hoteliers to aggressively maintain existing fixed-place regulation; they usually lose in the face of Uber drivers and Airbnb users and hosts, who claim the right to deliver services on their own terms. The battle over business regulation is still being fiercely fought. The Organisation for Economic Cooperation and Development wants governments to regulate the activities of multinational companies more rigorously. Brexit supporters believe that the European Union is over-regulating and unjustifiably interfering in society. How much and what to regulate is an ever-developing issue in contemporary society.

Notwithstanding these fears, there is such a thing as 'regulatory capture'; here, the regulating body cedes territory to the interest groups whose activities it is charged with regulating. This undoubtedly happened prior to the economic crash of 2008 in Ireland, when the banking regulator could no longer determine whether the banks were insolvent or simply temporarily short of cash.

There is a new standard-setting agenda in the field of disability rights. In his review of international developments from the 1980s, Arthur O'Reilly notes that by 2002 'there was wide agreement on the need for a focus on the human rights dimension of the issues involved' (O'Reilly, 2003). A third driver of regulation is state concern as to whether they are getting value for money in subsidising services and employment supports. Despite the difficulties in actually measuring value-for-money, the preoccupation persists in public policy. The need to obtain some minimum standard for services and supports to people with disabilities is a fourth driver of regulatory processes. Without a high level of trust, social services cannot function.

The Arrival of Social Service Inspection

The promise of a social service inspectorate in law reached back to 2007. Yet, there was still scepticism and disbelief that it would happen. There was considerable friction between the new 'outsider' agency HIQA and some of the voluntary bodies to be inspected. Inspection standards were drafted, redrafted and drafted again. The process of registering all residential services for people with disabilities proved very difficult initially. To date, HIQA has registered just under 1,000 residential disability services. The 2007 *Health Act* defines a 'designated centre' not as a single building but potentially several houses/buildings/residences spread out over a wide geographical area or on a single campus or adjoining neighbourhoods. When inspections are conducted, some but not all residences may be inspected. The ensuing inspection report may relate to some but not all residences, leaving the reader perplexed as to whether the report covers all residences within a 'designated centre'. This confusion, which arises from the law, is likely due to parliamentary legislative drafters imagining that residential services for people with disabilities are similar to nursing homes: single buildings with a single entrance. They are not.

A further difficulty in the initial stages of the inspection regime included communication with service users/residents with disabilities. It was not clear at the outset that inspectors were able to communicate with the residents or were familiar with the types of communication that might be used by some residents, such as the manual signing system called Lámh, picture boards or typing on screens. Some of these early difficulties have since been addressed, and the voice of the resident is now given more attention.

Inspection also has its costs. Services are expected to pay an annual fee of €500 for inspection and a fee of €100–€200 for a small or large variation in their registration as a service provider. The inspection fee is based on how many approved or 'designated' centres the provider is operating. This unintentionally provides an incentive to service providers to group their residences into fewer 'designated centres' and save money from having each residence classed as a 'designated centre'. Some services have more than forty distinct residences. If each were designated, registration fees alone would amount to €20,000. This excludes the cost in time of assembling a large amount of documentation for an inspection of each residence.

The issue of whether all residences in a service are inspected came to the fore in the case of the Áras Attracta service in Swinford, County Mayo, investigated in an RTÉ *Prime Time* investigation in 2014 entitled 'Inside Bungalow 3'. *Prime Time* had a camera placed inside the living room of the residence by an undercover staff member. The camera recorded staff and resident interactions over a period of days. The results were edited into a shocking programme revealing elderly and disabled residents being mocked, teased, slapped, sat upon, shouted at and humiliated. The service was operated by the HSE. A two-day inspection of the service had been undertaken by HIQA some months earlier and had reported that residents were treated respectfully and that measures were in place to prevent the abuse of residents.

Following the programme, nine staff were removed from duty on paid leave. The programme was followed by several investigations, including one by an Gárda Siochána, who collected evidence for prosecutions against five staff. Interviewed by *Prime Time* presenters after the broadcast, the HSE director of social care described the service as being 'totally unacceptable', having 'shortcomings' and that it was 'a significant challenge'. He did not clarify what the 'challenge' was. Paddy Connolly of Inclusion Ireland, also interviewed, described the situation of the residents as 'inhumane and degrading' while Judge Peter Kelly described it as 'inhuman' (RTÉ, 2014; Carolan, 2017, 7; Áras Attracta, 2016). The contrast in language is remarkable. 'Inhumane' and 'degrading' are adjectives that describe serious breaches of human rights. 'Shortcomings' and 'challenges' imply the service was less than optimal. This may not have been what the director of social care intended to convey, but this was what was implied by the terms used. The Irish Nurses and Midwives Organisation deplored the treatment of patients by staff at Áras Attracta and called for the use of fitness to practice hearings in relation to the staff of Bungalow 3.

This was not the first time that RTÉ *Prime Time* had used undercover methods to obtain evidence of the poor treatment of people with disabilities. An RTÉ *Prime Time* television programme on the North Dublin private nursing home, Leas Cross, had been broadcast in 2005. The death of a resident of Leas Cross in Beaumont Hospital attracted considerable public attention. The resident had intellectual disabilities, was a ward of court and died just twelve days after he was transferred to the nursing home with the permission of the High Court but against the wishes of his family. Staff at Beaumont Hospital are reported to have seen a series of residents of Leas Cross whose health suggested poor-quality care. These concerns were not communicated to Leas Cross or to the health board (O'Donovan, 2009). The nursing home was closed down in 2005; part of it was levelled and another part was converted to a nursing home under new ownership and management. These events occurred prior to the establishment of HIQA. Leas Cross had, however, been inspected by the area health board and had passed these inspections, just like Áras Attracta. The director of nursing at Leas Cross was struck off the Nursing Register in 2012. A regime of inspection and the enforcement of standards does not necessarily mean they will be adhered to.

The Fear of Regulation

Despite the drive to regulate health, social and educational services, inspection and inspectors conjure up an image of dread, tyranny, annoyance and unwarranted judgement for many professionals working in these fields. Yet the scandals of care are mounting up. 'Grace' was a child with complex disabilities who had been in foster care for most of her life. She was a child and then adult in need of protection in the southeast of Ireland. Complaints against the foster family appeared to have prompted the removal of other foster children from the foster home, but 'Grace' remained in their care. Eventually her situation came into the public domain, revealing the need for vigorous inspections and the enforcement of standards. Interestingly, the scandals mentioned above arose from the work of whistle-blowers, including psychologists and social workers in various services, and reached journalists in RTÉ's investigation unit. The scandals did not arise directly from inspections.

In relation to people with disabilities, the HIQA was not particularly satisfied in 2016:

> The experience in residential services for people with disabilities is somewhat mixed. While many are receiving a quality service and enjoying a good standard of living, a significant number of people are experiencing a quality of life that is well below that which would be expected for citizens in this 21st Century Ireland. These people have been living over a long period of time in institution-alised services that do not promote person-centredness and where abuses of their rights have happened. In some instances, HIQA has assessed the care being provided as unsafe (HIQA, 2017a).

In 2016, HIQA inspectors witnessed situations where patients had been placed in services that were not appropriate to their needs. This practice often results in an increased risk to the safety of the patients concerned and the people they lived with. The HIQA continued to witness routines and practices that were determined by the needs of staff – as opposed to residents' needs – in more densely populated settings as well as in some community-based houses. As a result, and in order to protect residents, the Office of the Chief Inspector took legal enforcement proceedings against a number of providers in 2016 and will continue to act to promote and protect the rights of residents (HIQA, 2017).

In April 2017, the HIQA reported on inspections they carried out in centres where people with disabilities resided. This is what they found:

> In one of these centres, the inspectors found that the institutional practices observed were seriously impacting on residents' rights, safety and quality of life. The residents at this centre were subjected to peer-to-peer assaults and witnessed serious incidents of aggres-sive and challenging behaviour. In another centre operated by this provider, the inspectors found that the residents were in receipt of poor quality services and that the governance and management

arrangements in place did not adequately ensure that residents were safe in their home (HIQA, 2017a).

Multi-Inspection of Disability Services

The HIQA is not the only regulator in this regard. The Department of Education has its own inspectorate, which visits special schools, special classes in mainstream schools and mainstream classes that may contain children with disabilities. The inspection of educational provision dates back to the early nineteenth century but was updated by Section 13 of the *Education Act, 1998*.

The field of mental health has its own separate inspectorate under the *Mental Health Act, 2001*, which established the Mental Health Commission and gave a statutory basis to the Inspector of Mental Health Services. The Mental Health Commission keeps a register of approved centres where mental health services are provided and can recommend that approved centres be restricted in their services or the number of people to whom services are offered. It can propose that new admissions be refused for a named mental health service or that specific centres be closed down via cases brought to the High Court.

The *Mental Health Act, 2001* introduced the establishment of mental health tribunals to determine whether the involuntary admission of patients with a mental disorder to hospitals had been done so in accordance with the law. It took five years (late 2006) to get the mental health tribunals up and running.

Despite the clear aims of the various new regulatory laws, policies on the ground have drifted as the inertia of the reformation of systems has slowed change. Parts of the 2004 law, *Education for Persons with Special Education Needs Act (EPSEN)*, have never been implemented. The registration of all residential centres for people with disabilities had not been completed by 2016 , and in 2016 an amendment was passed to the *Health Act* to give additional years to allow not-yet-registered disability services to reach minimum standards under the *Health (Amendment) Act, 2016*. This may have sent an unintentional message to service providers that delaying and lingering over registration pays off, or alternatively, that HIQA does not have the resources to do its job.

Once the regulation of services has been installed, there are strict limits on who can provide services and what precisely constitutes a service. For example, the *Mental Health Act, 2001* bans the establishment or running of unapproved centres or hospitals for people with a mental illness unless they have been approved and registered. The same applies to residential social care centres, residential social care houses or children's homes in the community for people with disabilities.

One of the primary aims of service regulation has been to designate, legally, what constitutes a 'service'. Services that fall outside the fixed standards are effectively unregulated, may be illegal and are not entitled to public funding. Hypothetically, if a couple decided to rent a large house in the countryside and provide two people with mental illness a home and interesting activities, they could find themselves outside the law. They would lack the specified care qualifications, governance of their 'service', specialised training, etc. The same regulations that ensure high standards of services for people with disabilities can also inadvertently discourage innovation or new person-centred living solutions. There is evidence that this is already happening. The HIQA has signalled a trend toward new, unregulated services: 'An issue that has arisen from the transition away from congregated settings is the emergence of new models of services or existing services caring for vulnerable people that do not fit within the definition of a designated centre as contained within the Health Act' (HIQA, 2017, 26).

The HIQA has observed this trend in personal assistants, home care, sheltered housing, respite care, day care and home sharing. According to the HIQA, people with disabilities were accommodated in centres using extensive, restrictive practices that might fall outside the definition of a designated centre. How innovative and progressive social developments are to be regulated in the interests of the welfare of people with disabilities is an issue of considerable importance.

The Regulation of Charities and Not-For-Profits

The British government has been regulating charities for over one hundred years, but this has not been the case in Ireland. There are 19,505 not-for-profit bodies, groups and associations in Ireland (Benefacts, 2017). They range from multi-million-dollar hospitals and universities to small-scale local groups. Some are charities and friendly societies, others are trade unions or are unincorporated. Attempts to regulate charities have been ongoing since the 1990s when the Law Reform Commission included charity law in its work plan for the period 2000–2007.

The scale of the not-for-profit phenomena varies between the numbers provided by the Charity Register, the Revenue Commissioners and new Benefacts' research. The Charity Regulator has registered 8,584 charities compared with the 19,505 monitored by Benefacts and the 7,750 registered by the Revenue Commissioners. There are different ways of defining a charity, depending on its purpose.

The 2007 Charities Bill was an attempt to provide greater accountability of charities and protect the public against fraud while also updating the *1962 Charities Act*. The Law Reform Commission produced a series of researched papers on how to regulate and define charities and charitable trusts (Law Reform Commission, 2006). To successfully regulate charities, charitable activity must be defined in such a way that what is regulated is not merely an intention to do good but also the actual activities of the charity. After many discussions and debates, the *Charities Act* was adopted by the Dáil in 2009 and was brought into effect gradually, up to 2016. The act established a Charity Regulator and a Register of Charities and set minimum standards for the conduct of their business (Oireachtas Library and Research Service Note, 2015).

Until quite recently, the not-for-profit sector was a tangled maze of organisations. Now, analysis is clearly displaying how non-profit agencies, groups and associations function. This is partly due to the high-profile scandals coming to the attention of the public. One example was the Central Remedial Clinic scandal, a second was the Console charity scandal, where the charity was placed in liquidation.

The activities of registered charities were separated into four categories in 2009:

- Combatting poverty and economic hardship
- Advancing education
- Advancing religion
- Other purposes of benefit to the community including environmental protection and animal welfare

Activities that are excluded range from political activism (apart from lobbying for a charitable cause), activities for the benefit of one's own members (such as sporting organisations) and certain membership bodies such as the chambers of commerce or trade unions. Having defined what a charity consists of, those bodies outside the terms of references are NOT registered charities and cannot describe themselves as such, although they will remain not-for-profit. Charities can be removed from the Register of Charities if they refuse, without justification, to implement their obligations such as publishing annual accounts and reports of activities, maintaining books of accounts, mismanaging their funds or having unsuitable persons as trustees. The regulator can refuse to register, or remove from the register, bodies that fall into the categories below in Section 44 of the *Charities Act*:

> 43.(1) Where the Authority, after consultation with the Garda Síochána, is of opinion that a body registered in the register is or has become an excluded body by virtue of its promoting purposes that are—
> (a) unlawful,
> (b) contrary to public morality,
> (c) contrary to public policy,
> (d) in support of terrorism or terrorist activities, or
> (e) for the benefit of an organisation, membership of which is unlawful, it shall remove from the register all of the information entered in relation to that body and the body shall thereupon cease to be registered.

However, some charities are more equal than others. A relatively small group of 347 bodies get 70 percent of all state funding for not-for-profit organisations. These are forty-four of the largest health and social care service providers; twenty-two higher education institutions; and 281 local providers of family support, addiction services, citizens advice and local development supports. These are quasi-state and quasi-market bodies. The remaining 19,258 bodies have to make do with the leftovers of state finance.

Disputes over charity funding continue to be aired through the media and Oireachtas committees. Some universities (UCD), hospitals (the

National Maternity Hospital and St. Vincent's University Hospital) and disability service providers (Rehab, the Catholic Institute for Deaf People, the Alzheimer's Society and St John of God's Community Services) did not believe that the state had the right to tell them how to spend their privately generated income from their own fundraising and fees. For example, these bodies believed that they had the right to pay staff members, doctors, managers or lecturers above the going rate for senior personnel where that payment was sourced from privately generated income. In the view of some bodies, the state was not so much trying to regulate them as trying to exercise control over them, ignoring the fact that they were voluntary bodies with their own governing structures.

One of the ironies of the *Charities Act* is its prescription of who may become a charitable trustee. It excludes persons who have convictions or have served prison sentences. When one charity, in the name of inclusivity, attempted to put an ex-prisoner on their board, they ran into difficulty because he was an 'excluded person'. This implied that he would forever be excluded.

The Regulation of Professionals

Between 47 and 50 million Europeans now work in roughly 6,000 regulated professions. About 42 percent of these professions are in the health and social care sectors. The proportion of professions in the European workforce under regulation is growing as more professions become regulated by law. Regulation impacts on the length of time and study necessary to become professionally qualified. Regulation determines whether the title of a profession, such as a 'social worker', can be used by anyone to describe themselves or whether it is restricted to those who have officially registered as a professional social worker and have been approved by a regulatory body.

Occupational regulation refers to legally defined requirements that govern entry into occupation and subsequent conduct within said occupation (Koumenta and Pagliero, 2016). In the European Union, there are three broad types of regulation:

- Licensing, which legally regulates specific activities such as those of a nurse, doctor or pharmacist.
- Certification, which uses a protected title such as taxi driver or security guard.
- Accreditation though a voluntary agreement of compliance with standards.

Some believe that the European Union is overstepping its powers in seeking to regulate certain professions when the European treaties do not give the EU power to regulate health services and systems. It could be argued that overregulation of health professions is a form of creeping control of an area that the EU should stay out of (Baeten, 2017).

In Ireland, more and more activities are legally regulated by defined requirements that determine entry into an occupation and conduct within that occupation. Entry into a profession can be successful by having the minimum education requirements; meeting experiential requirements such as fixed-length internships; completing annual and approved professional training; registering membership annually; exhibiting behaviour of a high standard that avoids bringing disrepute to the occupation; having professional indemnity insurance or agreeing to random inspections. These detailed standards vary from profession to profession and from country to country.

In some countries, activities are regulated by licensing; certain countries are keen on licensing occupations and others are more relaxed about it. Table 16 shows the top five countries where the highest proportion of persons are in licensed occupations and the five countries with the lowest proportions of licensed workers. Ireland ranks third out of twenty-eight countries for a high level of licensed occupations. Licensing of occupations is one of the contributors to inequality in Europe. For people with disabilities who have an incomplete second-level education or no third-level qualification, licensing makes entering the labour market and competing for jobs quite difficult.

The level of regulation of a country's professionals has no relationship to the level of social and economic development of that country. Germany and Croatia have little in common as high regulating states. Sweden and Latvia have equally little in common as low regulating states. In this sense, regulation is a phenomenon which occurs culturally or socially but is not a result of economic development. If the regulation of occupations were easier to understand, professionals could easily move from country to country by merely checking a chart. This is not possible at present. However, some countries are more attractive to mobile professionals than others.

Table 16: Selected member states of the EU ranked according to prevalence of licensing of occupations.

Countries with highest proportion of persons in licensed jobs	Percentage of workers licensed	Countries with lowest proportion of persons in licensed jobs	Percentage of workers licensed
Germany	33	Denmark	14
Croatia	31	Latvia	15
Ireland	29	Sweden	15
Slovakia	27	France	17
Hungary	26	Finland	17

Source: Cited in Koumenta, M. Pagliero, M. (2016) *Measuring Prevalence and Labour Market Impacts of Occupational Regulation in the EU*, European Commission, Brussels. Table 3.4. p. 29.

Regulating occupations should ensure higher standards of service for consumers. In Ireland, there can be a lack of professional oversight and professional and effective enforcement, which stems from a lack of deterrent sanctions and a failure of self-regulation. The fines for polluting waterways can be very small compared with the investment involved to replace fish and wildlife killed or damaged by pollution.

Besides the regulation of services, the regulation of professionals has added to the complexity of this field. CORU is a body that has been established in Ireland to regulate a wide range of professions within the health and social care sectors, including social workers, social care workers, occupational therapists and speech and language therapists. Those who wish to be employed as social workers now have to register with CORU on an annual basis and keep their qualifications up to date. They are bound by a code of conduct and ethics and must have graduated from a CORU-approved educational course. CORU now has registers for thousands of health and social professionals.

One of the biggest challenges CORU faced in 2018 was the registration of 10,000 care workers. This was by far the biggest cohort of to-be-regulated professionals to date. In 2017, a social care registration board was established, and CORU examined the various university and college courses to establish an educational standard of equivalent courses of equivalent length for the registration of social care workers.

The registration of professionals ensures that their conduct is regulated by their own profession. Fitness to practice regimes now function across a wide range of health and social care professions. These quasi-judicial bodies exercise great power and can effectively 'police' the workforces. This is achieved by setting codes of good behaviour and standards, known as 'codes of conduct'. The codes may be lengthy and detail how confidentiality is to be achieved, how the consent of service users can be obtained and how communications are carried out.

A breach of these standards may lead to a complaint, which, if upheld, could generate sanctions against the person by the professional body. Trade unions representing social care workers now offer a specialised legal service to advise members against whom complaints are made. Sanctions may be mild, with the employee receiving a censure, or they may be very serious, with their name taken off the register and a consequent ban on employment in the sector. Once off the register, that professional cannot practice in Ireland or in any other countries around the world where reciprocal arrangements are in place.

The Rise of Credentialism

Credentialism concerns the preoccupation with formally accredited systems that demarcate levels of learning, regardless of whether the credentials are required for a job or not. Credentialism is closely aligned with what Pat McDonnell calls a preoccupation with 'expertism'. The growth of expertise and 'expertism' is a historical development of rationalism away from the moral and religious domination of ideas. Expertism is based on objective or technical capacities, competencies or qualifications.

Credentialism has far-reaching implications for all types of education. Allegedly neutral expertise can create a significant social and economic distance between an expert and the object of his or her study or work.

This can happen in social care where barriers between the care workers and cared-for can widen. Credentialism occurs when high-level job specifications and qualifications are disproportionately applied to lower level jobs which have no need for them. Credentialism often creates new forms of social exclusion by raising the bar for entry into a job or employment post ever higher. Credentialism ultimately devalues the qualification which has been sought, since the work being undertaken does not require a high-level qualification. An example is when junior lecturing posts in third level education are advertised as requiring a PhD of candidates. A PhD qualification may not be required at this level of teaching. Credentialism can be used to reduce the number of applicants applying for a job by setting the required qualifications at an unnecessarily high standard. This results in a displacement effect as those who have lower level qualifications find themselves squeezed out of recruitment when the job would actually have been suited to them.

Over the decade of the 2000s the European Commission began responding to complaints that professional regulation had become disproportionate to the standards for which it was designed: the evidence base for specific rules and regulations was absent from decision-making. The same profession can be regulated differently from country to country. A looser form of regulation may be called for, based on the requirements for registering as a professional. Different regulatory specifications exist across the European labour market, some of which are based on opinions, common sense or historical factors rather than evidence. In order to ensure the effective free movement of professionals across Europe, said professionals must be able to foresee whether they can work in other European countries. Over-regulation can create market restrictions, limit consumer choice, raise prices of services and reduce the number of people who are able to enter the jobs market (European Commission, 2015).

Conclusion

To reinforce standards in social care, parents, relatives, resident groups and associations can pool experiences; report on planned changes in policy or development by service providers; participate more in HIQA inspections; and be recognised advocates for family members. Such groups will not and do not emerge spontaneously; they require promotion, facilitation and support to find a method of operating that will give them the confidence to speak out when necessary. One of the lessons learned from Leas Cross and Áras Attracta is that an inspection regime does not dispense with the need for active citizenship in relation to the provision of services. In other words, inspection does not do away with the need for close monitoring of service provision. To be effective, inspection needs on-the-ground monitoring by those close to the service, particularly services where users cannot fully articulate their opinions and require independent advocacy.

In the twenty-first century, the entire landscape of social services and services for people with disabilities has altered. The state prescribes who may open a service, who may work in that service and how its activity and expenditure is operated. Regulatory investigators of non-compliance are now being employed by the Office of the Data Protection Commissioner, the Charities Regulator, the Anti-Money Laundering Compliance Unit, the Office of the Inspector of Prisons and the Property Services Regulatory Authority. The new inspectorates are in some cases still in their infancy and are adapting to new realities. However, compliance and innovation do not necessarily go hand in hand. This is an area ripe for improvement to ensure that services by, with and for people with disabilities do not become standardised and unsuitable for individual preferences.

The discovery of serious abuse and neglect in disability services has been amplified by the media. This neglect has occurred even where staff had attempted to disclose the abuse but were ignored. The accuracy and effectiveness of inspections could be enhanced if people with disabilities were part of inspection teams.

In terms of the regulation of professions, some regulation may be disproportionate to the activity or service being regulated and should be reduced through law reform or amendments to statutory instruments. Without an examination of what is a proportionate measure of a good service, we risk veering toward an autocratic state.

Chapter 10 References

Áras Attracta Swinford Review Group (2016) *What Matters Most – Report of the Áras Attracta Swinford Review Group*, HSE, Dublin, July.

Baeten, R. (2017) 'Was the Exclusion of Health Care from the Services Directive a Pyrrhic Victory?' *Opinion Paper 18*, European Social Observa tory, Brussels: ww.ose.be/files/publication/OSCEPaperSeries/Baeten_ 2017_OpinionPaper.pdf. Accessed April 22, 2017.

Benefacts (2017) Non-Profit Sector Analysis, Dublin: www.benefacts.ie. Accessed July 11, 2017.

Carolan, M. (2017) 'Treatment of Woman in Mayo Home "Inhuman"', *Irish Times*, November 17, 2017.

Dáil Éireann Debate (1925) Vol. 10, No. 15. Thursday, 19 March.

Dáil Reports (1923) Vol. 2. No. 10. January, Paragraphs 639–640.

Department of Health (2012) *Value for Money and Policy Review of Disability Services in Ireland*, Dublin, July.

Electoral Act (1923) Section 1(8).

European Commission (2015), A Single Market for Europe – Analysis and Evidence, SWD (2015) 202 Final.

European Commission (2016) Brussels, January 10, 2017 COM(2016) 820 Final, *Communication from the Commission to the European Parliament, the Council, the European Economic and Social Committee and the Committee of the Regions on Reform Recommendations for Regulation in Professional Services*, SWD (2016) 436 Final: SWD-2015-202-FIN-En-Text%20(1).pdf. Accessed February 1, 2017.

Fiennes, C. (2017) 'The Threat of Godzilla Charities', *Financial Times*, London, July 29, p. 7.

Health (Amendment) Act of 2016.

HIQA (2017) Overview of 2016 HIQA: *Regulation of Social Care and Health Care Services:*hiqa.ie/hiqa-news-updates/disability-publication-statement-12-april-2017. Accessed April 27, 2017.

Koumenta, M. Pagliero, M. (2016) *Measuring Prevalence and Labour Market Impacts of Occupational Regulation in the EU*, European Commission, Brussels.

Law Reform Commission (2006) Report: *Charitable Trusts and Legal Structures for Charities*, No. 8, Dublin. LRC.

Le Grand, J. and Bartlett, W. (eds.) (1993) *Quasi-Markets and Social Policy*, Palgrave Macmillan, London.

O'Donovan, D. (2009) *The Commission of Investigation (Leas Cross Nursing Home)* Final Report, June.

Oireachtas Library and Research Service Note (2015) *Charities and Regulation in Ireland*, Houses of the Oireachtas, Dublin, June 16.

O'Reilly, A. (2003) *The Right to Decent Work of Persons with Disabilities*, IFP/Skills Working Paper No. 14, International Labour Office, Geneva.

Power, A. O'Connor, D. and Walshe, K. (2016) *The Irish Not-for-Profit Sector: Fundraising Performance Report 2015*, Mazars and Ecclesiastical Insurance: www.2into3.com.

RTÉ Interviews (2014) www.rte.ie/news/player/prime-time-web/2014/1209. Accessed December 12, 2014.

Saorstát Éireann (1927) *Report on the Relief of the Sick and Destitute Including the Insane Poor*, The Stationery Office, Dublin.

Stone, B. (2017) *The Upstarts: How Uber, Airbnb and the Killer Companies of the New Silicon Valley are Changing the World*, Bantam Press, London.

Walsh, D. and Daly, A. (2004) *Mental Illness in Ireland 1750–2002: Reflections on the Rise and Fall of Institutional Care,* HRB, Dublin.

Chapter 11

The Independent Living Movement

From Oakland, California to Boston, Massachusetts, and from Boston, Massachusetts to Dublin, Ireland – this was the route the independent living movement took when Martin Naughton decided it was time for change in the living arrangements of people with disabilities in Ireland in 1988. Describing his experience in the US, he said:

> I ended up meeting people who were just like me, who were running independent living centres for other people with disabilities. I spent time with them, exploring the whole notion of independent living. And I began to think about all the people back home, many of whom I had semi-reared in some sense when I was in Baldoyle, who were living in institutions. The temptation to do something became too great and I felt the pull back home (Marsden, 2010, 92).

The first Centre for Independent Living (CIL) had been established in the University of California, Berkeley around 1974 by Ed Roberts and his friends. Polio had paralysed Ed from the neck down and as he could not live in a student dormitory, he was given an empty hospital ward on the campus in which to live. In a short time, the CIL at Berkeley was attracting hundreds of people with disabilities to its doors, offering services such as housing advice and parenting counselling. The establishment of the CIL coincided with the end of the Vietnam War, in 1975. Thousands of veterans were pouring into California from South-East Asia. Some 153,000 young soldiers had been injured during the twenty-year war (Veteran Administration, 2017). They were now disabled, in need of support and did not know where to go or what would happen when they left Veteran Administration hospitals. It was an era of civil rights, but the rights of people with disabilities had never been articulated.

The US independent living movement was greatly encouraged by a very tiny paragraph – Section 504 – in the *1973 Rehabilitation Act*. Section 504 stated that: 'No otherwise qualified handicapped individual in the United States, as defined in §7(6) shall, solely by reason of his handicap, be excluded from participation in, be denied benefits of, or be subjected to discrimination under any program or activity receiving Federal financial assistance'. Here is how it is described in US law:

Section 504 of the Rehabilitation Act of 1973 is a national law that protects qualified individuals from discrimination based on their disability. The non-discrimination requirements of the law apply to employers and organizations that receive financial assistance from any Federal department or agency, including the US Department of Health and Human Services (DHHS). These organizations and employers include many hospitals, nursing homes, mental health centers and human service programs.

Section 504 forbids organizations and employers from excluding or denying individuals with disabilities an equal opportunity to receive program benefits and services. It defines the rights of individuals with disabilities to participate in, and have access to, program benefits and services (Health and Human Services, 2017)

Section 504 took many years to evolve into a programme of services and non-discrimination practices. President Nixon, as a conservative, was unhappy with Section 504 and did not want to approve its development into a practical reality, despite protests and sit-ins across the United States. Eventually, it was President Jimmy Carter who set to work on Section 504, planting the seed of the *Americans with Disabilities Act*, a law which Senator Edward Kennedy would later champion through the American Congress (Kennedy-Smith, 1996).

The thinking behind the independent living movement was that of peer support, where people could take control over their own lives with the support of other similar-minded peers. The independent living movement has been one of the more interesting social exports to Ireland. Its expansion coincided with the establishment of the Forum of People with Disabilities in Ireland, which explicitly rejected the charitable orientation of many disability services in favour of a self-directed movement.

A Centre for Independent Living in Ireland

With the help of others, Martin Naughton established the Centre for Independent Living at Carmichael House in Dublin in 1992. Like their counterparts in Boston, the members of the independent living movement began to canvass for the support that people with disabilities needed if they were to live successfully outside of residential institutions. These supports are as relevant today as they were back in the 1980s and 1990s. Foremost among these was the need for personal assistants (PAs) who could help people with disabilities manage their everyday lives.

The independent living movement was based on the belief and fundamental right of people with disabilities to live a life of their own choosing and not be obliged to live in a residential centre or with their parents upon reaching adulthood. Following a study of the US experience of employing people to support individuals to lead independent lives, a small programme of personal assistance was established in the early 1990s. The Irish Wheelchair Association later became the main provider of PAs to people with disabilities (Murphy et al., 2006).

The relationship between a person with a disability and their PA is very complex; it can involve intimate care, personal care, and formal and informal activities, with many hours spent in proximity to another person. Pat – an adult with a disability, described her experience: 'For me I'd rather fight to the death if I had to for my freedom, the personal assistant service has ensured my freedom, if I don't have the personal assistant service I would be in bed with bed sores, in one room, with very few possessions […] life wouldn't be worth living' (Murphy et al., 2006).

There are more than twenty CILs in Ireland. However, this number cannot provide national coverage. It has been difficult to establish significant and stable funding for independent living across the country. The Centres for Independent Living in Ireland questioned their members on how the service worked. Here is what some of them said:

Quite simply it allows people with disabilities to be people – to live real lives with real meaning. [It is] not accessible. [The] district nurse made [the] initial request. [A] Letter came back saying 'no' and no assessment [was] undertaken. Later in the year, hours were approved as I was in hospital for several weeks and it enabled me to come home. [It is] definitely not fair or user friendly. I regard the system as one in which the client is 'done to' – the assessment process is highly subjective. Recently, I have obtained copies of [...] policies from different parts of the country. Not only is the assessment subjective, based on assessment tools from 1965, in terms of policy it is biased on a geographical basis and depends on the skill and judgement of those handling the budget at local level. I believe it is very important to have legislation for personal assistance services as we are all citizens. It should be a human right for people to have this service as we can live independently and give back to society as a whole and not have to hear those words 'subject to funding' (CIILFC, 2016).

Thomas from Canada expresses his views:

[...] first, I spent many years living with my parents. So, on one level independent living means living outside the immediate family environment. I also spent three months living in a chronic care facility, which was an utter nightmare. So, I would say that independent living would be living in an environment that was my own, where I can choose to a greater or lesser degree, where I can control my lifestyle and the hours I wish to keep when I get up, when I go to bed (Gibson et al., 2009, 322).

The final report of the Commission on the Status of People with Disabilities was somewhat restricted in what it advocated in relation to independent living. The report recognised that personal assistance was a concept that emanated from the independent living movement but proposed that personal assistance services should be provided only for people with 'significant physical disabilities' (DJELR, 1996, 165). The report did not recognise that many people with physical, intellectual, neurological and psychological disabilities need support to live independent lives or live more independently. One essential support is personal assistance; a second essential support is payment made directly to the service user rather than the service provider. PAs are highly restricted in numbers and were available to just 2,200 people with disabilities in 2017. Of these, 990 had between one and five hours per week of PA care, or one hour a day from Monday to

Friday. A further 500 received between six and ten hours of PA care a week. Ten hours a week is not a lot of time to have a life (Oireachtas, 2017, 55).

The End of Mass Communal Living

For centuries, the sick, ill, poor, destitute, orphaned, unlawfully pregnant, deaf and insane were obliged to live communally in closed institutions, not just in Ireland but across the Western world. For these people, 'normal living' meant living with many other strangers in a quasi-military setting. In the nineteenth and twentieth centuries, closed institutions such as hospitals, prisons, industrial schools and laundries provided segregated living to defined and unwanted categories of people.

A number of factors gave rise to the growing critique of institutional living in the late twentieth and early twenty-first century. Among these was the growth of a human rights movement that argued against institutional living, believing it was contrary to the individual rights of people with disabilities. The importance of writers such as American sociologist Erving Goffman was another factor. His book, *Asylums*, undermined contemporary thinking about psychiatric hospitals as therapeutic places of care. Goffman's book was based on his experience working undercover in a large hospital (1961). Another (possibly mistaken) factor was the belief that community living might be cheaper for public authorities than spending money on institutions. Finally, living in the community was thought to contribute to better and happier lives for those concerned.

The Olmstead Case

In the US, a major civil rights court case, *Olmstead v. L.C.* of 1999 opened up the opportunity for community care for people with mental and intellectual disabilities living in institutions. Tommy Olmstead was the Commissioner for Health of the State of Georgia.

> The story of the Olmstead case begins with two women, Lois Curtis and Elaine Wilson, who had mental illness and developmental disabilities and were voluntarily admitted to a psychiatric unit in the

State-run Georgia Regional Hospital [...] However, the women remained confined in the institution each for several years after the initial treatment was concluded. They filed suit under the Americans with Disabilities Act (ADA) for release from the hospital.

On June 22, 1999, the United States Supreme Court held in Olmstead v. L.C. that unjustified segregation of persons with disabilities constitutes discrimination in violation of title II of the Americans with Disabilities Act... Confinement in an institution severely diminishes the everyday life activities of individuals including family relations, social contacts, work options, economic independence, educational advancement, and cultural enrichment (Olmstead, 2017).

When the case was first filed, twenty-six states joined the case with the state of Georgia to support institutionalisation. With pressure and awareness from the disability rights movement mounting, nineteen of the twenty-six states withdrew their support for Georgia. While many Americans associated segregation with racial segregation, in the Olmstead case, a new kind of segregation was highlighted: disability segregation.

The Olmstead judgement had a huge impact on the lives of people living in residential institutions in the US. With support, they could leave the institutions, even after many years, and live in a community setting. However, implementing the Olmstead judgement was to prove difficult. Under Title II of the Federal *Americans with Disabilities Act*, Justice Ruth Bader Ginsburg, delivering the opinion of the court, ordered that

> states are required to place persons with mental disabilities in community settings rather than in institutions when the States' treatment professionals have determined that community placement is appropriate, the transfer from institutional care to a less restrictive setting is not opposed by the affected individual, and the placement can be reasonably accommodated, taking into account the resources available to the State and the needs of others with mental disabilities (Accessible Society, 2017).

My own experiences living and working at Boston State Hospital in 1966 was a confirmation that a 'total institution', in the words of Goffman, dehumanises individuals. The psychiatric hospital was a former lunatic asylum from the 1830s, and it admitted anyone and everyone in the 1960s: unmarried mothers, the intellectually impaired, disturbed teenagers, elderly people and involuntary patients committed by the courts. Some of the staff were legitimately armed and appeared quite ready to use lethal force. The hospital was like a little town of its own, self-sufficient and completely cut off from the outside world. Some of the older patients had not seen sunlight in a long time. As more and more patients moved to community residences, the hospital was closed down.

The deinstitutionalisation and independent living movement advanced at quite a fast pace in the US, leaving Europe with a lot of catching up to do in terms of the rights of people to live ordinary, everyday lives in their own homes with companions of their own choosing.

Living Independently in Europe

In 2009, the European Council, the supreme decision-making body in the European Union, reflected on the implementation of the 2006 UN Convention on the Rights of Persons with Disabilities. The importance of Article 19 of the convention is paramount: it recognises the right of all persons with disabilities to live independently and be included in the community. The European Council ordered that member states of the European Union needed to ensure that persons with disabilities had the right to choose their preferred living arrangements and to access services and facilities that met their needs and allowed them to be included in the community. This would require personal budgets, life projects, home care services and assistive technology (SPC, 2010; Eurolex, 2010).

Again in 2009, the European Council invited member states to recognise the role of social services in the economic crisis and to promote the active inclusion of those furthest from the labour market and society. This is just one of several tediously slow movements in Europe that aims to establish a social model of disability as the dominant model.

The European Union has produced a very detailed guide on how to achieve community and independent living and the transition involved in this move (European Commission, 2015). This interesting guide defines an 'institution' not by its size, scale, legal structure or ownership, but by its 'institutional culture'. The guide presents four characteristics of institutional culture:

- depersonalisation (signs of individuality)
- rigidity of routine (fixed timetables for waking, eating)
- block treatment (of categories of people)
- social distance (staff v. residents).

In Europe, the argument that community care is cheaper than institutional care is not presented very often. If community care operates to high standards and quality, then this may not be the case. There is worry among service providers at the (expensive) risks of maintaining services, both inside and outside of communities, with the risk of leaving persons facing significant difficulties in residential care. New community care arrangements – even in small clusters of sheltered housing or community 'homes' – can acquire an institutional culture quite quickly if staff skills and attitudes are not revamped and adequate preparations are not made for those patients who are transitioning.

The European Union Agency for Fundamental Rights also signalled its interest in the rights of people with intellectual disabilities and mental health problems. The agency defined the exercise of the right to independent living as the first theme on its list of research specifications for a project concerning persons with intellectual disabilities and mental health difficulties in Europe. It has adopted the newer definition of institutionalisation as a culture, not a place.

At a grassroots level, the European Network for Independent Living (www.enil.eu) has kept the pressure on at the European level by organising a 'freedom ride' to Brussels or Strasbourg every two years. Men and women with disabilities come from all over Europe and spend a week meeting with members of the European Parliament, visiting the Council of Europe (when in Strasbourg), and talking with the European Disability Forum. Of particular interest in these discussions is to stop public money being spent on more large institutional residences.

At both a European and an international level, there is another stream flowing into this river of change, namely concern over the long-term care of aging populations. This concern stems from the demographic trends of fewer babies and fewer adult workers to care for the next generation of retired and older persons. The subject of who is caring, how care is organised and who is paying for it has been examined internationally (Colombo, 2011). A most interesting feature is how institutional care consumes public funds at the same time as the rhetoric of home-based care beams out. In Canada, for example, just 0.7 percent of the population lives in an institution, but that care consumes over 80 percent of the public expenditure on care. Could this be the case for Ireland too? The funding of nursing home care in Ireland is about three times the amount of funding that home care receives: €900 million is spent annually on nursing home care compared with €324 million spent on home care.

'Congregated' Settings

One of the successes of the independent living movement in Ireland was its contribution to the establishment of a working party on the subject of the future of institutional living for people with disabilities. The Working Party was composed of representatives of bodies and services operating institutional residences and representatives of the public sector. Curiously, the word 'institution', was not to be mentioned by the Working Party; instead, institutional living was described uniquely across the western world as a 'congregated setting'. Is this quibbling over words necessary? Yes. It is vital to identify the problem with a clear name. The working party was chaired by the head of a residential service provider rather than by a person with a disability. After extensive deliberation, the group produced a report confirming that a deinstitutionalising policy would be undertaken over several years (*Report of the Working Group*, 2011). This report implied a situation of expensive parallel funding, with existing residential services maintained while alternative services in the community were put in place. The HSE describes its policy as follows:

> The overall objective of the national group is to ensure that following implementation of the recommendations of the report people with disabilities will be actively and effectively supported to live full, inclusive lives at the heart of the family, community and society. They will be able to exercise meaningful choice, equal to those of other citizens, when choosing where and with whom they

live. People with disabilities will have the right to direct their own life course.

> In line with the report's recommendations, it is proposed over the seven- year time frame 2013 – 2019 to offer residents (living in congregated type setting defined as living arrangements where ten or more people share a single living unit or where the living arrangements are campus based) alternative housing in mainstream community and to close progressively the remaining institutions and residential campuses serving ten or more people.[1]

The policy change did not apply to most of those who were receiving long term mental health services in hospitals, nor did it apply to long-stay hostels, homeless accommodation, refuges or people with disabilities located in nursing homes. According to the census of 2011, there were almost 40,000 individuals with disabilities living in hospitals, prisons, nursing homes, shelters and refuges (CSO, 2017). The deinstitutionalisation policies were to apply to only 10 percent of the individuals living in communal residences.

In stark contrast to this policy, which was to apply mainly to people with intellectual disabilities, those who were elderly and fragile were offered an entirely different policy. With this policy, tax-incentivised support was offered to institutions (mainly private nursing homes), where means-tested access to subsidies would pay for a place in the nursing home. So, under the age of sixty-five years you could be disabled and helped to live in the community, but over the age of sixty-five years you might not be disabled but were offered a residential service. The mainly private nursing homes are not also classed as 'congregated settings' where more than ten people are living: this is quite confusing. In 2016, there were approximately 1,200 nursing homes and children's homes in Ireland – a slight fall from 1,266 in 2011. However, the number of persons in nursing homes and children's homes actually increased in the same period (census, 2016). The reason for this increase is not known.

Moving individuals out of institutions has proved extremely complex. Some service providers have seen this as an opportunity to develop more

---

[1] Hse.ie/eng/services/list/4/disability/congregatedsettings/

innovative and person-oriented care. Other providers have developed a single model of community care homes in rented houses where between four and nine individuals live, often in proximity, and always together with care staff. However, this system has not worked out as planned in every case. The number of persons per residence appears to be arbitrary: the average size of an Irish household is 2.7 persons per household, so a community residence should have no more than three persons for it to resemble an 'ordinary' household. Some individuals who left congregated settings asked to return to their former residential settings and had to be readmitted. Some individuals were moved to large-ish residences, with eight, nine or ten people living together. This quickly and unsurprisingly acquired an institutional culture. As described in a European report, this is quite common:

> These include the replication of institutional culture in community-based services, and the long-term persistence of parallel services (failure to close the institutions). Conversely there is a risk of failure to create appropriate community-based services due to unrealistic targets and timetables which exceed the capacity for their development (*Report of the Ad Hoc Expert Group*, 2009).

The Muiríosa Foundation in County Kildare (www.muiriosa.ie) decided it was time around 2016 to strike out with new ideas concerning independent living. Some individuals in residential services were offered the option of moving to individual homes supported by non-traditional care workers and in close collaboration with their families. The experiment involved a number of 'natural' supports from the community, including neighbours who offered help with shopping, money and even housing. The experience was costed, and in some cases, it cost thousands of euro less than the more conventional arrangements.

In the first year of the deinstitutionalising policy 2012 to 2013, the Department of Environment, Community and Local Government did not have a budget to rehouse people and was provided with €1 million by the HSE. The Department spent the budget on de-congregated settings; they reported that they had also spent some of the budget on those already living in the community who needed housing adaptation grants (DECLG, 2014). This diversion of funds is not uncommon when new social programmes begin. The implementation of the policy to support individuals moving out of large residences was, in a mood of spirituality, called 'Transforming Lives'. Queried about its progress in the Dáil, the then Minister Kathleen Lynch TD reported that the 'decongregation' target for 2016 was for 165 people. She reported that €20 million had been allocated for the process of acquiring or renovating properties in addition to another €10 million from the Department of the Environment and an additional €1million for what was called 'transitioning'. This came to a total of €31 million or €187,878 per person.

In a study of transitions to community living in Ireland for people with intellectual disabilities, The Department of Health Sciences at Trinity College observed in a study that those with greater abilities were the first to leave institutional residences and that the remaining residents faced considerable obstacles. This phenomenon was avoided in the case of Muiríosa, which included those who should never have been living in an institution as well as those who faced substantial challenges in self-determining their lives. The Trinity study noticed that the ability of residents to undertake daily activities, such as cutting up your own food or getting dressed, varied significantly depending on where you were living, whether at home, in a community house or in an institutional setting. Those in an institutional setting showed less of a capacity for the activities of daily living than those who lived at home or in a community house (King et al., 2016).

Muiríosa identifies a number of ordinary goals that can be achieved by individuals with a disability, especially intellectual disabilities. These include having friends that include people who do not have disabilities, securing work placements, securing paid employment, being a homeowner and being active club members. A significant feature in the Muiríosa approach is a changing attitude toward taking risks in social care services and a challenge to the assumption that most individuals in residential care need constant support.

Between 2012 and 2014, 364 individuals moved out of institutions. Some 61 percent of those who made the transition moved to accommodation with more than four people sharing, which was contrary to recommended policy. The majority of those who moved before the end of 2013 did not obtain mainstream social housing. The single biggest housing option was private, rented accommodation. The second largest option was private voluntary housing bodies. In addition, as some residents moved out of institutions, others were admitted or readmitted. In the first period of the deinstitutionalisation policy, 55 people were admitted or readmitted to a congregated setting (Moloney, 2014). At the current rate of change, it could take roughly 20 years to close down institutional living arrangements.

Here is how Paul Alford described his move to independent living in 2015:

> I have worked for Inclusion Ireland for the last ten years as a self-advocate. I believe all people should live as independently as possible and live the way they want to live [...] This does not happen for so many people with intellectual disabilities and I want change to happen right now because it is taking too long. For so long people with disabilities have not had any power in their lives [...] we have decisions made for us every day. I have been fighting to live my own life independently for a long time. Now I am going to move into my new apartment and live on my own. I am buying my own place so I will own it for the rest of my life. I am leaving a disability service where I have lived for over thirty-two years (Alford, 2015).

In relation to de-congregation, the HSE aimed to accelerate the movement of people from outdated, institutionalised settings to the community. They set a target to move 160 people in 2016. However, only 97 moves were projected to have been completed by the end of the year. The target of 223 people for 2017 included those 63 people who were due to move in 2016. The plan, rather worryingly, indicated that the HSE expected to deliver fewer home support hours and personal assistant hours in 2017 than in 2016 (McCullough, 2017). In a small study undertaken by people with disabilities and researchers, the choices available to those moving out of institutions, group homes or the family home were explored. The study found that 18 people had chosen to move out of the house where they lived and 11 people had no choice about moving out (IRN, 2015).

Independent Living and Community Living

Moving into a community group home is not the same as independent living. Research suggests that:

Of most concern is that a primary mechanism of community integration and engagement, movement to community group homes, in many areas more resembles experiences in institutional settings rather than other community-based-living arrangements such as family care or independent living [. . .] movement must not simply be about a change of address (Burke, 2014, 57).

Some of the individuals who moved into community group homes arrived with low levels of literacy and numeracy skills, little familiarity with handling money and few, if any, spouses or children to offer them help with community living. Unsurprisingly, reliance on care staff to organise everyday living was extensive. Living in one house with five or six others means the interests of each has to be pursued in rotation. If not located at the edge of a town or village, transport to activities, events and amenities also becomes an issue.

Many of the residents in institutions were placed in institutions on the advice of professionals. Parents were given to understand that it was the right thing to do for the sake of the whole family. They believed that their child was so physically or mentally different that for the child's sake, they would be better off in an institution:

The non-porous nature of institutional walls ensured that the public heard little, if anything, of institutions' inner workings. Despite institutions' vast geographic, historical and emotional reach, people who experienced institutionalisation have, until very recently, borne this formative piece of their personal and familial history in silence and alone (Burghardt et al., 2015, 1081).

Moving out of an institution after many years in the company of the same co-residents and staff was both a physical and cultural shock for residents in the opinion of this author. Moving on from a congregated setting and into community or independent living is not automatic. For profound changes to occur, there needs to be a rebalancing of the relationship between community group homes and their local environments. Greater personal control by residents over their living circumstances will be required, such as leaving some doors in their homes unlocked, so that they can move toward living independently.

For individuals who want to move into community living with more independence or move out from their parent's house, there needs to be a PA and/or other home supports such as a health care assistant or home help. Asked about their assessment for a PA service, people with disabilities already using personal assistance schemes in 2014 had this to say:

> If I had to apply using the new [HSE] application form, I wouldn't get as many hours as I do. That form induces a guilty feeling if you're seeking more than personal care – like you don't deserve support.
>
> The assessment doesn't respect my right to independent living as my partner has to do all the night-time work plus other tasks such as shopping.
>
> People who live alone get more hours because the HSE can't shift the burden onto family members.
>
> I now need more hours [due to worsening condition] but I don't trust my provider to appreciate my needs. They are stuck in the medical model of care.
>
> It's hard to get hours to support me in raising my kids. Unless it's a welfare issue, the HSE doesn't want to know.
>
> I had to fight the medical authorities [after acquiring a disability] to live [alone] in my own home.
>
> I was urged to shop on the internet to reduce PA time enabling me to get out.
>
> My request for additional PA hours [for 'social' purposes] was denied recently. I was told there were higher priority needs, namely, out of hospital, a change in personal care needs or in informal supports. Quality of life was at the bottom.
>
> My needs haven't been reassessed in recent years since the provider has nothing to offer (Buchanan, 2014).

These views illustrate the demand for supports that enable them to live independently as much as possible. The planned closure of residential institutions was an opportunity to think differently as to how people with disabilities could live ordinary lives in ordinary places. It offered a chance to reflect on the experiences of the independent living movement and its emphasis on self-directed living. This opportunity was explored and put into practice by just a handful of service providers, who took a risk and developed the concept of person-centred services into a form of supported independent living.

The criteria suppose that service providers individually, in groups or in consortia provide ongoing skills and competence training for staff. Since there is no mention of particular hierarchies, one may assume it is for all levels of staff. Again, the plain wording opens up a multitude of possibilities. For example, 'Meeting the changing needs of individuals' might mean very different things. A study commissioned by the Mental Health Commission found that the majority of residents in their study were willing and ready to stay in their current accommodation. This may be a fateful acceptance or lack of experience of alternatives.

From an educational perspective, meeting the changing needs of individuals must involve a critical understanding of the limits of deinstitutionalisation as well as the dangers and risks for people with disabilities. This is explored in a recent paper:

> The less palatable reality for many people with disabilities is that they often take significant psychological and sometimes physical risk being in many mainstream contexts because[...] their spatial and economic inclusion also includes the 'normality' of discrimination, abuse, intolerance and more subtle forms of personal exclusion (Milner and Kelly, 2009,53).

Policy moves to break up 'congregated settings' and establish 'living in the community' immediately raises issues, such as the protection of service users. Individuals have a right to be unwise and make mistakes as part of autonomous living, but will staff be blamed by superiors or families when such mistakes are made? Competing rights and obligations do not easily fit into a one-size-fits-all protocol; careful acts of judgement are required.

The European Accessibility Directive

The EDF represents 80 million individuals with disabilities in Europe and has made accessibility its number one priority. It wants European funds to be spent on making Europe more accessible to people with disabilities. It wants accessible buildings; access inside buildings; accessibility in communications and information technology; in state use of European structural, social and regional funds; and in public procurement. The EDF considers accessibility an essential and core prerequisite for independent living and a basic underpinning of the free movement of labour in Europe. Individuals should not have to ask for help to get into a building and then find themselves subsequently stranded on the ground floor. As the use of digital technology increases, websites need to be accessible. They should not be covered in pictures that will not translate for blind users. A separate directive on public sector website accessibility was adopted in 2016 by the Council of Ministers and is to be implemented by the end of 2018.

The European Commission, while accepting the need for greater accessibility in Europe, opted to place the accessibility discussion within the framework of Europe's internal market. On its passage through the European parliament in 2017, the Draft Accessibility Directive was limited in the field of transport: it excluded metros, trams and local buses from the accessibility requirement. Micro enterprises were also excluded from the requirement.

The directive proved all the more necessary when it was discovered that some member states were using EU funding to further develop institutional living arrangements, as shown in Chart 1 instead of developing community living. The discovery was largely due to the European Network for Independent Living's monitoring activities. The European Coalition for Community Living strongly denounced the use of European funds in Central and Eastern Europe for the renovation, restoration and construction of segregated residential centres for children and adults with disabilities. This happened despite the support for the rights of people with disabilities and for the UN Convention across large swathes of European society. The coalition argues that this practice is contrary to EU policy and to international human rights standards. The coalition noted with concern the situation of 1.2 million adults and 150,000 children still living in institutions across Europe.

Independent living demands a new way of funding living arrangements. It should involve personalised budgets and include a readiness to take risks. Personalised budgets are payments made to individuals rather than to those who provide services. Having personal budgets for individuals is part of the self-determination and autonomy that people with disabilities need. It is at the centre of civil rights for them. The personal budgets provide purchasing power to individuals who often find that existing services do not meet their needs. It moves service development toward the service user and away from a rigidly operating 'disability system'. Brendan Broderick has described this process as getting a life, not a service. He does not argue that it is easy.

Chart 1: Examples of misuse of EU funds

Czech Republic (2015)	…continues to invest more resources in institutional settings than in support services that would enable persons with disabilities to live independently in their respective local communities (para 38).
Denmark (2014)	…end the use of State-guaranteed loans to build institution-like residences for persons with disabilities; that it amend the legislation on social services so that persons with disabilities may freely choose where and with whom they live, while enjoying the necessary assistance to live independently; and that it take measures to close existing institution-like residences and to prevent the forced relocation of persons with disabilities, in order to avoid isolation from the community (para 43).
Hungary (2012)	…has dedicated disproportionally large resources, including regional European Union funds, to the reconstruction of large institutions, which will lead to continued segregation, in comparison with the resources allocated for setting up community-based support service networks (para 33).

Source: Parker, C. and Bulic Cojocariu, I. (2016) *European Structural and Investment Funds and People with Disabilities in the European Union*, European Network on Independent Living, European Parliament Committee on Petitions, Brussels, Belgium

In the Person-Centred Wing individuals and/or their families have made a very conscious decision to be supported in this way. They want to be involved. They want to remain in charge of their lives. It is an altogether more collaborative engagement, a joint venture, where both parties collaborate across all fronts – on resource allocation, on the orientation of risk management… the individual, his or her family and support network, bring something to the party – real engagement in planning, in oversight, in navigating uncertainty. Many families make a contribution to running costs (usually via rentals, utilities, supporting certain kinds of social experiences). There are even situations in which families partner with us in sharing some of the direct support (for example, stepping in to cover certain 'shifts'; one family takes complete responsibility for Sundays). This is work of high ambition, pursued with serious intent. It does not suit tidy-minded people. It's about individuals accessing a life, not a professional service. A life that is going somewhere (Broderick, 2016).

Personalised Budgets

There are already some payments allocated to families, namely the Domiciliary Care Allowance and the Carer Support Grant, which resemble a direct payment and were discussed in Chapter Six. Direct or personalised payments will lead to a reduction in the funding for some service providers. Such uncertainty may lead to a reduction in conventional services. All of this was intended to be addressed by the government Task Force on Personalised Budgets, established in 2016 under the auspices of the Department of Health, chaired by the CEO of a large service provider. It was to report in 2017–2018. In the *Programme for Government 2016*, the following was planned for the Task Force on Personalised Budgets:

- The adoption of a single, national, coherent application system to develop budgets before the end of 2017.
- The adoption of a single, national, coherent system of accountability for the spend.
- Exploring brokerage models whereby people are assisted to connect with and purchase the services that actually meet their own needs.
- Actively monitoring practice, usage and trends and especially the link between personalised budgets, employability and employment rates, as well as community living

Curiously, the core goals of the task force do not include independent living but include employment/employability, which have no obvious relationship to independent living. Ironically, 'a single national coherent system of accountability' is to be devised by a body under the Department of Health, which has been unable to provide a coherent summary of their own funding in the field of disability services. The Task Force reported in 2018.

Independent living has been clarified by the UN in an extensive guidance document for member states (UN Committee, 2017). The document specifies that institutionalisation is not about size but culture. If individuals cannot choose who they live with, do not have the means to integrate into their community, have their day planned in detail and have to seek permission to undertake activities of daily living, then they are not living independently, according to the UN. The guidance document rejects the practice of shared personal assistance services as being incompatible with independent living on an individualised basis. It warns against assuming that services calling themselves 'community living' or 'independent living' actually function in a way that their title describes. The document insists that the size of an institution is not the determining factor in deciding whether it provides independent living; it is a matter of the culture of the institution.

In response to RTÉ's *Inside Bungalow 3* documentary, a review group was established by the HSE to examine how residents with disabilities at Áras Attracta were physically and psychologically abused. As part of the review, relatives of the residents engaged in group discussions (Áras Attracta, 2016, 77). Their views on independent living were explored and were quite revealing. The status quo of Áras Attracta as an institution was viewed as a given and no transition to community living was discussed at that time in 2016. Relatives took for granted that Áras Attracta would remain as it was, with the services improved or reformed. A review of the opinions of staff members of Áras Attracta revealed views of social care practices that were not conducive to community-style living for residents. Examples cited included the lack of opportunities for resident attendance at local community events, poor time allowed for staff training and overcrowded living arrangements. Yet, this review occurred four years after the publication of a policy designed to eliminate congregated living on sites like Áras Attracta's.

The Costs of Disability

Living with a disability costs more than living without a disability. The core, recurring and essential extra services and goods that need to be acquired to live a decent life are termed the costs of disability. The topic of the costs of disability was addressed and recommended by the Commission on the Status of People with Disability in its final report (1996, 129) and earlier by the former National Rehabilitation Board. The report's argument that the state should acknowledge its role of supporting people with disabilities and their families in meeting the additional costs arising from disability was never conceded. Households with a disabled person frequently teeter at the edge of poverty due to the depletion of savings, the absence of two salary earners and the additional costs of goods and services.

In 1993, the then National Rehabilitation Board researched the costs of disability among a small group of people with disabilities using a methodology that still has value today (Murray, 1993). The research put a monetary value on benefits and services and calculated the difference between the income of individuals and the costs of disability. The study found that individuals were borrowing money to meet their additional coasts; over a fifth said they were always in debt and almost half described their standard of living as poor or very poor (Combat Poverty Agency, 1995).

Conclusion

The struggle over so-called congregated settings, the segregated institutions in which some people with disabilities are obliged to live, is illustrative of the slow rate of change in disability policy in Irish society. It epitomises the deep roots within society that are hostile to change. Segregated institutions have become part of the fabric of the local economy.

The failure to take account of the additional costs of disability is part of the same closed attitude of mind toward disability issues since the costs of disability are inextricably linked with independent living and personalised budgets. Impairment impoverishes, and that is a fact. Once all the individual or familial reserves of savings and borrowings have been depleted, being unable to participate in daily life is a terrifying and likely prospect. Opportunities for young people with disabilities are very problematic. They and their families are supposed to accept services in the HSE area in which they live, regardless of their needs. So, while brothers and sisters go off to college, the teenage sibling with a disability is trapped inside their community care area, which means they are also unable to participate in daily life. Sometimes there are not enough day services and the young people have to stay at home most of the time. Independent living is a citizenship right – it is a civil right that should be supported.

Chapter 11 References

Americans with Disability Act 2017: https://www.ada.gov/olmstead/olmstead_about.html. Accessed May 5, 2017.

The Center for an Accessible Society (2017) A Clearinghouse for Journalists. http://accessiblesociety.org/topics/ada/olmsteadoverview.htm. Accessed May 5, 2017.

Alford, P. (2015) 'My New Life in My New Apartment', *Frontline*, Dublin.

Áras Attracta Swinford Review Group (2016) *What Matters Most – Report of the Áras Attracta Swinford Review Group*, HSE, July.

Broderick, B. (2016), *Speaking Notes for a Presentation to Personalised Budgets Working Group*, Thursday 17 November: www.muiriosa.ie.

Buchanan, L. (2014) *Access to Life: Personal Assistant Services in Ireland and Independent Living by People with Physical and Sensory Disabilities: Full Report*, Disability Federation of Ireland, Dublin.

Burghardt, H. (2015) *Disability and Society*, Vol. 30, No. 7–8, May, Taylor and Francis, UK.

Burke, E. McCallion, P. McCarron, M. (eds.) (2014) *Advancing Years, Different Challenges: Wave 2 IDS-TILDA, Findings on the Ageing of People with an Intellectual Disability*, Trinity College, Dublin.

Centre for Independent Living Leader Forum Consultation (CILLFC) (2016) Report: Personal Assistance Services, Carmichael House, Dublin.

Central Statistics Office CSO (2017) *Census 2016*, Statbank CD82.

Central Statistics Office CSO (2016) *Census 2016*, Profile 4, Table E4004, Profile 5, Table E4035 (Statbank).

Combat Poverty Agency, Forum of People with Disabilities (1995) *Disability, Exclusion and Poverty – Papers from the National Conference:* Disability Exclusion and Poverty – A Policy Conference, National Rehabilitation Board, Dublin.

Commission (2015) *Common European Guidelines on the Transition from Institutional to Community Care*, Luxembourg.

Colombo, F. Llena-Nozal, A. Mercier, J. Tjadens, F. (2011) *Help Wanted – Providing and Paying for Long Term Care*, OECD, Paris, DOI 10.1787/2074319x.

Department of Environment, Community and Local Government (DECLG) (2014) *National Housing Strategy for People with a Disability 2011–2016. First Report on Implementation: September 2012–December 2013.*

Department of Justice, Equality and Law Reform (DJELR) (1996) *A Strategy for Equality – Report of the Commission on the Status of People with Disabilities*, Dublin.

European Council (2010) SPC_QF_document_SPC_2010_10_8_final[1] PDFEUR-LEX.europa.eu/legal-content/EN/TXT/PDF/?uri= CELEX:32010D0048&rid=1 See also: Presidency Conclusions – Cologne 3 and 4 June 1999, page 11.

Gibson, B., Brooks, D. De Matteo, D. and King, A. (2009) 'Consumer Directed Personal Assistance and "Care": Perspectives of Workers and Ventilator Users', *Disability and Society*, Vol. 24, No. 3. Taylor and Francis.

Giddens, A. (1991) *Modernity and Self-Identity: Self and Society in the Late Modern Age.* Stanford University Press. Stanford.

Goffman, E. (1961) *Asylums: Essays on the Social Situation of Mental Patients and Other Inmates*, Doubleday, Random House, New York.

Health and Human Services HHS (2017) US Department of Health and Human Services Office for Civil Rights Washington, D.C. www.hhs.

gov/sites/default/files/ocr/civilrights/resources/factsheets/504. pdf. Accessed May 1, 2017.

Inclusive Research Network (IRN) (2015), Our Homes: Home and Independence Project. Dublin: School of Social Work and Social Policy, Trinity College Dublin and Department of Clinical Therapies, University of Limerick; with the National Federation of Voluntary Bodies.

Kennedy-Smith, J. (1996) Communication with Author at UCD, Dublin.

King, E. Okodogbe, T. Burke, E. McCarron, M. McCallion, P. and O'Donovan, M.A. (2016) 'Activities of Daily Living and Transition to Community Living for Adults with Intellectual Disabilities', *Scandinavian Journal of Occupational Therapy*.

Marsden, J. (ed.) (2010) *Extraordinary Lives: Celebrating 150 years of the Irish Wheelchair Association*, IWA and Dyflin Publications, Dublin.

Murray, B. (1993) *Costs of Disability Study*, National Rehabilitation Board, Dublin.

Murphy, N. Conroy, P. Dixon, S. McGrath, C. (2006) *Extending the Boundaries – Our Experience of Independent Living*, CIL, Carmichael House, Dublin.

Muiríosa Foundation, (2016) *Annual Report 2016*, Co. Kildare.

Moloney, S. (2014) 'Congregated Settings, Implementation, Oversight and Support', Presentation to the Moving Ahead Seminar, Cork, November 25, 2014.

Milner, P. and Kelly, B. (2009) Community Participation and Inclusion: People with Disabilities Defining their Place, *Disability and Society*, Vol. 24, No.1, Taylor and Francis.

Oireachtas (2017) Joint Committee on Health, Debates, 18 October.

Parker, C. and Bulic Cojocariu, I. (2016) European Structural and Investment Funds and People with Disabilities in the European Union, European Network on Independent Living, European Parliament Committee on Petitions, Brussels, Belgium: http://www.europarl.europa.eu/RegData/etudes/STUD/2016/571386/IP OL_STU(2016)571386_EN.pdf. Accessed May 1, 2017.

Report of the Working Group on Congregated Settings (2011) *Time to Move on from Congregated Settings – A Strategy for Community Inclusion*, Dublin: Health Service Executive. Hse.ie/eng/services/list/4/disability/congregatedsettings/. Accessed May 9, 2017.

Report of the Ad Hoc Expert Group on the Transition from Institutional to Community-based Care (2009) European Commission Directorate-General for Employment, Social Affairs and Equal Opportunities, September.

UN Committee on the Rights of Persons with Disabilities, Eighteenth Session, August 14–31, 2017.

Veterans Administration (2017) www.va.gov. April 26, 2017.

CHAPTER 12

Conclusion

We are good at renaming what we want to avoid. The Respite Grant became the Carer Support Grant. The Portrane Asylum became St. Ita's Hospital. Closed institutions became congregated settings. Unwanted people were annihilated by Hitler and banished as genetically inferior in Norway and Romania. Infants were left unburied and unnamed in Tuam. Irish soldiers, sailors and aircraft operators who became deaf were disbelieved and ridiculed. It is not a happy history. We have inherited a legacy steeped in prejudice. We have inherited a legacy of rejection for those who look, sound or appear a bit different from the image we hold of ourselves.

The legacy includes a belief that some people with disabilities are less human, less equal, less entitled to equal treatment and less entitled to the right to life compared with the majority of citizens and residents. They are cast as other, as another kind of people. These ideas and beliefs were not and are not unique to Ireland. They have drifted like a sea haze across Europe and further afield, dulling the outline and clouding over the enforcement of rights.

The eugenics legacy of Europe, the Nordic countries and the United States still affects the thinking and practices of public policy, namely that people with disabilities can wait longer for their right to equal treatment and can be contained in a variety of closed institutions. In the case of Tuam, we are so often invited to see things in the context of their time. In the context of pre- and post-Second-World-War-Ireland, no public or private body had the right to neglect infants and children and refuse them a decent burial, especially those children who were in the care of the state.

These legacies have led us to passively tolerate the confinement of people with disabilities to closed spaces and institutions, to build more closed institutions and to permit an institutionalised culture to permeate the community homes that are supposed to guarantee individualised, person-centred lifestyles. We have not been challenged enough to think and reflect about what we are doing and endorsing with docility. These legacies are not particularly religious or faith-based and are to be found in countries that are widely divergent in thinking and culture.

There remains a legacy of ignorance and a refusal to listen, exemplified in the army deafness cases. Worryingly, they revealed a deeply embedded prejudice against people who are deaf or have damaged hearing. There was a pervasive view that the entire issue was a scam. The idea of people with disabilities being deceitful is not new; it goes back hundreds of years, when disabled beggars had to wear a 'badge' declaring that they were 'official' beggars. In so many ways the past is now before us in new forms: the regulation of social services, the low employment rate of people with disabilities and the unburied babies of Tuam.

It is not that people with disabilities should be treated the same as everyone else. Rather, they are entitled to those adjustments which place them on an even playing field with everyone else: a counter they can reach, an adjusted car, accessible buildings. Yet it has proved extremely difficult to persuade many public and private bodies, who are otherwise in favour of diversity, that business and life will not collapse from the granting of some reasonable accommodations.

Legacies of the past have held change to ransom, have blocked legislative enactments, have held back the implementation of reforms and have resulted in the refusal of services for those without 'priority status'. Equal status eludes people with disabilities. And yet in many instances, the Dáil has done its job. It has enacted legislation for addressing special educational needs; however, much of it never came into operation. The *Disability Act, 2005* still has sections in the legislative freezer which excludes thousands from needs assessment as a result. The *Assisted Decision-Making Capacity Act* of 2015 was enacted but continues to leave individuals without rights. The right to exercise a vote at your local polling booth has still to happen for many. Televised government press conferences are conducted without sign language interpreters. As of June 2018, the *Irish Sign Language Act* of 2017 had still not been brought into force. The comprehensive range of disability rights remain ignored. On a brighter note, Ireland did ratify the United Nations Convention on the Rights of Persons with Disabilities, ten years after its signature in 2007.

It is somewhat ironic that two of the most significant strands of thought about disability have come into Ireland from the United States: the *Americans with Disabilities Act* and the Independent Living Movement. It took a long time for the European Union and its member states to realise and to accept that these two social developments put the US ahead of Europe in terms of social and civil rights. At the same time, Europe hesitated to accept that people with disabilities were, in the words of the OECD, living in a state of fragility.

There has been a mis-specification of the problem of disability rights, based on the personal tragedy scenario. Disability is viewed as a public misfortune, the consequences of which include dependency and an inability to earn a living. The focus is on a continuous struggle for state benefits and services to fill the gaps as a result. The question as to why so many people lose their jobs on becoming impaired is not asked. Why do such a high proportion of children with disabilities leave school with no qualifications? The answer lies not with the impairment but with the disabling environment and culture that the impairment is locked into (Agulnik et al., 2002).[1]

The voices of people with disabilities are heard as whispers, barely audible in the void between civil society and state and the state-controlled slightly non-governmental bodies. Competitive market principles and monetised services creep ever more into the fabric of everyday life for people with disabilities and their friends and families. They find that the charitable ethos has been converted into a pay-as-you-go mentality for many individuals and families who try to pay for assessments and services they cannot obtain. The formation of networks and parent groups, self-advocacy, meetings, fundraising activities, anti-discrimination complaints, publications, volunteer efforts, acts of kindness and public demonstrations: all of these make up a social capital which is invested freely via civil society organisations and informal associations. Social capital is constantly renewed and called on to renew itself through volunteering efforts.

Empowerment is an act of the powerless themselves that cannot be accomplished by other people on their behalf. Empowerment can never

---

[1] Phil Agulnik, Tania Burchardt, Martin Evans (2002) 'Response and Prevention' in J. Hills, Julian Le Grand and David Piachaud, (eds.) *Understanding Social Exclusion*, Oxford University Press, Oxford, pp. 163–170.

be a gift or donation, however well intentioned. This is why complaints systems are so important: they enable individuals to enforce their rights. This is why the advocacy movement is so important in facilitating people with disabilities to define their own agendas. The taking back of power ruptures pre-existing relationships and establishes a new balance of power with new priorities for reform.

The medical model of disability, despite the *Employment Equality Act* and the *Equal Status Act,* is still alive and well. The right to engage in paid work has barely moved on. For individuals with intellectual disabilities, the situation regresses each year. Even social inclusion programmes fail people with disabilities. The numbers using such schemes halved between 2010 and 2014 following changes in eligibility. [2]

In terms of public policy, there is no logic in moving people with disabilities into houses in the community while simultaneously moving older people with disabilities into collective living in nursing homes. This conflict of policy can be partially resolved: by enabling more older people to stay in their own homes and live more independently supported lives, while enabling people with disabilities to have more individualised living arrangements suited to their circumstances, the situation will improve. However, there will have to be provision for a cost-of-disability payment in both cases to put a stop to the risk of poverty as well as long-standing health conditions and age-related frailty. This path toward individuality is being quietly trodden by some large-scale services in co-operation with family members and the goodwill of members of the wider community. Such projects embedded in civil society do not fulfil the service provider model but lean toward a more promising new model of citizen-to-citizen engagement.

The implementation of laws for the protection of vulnerable adults and assisted decision-making will generate new public institutions such as the Adult Safeguarding Authority and the Office of the Director of Decision-Making. These in turn will require support from a wide range of people, including co-decision-makers, decision-making supporters, substitute decision-makers, self-advocates, visitors and personal advocates. People will be invited to consider the question of disability from

---

[2] Department of Social Protection (2015) *An Analysis of the Community Employment Programme*, p. 79.

a different perspective, perhaps mobilising some new technical supports and communication applications.

It would be unfair to brand all forms of inspection and vetting as intrusive and unnecessary. However, their proliferation, scope and administration may be disproportionate to their aim. That has to be examined on a case-by-case basis, and the time has come for a review of the *Health Act, 2007* as it relates to people with disabilities and long-standing health conditions.

The privatisation of services is a real menace. Once it gets into a system, you can supress it, but it keeps returning. It is not even clear to the Department of Health how many services it is funding and for whom. It certainly was not clear to the Value for Money Review of Disability Services established by the Department of Health. It is definitely not clear to people with disabilities and their supporters.

There was a reason why Ireland did not ratify the UN Convention on the Rights of Persons with a Disability for so many years. The reason lies in the profound mistrust of people with disabilities being able to determine their own lives and of families and supporters having the right of access to services and individualised supports. There is also a fear of fully dismantling and restructuring the disability economy with its closed spaces, closed buildings and closed minds. From asylums to Mother and Baby Homes to large residential institutions and nursing homes, they all form part of a local economy providing employment and the purchase of goods and services. Many of the reforms required for people with disabilities and long-standing health conditions require a breakup of these local economies in their present form and their rearrangement in a new configuration.

The dilemmas of social reform that we face in Ireland are not especially unique. Romania, Norway, Italy, Switzerland, Germany and the US have all had to face their own particular obstacles to equality for people with disabilities in specific cultural contexts. Sometimes it suffices to have the pressures of a social movement. Sometimes a court ruling, like the Olmstead case in the US or the soldiers' deafness cases, is sufficient to force a break with the past. Sometimes it needs both and more.

It is not always a question of budget or costs that holds back rights; it is how budgets are spent. An Oireachtas calculation of 2014/2015 indicated that the nursing home support scheme gets 75 percent of the care budget for 23,400 people while the remaining 25 percent has to be shared by 66,000 people.[3] People with disabilities are to be found in homeless shelters, prisons and in private homes. They are not all consumers of services. They are frequently under-served populations. When government departments succeed in sharing budgets and responsibilities, a greater outreach to underserved groups can occur.

This book has addressed a limited number of questions related to disability in Ireland. One of the topics omitted is our treatment of those with substance abuse problems. A second is the important contribution of Irish aid in promoting the rights of people with disabilities in the developing world, where the vast majority of people with disabilities are living.

The last two decades have seen the realisation of many civil rights in Ireland. Human rights for many are now better protected. However, full disability rights are among the last to see a new day dawning. An accessible society and independent living, including supports to independent living and decision-making, are what a new generation can and should expect in a new Ireland.

---

[3] *Home Care for Older People* (2016) Research Matters for the 32nd Dáil and the 25th Seanad, Houses of the Oireachtas Library and Research Service, Dublin, p. 19.

Index of Tables and Charts

Charts

Dr Pauline Conroy is a graduate in Social Science from University College Dublin and the London School of Economics, where she studied under Richard Titmuss. She has undertaken research and published on gender, equality, disability, labour-market issues and social exclusion with the Council of Europe and The International Labour Organisation. Pauline has worked and lectured at University College Dublin, the Open Training College and the Open University UK. She has spent four years working with the Mental Health Review tribunals and is currently engaged in activity that brings her into contact with prisoners; both of these activities reflect her interest in those who are socially underserved and detained in closed spaces. Her views on social policy are influenced by her years of travel in the poorest areas of Europe with the European Commission and her years of work and study in Italy, England, France, Belgium and North Africa.